Riding the Sugar High

LETIZIA LORINI

Copyright © 2024 by Letizia Lorini

All rights reserved.

No part of this book may be reproduced in any form or by any electronic or mechanical means, including information storage and retrieval systems, without written permission from the author, except for the use of brief quotations in a book review. To request permission, contact the author at letizia@letizialorini.com.

ISBN: 9789198853315

Cover Design by Sam Palencia at Ink and Laurel

Editing by Britt Tayler

Formatting by Letizia Lorini

This is a work of fiction. Names, characters, businesses, events and incidents are the products of the author's imagination. Any resemblance to actual persons, living or dead, or actual events is purely coincidental.

author's note

This book contains on-page intimate scenes and mature content and is intended for mature audiences only. For more details on the content warnings for this novel, please visit: www.letizialorini.com

To all the girls who dream of being chased through an orchard by a man in a black helmet, cause it can't just be me.

playlist

Lose Control - Teddy Swims
Dog Days Are Over - Florence + The Machine
Pink - Lizzo
Fresh Out of Love - E^ST
Show You My World - Upstate
Fighting with Myself - Declan J Donovan
Not to be Dramatic - Zoe Clark
Strawberry Wine - Noah Kahan
Watermelon Sugar - Harry Styles
Heat Waves - Glass Animals
Do I Wanna Know? - Arctic Monkeys
Too Sweet - Hozier
Sweet Love - Myles Smith
Beautiful Things - Benson Boone
Pour Some Sugar On Me - Def Leppard
Real Love Baby - Father John Misty
Dazed & Confused - Ruel
Delicate - Taylor Swift
Ho Hey - The Lumineers
You Put a Spell on Me - Austin Giorgio

Wildest Dreams - Taylor Swift
Budapest - George Ezra
Come Back . . . Be Here - Taylor Swift
Home - Edward Sharpe & The Magnetic Zeros

dicktionary

Chapter One
Chapter Two

Chapter 18

Chapter 23
Chapter 24
Chapter 30
Chapter 31
Chapter 32

For more books featuring the Dicktionary, check out @thedicktionarybookclub on Instagram!

you can't drive

. . .

Logan

FUCK, tonight's just not doing it for me.

The moon is high in the sky as I rev the engine, the sound echoing through the quiet night. The deserted road blurring on either side of me always does its trick in helping me clear my head, and the cool night air is usually like a calming balm.

I've ridden along Elm Avenue a hundred times before, but tonight, the vast, poorly illuminated road feels different. The wind is whipping through the tips of my hair, and adrenaline is coursing through my veins, but the freedom that comes from riding at night, alone with my thoughts, just isn't there.

The same tightness I've been feeling in my chest for months doesn't vanish like it should. The bills that are accumulating, the dozens of people whose livelihoods depend on me, the animals who are bound to get sick and need medication—they all pile up until the crushing sense of failure vibrates through me like an electroshock.

Something's not right.

And I can't, tonight of all nights, be sick.

The engine's roar is deafening in my ears, but it's not enough to drown out the cacophony of thoughts racing through my mind.

A vice squeezes around my heart, and I can't seem to catch my breath.

Focus on the road, I tell myself. But as I blink, the blooming trees at the edges of the road blur, and I know I need to stop.

My hands are shaking hard—too hard to pull the brakes—and as another wave of gut-squeezing pain crashes through me, I clench my fingers around the handlebars, waiting for the tingling to subside.

I'm fine. I'm *fine*.

Pushing the throttle forward, I try to overtake the fear. But it's like I'm running in quicksand, and whatever's wrong with me is gaining ground with every passing second.

Why is my heart beating so fast?

God, my chest hurts. I think I'm having a heart attack.

Appealing to every bit of strength I have, I pull over to the side of the road, my hands trembling as I try to steady myself. My eyes burn, and my ears ring loudly enough to cover the engine's rumble.

Clutching my chest, I lean forward and rest the top half of my body on the bike. *This is it*. I'm fucking dying, and I won't be able to call anyone. This road is always empty at night, so someone will likely find me in the morning.

It's almost a relief, for a second, that the all-consuming sense of doom following me around will stop.

But those two piglets.

My animals.

The farm.

I force my arm up, snap my helmet open, then throw it on the ground beside me. It helps—the cold air on my heated skin. Sweat trickles over my eyebrows, and I close my eyes, trying to focus on my breathing and slow down the quickened beats of my heart.

For a moment, all around me is silent, until the screeching of brakes against asphalt has me looking over my shoulder, right into a blinding beam of light. In the split second it takes me to realize a car is colliding with my rear end, my bike jolts forward, and I lose balance.

I'm tossed off the side, and the hit knocks the air out of my lungs, then my breathing fails me again as the bike falls over my leg.

"Fuck," I grunt, my vision tunneling from the intense wave of pain. I blink up at the sky, trying to get my bearings.

"Oh my god, are you okay?" a high-pitched voice calls out. The engine of the car dies, and there's the sound of a car door opening, then shoes slapping against the asphalt. A woman leans over me, her features hidden by the headlights casting a shadow over her face. Like a fucking angel of death.

"No, I'm not okay," I choke out. "You ran me over, you moron."

She hesitates, then circles the bike to stand next to where I'm sprawled, her blonde hair falling past her shoulders and fading into a bright pink. "You stopped in the middle of the road," she mumbles, and as she leans down to study my face, I finally put hers into focus. She must be in her mid-twenties. Her eyes are the same blue as a spring sky, and there's a healthy dose of freckles over her cheeks. "Did you hit your head?" she asks, lips coated in pink lipstick and bent into a frown.

"No," I say through gasps. Of course, being run over by this blind idiot didn't help the heart attack I'm experiencing. "The bike —my leg."

Her brows knit tight as she turns back, then with a muttered curse, grabs onto the bike handle and pulls, achieving no tangible result. "It's so heavy! How can you drive this thing? And where is your helmet? And why—*why* did you stop in the middle of this dark, deserted road?"

"Shut up," I croak. I lean forward, trying to get my muscles to cooperate. I need to lift the bike an inch off my leg, but I'm shaking even more than before the crash, and this tiny woman is useless. "Pull."

She does, grinding her teeth with effort, and I push at the same time. The bike lifts just enough for me to slide my leg out, and with a sigh of relief, I close my eyes and fall back, trying to catch my breath.

"Please tell me you're okay," the woman says as she comes to kneel beside my chest. She shakes my arm when I don't respond, and as she speaks again, she sounds a moment away from breaking into tears. "Please, I'm sorry, I . . ."

I slowly sit up, holding a hand to my chest and looking into her eyes. "I'm . . . I needed to stop. My heart."

Her gaze settles over my chest. "Your heart? Are you . . ." She studies my face, then gasps. "I'll call 9-1-1."

"No . . . reception."

"Shit!" Eyes stuck on her phone, she throws her other hand up. "What *is* this place?" She tosses her phone aside and looms over me again. "What do I do?"

And how would I know?

When I shake my head, her brow furrows. "Don't you have a heart condition?"

I grip my throat, at this point almost completely closed. This is it. These are my very last breaths. "Not . . . that I know . . . of."

"Oh—*oh!* You're not having a heart attack!" She works on the zipper of my jacket until it opens, and it relieves some of the pressure immediately. "You're having a *panic* attack."

A panic attack?

She rises to her knees, then takes big, exaggerated breaths. "Do what I'm doing. Focus on breathing in and out, and it'll stabilize your heartbeat."

Her voice almost sounds like an echo, hard to hear with the way my ears are ringing. She can't be right. This can't just be panic. It feels like I'm staring down the barrel of my final minutes.

"I promise you're okay," the woman insists as she cups my shoulder. When I flinch, she pulls her hand back. "Sorry. I won't touch you."

I hold my head between my hands, trying to breathe the way

she showed me. My hair curtains around my face, and it helps to be separated from everything else, but I also need to know she's here. That she's going to help make this feeling disappear. So I hold my hand out.

When she takes it, her soft fingers sinking into my much bigger gloves, I squeeze it gently. It soothes the shaking a little, knowing whatever is happening to me, I'm not going through it alone.

The wind, crisp and fresh, gently picks up, carrying hints of blossoms and damp earth. I open my mouth—maybe to tell the woman that my business is failing and I'm the only one who knows just how deeply screwed we are. How it's all my fault, and the thought of disappointing everyone is slowly killing me with its inevitability. But nothing comes out except for strangled breaths—none of which manage to bring any air into my lungs.

"Is it your first time having a panic attack?"

I nod stiffly.

"It happened a lot to me growing up. Your life isn't in danger." She looks firmly into my eyes, her full lips pulled into a tight line. "I know it feels like you can't breathe, but you can. I promise your throat and lungs are perfectly fine."

She approaches with her hand, then stops before it touches my chest. "Can I?"

When I lean back on my palms, giving her room, she lays it over my sternum.

"Take the deepest breath you can, and watch my fingers."

As I breathe in, her hand rises, then falls once I breathe out.

"See? You're breathing just fine." She gives me an encouraging smile, then continues. "Here's a little beginner's trick. Ever heard of the three-three-three rule?" Without waiting for an answer, she sits on her heels, her pink dress draping over her thighs. "It's easy, and it'll help you focus on something else. Tell me three objects you can see."

I breathe in, out, in, trying to remind myself that though it doesn't feel like it, air is inflating my lungs all the same. "Scrunchie," I choke out. She pinches the pink scrunchie with yellow flowers off her wrist and nods, holding it in her hand. "Dress." Looking up at her face, I mutter, "Pink hair."

Still with a hand to my chest, she utters a soft 'mm-hmm.' "Now, three sounds."

"Your voice." Her bracelets jingle as she tucks some hair behind her ear. "Bracelets," I whisper, and when I struggle to find a third sound, she starts whistling. "Whistling."

"Almost done. Now, I need you to move three body parts."

I take her hand in mine, the pink scrunchie trapped between our palms. It makes her smile in a soft way and—*fuck*. I like that. Focusing on her is distracting me enough that my breathing is almost back to normal.

"So good. Just like that, deep breaths." Cute dimples appear on her cheeks. "Two more."

She's so pretty. I wish this wasn't happening in front of her, and at the same time, I'm thankful she just ran me over because the tingle under my skin is disappearing, and adrenaline is replacing the strangling fear.

My other arm moves up, then my hand is holding on to the back of her neck, and I only realize my heart rate has slowed down because it picks up again. What am I doing? Maybe I *did* hit my head, because as her relieved expression dissipates and her eyes dance over my lips, I think I want to kiss her. I think she wants me to kiss her too.

"One."

With a slow pull, I drag her forward until her mouth is on mine. I guess it's technically two movements because my lips dance on hers. Three, when my fingers shift to her hair and use it to direct her the way I want her.

Her hands fist my shirt, and her body roams closer until her chest is pressed on mine. I slide my hand down to the spot over her ass, urging her closer.

Fuck, this is a kiss. A proper kiss.

A kiss like only a few others in a lifetime.

The road is pitch black except for the moonlight, casting gentle shadows and illuminating patches of wildflowers. With only the symphony of nighttime creatures around us, the delicate sounds of our subtle breaths and pressed lips are all I can hear.

Her tongue keeps teasing mine, and with each flick, I want to deepen our contact. I want to flip us over and do more, as if we're not sitting in the middle of a road on the town's outskirts.

With a soft moan drowned by my mouth, she pulls back a little, and her eyes look nothing like they did when she was helping me through my panic attack. They were sharp-focused then, and they're cloudy now. Hungry and pleased at the same time.

God, I can just picture those eyes looking up at me while I take her.

She opens her mouth, and I glance at the bright pink lipstick smeared over her chin. Her lips are swollen, bruised by my kiss, and the skin around her mouth is red with the friction of my beard.

"That's a very unhealthy way to process your anxiety," she whispers, and I nearly laugh, but it's like my body's too tense for it, my fingers rubbing the scrunchie I'm somehow holding. "Did it work? Did all your blood rush from your brain to your groin?"

"Yes." But I haven't kissed anyone in five years, and I'm unsure how to behave now. The woman nearly killed me, then saved my life, and then I kissed her. And I can't bring myself to check my bike, because I'm pretty sure that will cancel out my gratitude for her.

"You shouldn't be riding. Can someone come pick up your bike? I'll drive you home."

As if. "I'm not leaving my bike."

"You're joking, right?" She scoffs as I tentatively stand, then locate my helmet next to a bush. "Ah, so you *do* have one of those." Following me, she powers on. "You can't get back on that bike right now. It could happen again—it's not safe."

"I doubt getting in a car with you would be safer," I say distractedly as I dust the helmet off.

A sense of dread tightens my chest when I turn to the bike and force myself to walk closer. After I pull it up, I run my fingers along the frame, feeling the imperfections beneath my touch. The once smooth surface now bears scratches and dents, and one of the mirrors hangs at an awkward angle. But overall, the damage seems primarily cosmetic.

Relief floods through me, and besides some stiffness in my muscles and a sense of sleepiness, it's almost as if whatever that . . . attack was, never happened. My heart is back to its normal rhythm; my vision is sharp. Like it's all been a nightmare.

"Seriously? You're being very irresponsible."

"Who, me?" I ask as I give her a dry smile. "That would be a first."

She crosses her arms, tilting her head as her eyes gently scold me. "So that's it? You involve me in an accident, then *kiss* me, and now you're going to head off into the sunset?" Eyes bouncing around, she shrugs. "Or . . . night?"

"Look, what do you want? A date or something?"

"Who says I don't have a boyfriend already?"

Oh, shit. She has me there. And though she definitely kissed me back, it doesn't feel right to know I've kissed someone else's girl. "Uh, sorry, I . . ."

"I don't." She taps a foot on the ground. "I'm just saying."

Saying what, exactly? "Okay, well . . . I'd ask for your number, but trust me, you don't want me to call." I slide my helmet on. "And besides, you're not from around here." I'd remember her if I had seen her before. "Judging by your accent, you're not from Roseberg either."

"Mayfield."

There you go. What's that, a six-hour flight from here?

It makes it easier for me because she could be living inside my house, and I still wouldn't date her—or anyone else, for that matter.

"Well, thank you for . . ." I vaguely point at the ground, where we were sitting just a minute ago, and her small shoulders hunch. "If you notice any damage to your car or need anything while you're in town, Farm Coleman."

"Farm Coleman? You're a *farmer*?"

The disgusted grimace on her lips makes me regret my offer instantly, and she must notice, because she quickly waves both hands.

"Oh my god, sorry. No—my ex, he . . ." Studying me suspiciously, she shakes her head. "Anyway, the car is a rental, and I'm leaving tomorrow. Are you sure you're fine to drive?"

"Sure."

"Okay." She still doesn't look convinced, but she takes a step back. "Well, it was . . . nice? To meet you."

"Yeah, I'm not sure how I feel about it either," I say as I hop onto my bike. I should leave, but for some reason, I can't.

"I think I can help with that. You feel grateful." Dipping her chin, she adds, "And a little turned on."

"That sounds about right." I start the engine, and when it sputters with a rocks-in-a-tin-can sound, I glare at her through the gap in my visor. "Mostly turned on. A little grateful."

"Stop on the side of the road next time."

I grin, and though there's no way she can tell, she does too. With one last wave, she spins on her heel. "Bye, then."

"Hey."

She twists to glance at me over her shoulders, her blue irises even brighter now that the bike lights are shining directly on her face.

I hold up her scrunchie. "This is yours."

With a little "hm," she walks closer. I hand it over, and her eyes study mine for a long moment before she turns to leave.

My eyes dip down her dress, the same pink of cherry blossoms in spring, gently hugging her upper body before flaring out slightly at the waist, and settle on her ass. Once she enters the car and her headlights flash on me, the engine emits a feeble sputter, like a tired cough struggling to gain momentum.

Then the headlights turn off.

With a mumbled curse, I kill the engine.

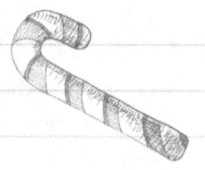

be my partner in crime

. . .

Primrose

"LOOK, just call road assistance. That's what they're for," the man says in a gruff voice as he exits the car. He's been trying to start the engine for the past ten minutes with no result, so it's safe to say something important is broken.

This is just perfect, isn't it? Just brilliant.

"It's a rental."

"Then call the rental company." He studies me for a few seconds through the slit in his helmet and shrugs. "See ya."

My eyes flare.

This guy can't be serious. The car is broken because of him, and now he's just going to leave me out here to fend for myself against wild beasts in the middle of the night? "Wait—where the hell are you going?"

He keeps walking. "Uh, none of your business?"

"You *can't* leave me here."

"I can, and more importantly, I have to. There's somewhere I need to be."

"Well, same." And I can guarantee my plans are more important than whatever he has going on. "It's your fault I'm stranded in the middle of nowhere. Now, you're going to leave me in the hands of potential serial killers?"

"In Pinevale?" He snorts out a laugh. "You're talking to the only criminal in the area."

Eyes bobbing left and right, I shake my head. "That's not reassuring!"

"Let me ease your concerns." For a moment, his eyes stare into mine, then he hops on the motorcycle. "Bye."

"No—no!" I rush in front of the wheel. "You're *not* leaving. You hear me? If I'm stuck here, you're stuck here."

He rubs his brow as if appealing to deeply buried patience. "You know when you see those tiny-ass chihuahuas barking at Rottweilers and Pit bulls and think, 'man, those rats should choose their battles?'"

"Are you comparing me to a dog?" I hiss.

"I'm comparing us both to dogs. I'm comparing *you* to an annoying dog unaware of its size."

Though I'd love to argue, with his helmet and those broad shoulders, he's pretty reminiscent of a Rottweiler—silent, dangerous power.

And I do feel like quite the chihuahua right now.

"Fine. You know what? I don't need you. In fact, you'd probably get in the way. Go. Thank you for absolutely *nothing*."

With a flip of my hair, I turn around and walk back to the car, then take out my phone. I've never dealt with anything like this before, seeing as in a big city like Mayfield, we mostly move around with public transportation, but it can't be too hard. They'll have to send someone out here.

Not sure where *out here* is exactly—around me, there are trees upon trees, endless silence, and a sweet, spring melody created by the buzzing of insects all around—but I can check online.

Holy shit. No reception.

He said there's no reception.

Why did I come here? I knew it was a bad idea. But with my two-week-long work trip to Roseberg, a visit to its neighboring town Pinevale was too tempting to pass on.

"You have to walk to the end of the road." Arms crossed, he stares at me with his back against the bike. He's taken his helmet off, and now that my eyes have adjusted to the darkness, I can see his high cheekbones and broad forehead. His eyebrows are thick and well-defined, sitting above striking almond-shaped eyes. With his straight and slightly narrow nose, long beard and mustache, and dark brown hair falling over his shoulders, he's the most astonishingly attractive person I've ever seen in real life.

And for some reason, he kissed me.

"Great," I mumble.

"You know, there's no way a little bump caused this. It would have happened regardless of our accident."

"I thought you were leaving?"

He shrugs, then walks. "And find out in the morning that you've been a victim of the local Hannibal Lecter?" He raises the hood of the car. "Wouldn't be able to live with myself."

"Ha-ha." I step closer, then look down at the incomprehensible cables and boxes. "Do you know what you're doing? I don't want more trouble with the rental agency."

"Happy to leave you to it yourself if you'd like."

I'd like him to go to hell, but 'the end of the road' feels like a whole lot in these heels, and I can't deal with how dark and silent this place is. With nothing around but fields, the thought of being alone out here is terrifying.

As casually as I can, I twist my neck and watch him, the kiss flashing through my mind. How his beard scratched my skin, and his taste, which I can only describe as "wild nature." He has the most beautiful hooded bedroom eyes I've ever seen, and while I'm usually more into metrosexual men than gruff, rugged types, I'm pretty sure he rearranged my chromosomes.

"See if there's a toolbox in the trunk."

I walk around the car, then stand in front of the trunk, looking for the handle. By the time I finally find the hidden button, he's glaring at me over the car's roof. "Got it."

"Congratulations."

Ugh, why does such a good kisser have to be an ass?

There's a small green box, so I bring it over, and with a relieved sigh, he opens it. "No flashlight."

Flashlight? "I have a flashlight."

He cocks a brow at me, and with a huffed chuckle, I take out my phone.

I turn the flashlight on, eyes narrowing when he goes 'huh,' then point it at the hood. He's already removed a black piece that looks identical to all the other black pieces, and grabbing a wrench from the toolbox, he begins working.

Once again, I lose myself watching him, but I guess I'm excused. Finding someone who kisses you that well is not an everyday occurrence. In fact, I'd say if ever, it takes someone a good amount of tries to get it exactly right. But this guy had never met me before, had definitely never kissed me, and yet he just knew. There's something to it, isn't there? Like chemistry.

"Quit staring at me."

Okay, maybe not *chemistry*.

I scowl, and for a while, I watch his hands at work, though I have no clue what he's doing, and all I can do is pray that *he* knows. But it feels like forever, especially with the soft rustling of leaves and grass as unseen creatures navigate their way through the darkness.

Swallowing, I lean with my hip against the car. I focus on the noises I hear, shifting left and right, until my heart is thumping and I'm as tense as a bowstring. "Tell me something about yourself," I burst.

Wrench in hand, he cocks a brow at me. "Huh?"

"I can't stand the silence. The darkness." I look around, picturing what could be hiding behind the bushes and tall grass. "Just say something."

"*You* don't like the silence and the darkness. *You* say something."

Fair enough. He just had his first panic attack, and I'm here trying to make conversation. He must be exhausted, scared, confused—of course, he doesn't want to talk. But I don't mind talking, and it's not like I'm dying to get to know this guy. "Uh, fine. I . . . I love making candy. Do you like candy?"

His lips press tight together.

"I've never ridden a bike," I say, figuring I should aim for the one thing I know he likes. "How did you learn?"

He rubs his forehead with the sleeve of his jacket, his hands black with motor oil.

I give up. I have absolutely no idea what to say, and I'm willing to bet 'How old are you?' or 'What's your zodiac sign?' won't achieve better results.

"I have a love bucket list," I offer when the silence turns quieter and the night darker. His eyes dart to me, and I give him a tight-lipped smile. Seeing as this has attracted the attention of millions of people online, I figured it was a safe bet even with this ray of sunshine.

"A *love* bucket list?"

With a timid shrug, I say, "A list of things I'd like to do with a boyfriend. Or that he'd do for me. With me. *To* me." I tap my fingers on my knee. "You get it."

His eyes study me. "Are you dying?"

"What? No!"

"I had to make sure. Who has a bucket list at your age?"

"What's the point of a bucket list if you write it on your deathbed?" I ask. When he tilts his head in a 'you have a point' motion, I continue. "There are certain things I want from love, and they haven't happened yet, which can get depressing real fast. When I feel down, I look at the list, and I can see my future. The one I want, anyway."

He pauses. "But you're not dying."

"No, I'm not dying," I confirm, my voice taking an annoyed edge.

When he smirks, I roll my eyes. He's mocking me, and I'm making it easy. "What's on the list?"

"A lot of things."

"Tell me one."

Pressing my lips tight, I hum. *"Kiss my forehead."*

"Tell me one you *haven't* crossed off."

Eyes lowering to the ground, I pause for a long moment. "Uh, I guess . . . *Fight for me.*"

He says nothing, and I could kick myself for choosing something so depressing.

"How about *Kiss someone I just ran over*? Do you have that one?"

Laughter blossoms out of my lips, and thankful for the quick change of topic, I tilt my head. Though I'm afraid it isn't on my bucket list, that kiss should be. It was like nothing I've ever experienced. The low vibration of pleasure out of his mouth and right into mine. The way his hand inched down my back.

"Kiss me until I can't breathe." I look up at the clear sky sprinkled with stars. "I could cross that off now."

He clears his throat, but I see how his chest puffs up with pride. "Could?" he asks. "You won't?"

"I don't have my list." I bring a hand to the back of my neck. "I lost it a while back."

"So write it again."

"Yeah. I should." The muscles beneath my fingers stiffen, and I quickly regret mentioning the list at all. It's all I've been thinking about—that stupid list. It was supposed to represent my hope, to give me comfort. Now, it's a nightmare, following me wherever I go. A reason for ridicule. A scar.

"Okay. Let's test this out," he says. When I stare at him wordlessly, he points at the car. "That means get in and try to start this piece of junk."

"Oh." I settle on the driver's seat, then turn the key in the ignition. Though it makes a slightly more encouraging noise than before, it's still not what I'd like to hear.

"—re gas."

"What?" I ask.

"Give it—"

"I can't hear you!"

"Goddamn it," he grunts as he appears by my side. "Let me try."

"You think I don't know how to start a car?"

His eyes narrow, his lips pressed so hard it looks like his head might explode. Taking pity on him, I get out of the car and let him in.

In two seconds, the car engine is *roaring*.

He's right. It *is* a piece of junk.

"There." He steps out of the car. "It needed more gas."

"Oh." I nod, then throw him an awkward glance. I guess this is it. Maybe I should ask his name—I'd like to have something to call him when I reminisce about tonight. About our kiss. "Thank you so much."

He barely acknowledges me as he walks to the hood and pulls it down. Then, brushing his hands together, he stands silently for a long moment. "Well, all right. Goodbye. Again."

"I'm Primrose," I say to his back once he turns.

He stops, then throws me a head-to-toe glare. "Of course you are."

I've been told my name fits my aesthetic well, but never in *that* tone. Is he just not going to tell me his name? "And you?"

He shrugs. "Logan."

Ugh. Logan. Even his name is hot. He doesn't *deserve* a hot name.

When he slides his helmet on, I enter the car. By the time his engine roars, I'm holding the seat belt, unable to look away from Logan. Though the dark helmet shields his face completely, I know he's staring at me.

I wave, and without as much as a nod, he takes off. Before long, he disappears around the corner.

Gone.

Trying to release the adrenaline sizzling inside me with a deep sigh, I focus on the car dashboard. This was a minor detour, but tonight is hardly over. I have a love bucket list to retrieve, and I'm not leaving this podunk of a town until I have it.

I pull into first gear, then release the handbrake, and after moving half a foot forward, the car engine sputters and dies, leaving me in the utter silence and darkness I spent the last half hour trying so hard to avoid.

Huffing out a breath, I throw my head back.

Fuck. My. Life.

The cab stops, and on one side of me are vast fields sectioned by rows of fruit trees, while on the other, a gate leading down a long, dark driveway. Though the weather might not have gotten the note about spring starting a few weeks ago, nature has, and the rolling hills in the distance are covered with blankets of lush green grass and dotted with colorful wildflowers.

"Is here okay?" the driver asks.

"Uh, y-yeah." I have no idea, actually. "Is that Derek Gracen's farm?"

He nods. "Well, it's his dad's farm, but he retired a couple of years ago, and Derek has taken over." He throws a concerned look at me through the mirror. "He's not a great kid, you know, sweetheart?"

Through the rearview mirror, I glance at the driver, whose worried expression reminds me of my dad. Where was he six months ago to warn me about this demon of a man?

"Oh, I know."

He nods, then points at the black gate. "That's him."

With a "thank you," I get out of the cab, clinging to my bag, then walk to the gate. There's a doorbell, but I'm sure he'd refuse to see me if I rang it. He's been avoiding confrontation for so long; I doubt he'd be keen now.

But I'll *make* him.

Sure, I planned to show up here at eight, not at midnight. But with the accident, then having to walk for miles, call the rental company, then the cab, I'm not left with much choice. I'll have to find a way back to Roseberg tonight, because my flight back home is tomorrow.

So it's happening. Tonight. I'm getting my list back.

I hold on to the metal gate, then pull myself up and climb over another horizontal metal piece, praying to god I don't fall and break my neck.

"Okay. Almost there," I mumble as I swing my other leg over. I find the same piece of metal to stand on and release a deep breath, hopping to the ground.

Done. Wasn't so bad either.

Silently, I walk down the driveway, my lips parting as the villa comes into view. It's gorgeous. Its large windows emit a soft yellow light, painting the surrounding grounds with a warmth that reaches out into the darkness. The sturdy wooden beams and expansive wraparound porch make it look even more imposing as I step closer, the scent of wood smoke and earth filling my senses.

Following along the well-kept driveway, I reach the front porch, my hands sweating as my heart thumps faster.

I need to do this.

Yes, it's downright idiotic, especially with everything he's been saying about me online. But that's *my* list. *My* stupid piece of paper.

"I want it back," I mumble, and when I hike my bag up my shoulder, its contents spill onto the porch. Because of course they do. With a silent 'Fuck!' I lean down, then hastily shove my makeup and keys back inside. I silently wait for Derek to open the door and find me on my hands and knees on his porch, but nothing happens besides a noise in the distance.

Thank god he didn't hear me.

I grab the lighter that landed next to the flower pot, only now realizing I still have that pack of cigarettes I confiscated from my dad last month when I visited him.

I'm not a smoker, but I'm also not a trespasser, yet here we are. So, hoping it'll help calm my nerves, I take out a cigarette, bring it to my lips, and flick my thumb over the spark wheel, igniting a flame on my fourth try. When I breathe in, I almost immediately explode into a coughing fit.

"Shit!" I choke out as I try to cough on the inside. The smoke from the cigarette makes my eyes tear up, and smelling it only seems to worsen my cough. I stand, rushing down the steps and onto the front yard, then drop it and hack into my elbow.

Why do people smoke?

When my throat is done spasming, and my lungs feel clear, I register the smell of the cigarette, only to notice a small pile of dry leaves catching fire.

Seriously?! Of all the places it could have landed on?

"No, no, no," I whisper-shout as I approach it, then hold my foot over it. I think of stomping on the flames, but they're rising too quickly. Next best option is to smother it, so I gather more leaves in my hands and throw them on top. Unfortunately, it has the opposite effect.

"Holy shit," I breathe out as I watch the fire grow higher, the flames licking the trash can next to the porch.

A loud noise nearby has me flinching, and with my heart in my throat, I run. Fast, ignoring the bouncing of my boobs—hardly supported in a bra that was not made for sports—or the fact that my heels are sinking in the mud, and I can't see a single thing.

I run, knowing that if I'm found here, trying to set my ex-boyfriend's property on fire, my life is officially over.

When I make out a long fence in the distance, I sprint toward it, hoping there's safety on the other side. By the time I reach it, my lungs burn, and my muscles tremble so hard that I'm not sure I can pull my leg over it. I gasp, catching my breath as I look behind me at the flames casting an orange glow in the night.

The sound of a gate clacking shut has me turning to the right, where a man in all black is running away from the house in a very similar fashion as what I just did, except it looks like he's escaping from the back of the property.

"Oh crap," I whimper when I realize he's running my way. It must be Derek, and the thought of being caught paralyzes me on the spot.

I'm so screwed.

My heart gallops in my chest as he stops a few feet from me.

Are those . . . piglets tucked under his arms?

"You *must* be kidding me" comes out of his lips, and with a flinch, I realize this man is definitely *not* Derek. He's taller—his shoulders much broader. Broader than the average human, actually. And his voice is gruff, stern—nothing like Derek's slightly nasal tone.

I can't see his face, but I don't need to. It's him. The man I hit. The one who panicked. The one who kissed me, then abandoned me.

Logan.

Why is he here? And why is he holding a piglet under each arm?

When a loud voice comes from the house, Logan turns around, his eyes bulging as he probably sees the flames.

He steps onto the fence, then tries to get one leg over it, but the squirming piglets restrict his movements, and he wobbles back down. "Shit—" He turns to me. "Grab her."

"What?" I hiss, cowering away from the small pink animal he's holding out.

"Grab the piglet and climb over."

"I'm—I'm not touching that . . . that *wild beast*."

"It's a pig, not a bear," he grits.

I open my mouth to quip back, but the sound of police sirens shuts me up instantly. I grab one of the piglets, tuck it under one arm exactly like he did, and climb over the gate after him.

He grasps my arm to help me ease down, and I land in front of him just as someone turns a light on outside Derek's house, illuminating Logan's face just enough for me to make out the gray-blue irises of his hooded eyes, the sharp line of his jaw. Geez, he's handsome.

By the time I remember myself, his full lips—which have been pressed into a rigid line—open in a snarl. "You want a picture, Barbie? Fucking run."

"What?"

"Run," he barks. "And don't look back."

you kick during sex

. . .

Logan

WHO *IS* THIS WOMAN?

I follow Primrose through the dense patch of forest that separates the Gracen farm and mine, the crunch of leaves and broken twigs under our feet mixing with our ragged breathing and the occasional squeal from the piglets.

Fucking piglets.

I almost lost it when they hid from me behind some giant, pissed-off, territorial pig. It tried to bite my hand off, and the scene must've been loud enough to alert Derek, because I distinctly heard someone running toward the sty.

Then something else happened. Something that distracted Derek Gracen enough for me to run the fuck out of there with the piglets. This woman. I was either leaving with them or getting arrested trying, and now thanks to her, I'm one step closer to the former.

Did I dream up that orange glow? Was it a fire?

"Crap!" Primrose hisses as she trips. She manages to turn before she hits the ground, the piglet held high, but it doesn't prevent me from dropping too, my arm ending up in a thorny bush I might never extract it from.

There's silence for a moment, and though there are plenty of nightlife creatures making all sorts of noises around us, I can't hear any with the way my heart is beating in my ears.

"My ass," she whines, and after taking a deep breath, I pull my arm out, ignoring the sting of the thorns digging into my skin.

God, I'm lightheaded.

"You good?" I ask as I get to my feet, holding the screaming piglet to my chest.

Her full lips are bent into a grimace as she mutters, "Yeah, I'm *fuck*-tastic."

I help her up next, her small palm getting lost in mine. Her wide and deep blue eyes stare back at me as her straight, slightly upturned nose twitches. She must be over a foot shorter than me, and as my eyes run down her body, searching for potential damage, I notice her hourglass figure— her full bust, slim waist, and rounded hips.

Pretty, even in that ridiculous glittery pink dress.

I look away, deciding it's easier to concentrate when I'm not obsessing over our kiss. "We're almost clear," I whisper. "But we need to run fast. The police will know to come to my farm, and they'll be quicker by car. Can you keep going?"

When she nods, I gesture at her to go before me and follow her through the dense trees until my wooden fence comes into sight. I hold her arm to stop her and bring my index finger to my lips. I need to make sure the police aren't already here.

I hop over the fence and slowly walk along the back wall and to the side, and once I confirm the driveway is clear, I tell Primrose to come. She awkwardly jumps over the fence and joins me, shushing the piglet, who emits a continuous screech, as if it will suddenly start listening to her.

She opens her mouth to speak, but is immediately silenced by faded red and blue intermittent lights in the distance. Her face turns whiter than a sheet, and it spurs me to fit a hand into my pocket and look for my keys.

Which I can't find.

"What do we do?" she asks in a trembling whisper. "I can't be arrested. I'm too soft. They make you wear pants in prison, don't they?"

My eyes narrow over her face as I search the other pocket.

"Of course they do," she whines. "It's not like it's tennis."

Where are my stupid keys?

"The food must be terrible too. And I can't sleep without my pillow. Oh!" She gasps, cupping her mouth. "I have a shy bladder. How do people with shy bladders survive prison?"

"Shut the fuck—" I cut myself off with a groan. I must have dropped the goddamn keys when we fell, and finding them would be hopeless even if the sun were shining, but in the middle of the night? No way.

I walk to my pickup, happy to see I left the window open like always, and I reach in to pull the lock, then set the piglet on the driver's-side floor. Thankfully, Primrose followed me, so I set the other piglet inside and shut the door. Enclosed in the comfortable space, they immediately settle down.

If they squeal, we're toast.

"You have to hide me, okay? I can't be arrested. I'm somewhat of a public figure and this would ruin me. *Ruin me.*" Primrose rushes out. "I'll pay you. What do you want? I'll do anything. Anything, please—"

Oh my god, she won't shut up, and the police cruiser must be at the top of the driveway because the lights look static now. We're out of time.

Grabbing her hand, I drag her to the backyard as I start to undo my flannel top. By the time we reach my old outdoor wooden table, she's looking at my naked chest with wide eyes. "Take off your dress."

"What?"

"Your dress," I insist. "We have less than a minute."

"I'm not—" She crosses her arms, a scowl on her heart-shaped face. "Okay, look, I let you kiss me, but when I said I'll do *anything*, I meant—"

"Fucking take off your dress, or pee in front of a pants-wearing murderer in your new cell." I pull my shirt off and drop it on the table behind her. "Put this on."

We're standing so close, every quick breath makes the tip of her tits brush against my stomach. Her eyes run down my body, her pupils dilating ever so slightly, as if deciding whether I'm worth having sex with to evade prison.

She winces, her body vibrating with indecision until she grabs my shirt from beside her. "Turn around."

"You can't be serio—"

"Turn around!"

Oh, for the love of god.

I turn my back on her, listening to gravel crunching under the officers' shoes. They'll knock at the house first. Then they'll check the pickup. So if Purity Princess can get sorted quickly enough, I'll make a noise that will drive them out here before they think of flashing their lights through the car window.

"Okay," she whispers. "I'm done."

I'm mid-turn when I hear knocking from the other side of the house. They're at the door, which means I need to make this happen *right now*.

But as I stare down at the pocket-sized Barbie wearing my shirt, the fabric brushing past her knees, I forget it all for a second. She looks exactly the way she should. Disheveled, dirty, out of breath. Wearing something of mine, in which she looks much better than I do.

"What now?" she mouths, and even though she makes no sound, I can almost hear her desperation, and it helps me snap back into focus. Grabbing both of her thighs, I pick her up and set her down on the table, her legs hanging over the edge as her ass lands on it. She lets out a little gasp, and once I smack my hand against the table, her mouth opens to form a small O. The noise that reverberates is so loud I'm expecting the cops to wander back here any second.

Fitting between her legs, I lean forward, my eyes on her, and her shaky breath fanning over my chin. She maintains a safe distance from me as I advance, until the top half of her body is lying down on the table, and she has nowhere to escape.

Shit, look at those innocent, big blue eyes.

She's beautiful.

Dragging my gaze away from hers, I veer to the left and kiss her neck, hoisting her legs up until she takes the hint and wraps them around my ass.

My chest presses against hers, the cold night air doing nothing to cool the rising temperature of my body. I can't even tell what it is—if it's fear, uncomfortable intimacy, or such sudden arousal that I'm struggling to keep up with it.

I pepper kisses down her neck, then along my shirt collar, reminding myself to stop before my lips dip further down. But man, does she taste great. Smells great, feels great too, her wide hips squeezed in my hands.

When she sighs softly and goosebumps rise on the skin of her chest, I look up at her. Eyes closed, she's arching into me so her pebbled nipples brush against my skin.

Is she . . . enjoying this?

Her hands run up my shoulders to lock around my neck, and I fit one arm under her, her soft body clinging to mine in all the right places.

She *is* enjoying it.

Maybe danger-infused sex with a stranger as the police watch isn't the worst idea I could have.

Someone clears their throat, and I flinch. I lift a shoulder, though not enough to expose Primrose, and connect with a pair of green eyes I'd recognize anywhere. In a second, my arms retract and she slams back down on the table with a thump.

"Fuck," I say as I look down at her. "Sorry. You okay?"

She glares, and with my heart beating wildly in my chest, I focus on Josie again.

"Didn't mean to interrupt." Josie walks closer, her vigilant green eyes on Primrose. Her gaze flips to me, and with her lips pressed together, she hooks one finger on the loop of her belt next to her holster. "Hey, Logan."

"Hi." *Fuck!* What is she even doing here? I thought she was stationed in Roseberg now. "Hi, Jo—what . . . what's going on?"

Primrose shifts between my hands, pulling at my shirt until she's sitting on the table. Another officer comes into the light, and I exhale.

Connor Harper.

Good friend to one Derek *goddamn* Gracen.

"We got a call from the Gracen farm. Someone stole their animals again." Josie's brows arch, a patient smile fixed on her face as she tucks a strand of fiery red hair behind her ear. "And they set his garbage on fire as a distraction."

I hum, turning to Primrose. No matter how much I try to picture it, I can't imagine this tiny, pink-haired woman committing arson.

"You happen to know anything about it, Coleman?" Connor asks.

I look at the pair again and shrug. "Not really, no. As you can see, I'm pretty busy." I drive the point home by squeezing Primrose's thigh, and she squeals in surprise.

Josie's circumstantial smile disappears, and she straightens the tie clipped onto her beige shirt with a sigh.

"Your rap sheet just gets more and more vivacious, doesn't it?" Connor continues, rubbing his salt-and-pepper stubble. "Break-in, burglary, and now arson?"

"All you can arrest me for is a little public indecency," I quip back. "Does that hold up if you're at your own house?"

Connor nearly sneers, and Josie steps in front of him, giving him her *Quit it* look. I know it far too well. "Okay, hm . . . What's your name?" she asks, looking away from me.

"Primrose—Bellevue."

"Primrose, did you spend all night with Logan?" Josie holds a hand up. "And please remember that lying to me could turn you into an accomplice to his crimes."

My crimes? Sure.

Primrose tilts her head to study me, and I clench my jaw, focusing on her clouded blue eyes. I'm not worried she'll rat me out, but she also doesn't look like a super-confident liar. "Y-yeah. We went to the bar, then we thought we could—we like to keep things interesting, you know? Sexually."

Josie's eyes flick to mine, and I try to cringe inwardly as I slowly nod. "Uh, yep."

"So you two are together?"

"Yeah," Primrose says as her small hand taps my chest. "Inseparable. I'm obsessed—no, not *obsessed*—just, hmm, I love him so much."

Oh, god. She's panicking, isn't she?

"Huh." Josie's eyes pierce mine. "And you didn't think a woman loving you was worth mentioning to your family?"

Primrose grasps my hand on the table, her fingers squeezing until my blood flow is cut off.

"I was going to," I say as I try to escape her death grip. "You know me. Privacy."

"Solve your family drama in your free time, Officer Lawson," Connor tells Josie as he walks past her, stopping in front of me and planting both hands on his hips. He jerks his chin forward, as if it can compensate for the half foot difference in our height. "Where are the pigs, Logan?"

"Pigs?"

"The animals that were stolen."

I suck in a quick breath. "Ohh. You mean the pigs that were weaned from the sow earlier than it's legal to do?" I click my tongue. "Yeah, I've heard about that. Horrible business, but I'm sure you guys are on top of it." I smirk down at the nearly bald man. "Aren't you, *Conny*?"

"Just because Derek *allegedly* did something illegal, it doesn't mean you can too, Logan," Josie says before Connor can interject. She sighs in the same way she always does when we find ourselves in this sort of situation, which might be a little more often than I care for. "It's up to the authorities to prove a crime has occurred, then take the correct measures against it."

"I'm aware." I turn to Primrose, then glance down at her plump lips. She's chewing on the bottom one, and I fight the impulse to pull it free with my thumb. "Which is why I was here taking care of my girl." I focus on Connor. "Several times. All night long. Right, cupcake?"

She swallows hard, then nods.

"Mind if we take a look inside?" he hisses.

"I do. A great deal."

Connor nods, and it's only when Josie tells him they should go for the third time that he disappears along the side of the house. Josie stays, watching us curiously for a moment longer before saying, "Come over next week, huh? Both of you? We can have dinner." Her eyes soften, and she adds, "Sadie would love to see you."

"Yeah, okay. We'll try."

She nods, giving me the sad look of someone who knows they're being lied to. Then she hesitates and says, "Logan, are you . . . bleeding?"

Shit. I look down at my arm and find blood streaming from a gash below my elbow. The thorns, if I were to guess. "Just a little scratch," I mumble.

"How'd you get it?"

I shrug, holding her inquisitive gaze. "You know . . ." I awkwardly pat Primrose's arm, and she's nearly shaking with fear. "Primrose likes to use her nails."

Her pupils blow as she stares up at me, her cheeks clamped between her teeth. Then, almost as quickly as it showed up, the expression is gone, and she's nodding at Josie. "Yeah. Scratching and—and slapping. And kicking too, or—"

"Anyway," I stop her, hooking an arm around her shoulders and squishing her against my chest. "If there's nothing else we can do for you . . ."

"No." Josie takes a step back, studying us. "I'll see you at dinner at our place, Logan. Both of you, since you're in a serious, committed relationship." Her chin dips. "Right?"

"Right."

"Great." She clicks her tongue. "Stick around. No skipping town." Then, without waiting for confirmation, she walks around the corner.

Shoulders falling, I let Primrose go.

"Oh, god," she whispers as she slowly reclines onto the table, her chest heaving with each quick breath. If she's experiencing half of the adrenaline crash I am, I get it. I can't get arrested again. It'll give my mom that heart attack doctors have been threatening her with for years.

Head tipping forward, I glance down at Primrose's legs. The shirt has ridden up her thighs and is now bunched around her hips, her green underwear on full display.

Are those . . . smiling sloths?

Yes, they are. Smiling brown sloths on an olive-green background.

"Hey!" she shouts as she shoves me, her other hand tugging at her shirt to cover up. "What the hell? Are you staring at my underwear?"

"Sloth—I mean, *shit*, no." I turn around, searching the ground as she hops off the table, my cheeks heating.

Really smooth, Logan.

"Yes, you were." There's a moment of silence, then, "What are you doing?"

"I'm looking for a rock."

"A rock? What for?"

I find one that's big enough and walk past her to the back door without a word. I hold it up, then send it crashing against the glass as I keep one arm over my face. Careful to avoid the jagged shards still attached to the window frame, I fit one arm inside and twist the lock.

She's at my side in the next breath. "Wait a second," she whispers, her big, worried eyes studying me. "I don't know what impression I gave you, but I'm not a criminal, okay? I can't even lie. I'm family-rich, and I've been shielded from everything my whole life. My dad made us cross the street when a homeless man was on the sidewalk, you know?"

I pull my arm out, shaking my head. "What the hell are you on about now?"

"I can't break into another house."

"This is my house. I lost the key."

Her lips part, and I open the door. "Wait here. I'll clean up." My boots crunch on the glass as I turn on the light. I walk the corridor to the entryway closet, and when I return with the broom, Primrose is leaning against the doorframe, her naked legs crossed in front of her. All the way to her knees, her skin is scratched and dirty with blood and mud, and her hair is ruffled on the back of her head. As her eyes burn into mine, I have to remind myself the nearly naked woman in front of me is only wearing my shirt because of the stupidest turn of events in history.

"What?" she asks, her head barely lifting.

"Nothing."

"I'll go get my dress, then I'll call a cab and be out of your hair."

Brows screwing tight over my eyes, I shake my head. "You what? You can't leave. You just told Josie we're together, and she'll be back in the morning, trust me."

"Oh. So . . . do I need to sleep here?"

"Afraid so."

She hesitates as I sweep around her. "Are you . . . are you a criminal?"

"No more than you."

She seems to want to disagree but stops before saying a single thing.

"If I'm going to sleep here, I need to know I can trust you," she murmurs.

I clean some more shards off the tiles, her eyes on me, and I'm not sure what she's expecting. *She* told the cops we're in love, and now I have to prove myself to her? "You know, you hit me with your car. And *you're* the arsonist. I'll be lucky if I don't wake up with smoke down my lungs, so maybe you should be the one to prove you're not dangerous."

"I am not an arsonist." She points up and down her body. "Look at me."

Yes, she looks ridiculous.

Yet shit went up in flames.

"Fine," I say as I drop the broom on one side. "You want me to prove I'm honest?" I shrug. "I *was* staring at your underwear."

"I knew it!"

"Yeah, give me a break. If there's a half-naked woman in front of me, I'm going to look. Okay? It's biology."

"Yeah. Perv biology," she mumbles as she looks away.

Fucking unbelievable.

"No, not perv biology. The same biology that makes you grind against a man you're fleeing a crime scene with." I shoot my brows up my forehead. "Because biology works like that. If I kiss your neck a certain way, I end up feeling your nipples against my chest."

She opens and closes her mouth a bunch, her cheeks turning redder by the second, until I walk into the corridor and open the first door to the right. "Guest bedroom. Bathroom's the next door. Good night, and don't touch the matches."

"I am *not* an arsonist, you dick," she calls after me.

Turning around, I say, "It brings out the pink in your hair, you know?"

She narrows her eyes. "What?"

I wink. "Your green underwear."

make me feel better after a bad dream
. . .
Primrose

THIS IS OFFICIALLY the worst night of my life.

The events of the last few hours keep running through my head, each more unrealistic than the next. Why did I rent that car? I never drive. I've also kissed three people in my life, and tonight let a stranger grope me. And why—*why* did I decide to pick up smoking?

It feels like even showering didn't help with the crippling terror.

I'm a criminal. Lying to the police makes it official, and I spent the last few hours twisting and turning in bed, trying to make my mind up.

I can't be arrested. It's not like I meant to set anything on fire anyway. Sure, I'm guilty of trespassing, but people don't go to prison for that, do they?

I grab my phone to do a quick online search, but there's no service, and after watching the screen buffer for a few seconds, I set it back down.

Just when I need to know if there's such a thing as "accidental arson."

I peer around the small room, trying to decipher something—anything—about the man whose house I'm currently sleeping in, but there's not much to go on. A bookshelf, a desk, and a crate full of toys. The fact that they're neatly stacked in the guest room probably means whoever the child is, they don't come here often.

Those two cops seemed to know him. The man, whom Logan called *Conny*, definitely wasn't a fan, but Josie? Connor said she and Logan are family. Could she be an ex-wife? He looks older than me—maybe thirty.

Oh my god. What if she makes it her life's mission to prove I'm guilty of my crimes because she thinks I slept with her ex-husband?

"Shit," I mutter as I sit on the edge of the bed. Maybe I should leave this house and never come back. If I get a cab to the airport, will they contact the authorities back in Mayfield?

We need to figure this out—right now, I decide as I stand and open the bedroom door. Everything's dark, but the door to what I presume is Logan's bedroom isn't fully shut.

Approaching with as much stealth as I can muster, I look through the sliver and locate the two piglets sleeping in a bundle of blankets on the floor. The moonlight hits the bed directly, and Logan's lying face down, his long hair strewn over the pillow and a sheen of sweat covering his broad back.

Everything I can see from here is covered in intricate black tattoos.

For a moment, my eyes run over the muscles and furrows. I haven't personally seen a whole lot of naked men, but none of what I *have* seen comes close to the near perfection that is this man's upper body. I didn't even know people this sculpted existed, and it's as thrilling as it is intimidating.

Pushing the door open, I walk to one side of the bed and call his name. Nothing. I do it again, a little louder, but he makes no sign of having heard me, so I climb onto the thick mattress and sit on my heels.

"Logan?" I insist as I gently shake his arm.

He flinches. "Hmm?" He turns over and narrows his eyes, his

long brown locks caught in the crease of his neck. "If you're going to set me on fire, have the decency to let me sleep through it."

"I'm *not* an arsonist," I insist.

"Whatever you are, you're in the wrong room."

He turns his back on me, and I have to press my lips tight at the sight of his rippling muscles. "Logan, what happens when the police come back?"

He inhales. "Normally, they'd drop it. The police department can't waste resources on two stolen piglets, and Derek knows better than to try to take me on by himself. But your little pyro-show spices things up."

"So what will we do?"

"Same as we did last night," he mumbles in a sleepy voice. "Lie our asses off." He twists his neck to look at me over his shoulder. "Which, by the way, you suck at. Do I look to you like someone who'd let you kick him during sex?"

Ignoring him, I shake my head. My chest feels tight, and there's a fluttering sensation in my stomach that won't disappear. "Listen, I think I should just tell the truth."

His head drops on the pillow, and after a groan, he pulls himself up. The blanket bunches at his waist as he leans against the headboard, a hand rubbing the side of his beard. "What?"

"It's not like I meant to set Derek's garbage on fire. It was just an accident."

"But *did* you set it on fire?"

"Yes."

"Afraid it still counts as a crime." Hand dropping from his face, he studies me for a few seconds, then he shrugs. "You do realize you're not even a suspect, right? They think I set that asshole's garbage on fire so I could steal the piglets."

"But there must be my DNA on the crime scene. And if they search the woods, they'll find my blood. Look," I say, pointing at the scratches on my legs.

"Search the woods?" He huffs out a laugh. "Does that happen before or after the FBI sends a helicopter?"

How am I supposed to know?! "Before?"

With an eye roll, he stands and walks to the piglets. He gives them both a cuddle, and then he's out of the room. Unsure of what to do, I follow after him.

The light in the kitchen is on, and as I walk closer, I find Logan reaching into a cupboard and pulling out a white mug. "Tea?" When I nod, he mumbles, "Maybe I should get you some Valium to go with it."

I sit at the old kitchen table, tapping my fingers on my leg and wondering how he's so calm. It must mean he's broken the law before, right? Because I'm pretty sure my reaction is perfectly normal. And now that I think about it, Josie said it's not the first time someone stole Derek's animals.

"Do you do this a lot?"

He cocks a brow at me. "*This*?"

"Just . . . burglary?"

With a wide smirk that turns into a chuckle, he nods. "Now and then."

I can't tell if he's serious, so I bite the inside of my cheek and look out the window.

"Do *you* often—"

"I'm not a fricking arsonist, okay?"

He sets the kettle on a burner and turns with his back to the yellow counter, arms crossed. "That's not how the police will see it, though. All they know is that you trespassed in the middle of the night, set his property on fire, then escaped and lied about it."

"It was an accident. I wanted to talk to him."

He hums as if he doesn't believe me. "Irrelevant."

"Look, I can't go to prison, okay?" I know Logan will eventually find out what's been happening between Derek and me, and trying to convince him tonight was just an accident will be impossible. "It's an important moment for my career, and everything's already falling apart, and I can't . . ." I shake my head, eyes fiercely stuck on his. "I can't go to prison."

"Do what I say, and you won't." He points a thumb behind him. "Starting with, drink this tea, go to bed, and let me sleep."

Rude.

"Why did you take those pigs?"

"Because he was going to kill them."

At this point, I'd accept pretty much any excuse to hate Derek some more, but a farmer killing pigs is hardly newsworthy. "And?"

His jaw is set as his eyes turn darker. Somewhere in the periphery, the kettle begins a low hiss. "*And?*"

"I mean—aren't you a farmer too?"

"*And* he weaned them before it was time," he mumbles, then must notice it means nearly nothing to me, because he continues. "If piglets are separated from the sow too early, the changes in feed and environment will harm their development." He fills the cups with water. "Those pigs were going to become bacon one day. At the very least, they deserved to live their life without any added stress. Don't you think?"

"Sure," I whisper. I can't say that I've ever thought about pigs' well-being a whole lot, but when he puts it that way, it's hard to argue against it. "Then why did he do it?"

"Because he's a cheap asshole who cuts corners, takes what he wants, and doesn't care who or what gets hurt in the process." Looking over his shoulder, he holds the tea bags over the cups. "Sound familiar?"

Awfully so.

"Look, there's going to be an investigation, but they have nothing on us."

"Except for the piglets. What about them?"

"No one will find the piglets."

I chew my nails. I'm not a huge fan of farm animals, and if I could go the rest of my life without touching another pig, that'd be great. But thinking of those two tiny things becoming someone's lunch is almost sickening. "What will you do with them?"

"What, you think I almost got arrested so I could use them for breakfast?" He rolls his eyes. "This is a vegan farm. All the animals here are safe."

A *vegan* farm. That makes more sense.

"There could have been cameras."

He shakes his head firmly. "No cameras."

I exhale, propping my legs on the chair and hugging my knees. "What about the cab I took to Derek's farm? I talked to the cab driver—he'd definitely be able to pick me out of a line-up."

"I'll take care of him. He'll be sleeping with the fish come nighttime," he says with a dramatically creepy voice.

Pretty sure that he's joking, I rest my chin on my knees, but I can't get rid of this weight pressing on my chest. If any of this gets out, I'm screwed, and knowing Derek, he's probably itching to cry about it online.

"Relax, okay? This is a small town, and people know how Derek and I feel about each other, so they'll pin last night on me." He takes a sip of his tea. "And besides, any cab driver would look at you and think you're more likely to water someone's flowers than set anything on fire."

I guess a short, blond, chubby woman isn't exactly the typical criminal profile people look for. "But Derek! If he finds me here—"

"Look, Primrose. You know the policewoman from tonight?"

"Josie?" When he nods, I ask, "Is she your ex-wife?"

He scoffs and shakes his head. "Where the hell did you get that from?"

"Yeesh," I say with wide eyes. "Forget I said anything."

"She's my sister-in-law. She won't let that interfere with her work, but she's also not exactly out for blood." He pushes my mug closer as if to invite me to drink. "So it's in our best interest to do what she says, carry on the way she expects two people madly in love would, and hope this doesn't reach her bosses."

"So what, I should stay here indefinitely?" I ask before blowing on the hot tea.

"No, thank you." He hums, tilting his head. "Maybe a couple of weeks."

"A couple of *weeks*?"

"Well, I wasn't the one to tell her we were starting a family together, was I?" He narrows his eyes at me. "And I'm not exactly thrilled at the idea of you sticking around either."

"This isn't my fault. You had the stupid idea of pretending we were . . ." I gesture wildly, and his hooded, tired eyes follow the movement of my hand.

"Except it worked."

"Worked?" I shriek. This guy is unbelievable, isn't he? *"That's* why she asked if we were together, Logan. What was I supposed to say?"

"Plenty of things. Like that we met at the bar and you came back to mine to have your ass fucked." He shrugs. "Which, by the way, is much more credible than you being a dominant kicker."

Heat moving to the tips of my ears, I take my cup into both hands and raise it to cover my face—anything to avoid looking him in the eyes. "God, you're so vulgar! I don't . . . do *that*," I hiss. "And besides, how are we supposed to convince anyone we're together? Look at us."

Though he cocks a brow, he doesn't say a thing, and with a sigh, I drop my head.

"Give it a couple of weeks," he insists. "That'll be enough for them to exhaust any lead. And enough for Josie to believe you're my long-distance girlfriend who came to visit." He levels me with an unimpressed stare. "Do this for me, and I promise I won't let anything happen to you. I *swear* it."

I guess I don't have much of a choice, do I?

"Fine," I agree, his shoulders relaxing instantly. "But I'll need to be back home in twenty days—I'm starting a new job."

"In twenty days, we won't even remember each other's names."

How nice of him. "And we'll need rules," I continue.

"Rules? What rules?"

"Well, I've watched movies. Read books. I'm pretty sure every good fake dating story has rules."

Can an eye roll be loud? Because his sure is.

"I think the whole point of those *rules* is for the character of the story to break them."

I guess he's right. "Okay. No rules."

He dips his chin with a curt nod.

"Okay, one rule."

"I don't follow rules, Primrose," he says, frustration bleeding out of his voice. "I barely take suggestions."

"You can't do what you did out there," I say, pointing at the back of the house.

"What, save your ass?"

"No, just . . . touch me." I trace my finger over the rim of the mug. "And, and . . . kiss me."

"I didn't kiss you out there."

"You kissed my neck."

"Okay." He rests his elbows on the table. "So I can kiss your lips, but not your neck?"

"N-*no*," I say, and the memory of his beard scratching the skin of my face makes my stomach tumble. "I don't want you to kiss me. At all."

"Could have fooled me."

I open my mouth to quip back, though it's not exactly easy to argue with him. I wanted that kiss. Sure, it took me by surprise, but as soon as his mouth landed on mine, I wanted it to stay there. Which really, is all the more reason to set this rule. We don't want things to get confusing, and I don't need to be disappointed by yet another man.

"Fine. No kissing." He snaps his fingers. "Oh, and one more rule."

"Yes?"

"No falling in love," he says in a corny voice. When I give him a dry look, he shrugs. "What? Isn't that basically mandatory in the script?"

Whatever. Let him make fun of me. I have *much* bigger problems in my life.

"Forget about Mayfield for a while and get comfortable, Primrose, because you're not going anywhere. The police said so."

How is this my life?

Closing my eyes, I breathe out.

"See you tomorrow." He sets his cup in the sink, then throws me another glance before stepping to the door. "Don't run away, okay? I like the chase."

you're a walking red flag

. . .

Logan

A FAINT KNOCKING sound wakes me, and only after I open my eyes do I realize the knocking isn't faint at all, only far. Specifically the front door.

I stand, rubbing my eyes to get rid of the sleepiness. The piglets are still bundled in the blankets I put out for them, and the male one opens an eye as I walk out of the bedroom.

Who could it be at this hour? Kyle and Simon have a key for emergencies they regularly use for non-emergencies, so it can't be them. Besides, they won't get to the farm for another half hour.

Could it be Derek?

Maybe he's stupid enough to risk a fight with someone twice his size. Or maybe he's brought his friends along.

Either way, if it's him, I'll have to make sure it stays outside. I promised Primrose I'd make sure nothing happened to her, and I meant it.

I reach the door, mind and body alert, and open it. Unfortunately, on the other side, I'm met by eyes just like mine.

Aaron.

"What the *fuck*, Logan?"

Here we go. "Good morning."

"Arson? Seriously?" he asks as he barges into the house.

Crossing my arms, I close the door and try as hard as I can not to laugh at his hair, glued on his head. Did he dip his head in Vaseline? "Keep your voice down. I have a—"

"A girlfriend? Yes, I heard. Is she also a criminal? Is that why she's covering for you?"

Thinking of her rainbow earrings and the sloths on her underwear, I can't help but smirk. "Oh, yeah. A real mobster." Before he even opens his mouth, I raise a hand. "Look, I'll tell you the same thing I told your wife. I had nothing to do with it. Now get lost before you wake Primrose up."

"Primrose?"

"Yeah. The killer-for-hire I'm dating."

"Not . . ." He swallows, then joins his hands together in front of his mouth, the smell of his fancy aftershave making my nose scrunch. "You don't mean Primrose Bellevue? *Sugar High*?"

Uh, shit. Do I? What's a sugar high?

"Logan?" Aaron presses his lips tight for a moment. "Tell me you're not dating Derek's stalker."

My brows raise. "Huh?"

"The woman who keeps harassing him? The influencer?"

She's an *influencer*?!

Oh my god. I don't know how it took me so long to realize. She said she's a public figure, and with those clothes? The amount of words that roll out of her mouth? Of course, she's an influencer. Sugar High must be her username on whatever platform made her famous.

As if I needed another reason to lose what little respect I had for a woman who would ever date Derek Gracen.

"Wait—is she the one who tried to set his house on fire?"

I shake my head, trying to bury my concern under a mask of indifference. Aaron has always been too smart for his own sake. Smarter than me, for sure. With the fact that he's five years older than me, he's also convinced he knows better. "She's visiting me from Mayfield, and we spent last night fucking in every position I could bend her in, okay?"

He looks away, shaking his head as if he knows I'm lying. "She threatened to kill his dogs. Did you know that, Animal Lover?"

Primrose? Threatened to kill Derek's dogs? I'm pretty sure she wouldn't even pet those two old bulldogs, let alone hurt them.

"She hacked his phone. And slashed his tires. And—and—" He looks away as if he's remembering an old conversation. "She called and texted so many times he had to get a restraining order. She can't even be here by law."

"Hm. And you know all of this because . . ."

"Because Derek told me. Logan, they met *once*." His hands join. "She's known on social media for being some psycho, and people are bashing her all over the place. If you're covering for her—"

I raise a hand. "I thought she was covering for me."

"Look, I know you're not dating," he hisses. "But if you are, maybe you should consider whether you're part of some scheme to get to Derek."

"Are you worried about my heart getting broken, big brother?" I snap back. "'Cause you've always had a funny way of going about that."

His jaw tenses as he looks down, his lips pulled into a rigid line.

A movement in the corner of my eye has me looking past him and into the corridor, where Primrose is hiding against the wall, fearful eyes staring at me.

So maybe she *is* a little eccentric. If anything, it makes me dislike her less.

"If there's nothing else . . ." I point at the door. "I have a day of meaningful work to look forward to." I snap my finger. "You? Still crunching numbers at the loser factory, right?"

Aaron flips me off, and as he opens the door, he mumbles a "Fuck you" as if he wasn't clear enough.

"Oh, hey."

He looks over his shoulder.

"Is Josie working the morning or afternoon shift today?"

"Afternoon." He turns to face me, eyes narrowed. "Why?"

Without uttering another word, I close the door.

Primrose is slinking back down the hall when I call out, "Hey, giant red flag. Wanna come out here for a minute?"

She stops, lips pulled into a little frown when she steps toward me. "Yeah? What is it?"

I huff out a chuckle, and as I'm about to speak, there's another knock at the door.

With a groan, I swing it open. Kyle and Simon are standing on the other side, eyes widening as they land on Primrose.

"What the f—"

Nope.

I slam the door closed, then focus on Primrose again, awkwardly standing beside the couch. "Hungry?"

"A little," she says, studying the door with taut brows.

I walk to the kitchen, then open the cupboard. "Oats okay?"

"Mm-hmm. Who were those people?"

"Kyle and Simon. They work here."

"Oh, all right." She sits at the table behind me, and once I've put milk and oats into the pot, I set the coffee machine. We're both silent as the bitter aroma takes over the kitchen, the low purring of the machine turning louder as the carafe fills.

"It's not what it looks like," she mumbles eventually.

I turn to her, apple and knife in hand. "Hm?"

"I didn't threaten his dogs."

Yeah, no shit. "So why does my brother think you did?"

"I don't know. Because Derek is a liar? And . . ." She looks down at her nails. "I might have said I hoped his dogs would eat *him.*"

"Given the right opportunity," I say as I cut up another piece of apple, "they probably would."

When I throw another look over my shoulder, there's a sad little pout on her face. "Did you slash his tires?" She shakes her head, so I continue, "Hack his phone?"

Her eyes meet mine. "I had to."

"Did you?"

"Yes." She sighs loudly, crossing her legs as she fidgets with a kitchen towel. "He broke up with me without a real explanation, and I'd shared a lot of professional and personal things with him. I had to know what was going on."

"Uh-huh." I fully turn around, unable to help a smile. "How did you even do it?"

"I hired a hacker," she says, biting her fingernails as she sheepishly glances at me.

Yeah, she's . . . *something*.

"Okay. And? What did you find out?"

"Uh . . . That he's dating this girl. They use sweet nicknames for each other. And that they went on a trip together last month. Oh, and that—"

"I thought you were looking for *your* secrets, not his."

Lips pinching, she nods. "Right, yes. I didn't find anything. He never even mentioned me or my recipes."

"Recipes? Aren't you an influencer?"

"A foodie influencer. I make candy."

I try to rein in my disappointment, but that's hardly a job, and my thoughts must be pretty clear because her lips twitch.

"I'll have you know my audience didn't just pop up overnight. I've worked hard on my platforms, and my social media landed me the job of my dreams, assuming Derek doesn't run online and shout about this."

"He can't," I reassure her. "Pending investigation." She seems lightened up by the information before I ask, "What about the restraining order?"

"He tried to get one after I hacked his phone but was denied." She bites her bottom lip. "But I haven't even talked to him in weeks. And—okay, I broke into his farm last night . . . but I *just* wanted to talk."

Dropping her head forward, she whines.

I turn the stove off, scoop some oats, and set them into a small bowl. Once I add apples and strawberries, I hand it to

Primrose. As I prepare my own, one of the piglets enters the kitchen and moves under her chair, and she flinches, pulling her legs up.

She can't seriously be scared of a pink fuzzy piglet, can she?

"Do they bite?" she asks, distrustful eyes studying the small animal.

"Bite, kick, and trample," I say as I join her at the table. "Better not piss them off."

When she swallows, her worried gaze darting under the chair, I clear my throat. "What are your plans for today?"

She energizes at the question, her face breaking into a wide grin. "I have a meeting about my product. The company I'll work for—Marisol—wants to define some details."

"Your own product?" I assume that's the dream she was referring to. "What's that?"

"Not sure—I'll have to submit a few of my recipes." When I nod, she seems disappointed by my lukewarm reaction, and insists, "I've been waiting for one of these big candy producers to notice me. I've networked, collaborated, worked my ass off, and it took years, but I'm finally there now." She seems giddy with excitement and nervous tension, but just as quickly as it appeared, her enthusiasm flattens out. "I doubt they'd want to work with me if I was arrested, though."

"Then you better learn how to lie quickly."

Her nostrils flare as she stares down at her bowl. When her lips wobble, I set my spoon down, reminded of the reason why I hate dealing with people.

"*Don't* cry."

"I'm not crying," she whines as tears fall down her cheeks. "I'm just—just . . ."

"Crying?" I suggest.

She furiously wipes away her tears. "Strong girls cry when they're angry, okay?"

"No. Not okay." I lean forward to stare right into her eyes. "You cry, and he wins. You show you care, and he wins. If you let any emotions slip out, you're the weak one. And if you're weak, people know they can take advantage of you."

She sniffles, slowly shaking her head. "Emotions are normal, Logan. If you don't express them, they build up until your mind can't take it anymore, and they explode."

I hold her stare for a while, knowing she's referring to the episode I had last night, and once I'm sure she's done crying, I pick up my bowl and continue eating.

Emotions are normal, yeah. They're also inconvenient, and whether she cries over this or not won't change the fact that Derek is a piece of shit who lied to her and humiliated her. So, what's crying good for?

Nothing.

Nobody deserves her tears.

"She set Derek's trash on fire?" Simon asks before breathing in his open hands to warm up. The spring morning is alive with the chirping of birds, the rich aroma of fertile soil mingling with the sweet fragrance of blossoming flowers and the tang of manure from the barns. Though it's cold right now, we'll be drenched in sweat in a handful of hours.

"By accident." I fill the trough with feed as the goats gather eagerly, their soft, warm bodies brushing against me.

"What was it? Compost? Paper?"

My eyes roll. "*That's* what you want to know?"

Kyle pops up next to me, piercing brown eyes as wide as the moon. "Wait, so she's Sugar High? *That* Sugar High?"

I can feel the excitement bursting out of him from his voice alone, which means that prefacing my story with "It's not a big deal" and "No, really, it's not a big deal at all" didn't work as planned.

"How many Sugar Highs do you know?" I ask as the five

goats approach, and after making sure Russ's injured thigh looks good, I store the feed away and hop over the fence.

"Is she famous?" Simon asks Kyle as he runs his finger through his orange-blond hair. "Like properly famous?"

"She's got two million followers on Instagram alone." Kyle hesitates. "Though, lately, she's been known as . . ."

"As a *psycho*," I fill in, my lips twisting at the horrible word. Simon's chin jerks back, and he straightens his shoulders. "She didn't take the breakup with Derek the . . . conventional way."

"Well, he obviously used her," Kyle offers as he hops onto the fence and sits. "I mean, he had five hundred followers when he started dating her. And now? Forty thousand. And he was *flaunting* the relationship—it was transparently fake." He keeps scrolling on his phone. "I wouldn't have taken the breakup well either."

When he notices both Simon and I staring at him questioningly, he brushes invisible dirt off his light blue jeans.

"What? It's the latest Instagram drama." He hops off the fence. "But, on a bitter-sweet note, we do kind of have a cheat sheet to her innermost fantasies. Which, if you're not planning on using, I might—"

"What does that mean?"

"Just that if you're not into her, I'd like to—"

Eye rolling, I raise a hand to stop him. "I know you're a thirsty teenager in a man's body, Kyle. What's that cheat sheet business?"

"Oh." He taps on his phone. "Well, last week, this list was leaked online. She confirmed it's hers."

I grasp the phone from his hands, my eyes widening as I read line after line. *Act silly around me, Cuddle me, Introduce me to his family*.

It's her love bucket list.

And it's been made public.

"Look at the last ones. Spicy stuff," Kyle says with a suggestive tone, my eyes instantly piercing his face.

Though it takes every drop of self-control, I hand the phone back, my jaw ticking. "This is private shit, Kyle. What the fuck are you talking about—cheat sheet? You have no right to read any of that."

"It's online!" He turns to Simon, lips parted. "Explain it to him."

"Nah. He's right. Just because someone posted it, it doesn't mean you should engage."

"Well, you two are no fun." Pocketing his phone, he pulls his chocolate brown hair back. "I can't exactly *forget it*."

"Who leaked it?" I ask, the answer coming to me before Kyle can open his mouth. "Derek, of course."

Kyle nods.

So when she said she wanted to *see* Derek, when she said she just went to his farm to *talk*, that's what she meant. She's trying to get her list back.

"He said that Primrose sent it to him, begging him to take her back. In her version, she accidentally left it behind when he dumped her." He rubs his five o'clock shadow. "Wanna know what's *really* happening?" His eyes narrow. "Derek thought his newfound audience was actually about him, while it was not. And once everyone moved on from the breakup and onto the next gossip, he made up all these lies to have five more minutes of fame."

"And apparently, it worked," I say as I think of this morning's conversation with my brother.

"Oh, yes." With a scoff, he crosses his arms. "People will believe anything as long as it's entertaining, and now Primrose is suddenly a pariah." His eyes roll. "She doesn't deserve all the shit she gets."

Goddamn it. "Kyle, you bring up this list in front of her, and you'll be looking for your teeth in the grass," I tell him as I point a finger at his face.

"Why would I—"

"You seem awfully protective of this . . . stranger," Simon

interrupts as he takes a step toward the stables, and his deep-set eyes scan me the way they always do. It's infuriating.

"Don't make this about her," I warn.

"Who should I make it about?"

"About bullies. Assholes like Derek Gracen." I rub a tired hand over my face. "God, I'm going to kill that piece of shit."

"Is her reputation completely shattered? Or could she . . . you know . . ." Simon trails off. When Kyle and I turn to him with a confused expression, he shrugs. "Seriously? Am I the only one who's thinking it?"

Thinking *what*, exactly?

"She's a famous foodie influencer."

"And?" I insist, gesturing impatiently at him to speak.

"*And*, you might act like the farm isn't struggling, but we're not idiots, Logan," Simon says as he follows me. His voice has taken that serious edge he's developed since he became a father, and I can't say I love it. "You've got half as many guys as last year working here, and the rescues have doubled. It doesn't add up."

Swallowing past the lump in my throat, I grab the bale and turn to him. He's tried to broach the subject before, so he knows I have no intention of discussing it. "You want her to promote us."

"Yes, of course I do. You should too."

Shaking my head, I hold back a chuckle. "Well, I don't. And besides, she's been deceived by her ex for followers, and you want me to use her for promotion?"

"No, not *use* her. Ask her. You won't sleep with her, so it's not even remotely the same situation." He rolls his thin lips. "*Unless* . . ."

Unless? Unless what?

Noticing Kyle and Simon's eyes on me, I sigh. "There are as many chances that I'll sleep with her as there are that I'll sleep with you."

Kyle perks up. "So she's fair game?" He shoves his phone in front of Simon's face. "Because look at this. Just look at the bikini."

"Yeah, she's cute," Simon mumbles, and Kyle immediately smacks him in the chest.

"Cute? She's *hot*."

"Okay, hot." Simon throws a worried look at me. "Tread carefully, Kyle."

A familiar, hot anger moves up my throat until it morphs my lips into a sneer. "Did you not hear what I said?" I ask as the two of them share a look. "Why would I care? Say whatever you want."

Kyle fits a hand into his pocket. "Nothing happened between you two?"

I shake my head, though my mind floods with memories of her lips moving against mine, her body arching toward my chest, of her thick, soft thighs in my hands. "No, Kyle. She's all yours—in private." I point a finger at him. "If Josie finds out we lied, I'm screwed. Don't send me to prison because you need to wet your dick."

"Sure, sure." Kyle looks down at his phone again, a big, idiotic grin on his face. "God, look at her. How long did you say she's staying?"

"Seventeen days. She exchanged her ticket this morning."

"Nice. I think this is valley worthy."

Lucky Primrose. She gets the treatment reserved for the *crème de la crème* of Kyle's sexual escapades.

I walk into the stables, ignoring Kyle and Simon as they discuss Primrose's pictures and videos. Though I'm curious, I can't think straight.

I can't believe that asshole posted her list online. It's a stupid piece of paper, but it's important to her. Important enough to break into his farm to get it back. Important enough to commit a crime that could jeopardize her future.

She should have saved herself the trouble and asked me.

Be it the last thing I do, I'll get her list back.

kiss my forehead

. . .

Primrose

BALANCING the laptop on my legs, I bring up the screen brightness. With the sun shining behind it, I can hardly see the video conference room.

I check my face in the small square on the bottom of my screen, and there's sweat over the top of my lip, so I wipe it with the back of my hand and mentally curse the overly warm midday sun. Which is one of the many reasons I'd rather not have this meeting outside, but it's the only place where my connection works, and I haven't asked Logan for the Wi-Fi password yet.

I nervously check the time, but there's still a couple of minutes before the meeting is scheduled to start. I'm about to pick up my phone and mindlessly scroll when a light rattling from the speakers has me perking up, the bigger square buffering. "Primrose?"

"Yes, Chloe, hi." Her slender face appears on the screen, and she waves excitedly. "Can you hear me?"

"I can hear you fine. Where are you?"

"On a . . ." Thinking of my giant temporary roommate, I mumble, "Porch."

With a doubtful expression, she nods, then looks down at a sheet of paper before focusing on me again. "All right, so . . . we have a lot to go through. First of all, thank you so much for agreeing to jump on a call with me. We can't wait for you to meet the team."

"Neither can I," I answer sincerely. Marisol is *the* biggest candy-making company out there, and landing a job as a culinary developer for them is basically like winning a very exclusive lottery. Though I love the independence social media allows for, I'll happily give that up to see my candy in stores.

My *own* candy.

I've been dreaming of this moment for a decade. This is what kept me from giving up when Derek turned half of my fans against me. I've fought for this moment—I craved it. And now it's happening.

"And I'm sure Jessica already mentioned during your meeting that this isn't a home office position."

"Absolutely." Nine-to-five at the office nineteen days from now, which means I *really* can't get arrested. "I've already been given a tour of the offices too."

"Wonderful." She pauses, then her smile dampens. "However, we do have some concerns."

It's like a sudden blow to the chest, leaving me stunned and paralyzed with fear. My body goes rigid, but forcing a neutral expression on my face, I ask, "What do you mean?"

An angry furrow appears between her brows. "Our social media manager informed me of the situation between you and, uh . . ." She lifts a post-it. "Derek Gracen?"

I feel my stomach clench. She knows about the list. About the lies that foul man keeps spewing. "Oh, right. Yes. I know this is all very . . . inconvenient, trust me. But it's a big misunderstanding, and—"

"Misunderstanding?" She rests both elbows on her white desk, her hands steepled at her lips. "Primrose, you've been around a while. You know the truth doesn't matter. What matters is what people believe."

"I—sure, but—"

"You're supposed to sell candy. Happiness, childlike innocence, colorful hope. Not . . . tire slashing and, and . . ." She glances at the stupid post-it again. "And stalking, and *explicit*, private fantasies."

God, she's talking as if I chose to have something so private posted online.

"He's been making post after post about you, and people are believing his side of the story. So unless you can convince me and everyone else that you are done with this man, we can't have you jump on board."

Though there's a chasm in my chest, I fight to hold myself together. This is supposed to be my moment—my chance to prove myself and get my name out there. But it's slipping through my fingers, and I have no power to stop it.

She opens her mouth, but her voice is muffled by the sound of an engine. Turning the volume up, I glance behind the screen, where Logan's pickup is approaching. Great. Just who I wanted to see during this meeting.

"—me."

"Excuse me?"

Logan's pickup stops at the top of the driveway, and with the farm back to the usual silence, Chloe's voice blasts out of the speakers. "I said, convince me. Convince me you're done with that man."

I take a shaky breath, trying to push back the overwhelming wave of despair threatening to consume me, as the pickup door opens. Logan pops out, studying me, and at this point, I don't even know how to feel about him. Since that first, amazing kiss, we've had plenty of unpleasant interactions to cancel out that one good memory.

It brings out your eyes.

The green of your underwear.

Asshole.

"I'm, uh . . . I'm really done with him."

Logan steps in front of me, but I hold a hand out. If he walks past me on the steps, Chloe will see him on camera. Having a meeting to discuss my fuckups on a porch is unprofessional enough without some dirty boots peeking behind me.

With a loud sigh, he crosses his arms.

"Is that the best you've got?" Chloe asks.

"No. Of course not. Look, Chloe, Derek and I, we . . . we barely even had a relationship, okay? While we were together, I thought it was everything, but truly, all we had was an irrelevant, online flirt. We only met once, which is when we broke up."

Her expression is coated in pity, and I can tell it's done. I just lost the biggest opportunity of my life, and I have Derek Gracen to thank for it.

In fact, I have him to thank for my whole life going to hell.

"Look, Primrose, as much as I appreciate your work, I don't think this—"

Logan takes a step, and I nearly incinerate him with my glare, trying to communicate that he shouldn't walk past me, but he leans forward, and his hand cups the back of my head. "Hey, Barbie," he says softly before his lips press on my forehead, causing shivers to rain down my scalp and neck. It lasts but a moment, yet I distinctly feel my heart skip one long beat before it goes back to spasming inside my chest.

Then his hand and mouth are gone, and he's hopping up the stairs.

He kissed my forehead.

When I look down at the camera, quick breaths puffing out of my lips, I see his lower half as he enters the house, then closes the door behind him.

"Oh, well." Chloe says, a light giggle bursting from her lips. "Consider me convinced."

"What?" I ask, my skin still tingling.

"I'd hardly be thinking about this . . . Derek person if I had that hunk of a man lying around."

I smile awkwardly, then nod. "Yeah, it's still pretty new, but . . . it's been going well."

She opens the folder again. "Okay, well, good for you. Now, we need to convince everyone else."

I nod, but I can hardly focus on her words with the way my forehead tingles. It was a quick, chaste kiss—nothing like the scorching hot way he took my mouth with his last night—but I can almost feel the imprint of his lips.

Fine. I guess we have two positive interactions now.

A breath-catching kiss, and a seriously impressive ass saving.

"Come on, then."

I turn to Logan, sliding into a pair of boots by the door, then set my book against my chest. After my meeting ended, we ate lunch, and through all of it, he hasn't said a single word. Not *hello*, not *pass the salt*. Nothing for two whole hours, until "Come on, then."

I also didn't thank him, because though what he did was nice, he's been otherwise despicable.

"Come where?"

He points at the door. "Out."

"You must realize that's not enough information."

"Josie works the afternoon shift today, and I can guarantee she'll pay us a visit. So unless you want to face her alone, you need to come with me."

That's enough information. "Wasn't that difficult, was it?" I mumble as I stand and drop my book on the couch. He seems annoyed as I join him at the entrance, but who can tell. He's had this expression on his face for twenty-four hours.

Tennis shoes on and cardigan in hand, I look up at him, but he doesn't move. Instead, his eyes run down my body slowly. "No."

"No?"

"No."

God, give me the strength. "Are you used to people bending over at your monosyllabic orders?"

He says nothing, and it's all the confirmation I need.

"Well, I'm not a goat. So if you have something to say, use your words."

He cocks a brow at my A-line miniskirt, and my shoulders hunch uncomfortably. What's the problem with my outfit? I love this skirt—it has yellow, white, and pink flowers on a background of pastel green. And with it, I'm wearing a simple light-pink T-shirt. He can't have anything against that.

"You're not having a picnic. This is a farm. Put some clothes on that you don't mind getting dirty. Boots."

"All I have in my luggage is more of this," I say as I pinch the hem of my skirt. I packed what I'd need for two weeks of work in Roseberg—never at any point did I plan to spend seventeen more days on a muddy farm on the outskirts of tiny Pinevale. "You've picked it up this morning—it's a tiny piece of luggage."

"How's that—" He raises his brows in disbelief. "It's bigger than you." I'm about to point out that I'm also quite small, but he raises his hand in a dismissive gesture. "At least wear some pants."

"I don't have pants."

He scoffs. "Jeans, then."

"I don't have jeans."

As he processes what seems to be truly shocking information, I grab my big bag and watch him come back to his senses. "You wear skirts all the time?"

"Well, skirts or dresses or those cute shorts that kinda look like skirts but aren't. You know?"

His brow furrows so much, his forehead looks like crumpled paper, but he eventually waves toward the door, mumbling something under his breath. I'm pretty sure I hear a "princess" in there.

Once in the pickup, he plays some music and we ride in silence. I catch sight of an orchard, its trees heavy with apples, peaches, and cherries at different stages of ripening, and as soon as we move past it, the expansive fields of green stretch out in every direction, divided by neat rows of crops that dance in the gentle breeze.

"What are those?"

He points his thumb back. "We passed the fruit trees, and we're currently moving through wheat and other cereals."

Piece of cake.

"The farthest part of the property is for the animals. We have pigs, goats, sheep, chickens, cows . . ."

I bite my bottom lip to contain my excitement. The only cows and chickens I've ever seen were drawn on taco trucks, and I remember seeing sheep from a train ride abroad, but as much as I try to remember seeing a goat, no memory comes to mind.

"A few rabbits, horses—"

"Horses?"

"Yeah. You know. Long faces."

I definitely know what horses look like, but I've never seen one up close.

Gasping, I turn to him. "Wait—horses! Does that mean . . . Are you technically a cowboy?"

His brows descend over his eyes. "Uh, no. In no way at all."

"But you have horses," I protest.

"But I don't ride them."

"But you do have cows."

"But I don't use the horses to herd the cows," he says through gritted teeth. "You know what—fine. Whatever. I'm a cowboy."

I fight hard to contain a laugh, until I'm forced to hide a chuckle behind my fist. "Okay, cowboy," I say as casually as I can. "Can I get a yee-haw?"

He turns to me, and though he doesn't say it, I hear his *Fuck you* loud and clear.

With a satisfied sigh, I focus on the view, the fields morphing into acres upon acres of grass, and I nearly press my nose to the car window when I see the first white and black spots.

Livestock grazes contentedly in lush pastures—cows lazily chewing, sheep clustered together, and chickens scratching at the ground in pursuit of food. Through the open window, the farm seems to hum with the soothing sounds of nature—bells, bleating, the rhythmic clucking of hens.

It's beautiful. Harmonious in a way that makes me feel at peace.

"On this side are all the big animals. See that red building? Those are the stables."

"Where horses live," I say with a tentative voice as I glance at him.

"Uh-huh. Cows are there, there's ten of them. You can see Penelope sleeping."

I follow the direction of his finger, and indeed, a spotted cow is sleeping behind a tall wooden fence. "Penelope?" I ask with an amused voice.

"Mm-hmm."

"Do you know all your animals by name?"

"Yes."

"Did you name them?"

"Yes."

"Even Penelope?"

He scratches his neck as he awkwardly clears his throat. "Yes." Then he mumbles, "It's a name."

True, but picturing this unpleasant, hairy, giant of a man naming cows and goats he rescued makes me wonder how much of his stone-cold attitude is nothing else but a show for everyone's benefit.

"On this side," he says after a moment, "we have the main buildings. Where we store produce and machines. There's a cottage too."

Once he parks on the gravel strip, we get out of the car, and he walks past the little cottage, then points ahead. "Vegetables there. A little bit of everything. We started growing peas last year."

I let my eyes wander, but even from the higher point where

we're standing, I can only see more fields ahead. Crops and more crops and more crops. There's barely any sound either, if not for a low whirring noise and the chirping of birds. Compared to this, even a small city like Roseberg seems as loud as a club in Mayfield, and I'm not used to this level of silence.

Crazy to think all of this is Logan's place of work.

"It's beautiful," I whisper, and I only notice I said it out loud because he turns to me.

"Yeah, it is," he says with a sad sigh. Whatever he's thinking, he's gone to a dark place. Probably, that same place he went to last night, causing him a panic attack.

A lock of dark hair falls in front of his face with a gust of wind, and I guess since we're sort of talking, I should thank him for this morning. "What you did with Chloe was—"

"Not a big deal."

He keeps staring ahead, so I nod, but it *was* a big deal. She was about to drop me, and he totally damsel-in-distressed me. "It was to me."

He shrugs. "So, did you get the job?"

"Yes. She asked me to send her the recipe I'd like to begin with so they can approve it before I start. So . . . I'll have to decide what to submit."

He doesn't say a word, but stares at me with the utmost focus, so I continue, "She said I have full creative control—to go nuts. But should I go with something safe? Because my bubble gum fudge never fails to go viral." I hum. "Or maybe they expect something bold. A big company like that, they must see basic stuff all the time."

When he says nothing, I twist my neck to check his expression.

"Okay?" he offers.

"Pickle-flavored taffy," I explain. "That's a bold flavor. Either you love it, or you hate it."

"Pickle-flavored . . . what?" His chin jerks back. "I hate it. I don't need to try it; I just know."

"You'd be surprised."

"What else?" He walks, and quickly, I follow after him. "What other *bold flavors* did you inflict on the world?"

"Jalapeño lime hard candy."

"You're joking."

"Sriracha chocolate."

He huffs out a laugh as I manage to join his side, and noticing my struggle to keep up with his impossibly long legs, he adjusts his stride.

"Well, what's your favorite candy?"

"I don't eat candy," he says in a harsh voice. "Not since I turned twelve and went vegan. Candy is filled with gelatine, carmine—all sorts of animal-derived crap."

"Not *all* of it," I correct.

"No, not all of it, but most."

Fair enough.

"Well, I make vegan candy. It's kind of my specialty." I raise a hand to stop him when his cocks a brow. "Not *vegan*—just . . . candy for people who can't have candy."

With his pace slowing down, he shoves both hands in his pockets. "What does that mean?"

"That candy should be enjoyed by everyone, including vegans, people with dental issues, IBS, allergies, high blood sugar . . ." I roll my wrist. "You get it."

"So you make candy for people who wouldn't normally be able to eat it?"

"Yeah." I flash a wide grin at him. "I'll make it for you too."

"Thanks. I don't want it."

With an eye roll, I turn to the lush nature extending before us. "Right. God forbid it'd make you smile." I take a step, and a stray rock sends me teetering precariously on the edge of disaster. My heart lurches in my chest as my arms frantically move in an attempt to keep myself from falling until I find my footing again.

"What do you know?" he mumbles as he studies me with an unimpressed gaze and an amused grin. "You *did* make me smile."

He walks away, and as I watch him confidently strut, with

those broad shoulders and delectable ass, I dislike him so much, I'd actually love to make some candy for him, then administer it as a suppository.

Begrudgingly following him, I mumble, "I should have finished the job the first night."

you shit scrunchies
. . .
Logan

I TAKE out a joint and light it up, watching as the sun sets in the distance. The edge of the wooden step is digging into my back, so I switch positions and rest my elbows on the porch's wooden planks. I look up at the stars beginning to appear, then exhale and watch the smoke on its path upward before it vanishes in the backdrop of the sky.

I had to leave the house.

How has Primrose been here for twenty-four hours and managed to leave a mess in nearly every room? And on a related note, how many books can someone read simultaneously? Apparently, the answer is at least seven.

I'm also pretty sure she shits scrunchies. Blue with polka dots, pink with little cacti, a weird velvety red one. Scrunchies on my couch, on my table, on top of her books. None in her hair, though.

And the kitchen . . . good god, my kitchen. Every single baking item—even some I wasn't aware I owned—is scattered on the counter and the table. My fridge is nearly empty after she took everything out and started making her concoctions, and I'm pretty sure my house will smell like sugar forever.

It's only been a day, but it already feels like two weeks.

I bring the joint to my lips and inhale, feeling my muscles relax as the smoke fills my lungs again. I let it out, and a musky cloud surrounds me.

Josie didn't show up today, and I don't think it's the sign I want to believe it is. If they had nothing but suspicion that I'm behind what happened, they'd be here, poking around, like they have before. So what if they're not showing up because they do have something?

"Having a party?"

I straighten as Derek approaches the driveway on foot, his nasal voice and overconfident smirk irking me on the spot. I was expecting him, but seeing him still tenses me up in a way it's never done before. I guess learning he posted Primrose's list online is a key factor.

"Nah, looks like you're alone." He chuckles as he comes to a stop in front of me, rubbing his buzz-cut copper hair. "Can't even keep a woman around, poor fucker."

He leans forward, and my eyes follow the movement until he's squeezing my shoulder. God, I'm going to break his *tiny*, bony fingers.

"Get your hands off me," I say, glaring as he steps back and whistles.

"Yikes. Same temper too, huh?"

"Happy to provide a practical example."

He waves me off, still smirking like the asshole he is. Why is he staring at the house? Is he looking for Primrose? At this point, he must know she's here.

I want to rip his eyes out.

"So, look." He takes on a more serious tone. "I'm sure the trash can was a prank that went sideways, right? But I'll need those pigs back."

Oh, he needs the pigs back. Funny, because I also need something from him. Something that, like the pigs, should have never been his. Something he shouldn't have shared with the whole world on his stupid social media. "Pigs? What pigs?"

"Come on, Logan. You're not even making an effort to lie. I know you talked to the police."

Looking away, I nod. "Oh, right. Someone failed in their attempt to roast you last night—how unfortunate." I click my fingers. "Hey, question. Where did you get those piglets from?"

He bites his bottom lip as he looks away, adopting that same pleased expression I want to wipe off his face. He always looks so content with himself, like he's a prize for the rest of us. Like he's above shit like decency and empathy and respect.

"Did you happen to get them from Mikey? 'Cause I could've sworn his sow only gave birth a couple of weeks ago. And I don't need to tell you what that would mean."

"Yeah, well. You can report us if you're so concerned."

"Oh, I did, but you know better than me that cases like this can be dragged out for years if they ever get picked up at all. By then, the pigs would be sausage already." I lean forward, looking into his small, protruding eyes. "But, hey, I hope you find them."

The rhythmic chirping of crickets sounds around us as he stares back.

"I need those pigs, Logan," he says as he lazily kicks a small rock. "You keep stealing my animals, and my reputation is taking a hit. I don't want to have to start a war with you."

"Smart. You'd lose it."

His teeth are bared when he looks away, as if reflecting on what angle he can go about this from. He probably knows he's wasting his breath, just like he knows that the animals I keep stealing from him, he had obtained or dealt with illegally.

"So, is it true? Is Primrose here?"

My jaw tightens as I glare.

Bad, bad choice.

"She just can't take a hint, can she?" He breathes through his teeth. "I'm sorry she got you involved in her pathetic obsession with me, but—hey, I'm happy to get her off your hands if I get the piglets back."

Though my teeth clench so hard they hurt, I smirk. It's almost comical—he wants to get her off my hands, while I'd rather cut my hands off than let him anywhere near her.

"Unless you want my leftovers."

The word hangs in the air like a death sentence as he winks, and in an instant, my vision blurs, my ears ringing with the sound of my own heartbeat pounding in my ears. I can't breathe, can't think, can't do anything but feel so much fury, it's debilitating.

Derek's right. I do have a temper, and I spend eighty percent of my daily energy trying to keep it in check. But I'm exhausted. I haven't slept properly in months, and he said the one thing I really wish he hadn't.

I stand, then walk closer, jerking my chin down to look at him. "What did you just call her?"

When he laughs—a harsh, grating sound that feels like nails on a chalkboard—my fingers tighten into a fist. I try to remind myself of the consequences an assault charge would bring, but I keep hearing that word echo in my brain.

Leftovers.

I'm gonna fucking kill him.

I step forward, but the door opens, and I drop my charged fist to my side.

Holy shit, Primrose looks gorgeous. My eyes run up the pink dress she's wearing, and even with the blueberries on it, it's still the most beautiful piece of clothing I could picture her in. Her hips are wrapped in it like a Christmas present, and it pushes her tits up in a way that makes me feel lightheaded.

Her eyes blow wide as she stands against the door frame. "Derek?"

She's afraid. Why is she *afraid* of him?

He waves at her, the same slimy smirk on his face. "It's been a while, Prim. How are you?"

Turning my back on her, I set the joint down, then grab him by his shirt and pull him toward the gate, his feet stumbling back as he tries to keep up. "Give me the list," I hiss into his ear as soon as we're out of range.

"W-what?" He straightens, clawing my hands as he breathes hard.

"The list—fucking give it right now."

"I don't have it with me," he says, his nervous voice betraying him. "Let me—"

"Of course you have it. You brought it here so you could taunt her with it at the first opportunity." I tug him closer, his disgusting face an inch from mine. "Give it, or the next thing to burn down will be your dick."

"Fine, fine." His trembling hand sinks into his jeans pocket, and I relent my hold. "Here," he breathes out as he takes the piece of paper out of his wallet. He hands it over, and I keep my fingers relaxed around it to not crumple it. Even though everything in me is as tense as a bowstring.

I shove him back, and he lands with his ass on the ground. "Not one more word online. Do you understand?" I lean closer, then tilt my head Primrose's way and whisper, "Not one word."

After staring for a couple of seconds, he awkwardly stands. At first, it looks like he'll say something, but he eventually stalks away. Once he disappears behind the gate, I pocket the list and bring the joint to my lips again.

I need to relax. Need to remember there's someone I don't want to scare. That I have too much shit to take care of, and I can't afford to go to jail.

"Hey," Primrose says as she joins my side. "Are you okay? What happened?"

Ignoring her, I walk back to my porch and breathe out, trying to release some of the adrenaline that has surged through me. "Did you want something?"

"No, I . . . I heard voices."

"Are they telling you to start a fire?" I sit on the top step and exhale. "Because that would explain a lot."

"Voices *out here*. The ones I hear in my head can't get any reception." She throws a worried look over her shoulder, then turns to me again. "I made this." She holds out a small bowl filled with green candy. "Mint and thyme."

"No, thanks."

One corner of her lips drops. "Come on, try it."

"What's in it?"

"Well . . . mint, thyme, sugar—"

"White sugar?"

Her eyes narrow. "No. Refined cane sugars are likely to have been processed with animal products."

Huh. So she does know her stuff.

"Still not eating it," I mutter.

"Fine." She sets the bowl away with a sigh. "Kyle said you don't have Wi-Fi. Is that true?"

So she *did* hang out with Kyle. He told me he'd go see her when his shift was over, but by the time I came back home for dinner, she was alone.

My eyes drift over the blueberries on her pink dress, her thick thighs underneath, and I briefly wonder why she's wearing heels. "No Wi-fi here. If you want to use your connection, the front porch is the only place where the internet works."

Her nose scrunches, the same expression as if I'd condemned her to a life without oxygen. I guess it would feel that way to her. "Why was Derek here?"

Shoulders hunching, I shrug. "Just saying hi."

"Yeah, right." Light blue eyes scan my face, but I ignore them until she sits next to me on the step. "You said if I stayed here, I'd get to talk to him. Why did you chase him off as soon as I came out?"

"You don't need to talk to him."

She crosses her arms, her shoulders rolling forward. "Is that so? And why do *you* get to decide—"

I fit a hand into my pocket and hold the list between my index and middle finger. "You can talk to him if you want. But you don't *need* to talk to him."

For a moment, she looks at the piece of paper with her lips

parted, then she snatches it quickly as if she's afraid it'll suddenly disappear. She unfolds it, her thumb grazing the lines scribbled on it. "I . . . Logan, I—"

"It's fine."

She breathes out, as if she needs to get that 'thank you' off her chest. Really, she shouldn't be thanking me. That list is *her* stupid clump of romantic fantasies, and he shouldn't have taken it in the first place.

"Seriously, forget about it," I insist as I look away.

Though she remains perfectly silent, her eyes are louder than words. The way she keeps staring at the side of my face as if I'm the best person ever put on this planet, the gratefulness pouring out of her. I need her to quit it immediately, and she must perceive my discomfort because, without a word, she turns to her bag.

I watch her take out a pen, and after removing the cap, she strikes through one of the items on her list. I'm not sure why, as I don't usually care about much, but I need to know which one. "What was that?"

"Kiss me until I can't breathe."

Oh, right. I feel heat creep up my neck, but before I can find something to say back, she brings pen to paper again and strikes through something else.

Again, it kills me not to know. "And this one?"

Her eyes meet mine as she sets pen and list back into her bag. *"That,"* she says with a playful tone, "is the second item I get to cross off because of you, Logan. Thank you."

Unbelievable. She found a way to thank me after all.

After a moment of silence, she asks, "You don't have a TV, do you?"

"No," I mumble, trying to push any thought of her list away. "No TV, no computer, no cellphone, no technology."

"Wow." Her eyes widen, but she quickly brushes off her judgmental expression and waves. "You know, back home, I have three TVs."

"What—you live in a palace?"

"Just a two-bedroom." She chuckles. "I also have two computers. But on the other hand, the French balcony with a view of the mall doesn't compare to this."

I look at the hills in the horizon, overly aware of her shoulder a few inches from mine. And is that perfume? Why does she always smell like fruit?

"Seriously, though. How does someone live without the internet?"

With a shrug, I give her my least friendly glare. "There aren't a billion strangers calling me a psycho, so . . . so far so good."

She swipes her finger on the screen of her phone and begins typing. "What if you need to look something up?"

"What do you mean?" I ask as I breathe in the smoke.

"Say you need to check where Bangladesh is." She fidgets with the hem of her dress. "How do you do that with no internet?"

"Why the hell would I need to check where Bangladesh is?"

"To prove to someone that it's next to Myanmar."

I open my mouth, then close it. "I have an atlas."

She raises both hands as if to declare defeat. "All set, then. My mistake. Are microwaves allowed?"

"When my ex moved out, she took her TV back. I never liked computers, and when I realized I also don't like people, I threw my phone away." I inhale, rolling my stiff shoulders back. "Now, please shut up, Barbie."

She doesn't say a word, and lighting up the joint again, I wait for her to leave. But she doesn't. She keeps staring at me with those piercing eyes the same color as crystal clear waters.

I guess I hate to be stared at as much as I hate being talked to.

"What?" I hiss.

She huffs out a chuckle. "Why do you keep calling me that? Barbie?"

Brows arching, I throw a glance in her direction. "Blonde hair with pink tips. Blue eyes. Pink dress, pink heels." I gesture vaguely at her. "Barbie."

"Joke's on you, cowboy," she says with a long sigh. "I spent half my life wishing I could look like Barbie."

"Well, there you go."

She leans back on her elbow, stretching her legs in front of her and swiping her finger over the screen of her phone. Staring at the shiny pink heels on her feet, I purse my lips. What does she mean, she wants to look like Barbie?

When she crosses her ankles, goosebumps spread across her arms. My eyes drift to the strap of her dress, casually falling down her arm and exposing her shoulder. Pink bra too, I notice, as my eyes follow along the edge, to the few inches of her tits I can see, then the sinful groove between them.

She turns to me, and I quickly glance away, but I don't think it was fast enough for her not to think I was checking her out. And I wasn't. My eyes just went there.

Biology.

"Hey."

Fuuuuck. She's going to scream at me again, isn't she?

My body stiffens. "Yes?"

"Did Derek say something about the police?"

I give her a quick shake of my head. "Hm? No."

"Come on—he definitely said something. Is it bad? Will they arrest me?"

I study the side of her face, flushed cheeks and languid eyes. I don't want her to know what Derek said, but worrying about the police isn't a better alternative, and I'm sure with what's been happening on her social media, she's heard worse.

"He said nothing about the police, Barbie. He called you his 'leftovers.'"

"Leftovers?" she repeats in an uncertain voice.

"Yeah, you know. Like he's had you first, so I get his leftovers." I jerk my head toward her. "You."

"Oh." She blinks, looking away. "That's . . . What did you say?"

Nothing. I said nothing at all, busy as I was trying not to rip his head off. But I don't want her to know that, so I meet her gaze and say, "That you taste great once microwaved."

She rolls her big blue eyes, and it steals a smile from me. "Come on. What did you say?"

"I said . . ." My eyes run down her body, and this time, there's no way for her to miss it. "*I will.*"

Soft and hooded eyes settle on my mouth. Is she thinking about our kiss? And if so, how often does that happen? Because it keeps running through my mind. "That's a great answer."

"Hm." I watch her full lips—pink lipstick unmistakable under the porch light. I still remember the way she tastes—like summer and berries.

A car's engine interrupts the silence, and with her throat working hard, she stands. "Oh, here's Kyle. He's bringing me somewhere around the farm."

Wait, *what*? She's going out with Kyle? Is that why she's wearing that dress—those heels?

Mouth opened wide, I watch Kyle get out of the car in his one fancy shirt. She waves at him, says she'll grab her bag, then disappears inside the house.

He asked her out—hell, I don't know why I'm shocked. He's physically unable to be around a woman without trying to get into her pants, and he told me he would. I also know he's bringing her to the valley, which means he's about to impress her big time.

Good for him.

It doesn't bother me. Why would it?

Loosening a knot in my shoulder, I purse my lips.

It doesn't bother me *at all*.

With a long exhale, I glance up at Kyle, who waves. The only way to know for sure if this is a date would be to check if he tucked condoms in his wallet, and though I'm tempted to turn him upside down and shake him like maracas to see what comes out, I stand and enter the house instead.

Getting her bag, she said? Well, Primrose is refreshing her

lipstick, checking her reflection on the glass panel of the cabinet door.

Making herself even prettier.

For Kyle.

She turns to me, abandoning her lipstick on the table, and waits. I should tell her she looks good. *Have fun*, or *Be safe*, or whatever. Instead, I mutter, "Those shoes are ridiculous," and her smile falls.

"Nobody asked you."

"He's bringing you to the valley. It gets muddy there after it rains, and it's been pouring down for a week."

She shrugs. "Nobody asked you that either."

"Fine. Don't come crying to me when you get hurt."

"I wouldn't come to you crying or otherwise," she says as she struts past me.

Good. Maybe Kyle should deal with Derek then, since he's the one who gets to take her out. I don't need the headache.

Fuck. Why am I so annoyed?

"I'm going on a ride," I mumble as I grab my bike keys. The two piglets, resting beside the couch, scurry away, probably unnerved by the edge in our voices, and without looking back, I leave out the door, ignoring her quick steps behind me.

"A ride? Seriously?"

I ignore that too and strut to the garage.

"It's dangerous, Logan. What if you have another panic—"

"You don't *know* that it was a panic attack," I quickly interrupt. "And anyway, don't you have a date to go on?"

She flinches, then scowls. "It's not a date. He wanted to hang out."

"Yeah. 'Cause he wants to fuck you."

"*No*," she says pointedly. "Because I'm a nice person."

She crosses her arms, and I slip my helmet on. "I wouldn't know. I don't like 'nice.' I don't do 'nice.'"

"Yeah, clearly. Why are you so angry, huh? Are you weirdly jealous or something?"

"Jealous? Of Kyle? I don't even *like* you. We're not friends, or more than friends, or less than friends—we're nothing, okay?"

"Dude!" We both spin to find Kyle, arms wide and a shocked expression on his face. "What the fuck? Do you mind?"

Jesus Christ. *What* am I doing?

Primrose slowly exhales, her crystal blue eyes meeting mine. "For the record, I meant jealous of me hanging out with your friend. I understand how you feel about me." She shrugs and, before turning around, mumbles, "I'm microwaved leftovers."

you're stubborn
. . .
Logan

MY EYES open on the second ring, my heart immediately rumbling in my chest like a fully powered engine. I wasn't sleeping—only just managed to close my eyes after an hour of tossing left and right in bed.

I stand, rush to the living room, and grab the landline receiver. For some reason, the word 'police' keeps banging in my mind, though they likely wouldn't call this late. But knowing they're preparing a case against us is unnerving.

"What?" I bark as I bring the receiver to my ear.

"Hey, boss," Kyle says with an apologetic voice. "Sorry to wake you up."

"What happened?"

"Uh, nothing much. She was in a shitty mood after you insulted her, so I brought her to get ice cream. We just got back to the farm, right? But it's dark, and with the rain last week, the valley is still pretty muddy, and . . ."

My throat clenches. "Is Primrose okay?"

"Oh, yes. Totally fine. But she—uh . . . fell."

She fell. *She fell.*

I smack the receiver down, grab my helmet on the way to the door, and stop with the handle between my fingers. Looking down at the black helmet, my heart beats through the roof. The bike's faster, but if I use it to go to her, I'll also have to use it to bring her back here, and I can't let her ride with me.

I just can't.

I set it down and grab the keys, flying out the front door into the night—the pickup turned on before I'm even fully sitting.

I drive across the farm, testing the power of my pickup's engine like I never have before. It's either going to break down or take flight like a shuttle.

She fell.

What if she's hurt? Kyle said she wasn't, but he's a troublemaker. If she's so much as scratched, I'll waterboard him in cow piss. He's done hanging out with her—she's not here to make friends anyway. To go on dates and kiss Kyle. I want my eyes on her at all times.

She fell.

The closer I get, the faster I go, until in the darkness, the headlights flash on Kyle, waving.

I crank the handbrake and come to a stop in front of him. So close, in fact, that he bounces back with wide eyes. At least he knows exactly how I feel about him right now.

"Where is she?" I bark as I jump out.

"Logan, don't overreact. Nothing bad happened—" When he notices my flared eyes and nostrils, he raises both hands in defeat. "There. Next to that tree."

I rush past him, my chest so tight I can't breathe, and my eyes settle on her, sitting on the ground. I run, and Kyle's voice reaches me from behind. "That right there is an overreaction!"

"Two hours. I left you alone for two hours." Knees deep in the mud, I study Primrose's ankles, relieved when I see nothing horrendous like a bone sticking out.

"I slipped," she says with a pout. "And I didn't want Kyle to call you anyway. I'm fine."

Yeah, she's peachy, sitting in the mud. My eyes run up and down her no-longer-pink dress, looking for any damage. I still can't tell if she's regular pretty or if she made an extra effort to go out with Kyle.

Doesn't matter.

Focus, Logan.

"Can you rotate your foot?"

She does, then hisses, letting it drop back into the mud. "Yeah, but it hurts."

It shouldn't be broken. If it was, I imagine she'd be in much more pain. Maybe she sprained her ankle. "Well, why are you sitting here?"

"Every time I tried to pick her up, she screamed bloody murder," Kyle explains with a shrug.

My questioning gaze moves to Primrose, whose cheeks have turned a dark shade of pink. What's with that? I kissed her two minutes after knowing her, so I don't think it's an issue of not wanting to be touched.

"Can *I* pick you up?"

She shakes her head, and though my first instinct would be to scream at her to quit whatever this is, I breathe out, trying to remember what she said about not being a goat. Not that I'd ever scream at a goat. "Look, I'll pick you up and bring you straight to the truck, okay? Fifteen seconds, tops."

"No!" she squeals as I reach forward, her body cowering away as her hands sink into the mud.

What the hell?

I study her wide eyes, and the way her shoulders relax once she realizes I'm not going to grab her against her will.

Is she embarrassed? It looks like it, but I don't get what for.

I turn to Kyle. "Walk away."

Kyle's brows quirk, but with a nod, he turns around and walks until he's out of earshot. Only then do I focus on Primrose. "Well?"

She sheepishly glances at me. "What?"

"Why don't you want me to pick you up?"

She presses her lips tight, and when that doesn't magically convince me to leave her here to die, she sighs. "I'm too heavy, Logan."

Too heavy?

I look down at her thighs, smeared with mud all the way to the short skirt of her dress, but that doesn't help anyone, so I quickly focus on her face again. "You're not too heavy for Kyle, let alone for me."

"Yes, I am."

"No, you're not."

"Yes, I *am*."

I inhale, my jaw clenching. "So what's the plan, Barbie? Are you sleeping here?"

"Just help me stand, and I'll hop to the pickup."

"You'll slip on the mud again."

She shrugs, but then squints into the darkness like she's trying to measure the distance. "No, I won't."

Goddamn stubborn woman.

"Fine." I stand, then offer her my hand. She pulls herself up on one foot, and even before she can think of hopping anywhere, her one shoe slides forward in the mud, and she shrieks as she falls back.

I manage to let go of her hand and lean forward, wrapping an arm around her back and holding her up before her ass hits the ground. Unfortunately, it doesn't seem like the time and place for "I told you so."

She breathes hard, then looks into my eyes, and our faces are much closer than they should be, because I can smell the scent of strawberry coming off her skin—maybe her lips.

"Thank—"

I circle the backs of her knees with my arm and hoist her up, and with a final shriek for good measure, she settles against my chest.

She gasps. "You—"

"You're welcome."

"You know that's not what I meant! I told you not to pick me up, that I'm—"

"Too heavy?" I say as I lift her even higher. I could do lunges carrying her. I could prop her on my back and go about my day and I'd barely even remember she's there.

Too heavy. Fucking ridiculous.

She sighs and tries to shift away, but I can still detect the blush on her skin—redder than ripe tomatoes. Setting the thought aside for now, I walk to my pickup, and a cat-calling whistle resounds in the distance.

Kyle, of course.

"Watch your head," I mumble as I deposit her onto the seat, and once she's in, I close the car door behind her, then point a finger at Kyle. "I'm taking her back home. I'll deal with you tomorrow."

"Me? There's no need to deal with me."

But there is. He knows she's not dressed right for the farm. For slippery mud and thorns. We've got snakes here too, and they wouldn't think twice before biting her naked ankles.

I'm sliding into the driver's seat when I hear him call, "Can I come too?"

Without answering, I shut the door, then throw a look at Primrose.

"You okay?"

She nods, visibly upset. Is it because Kyle made her uncomfortable? Because she didn't get to kiss him? Because they *did* kiss, and it was horrible? Or because I picked her up?

No idea, and when my eyes dart to her mouth to check if her pink lipstick is there or if it's smudged, I find a smear of mud. Trailing up her face, I catch her eye, one brow arched.

I shake my head and start the car, focusing on the road.

Even if they did kiss, I don't give a fuck.

"I'm sorry," Primrose says as I grab a chair and sit in front of her, dropping the first aid kit and towel on the table next to me. Gripping the edge of the couch, she shrugs one shoulder. "I told Kyle not to call you, but . . ."

But he knew if he didn't, I'd shove his face in pig shit.

"You're fine." I pat my leg. "Foot here."

"No, you're angry. You told me those shoes were not suited for—"

"Foot. Here," I insist as I tap my thigh again.

She leans back and rests her tiny foot on my leg. It makes my mouth go dry, the awareness that now I get to—*have to*—touch her.

It's not like I want to.

I grab the wet wipe on my side and clean the top of her foot. She'll have to wait until she can stand to take a shower.

"Where are the . . ." She swallows, peeking past the table.

She's terrified of those damn piglets, isn't she? "Do you eat pork, Primrose?"

"Yes?" she says suspiciously.

I look into her eyes, trying to sound ominous. "Well, then. You may have eaten their mom at your last barbecue, but you won't let them nibble you just once?" I click my tongue. "Sounds unfair to me."

She studies me, eyes widening and brows tightly knit together, and only when I lift one corner of my lips, she exhales, then quickly chuckles. "Oh, you're the worst."

"Pigs love apples. Occasionally, they play—it's quite cute," I say, wiping her pink toenails. "Don't scare them, because then they will bite you, but pigs are prey animals. They won't do anything to you."

When she doesn't say a word, I look up at her, and I'm surprised to find a sweet grin.

Why is she looking at me like that?

My hand slips as I rub her ankle, and she flinches. "Damn—sorry. Does it hurt?"

"No, the wipe is just a bit cold. Do you think it's broken?"

"Likely just sprained. I'll bandage it now."

"Thank you," she whispers. She obviously feels guilty, and I guess she technically shouldn't. She didn't fall on purpose.

The silence stretches as I grab the white bandage and roll it around her ankle. Everything about her is so tiny that it feels like trying to paint a miniature with oven mitts.

"Logan?"

"Hmm?"

"Can you tell me what's going on with the farm?"

I glance up at her. "What did Kyle say?"

"Nothing." I cock a brow, and she shrugs. "He just mentioned . . . you're having issues."

Focusing on the bandage, I mumble, "We're a vegan farm, so our prices are higher than average. It costs more to grow produce when you're picky about what chemicals you use." I keep wrapping. "And we don't provide meat or eggs, which means that most customers working with us will have to get a separate supplier, and not everyone is willing to."

"And I guess all the animals you keep here are expensive." Her eyebrows are arched, and her eyes are rimmed with worry.

"Very. Food and vet bills. Medicines." I tape the bandage. "I've had to take on some loans."

I'm done with her foot, but she keeps it on my thigh.

"Plus, the competition is cheaper."

"You mean Derek?"

"And a few others, but mostly him, yes."

"Well, it's unfair." She pouts. "His produce might be cheaper, but he's . . ."

"He's the devil, but that's not how business works." I doubt I need to explain it to her, seeing as she's built an audience of two million. "And besides, I'm not such a great person myself."

Her face does something. It's a sort of amused twinkle in her eyes with a hint of *I'm not buying your bullshit*. Like she's telling me she knows me, which is ridiculous since forty-eight hours ago, we were strangers to each other.

Lifting her foot off my leg, she asks, "Aren't you?"

"No, I'm not." I watch her set her foot down, then check her face, but she doesn't grimace. Instead, she knowingly grins. "What?"

"Logan, you got my list back, and I didn't even ask you to. And tonight you showed up with that pickup flying across the field . . . You almost ran your friend over, then I saw with my own eyes the relief washing over you when you were sure I was okay."

I shift uncomfortably.

"And as you eloquently said tonight, you don't even know me. So, sorry if I struggle to believe you're this horrible person you want me to think you are."

Thinking of my lash-out, I grimace. A nice person wouldn't have told her any of that. "You're not leftovers," I mumble.

With a flick of her hair, she nods. "I know."

"And I don't think you're leftovers."

"I know that too."

Good.

"So . . . what's going to happen to this place?"

My heart twists, but I look away to hide my expression. "Uh, no idea."

"I can see why you'd have a panic attack over it."

With a glare, I snap, "We don't know what it was."

"Sure." She fidgets with the hem of her dress. "Does anyone know? Because Kyle didn't seem well-informed about the farm's financial situation."

So she *did* inquire, the snoop.

"No, not really." And I just know telling her is the wrong choice, but she has this way of looking at me when she asks questions. Makes it impossible to tell her to mind her business. "The farm wasn't vegan before I took over. My mom tries to understand, but..."

"You're afraid to admit making the farm vegan..."

"Is bringing it toward certain failure. Yes," I conclude in her place. It's the truth, as painful as it may be. And telling my brother he was right all along feels like punishment for something I've done in a previous life.

"Still, if we were to end up in prison, someone would have to take over. And they should be aware of the situation. Don't you think?"

"We're not going to prison." Not as long as we act coupley and don't give them any reason to look into our past. "I don't want you to worry about that."

She scoffs. "Easier said than done."

"I made a promise, remember?" I busy myself with the first aid kit, shoving everything inside. Then I force myself to stare back at her. "I keep my promises."

She nods, though I can still see stress lines on her forehead. "Well, you have to do something, right? About the farm?"

Oh, I've done more than something. I've hired an advertising company, run dozens of promotions, and reached out to any local business that might be interested in our produce. Good god, I even tried to get a table at the farmers' market, though I've been denied every week. "Trust me, this farm is the most important thing in my life. I'm doing everything I can."

"I guess I could..." She drums her fingers on her leg, indecision making her stop in her tracks.

I'll make it easy for her.

"I don't want you to promote us."

"Why not?" she asks suspiciously. "Everyone does."

"Because I think influencers are lazy freeloaders who didn't feel like finding a job, so they made their egotistical fantasies their occupation."

At her horrified expression, I laugh.

Even when she doesn't say a goddamn word, she's funny.

And pretty. She's pretty too.

"You're joking, right?"

"Yes. Primrose, this is something I need to fix myself," I explain. "And besides, you're busy with your own thing. Bold flavors or whatever."

It looks like she's about to argue, so I slap my thigh and stand.

"Do you want me to take you to bed?" She smirks, and I give her a dry smile. "You know what I mean."

"I can hop," she says, getting to her feet and taking two hops forward to prove it.

"Now I wish I had a phone to record you."

With a chuckle, she hops across the living room. "I'll see you tomorrow, cowboy."

"Try not to die before the morning."

She widens her eyes dramatically. "You'd miss me too much, wouldn't you?"

Sure I would. The tornado roommate who keeps falling and waking me up is just the addition to my life I didn't know I needed.

Two days down, fifteen to go.

lend me his crayons
. . .
Primrose

THE EARLY MORNING sun bathes the countryside in a soft, golden light, and around me, the farm is buzzing with life—chickens cluck and peck at the ground, bees hum lazily from flower to flower, and there's the gentle hum of a tractor in the distance.

I pick up my phone, adjusting the settings to capture the perfect shot of Kyle chopping wood before me. Five minutes into his task, he made a big show of taking off his shirt, so Logan might actually be onto something when he says Kyle wants to sleep with me.

His chestnut brown hair catches the sunlight, creating an almost halo-like effect around his head. Ensuring each frame is just right, I snap a few photos, until he must notice the click in between the thuds of his ax, and with a jovial beam, he looks up at me.

"Want me to take my pants off too?"

I chuckle, setting my phone down. "I think I'm good, thanks. Do you mind me posting it?"

He firmly shakes his head. "Not at all."

Kyle showed up at the house this morning, told me I couldn't stay there alone because Josie would likely come over, then dragged me out into the farm. We had fun last night, and even now, his proximity is comforting. Spending time with someone who doesn't make me feel as tense as Logan is a welcome change of pace.

I turn my focus to the recipe opened up on my tablet, until a growing rumble has me lifting my gaze off the wooden table and looking up, trying to identify the source. It sounds like it's coming from the road, so I glance over my shoulder, my jaw dropping as I see a motorcycle riding up the driveway.

Logan, I assume.

I've only seen him in his bike attire once, but just like that first night, he's dressed head-to-toe in black, exuding confidence as he slowly rides to the side of the house. A black helmet shields all of his features, and the leather jacket clings to his frame, accentuating his broad shoulders and hinting at the strength beneath the surface.

The rhythmic purr of the engine subsides as he smoothly parks the black bike, leaving a lingering echo in the air.

Damn.

I don't know much about motorcycles—never even ridden one—but that's hot.

He gets off the bike, and I bite my bottom lip when his black helmet turns my way.

Maybe he'd take me on a ride one of these days.

Maybe I should ask Kyle.

I turn, but Kyle's almond eyes are already on me, mouth open and brows tight as if I've personally insulted him. "What?"

"Are you kidding me?"

"What did I do?" I insist.

"Of course, she goes for the biker." He points a scolding finger at me. "You know, those things are dangerous. You could die."

I burst a laugh. "What—I'm not—" Oh my god. What if he tells him something? "I, uh . . ." I turn around again, and my pulse quickens when Logan removes his helmet, his long, brown hair tumbling over his shoulder. Even in the distance, I feel his blue-gray eyes boring into mine.

Kyle sighs loudly, then sits and rests both elbows on the table, sweat glistening his bronzed skin. He brings his frowny face against his fists and mumbles, "Well, good for you, Sugar High. He's definitely into you."

"What?" I squeal. "No, he's not. He can barely stand me."

"You don't need to be friends with someone to want to fuck them."

I smack his arm, feeling my cheeks warm. I can't deny it: just thinking about his size makes me squirm on the bench. Why is there something so hot about a man who could wave you around like a flag?

But a guy like that could get any woman he wanted, and he's certainly not going for the pink-wearing influencer who's robbing him of his privacy.

"You know, this is unfair. I'm much nicer, and I took you out on a date, and—"

"You what?"

He rolls his eyes. "Prim, I've been flirting with you non-stop."

"I guess, but . . ." I bite my lips. "I thought . . . I don't know. That you flirted with everyone."

"I do," he says matter-of-factly. "But I had my eye on you."

How thoughtful.

I pat his arm lightly. "Thanks. I'm just not looking for anything after Derek."

"Or . . . you're after a particular brand." He frames his words with his hands. "Moody-ass biker."

"I just turned around because it was noisy," I insist. When he gives me a who-are-you-kidding look, I glance down at my notebook. "And I thought Logan was your best friend."

"Not today, he isn't." With a sigh, he shakes his head. "You know, he hasn't had sex in . . . I don't know, decades. He probably can't remember how to."

Nearly choking on coffee, I cough before mumbling, "With a best friend like you, he doesn't need any enemies, does he?"

"Plus, he has some really weird kinks."

My eyes blow wide. "He does?"

"Oh, so you *are* interested." I open my mouth to tell him that I'm not, and mine is just morbid curiosity, but he powers on, "Rough sex. Not sure sweet little Prim would be up for it. Me, instead?" He wiggles his brows. "I'd treat you like a princess."

I roll my eyes.

"So? Are you going to tell him?"

"Kyle, I wasn't checking Logan out. I'm not into him, and he's definitely not into me, and—and . . . bikes aren't even that hot."

He stares at me, deadpan.

"Can we drop this now?"

"Of course," he says as he stands, both hands raised, and before turning away, he gives me a meaningful look. "But there is an efficient, infallible way to know if he's attracted to you. If you *are* interested."

"Well, I'm not." I tap on the tablet, trying to focus on the content I'm making. But now I'm curious. What is Kyle talking about? Not that I'd do it, especially because I can say with almost absolute certainty that Logan is *not* interested in me.

Even if I'll admit, his bike is hot.

"Fine. Fine. I'll let it be."

He returns to his pile of wood, and silence reigns for a few minutes. When I hear a door closing behind me, I do my best not to pay it any attention, especially as I feel Kyle's gaze on me, checking.

"Hello."

I flinch, turning to Logan, who distractedly waves before walking to Kyle. He's changed from the black outfit he wore on the bike to his usual brown boots, jeans, and flannel shirt. I'll get him to say "Yee-haw" at some point.

"Hey, boss."

"Did you take care of those radishes?"

The ax swings. "Mm-hmm. All done. And Damien is done with the fertilizer too."

"Good. The eastern fence has some damage. I'll—"

"Simon already took care of it."

"Huh. Great." He points at the house. "Then I'll do some office work."

Busy as I am avoiding his gaze, I don't notice Logan walking back to me until he stops by my side. If I look up, he'll *definitely* know what Kyle and I were discussing. "How's your ankle?"

"Oh, cool. Great. Awesome." I cringe, pressing my lips tight because I can't think of any other way to stop myself from blabbering. Why did Kyle have to make things weird? Now all I can think about is how Logan likes rough sex. How I'd probably like it too with a guy like him.

He throws a disinterested look at my phone. "You should keep it elevated."

"Maybe you could help her with that," Kyle calls from where he's chopping wood, and he's so serious that the meaning of his words hits me long after he's said them.

Then my heart drops in my stomach.

Logan faces him. "What?"

"Nothing," I blurt out, heat rising to my neck. Why did he say *that*? "Would you like some candy?" I glance at Kyle. "Both of you —just everyone. It's vegan friendly."

Kyle gasps loudly. "For real?"

At his enthusiasm, I perk up. "Yeah. Apricots from the farm. Brown sugar, no gelatine." I glance at Logan, who's thoughtfully staring at the bowl beside me. "Just try one." I can't leave this place without him trying and loving my candy.

"No, thanks."

Seriously? What's his problem? "Are you allergic to joy?"

Kyle swoops between us and grabs a handful of candy, then walks back. "Sorry. Keep going." His finger wiggles between Logan and me. "*Loving* this bickering dynamic."

After a perplexed glance at Kyle, Logan focuses on me again. "Is he having a stroke?"

Heart thumping, I set the bowl down. *Why* does he have to be so weird? "No, he's cool. Great. A—"

"Awesome, yes. I got it." His eyes narrow. "Anyway, Josie called. They want us to come in for some questions. I've already contacted my lawyer, and he recommended—"

"*What?*" I shriek.

Flinching, he tries again, "He recommended this, uh . . . Peter Miller? A colleague. They'll both come over to prep us for the police's questions tomorrow." He raises a hand to stop me from speaking. "Assuming you're comfortable with him. I figured you could look him up online."

Lawyers! He wants me to choose a lawyer while I'm still stuck on the portion of his sentence about the police wanting to question us.

I don't know why it surprises me so much—Josie told us not to leave town, and that other cop she was with clearly had a bone to pick with Logan. But so much has happened in the last couple of days, I almost let myself believe we got away with it.

And now I'm being questioned.

"Primrose?"

I meet Logan's gaze.

"Will you? Check out the lawyer?"

"Uh, yeah. Sure." I busy myself with my notebook, trying not to show him how nervous I am. He'd probably say I'm being dramatic anyway. "I'll go do that right now."

He grasps my wrist as I stand, then waits for me to look into his eyes before saying, "It'll be okay. I gave them some bullshit excuse for not being able to come in today, so we have plenty of time to figure this out." His thumb brushes the skin of my hand soothingly. Then, in a hushed tone, he continues. "Remember my promise?"

I won't let anything happen to you.

Once I nod, he lets go. Though I don't know Logan and have

Riding the Sugar High

no reason to trust him, I do. He got my list back from Derek without me asking, and he ran to my aid when I was hurt.

I'm so nervous, it feels like my stomach has been sealed shut, but hearing him say it'll be okay makes it better.

Once Kyle, who's been silently observing, walks closer, Logan steps away until the door shuts. Only then, I drop to the bench and look into Kyle's eyes.

"Feeling tense around Sugar Daddy, huh, Sugar High?"

Seriously?! He might not have heard the last thing Logan said, but there's no way he missed the first part. The police want to question me. Sugar . . . *Daddy* is the very last thing on my mind.

"Not in the mood," I mumble, resting my forehead on my fist.

"Oh, come on. Don't worry too much," Kyle says in a cheerful voice. "Trust me, Logan has been through this so many times." When my worried gaze meets his eyes, he makes a *pfft* noise. "Nothing ever happens."

Maybe he's right, and that's why Logan didn't look overly concerned either. Or maybe they're both crazy, and their carefree attitude will send me to jail. I guess I'll find out soon enough.

"So? Sugar Daddy?"

With a sigh, I try to focus on Kyle. "What about him?"

"For the love of—" He grabs an apple, winds back, and throws it at me. I manage to weave and duck, avoiding the hit. "Just admit you're into him!"

"Fine!" I exhale, then peer around to make sure Logan's gone. "I guess he's . . . good-looking. And the bike's hot. But that's all."

"Uh-huh." He rushes to sit back down, then smacks his hand against the table. "Okay, so here's what you do."

"I won't be doing a single thing, Kyle."

"Ask him to let you be his backpack."

I scrunch my brows. "Backpack?"

"Ride behind him." He smirks. "Bikers call their passengers 'backpacks.'"

Do they?

"Because you'd hold on to him while pressed against his back?

Your arms are the straps?" he hedges, speaking slowly as if to imply I should have understood already.

"Okay, uh... how's that relevant?"

"Logan won't let just anyone be his backpack." He shrugs as if he doesn't get it. "If he says yes, you're in. It means he's attracted to you. And now your bodies are in contact. There are sparks. He does his little trick where he only rides on the back wheel. Adrenaline is firing up."

Oh my god, this guy's nuts.

"He brings you to see the stars from someplace nobody else knows or some other dumb crap like that." He taps a finger on the table. "Guarantee the night ends *Top Gun*–style, with your arms around his waist. And then..."

I wave him off. "Yes, I get it."

"Uh-huh. So are you gonna?"

What? Ask him to take me on a ride? No. Hell no. If Kyle is right—and I have more than a doubt about it—then I'd be hitting on him, and I have no plans to be rejected by Logan. Sure, he kissed me that first night, but that was a knee-jerk reaction to panic. Since then, he's mostly looked annoyed by my presence. And besides, I have a deal to bring home and the police chasing after me.

"You know, as tempting as it sounds," I say, "I don't think so. No."

"Look, I'm not telling you to hit on him. Ask him to take you on a ride, and if he says no, you'll know he's not into you, but it won't be awkward."

"I'll think about it," I lie. I hope it's convincing, because I need Kyle to drop the topic. I don't even know why we're talking about this. There are rules in place—well, one rule—to make sure all he remains to me is a fake boyfriend. "Promise you won't bring this up with him either way."

"I swear," he says as he takes my hand in his and shakes. Then, with a clap, he stands again. "He's so lucky to have me in his life."

"Is peanut butter vegan?"

"Yes."

"Honey?"

"*Bzzz.*" Logan fits a forkful of eggplant in his mouth. "Therefore, no."

With a slow nod, I watch him chew dinner. I already know all of this, but I'll pretend ignorance over anything to make him talk. Having dinner in total silence is the worst.

"What?" he asks. "Is the mock quiz over?"

Oh, so he noticed.

"Gosh, am I annoying you?" I ask sarcastically. "Maybe if you talked a little more, I wouldn't have to carry the conversation."

Eyes narrowing, he silently stares at me.

"I thought vegans loved to talk about veganism anyway."

"Maybe vegans who love to talk."

With a sigh, I push the food around on my plate as one of the piglets lazily walks past me and toward Logan. It settles on top of his feet, but Logan doesn't seem to mind and keeps eating as if he has hardly noticed.

I throw the pink bundle another glance, wondering if it's the male or the female. I can never tell them apart. "Wait, what about your *leather* jacket? And the *leather* seat of your motorcycle?" I tease.

Setting his fork down, he rubs his eyes. "Okay. First of all, being a vegan isn't a religion, okay? There aren't rituals we follow to avoid eternal damnation." He levels me with an unimpressed gaze. "We live in a way that respects all creatures, but we're not perfect, and sometimes avoiding animal-derived products isn't possible."

So he *can* talk.

"But it's possible in this case. With faux leather."

Of course. *Faux* leather. Well, faux or not, they're sexy.

"Are you worried about tomorrow?" I ask, thinking of our appointment with the lawyers in the morning. We'll visit the police afterwards, and I'm not sure I'll be able to sleep until this is dealt with.

"No." He takes a sip of water, his eyes studying me over the rim of the glass. "Are you?"

When I give him a half-hearted shrug, he sets the glass down. "It'll be fine, Primrose. The lawyer will be with you the whole time, and he won't let you mess it up."

I hope he's right, but seeing as last time, it only took me two minutes around the police to start talking about sex-kicking, this lawyer would have to be a wizard to compensate for my built-in inability to lie.

"Think about something else, come on." He gestures at me to speak. "Ask me more annoying questions."

I glare, then resume eating. Though he doesn't deserve my sparkly personality, I'm also not sure he'll ever give me a free pass on my constant chatter, and I intend to take advantage of it. "What do you do around these parts once you're done working?"

He tilts his head like he doesn't understand the question.

"Well, you have no TV. No internet. Do you read? Listen to music? Go out with Kyle and his brother?"

"What do *you* do in Mayfield?"

"Plenty of stuff. One of my closest friends—Taylor—lives only a couple of streets away from me, so we go out for dinner, walk in the park, and there's this club . . ."

His brows furrow. "What?"

"N-nothing," I mumble, though truth to be told, I just realized I haven't seen Taylor in two months. Before that, *god*, we met for dinner about six months ago. "I guess . . . I mostly stay home. Listen to music, watch movies. Big city life means everyone is hustling around, and it takes forever to get anywhere."

"I sleep." He wipes his hand on a napkin, chewing as he studies his plate. "When I'm done working. I wake up at four every day, then work mostly in the fields for twelve hours. After that, I'm pretty much wiped."

I nod, hoping my expression doesn't betray how terrible that sounds. Working twelve hours a day and sleeping isn't a life, exactly. It sounds more like survival.

"I ride my bike," he mumbles. "Though you've kind of ruined that."

Fork frozen on the way to my lips, I go still. He's brought up the night we met, so it's my chance to ask questions. How do I just *know* he'll clam up? "You said it . . . it never happened before?"

He swallows hard. "What? Being hit by a reckless driver?"

"I was going ten miles an hour, Logan."

"Well, that's minimal comfort to me and my bike, isn't it?"

I open my mouth to quip at him, the words *you stopped in the middle of the road* on the tip of my tongue. But I'm determined to discuss this, so I try a patient, "Have you had any more since?"

He shakes his head.

"Are you sure?"

"We don't know if it was a panic attack, okay? Maybe it was a heart episode."

It says a lot that he'd rather think his heart is unhealthy than admit to a bit of anxiety. "So maybe you should see a cardiologist."

"I'm fine."

"I'm pretty sure you can ignore a stomachache or a headache, but your heart? You need that to live."

"I said I'm fine."

"Logan," I scold, and once his eyes are on me, I know I might as well be speaking another language. No matter how much I press him, he won't discuss this. Logan would much rather have an *actual* heart attack than talk about his feelings.

"How about this," I say, thinking one more attempt won't hurt. "I'll tell you something very private about me, and you'll tell me about your anxiety."

"I don't have—"

"I'll show you my list."

His parted lips shut.

The first night, as he tried to fix the car, talking about my list got his attention, and when he got it back from Derek, it killed him not to know which item he'd helped me cross off. I *know* he's curious, and at this point, one more person knowing my deepest fantasies and wishes won't change my life.

As he observes me, I grab my phone and take the pink cover off. I lift the folded list, then hold it out for him, and after a few seconds of what looks like deep consideration, he moves to grab it.

"And you'll talk to me?" I ask as I keep it just out of his reach.

He rolls his eyes, then, with a swift movement, snatches the list.

I'll take that as a yes.

He scrolls through the lines of text I know religiously until his brow furrows, and it's easy to guess what he's thinking. Only a handful of items on my list are crossed off: the ones he's responsible for. And among those, it's probably easy to guess which got struck through the night Derek came here.

"*Protect me from bullies,*" he reads out.

"Yeah."

His gaze darkens, but without a word, he resumes eating, still reading through my list. He doesn't say a word about the fact that so many of the things that most people my age have experienced have yet to happen to me, but I wonder if he's judging me for it. If he thinks it's as pathetic as it often feels. "Some of this is . . ." He scrunches his nose. "*Own a white horse*? You expect your dates in Mayfield to show up on a white horse?"

"I've compiled this list over the years, so some of it isn't as relevant anymore." He holds back a chuckle, and I strike him with a glare. "I liked it more when you were silent."

"Sorry." A few seconds of silence go by. "Why a *white* horse? What's wrong with brown horses? Black? Spotted?"

"Well, for starters, white is visible at night. I crashed against your *black horse*, remember?" I stab some zucchini with my fork. "And besides, twelve-year-old me was obsessed with Prince Charming."

He focuses on the list again. "Go downtown?"

Oh boy. "Um, that's . . . When I was younger, I thought 'town' was part of it, but it turns out it's not."

"Go down?" His brows rise as he straightens. "Oh, go down . . . on you?"

I tap the tip of my nose.

"But it's not struck through."

"I'm aware."

For a moment, he looks as appalled as if I'd told him I feed on human souls, but quickly collecting himself, he turns his focus to the list. "I guess number nine is also from your childhood?"

Number nine . . . *Lend me his crayons.*

"I wrote that one after Darrel Taylor refused to lend me his." I scoff, remembering my first crush, with his sandy-blond hair and cute chin dimple. "That was my very first heartbreak."

His eyes roll again, this time nearly disappearing into the back of his head. "What about number twenty-two? *Lend me his leather jacket?*"

Oh, dammit. I picture Logan's jacket, embarrassment creeping up my spine. I forgot about that one. "Teen years. I was in my bad boy phase."

"Huh." He looks around, then stands and opens the drawer. Once he's back at the table, he's holding a pen.

"Wait—what are you doing?"

"There's something better than a leather jacket, Primrose."

I squint, trying to read the word he's scribbling, until he sets the pen down and returns the list to me. *Faux*. That's what he added—a *faux* leather jacket.

Once I set the list beside my plate, I watch him expectantly. He can feel it, but he keeps his eyes on his plate for the longest time. Until my patience runs out. "Oh, come on."

He sighs, and I hope it means he's giving up. "What do you want to know?"

I'm not sure. I guess, first of all, I'd like him to acknowledge he had a panic attack.

He leans back in his chair. "You said it happened to you a lot growing up?"

"Yes. When I was in high school."

"Is that when you wrote number seven? *Protect me from bullies?*"

When I nod, he crosses his arms and presses them on the wooden edge of the table. "I've never felt anything like it before. It was like . . . like I was . . ."

"Dying?"

He blinks, his hands clenching into fists. "I kept thinking about everything that's going on. The farm, my family. And then, all of a sudden, it was like I couldn't breathe. My heart was beating too fast, and my eyes had black spots, and . . ."

I fight the instinct to touch him, because I figure it'll make him uncomfortable, and he's finally opening up. But I *do* want to, especially as I remember my first panic attack, when I overheard the classmate I had a crush on saying they shouldn't invite me to the cinema, as I'd likely take up two seats.

"How could it have been all . . . in my mind?"

"It wasn't," I explain, and when he meets my gaze, there's a vulnerable look in his eyes that makes it even harder not to offer some physical comfort. "Your heart was beating faster. It really *was* harder to breathe, and your vision was most definitely tunneling. But it all came from here," I say as I point at my head. "Not because your heart, lungs, or eyes don't work."

"So my brain wants me dead?"

"Your mind was overwhelmed, and it went into fight-or-flight mode. You tried to take in more oxygen, so you breathed harder. And your body released adrenaline, which made your heart beat faster, and your muscles tense up."

He seems to think it over for a moment, his shoulders dropping slightly. "Is there a way to . . ." He presses his lips tight. "I just can't have this shit happen to me randomly. I ride a bike and operate machinery—it's dangerous."

"Afraid you can't schedule them," I say, and when he gives me a flat "Ha-ha," I continue. "You could seek help, though. A therapist would explore with you the reasons behind your panic attacks and teach you how to deal with them."

Quickly, he shakes his head. "It was just once. I'm sure it won't happen again."

And I'm sure it's a cop-out, but I know better than to try to force therapy onto someone. When it's time, he'll get there himself.

"You could also tell me more about whatever is bothering you," I try after he resumes eating. "Your feelings and emotions. That could help too."

"I have a better idea," he says as he stands and opens one of his kitchen drawers. "Now, I'm going to give this to you, but it's not a gift. Got it? I want it back *promptly*."

I watch him walk back, then hold his hand out.

And boy oh boy, I can't help a massive grin from taking over my lips.

A box of crayons.

cuddle me

. . .

Primrose

AS I STEP through the heavy glass doors of the police station, my heart pounds with a mixture of nerves and apprehension. The fluorescent lights overhead cast a harsh glow over the sterile surroundings, illuminating rows of uniformed officers bustling about their duties. It's like all the light and warmth of the afternoon can't permeate the thick walls.

Beside me, Logan walks with a determined stride, his jaw set in a firm line as he follows the lawyers. His presence is reassuring, and when he turns to me and discreetly winks, I inhale. We're in this together. We can do this.

As we approach the front desk, a uniformed officer looks up from her paperwork and gives us a curt nod. "Can I help you?"

"We're here to speak with Officer Lawson," Logan replies, his voice steady despite the tension in the air.

The officer nods, scribbling something on a notepad before talking into her radio. "Lawson. Coleman's party is here for you."

Oh my god, I feel lightheaded.

How did I end up here? The more I ask myself this question, the more I can't wrap my head around it. I've never shoplifted. Never so much as got a traffic ticket. And now, I'm about to be questioned about my involvement in a felony. Which I'm *actually* guilty of.

"Look who decided to finally pay us a visit," a cop says as he walks through the corridor. Once he comes to stand in front of Logan, chewing a piece of gum with his mouth open, I recognize him as Connor, the officer who was with Josie the night of the arson. "I figured I'd have to come get you on your farm."

Logan barely spares the stocky man a glance. "What can I say? I'm full of surprises."

"Hey," Josie says as she emerges from a back door. "How's it going?"

Logan waves in her direction, and with a courteous nod, I keep my mouth shut.

Peter, my lawyer, said that I should talk only when strictly necessary and, even then, say as little as possible without arousing suspicion.

I plan to take his advice to the letter.

Connor walks to me, a hand scratching the fading hairline on his forehead. "You're with me. Follow—"

"No," Logan growls, stepping between us as his hand grasps my arm. I'm pulled behind him as Connor throws an amused look at the cop watching the scene unfold from behind the reception desk. "Not you."

"Can you believe this guy?"

"Don't you want to question *me*?" Logan insists, ignoring the lawyer's request to relax. "Let Josie handle Primrose."

"Either come with me voluntarily," Connor says as he tilts his head to look past Logan and straight at me. "Or wait for the arrest."

Heart in my throat, I try to swallow, but my saliva feels as sticky as glue.

Josie, who's been silently observing, walks closer when Logan sends her a silent plea. Her red hair is pulled up in a sober ponytail, and though her skin is bare, she's still painfully beautiful, even in her uniform. "Connor, come on. Take Logan and let us girls talk."

Connor hesitates for a long moment, studying his partner. The obnoxious smacking of his lips drives me crazy, but I'm much more concerned about Logan's reaction to the possibility of him questioning me.

Please say yes.

"Fine, Lawson. But this is the *one* friends-and-family discount you get." He spits his gum in a nearby bin, and the noise gives me shivers. "Ask for preferential treatment again, and I'll tell the chief to take you off the case."

"You got it." There's a quiet exchange between Logan and Josie as he and his lawyer follow Connor into the corridor. Then, clenching his fist, he glances at me.

Be strong.

I assume that's what he's saying, but I'm mostly thankful the lawyer will be with me throughout the interrogation.

Once they disappear into one of the rooms facing the corridor, Josie offers me a friendly smile. "Okay. We'll be in room two. This way." She leads me into the same corridor, then stops three doors away from Logan's and enters a small, poorly lit room. Naked walls, a table, three chairs, and a small window from which the sun struggles to filter through.

It's an actual interrogation room.

This is it. I'm going to be sick.

"Don't be nervous," Josie says as I step in.

Is it so obvious?

She closes the door, then sits at one side of the table, gesturing at the chairs on the other side. "You're not under arrest. I'll ask you some questions about what happened last Friday, and your lawyer will be with you the whole time."

He holds a hand out to her. "Peter Miller."

"Nice to meet you."

We all sit, falling into an uneasy silence as Josie sets a folder on the table, then laces her fingers together. "So . . . You and Logan. How did you meet?"

I watch Peter as he instructed this morning, and he nods. Though we spent all morning preparing for this, I still don't feel ready. How could he have prepped me for every possible scenario in just a few hours? But he swore he'd intervene if I were asked something unexpected, and god, I hope the money I'm paying him is well spent.

My life is quite literally on the line.

"Uh, we met in Roseberg a couple of months back."

"But you're from Mayfield, right?" When I nod, she taps her pen on the stack of documents. "That's a long way from Roseberg. What were you doing there?"

"Work. I travel a lot because of my social media. I'm lucky enough to collaborate with many businesses."

"Who were you working with at the time?"

I release a breath. Peter and I discussed all of this at length this morning, and besides the part about me meeting Logan, everything else is true. "Sodatron. They're a sugar-free soda producer who worked on a sour candy limited edition."

"Oh my god." Her eyes widen. "I love sour candy."

When I smile, she does too, then writes something down. "And your relationship has been long distance since then?"

"Yes."

Her eyes narrow. "But Logan doesn't have a phone, does he? How do you manage that?"

I check the lawyer's expression, and he offers a subtle bob of his head.

"He uses Kyle's phone to call me every day," I say. Peter promised we're making it harder for them by claiming we've been communicating through someone else's phone.

"Oh, that's cute." She writes something else. Her eyes focus on a spot behind me, and with a hum, she continues. "Tell me about Friday. What happened?"

My heart palpitates, but I try to keep my casual smile unbothered. "Uh, Friday, yes. I finished my job in Roseberg—I was hired to assist a cookie company with their social media—then drove here."

"Your car?"

"A rental." When she nods, I shift on the uncomfortable metal chair. "I arrived pretty late, and once I got to Logan's house . . . Well, we hadn't seen each other in a long time. We spent the night in."

"Where's your rental now?"

My mouth opens, but the accident with Logan comes back to me in flashes. Crashing against him. His panic attack. Our kiss. Him fixing my car.

Well, crap.

We didn't prepare for this.

I turn to Peter, and when he dips his chin, nausea assaults me. *If I nod, you can answer the question.* That's what he said this morning. But how can I explain what happened without our story falling apart? What—should I say I got into an accident with my boyfriend? How did she even know to ask?

"The car is at the repair shop," Peter offers. "How is this relevant?"

Josie shrugs. "I'm trying to piece together what happened. Did you get into an accident or something?"

An accident or something? She knows. She *must* know.

"No accident involved." Peter grabs his briefcase, swiftly opens the straps, and takes out a pile of papers. Once he finds the one he's looking for, he hands it over. "Mr. Coleman was understandably upset about his girlfriend's vehicle malfunctioning, so he got the mechanic's assessment. It looks like the car had a defective transmission sensor." He waves in dismissal. "I have no idea what that means, but . . . not Miss Bellevue's fault."

So Logan was right. The car didn't break down because of him.

Why did he get that document? I guess it's entirely possible he'd go through all that trouble to prove he was right, but . . . could he have done it for me? For *this* moment?

"Oh, that's . . ." Josie clicks her tongue as she studies the paper. "You should ask for a full refund."

I nod, but her friendliness is starting to feel corny. Is she just trying to put me at ease so that I'll lower my guard and mess up?

"You know, when we came to the farm last Friday, I couldn't help but notice that Logan's bike was pretty beaten up." She relaxes in her chair, her ponytail gently swinging with the movement and her emerald green eyes flickering with curiosity. "Do you know what happened?"

"Mr. Coleman fell from his motorcycle."

Josie's eyes flick to Peter. "Oh, come on, Mr. Miller. Give your client some credit—she can answer my questions herself."

"Officer," Peter says, "I won't tell you how to do your job, and I ask that you pay me the same courtesy."

The sudden rise of tension in the room has me swallowing, then trying to breathe through it though my heart is in my throat.

Josie sighs, her patient expression back in place as she asks Peter, "Why weren't the police involved? Ambulance? Insurance?"

"There was no need for any of it. The motorcycle only needs minor cosmetic fixes. Mr. Coleman will pay for those himself." Peter rolls his shoulders back as if he's suddenly remembered he should be somewhere else. "I struggle to see how this involves my client at all. If you don't have any more questions directly pertaining to her, we'll—"

"Tell me about Derek. He's your ex, right?"

I nod, slightly more comfortable because, at least, this portion of the story doesn't involve any lies.

"And you've experienced some backlash online after your breakup?"

"Some, yes." Reminded of Peter's recommendation not to be overly aggressive when discussing Derek, I shrug. "He's been sharing his version of the events between us online, and he doesn't often paint me in a great light."

"Yeah." She scrolls through the papers in front of her. "Not a great light indeed."

I wet my lips, then dry my hands on the flaps of my skirt.

"You mind if I ask you a few questions about that?"

I shake my head. Of all the things she could ask me about, Derek and his lies are the most favorable option, and I never thought I'd say that.

Once she leans back in the chair, I exhale.

This will be a while.

I twist and turn in bed, my blanket now entangled in a rope by the side of my body. Though I'm exhausted, my thoughts keep running to the three-hour-long informal interrogation I went through today.

God, I just want to sleep.

Logan always goes to bed early, and tonight was no exception. Once we got home from the police station, we had dinner and swapped information, and after that, he left for his room. From what I could tell, it looks like we didn't contradict each other—dare I say we made it unscathed?

Still, no sleep. It's like the tension won't wear down, and I keep replaying every second of it in my head, expecting to remember something I said that'll destroy our alibis. Is Logan doing the same? Is he really sleeping like everything's fine?

Fooling myself into thinking he might still be awake, I walk to his room and knock on the door.

Nothing.

Maybe it wasn't loud enough.

I try again, and this time I hear the squeak of his mattress springs, then the piglets grunting. "What's . . . What happened? Are you okay?"

Opening the door, I'm met with a pitch-black room and Logan's eyes squinting against the light coming in from the corridor. Does he always sleep without a shirt on?

"I didn't say come in, did I?"

"Sorry," I say as I enter the room and close the door behind me. "I can't sleep."

He sighs, dropping his face into his pillow, and though his words are muffled, I hear him clearly as he says, "Could have just abandoned you to that fire."

As if. He needed me to escape the crime scene.

"I keep thinking about today. What if I said something that will lead them to us?"

"Peter said everything went fine, Primrose. Go to sleep."

I sit on the edge of his bed, propping my leg up and under me as he studies me with a cocked brow. "You can't be sure."

"No, I can't. But I'm sure if you don't let me sleep, I'll deliver you to the police myself."

I press my lips tight, my finger drawing circles on his sheet. "Just five minutes? Please?"

With a sigh, he throws his head back on the pillow. "Fine."

"Tell me something to distract me."

He hums, eyes closed. "You know what's fascinating? The suspension system on my bike."

He launches into a detailed explanation of damping rates, rebound adjustments, and preload settings, whatever all of that is, his voice taking on a hypnotic quality. Try as I might, I struggle to muster up even a hint of genuine interest.

"Oh my god," I burst after a while. "Please stop."

He cracks one eye open. "Hmm?"

"This is the most boring combination of words I've ever heard."

"It's meant to make you sleep."

It might, but it's also killing any will to wake up.

Crossing my legs, I think hard of something else we could talk about. *Anything* else. "Do you date a lot?" I ask, then quickly add, "You know, when you're not fake-dating me."

He shakes his head. "At the risk of surprising you, no. I don't."

Right. I could have gathered that myself from—well, everything about him. "So you just kiss random people who crash into your bike?"

"Yes. In fact, I never even had a panic attack. It was all part of a long con designed to entrap you in my house, because I hate peace and sleep." He shifts his pillow up. "I don't want to talk about my dating life."

"Fine." I exhale. "So you admit you had a panic attack?"

He blinks, his shoulders tensing. "The last woman I dated was my ex. We broke up five years ago."

I guess we're back to the dating portion of the conversation. "Why did you break up?"

Holding himself up on his elbow, he looks up at me through a curtain of sleep-mussed hair. "We'd been together since we were kids, but as we got older, we started wanting different things. Can I go back to bed now?"

"Like what?"

He rubs his eyes. "Uh . . . she wanted to move. Focus on her career and all of that. I wasn't willing to follow her, but I was also very resistant to the long-distance thing."

Sure, with his love for phones. "So she left without you?"

Releasing a breath, he shakes his head. "She kept running away instead of facing our problems. She wouldn't come back home for days, staying at her parents' place to avoid seeing me." He pauses, looking down at the mattress. "Then she cheated. Screwed her way out of the relationship."

My lips twist. I've never been cheated on, but a lot about Logan makes sense now. How closed off he is—how distrustful and distant from everyone. "Did she confess?"

"I found out." Folding an arm behind his head, he looks up at the ceiling. "I flipped out at first, of course. Then I told her I understood. It wasn't even about sex—it was everything else. We were unhappy, and she searched for what was missing elsewhere."

Well, cry me a river. There's hardly ever an excuse to cheat, and this isn't one of them.

"I'm not saying she didn't fuck up," he comments when he notices my expression. "She knew it too—she was desperate."

"Did you dump her after that?"

One corner of his lips lifts, but it's not enough to distract from the melancholic look in his eyes. "I begged her to stay. Begged her to choose me. I told her I'd do long-distance. That I'd leave Simon in charge of the farm and go with her, but . . ." He swallows. "It didn't work out that way."

She dumped *him*.

She cheated on him, lied about it, then dumped him.

Maybe I am a violent person after all, because I'd like ten minutes in a room with her. Who *does* that?!

"Does she still live here?"

"Yup. With him. White picket-fenced house, cute kid. So she probably made the right choice." He closes his eyes, and I let mine trail up his chest, tracing the many tattoos intersecting all over his skin. With the silver moonlight coming in from the open drapes, he looks like pure art. "Lost something, Barbie?"

Skin heating, I look up at his face. "Uh, I was just admiring your—"

"Yeah, I know what you were doing." He huffs out a chuckle, then shrugs. "Was there anything else?"

"No. I'll let you, uh . . . get back to it."

"Thanks." He turns around, pulling a blanket over his body, and I watch the rise and fall of his shoulders for a while.

"I swear to god, Primrose. It's two in the morning, and I need to wake up in two hours. If you don't—"

"Can I sleep here?"

He turns to me, his brows scrunched so deeply his eyes are almost closed. "You want to sleep in my bed?"

When I nod, he shrugs. "And where do I sleep?"

It's my turn to look confused as I say, "Here, of course."

"You want to sleep in *my* bed, with me?"

I guess? It's weird—I know it is. Logan and I are basically strangers, and I've only ever shared a bed with one man. But the thought of lying in bed by myself, my heart in my throat as I think of today, is making my skin itch everywhere. "I don't want to be alone."

With a sigh, he scoots to the left. "Fine."

I slide under the blanket as he takes one of the two pillows under his head and sets it on my side. "Good night."

"No snuggles, huh?" I tease.

"I don't know, Barbie," he says as he tilts his head. "I reserve most of my snuggling for sex. Interested?" When I roll my eyes, he smacks his pillow and huffs out a "Thought so."

I still, tapping my fingers on my stomach as I stare at the ceiling. He wakes up early to feed the animals, and working in the fields is more forgiving when the sun isn't at its hottest.

Ugh, now I feel bad for having woken him up.

"Are you sure you don't want a cuddle?" I offer, breaking the utter silence with my version of an apology. "You can be the small spoon."

"Jesus Christ." He chuckles, low and throaty, then cups his face with both hands as he lets out a long groan. When he turns to me, he smiles wide, a hint of frustration the way his tongue rims his upper lip. Our faces are close together, and his blue-gray eyes are magnetic. "You're fucking ridiculous, you know that?"

"Am I?" When he nods, I shrug. "Is it a bad thing?"

"No."

"Because I think it's ridiculous not to have a TV."

"Hmm."

"In fact, if you had a TV, I probably would have put on a movie and fallen straight to sleep."

He clicks his tongue. "Now I *also* wish I had a TV."

I switch positions on the pillow to get closer to him. "So, number ten?"

"What's that?"

"*Cuddle me.*"

"I thought you were supposed to cuddle me."

"Do you *want me* to cuddle you?"

His mouth opens, then closes. "Just sleep."

"I can't," I say with a sigh as I cup my belly. "I swear I'm getting a stress-induced stomachache."

"Come on, close your eyes." When I don't, he scowls. "Right now, Barbie."

I do as he says, trying to breathe through my nausea. In the silence, my thoughts whirl until I can feel myself drift off, then the slightest touch to my forehead brings me back. I open my eyes to find Logan tucking a strand of my hair behind my ear, and when he notices I'm watching him, he rolls his eyes. "I said sleep."

I close my eyes, then smile.

I don't care what he says.

That counted as a cuddle.

you keep using the word 'snuggle'

. . .

Logan

"WHAT DO YOU THINK?" Primrose asks.

I lift my head, focusing on the tenth pair of identical brown boots she's tried. She moves around the mirror, turning one side and the other, lifting one leg, and crossing her ankles. It takes everything I have to limit myself to a simple, "Hmm . . . That this is the worst day of my life."

"*You* wanted to come," she says as she walks on the spot.

No, I want to make sure she buys appropriate footwear so she doesn't die on my farm, and that's the only reason I'm here.

"You understand you're not shopping for Paris Fashion Week, right?" I rest my forearms on my thighs and lean forward. "These boots will be nasty come tomorrow. Just buy the most comfortable ones."

"But it's not just a matter of comfort." She turns to me, and my heart squeezes at her defeated expression. "Do I want a zipper? And are they warm? Because mornings can get pretty cold around here. And what about water resistance? And durability!"

"You don't need durability."

She halts, seems to think it over, then turns to the mirror without saying a word. I didn't mean to sound like an asshole again, but it's the truth. Seventeen days. Twelve now. Simon even printed her plane ticket, and it's now sitting on my bookshelf, so it's official.

"I don't know. They're all so . . . brown."

"They might have them in black or gray. Afraid pink isn't an option."

With a sad pout, she mumbles, "I'll probably get those," and points at the first pair she tried. When was that? About an hour ago?

"Fine." I grab the box as she sits beside me and removes the boots. Once she's back in her pink tennis shoes, I look around, trying to locate the cashier, and instead my eyes land on the most *Primrose* pair of boots I have ever seen, on a plastic stand to my right.

I should just shut up. She chose her boots, and if she sees those, it'll prolong the torture.

"Let's go?" she says as she joins my side and pulls out her wallet, her lip stuck out. She looks so sad, and I can tell this is the least fun she's ever had shopping.

Damn me, I like it so much more when she's happy.

"How about those?"

"Hm?" She turns around, then gasps loudly as her eyes land on the white cowboy boots. "Oh—yes, yes! I want those!"

She walks over, her fingers brushing the complex beige stitch pattern. "They're so pretty. Aren't they pretty?"

"Dreamy."

Her big blue eyes wander around the shop. "I wonder if they also sell cowboy hats."

"I'll kick you off the farm."

"Come on, give me a 'yee-haw!' I know you want to." When I groan, she must take pity on me, because she raises a hand. "Okay, okay. Just the boots. I'll try them on; give me a second."

She walks back, then slides off her shoes. She fits the boots on quickly, and hands on her hips, stares at herself in the mirror.

Though my eyes briefly linger on her ass, wrapped in the shortest white dress to ever exist, I focus on her reflection.

Her blonde locks frame her face, the pink tips brushing over her round, dimpled cheeks. Joy radiates from her bright blue eyes, and I can't help but feel captivated by her genuine happiness.

It's a whole different sight.

"I love them. And they're made of faux leather." With a wink, she twists to look at me. "So you have to love them too, cowboy."

"Still not a cowboy, Barbie."

"Still don't care." She cheerily walks to the small bench and removes the boots, and once she approaches the counter, I step in front of her. "I'll pay for them. You're buying them to stay at my farm."

"But I'll keep them once I'm gone."

"But you wouldn't be buying them if it wasn't for *my* mud."

She elbows her way in front of me, then hands the cashier her card. I wouldn't need more than a pinkie to move her out of the way, but I step back and let her pay.

We leave the shop and join the influx of people walking around the mall. While it always makes me uncomfortable to be in such a large crowd, it feels like everyone's eyes are on me today.

"Think we can find a nice café in here?"

"I don't want coffee."

"Well, I do. And pastry—oh! Or cake!" She excitedly claps, then noticing my unimpressed gaze, bites her bottom lip expectantly. "Do you mind?"

This woman, I swear. Only because she's pretty, with those thick thighs and the bluest eyes I've ever seen, she thinks she can bat her lashes, and I'll do everything she wants.

"Fine."

Apparently, she's right.

She rushes to the right, then darts inside the first café we find, and I lazily follow. When she asks about vegan options and gets told all they have is coffee, she's out and on searching for the next one. I follow her to the next café, then to the next, and we keep receiving more of the same answers and curious looks. Until eventually, Primrose points at a small corner juice bar and shrieks. "That one! That must have something vegan!"

Gripping my arm, she leads me inside, then approaches the counter and asks the woman behind it to show us her vegan-friendly selection.

"Of course." The brunette woman in a green cap wipes her hands on a kitchen towel. Everything you see in this tray is vegan. We have cakes, cookies, and a couple of slices of pie." She points at the board behind her. "And all the drinks marked with the leaf are vegan, too."

"So many options," Primrose says with a cocky grin as she turns to me. "We'd nearly given up when we found you, but I was determined to find something for him."

"I'm Cassidy," the woman says as she looks up at me. Her smile softens, and her eyes stick to mine longer than I'm comfortable with. "I'm vegan too."

Great. Now she thinks we're instant buddies. Why is Primrose making friends with some random café worker?

"Primrose. And he's Logan," Primrose says. "Don't be fooled by his chattiness; he's quite moody."

When I glare, she gestures at me as if to show Cassidy this is what she meant.

"So, Logan, what can I get you?"

"Uh . . . a black coffee." Primrose's eyes widen dangerously, so I add, "And a slice of blueberry pie."

"And for you?"

I look away from Cassidy, who keeps glancing at me even as she takes Primrose's order.

"Okay, I'll warm up your pie and bring it out. You guys can take a seat."

"I'll pay," I rush to say. Primrose has already spent money on the boots, and I don't like feeling indebted to people. But I probably spoke with too much intensity, because Primrose takes a small step back with wide eyes.

"I'll wait at the table."

She walks to the back of the shop, and I approach the cashier. "Eighteen dollars," Cassidy says.

I take out my card, then tap it on the card reader.

"I haven't seen you around here before, have I?"

"Uh, no." The card reader buffers. "I hate malls."

"Really? Why?"

I think of answering with, *Because I don't like strangers asking me personal questions*, but settle instead on a mumbled "Too crowded. Noisy. And I swear everyone keeps staring at me today."

"You do look like an outdoorsy guy," she says, leaning against the counter with a grin I don't fully understand but makes me all sorts of uncomfortable. It's too . . . *friendly*. "But I'm pretty sure people are staring at you because of, uh, Primrose."

Noticing my blank stare, she cocks a brow. "She's Sugar High, is she not?"

"Yeah, that's her."

"She's quite the internet personality."

I check the machine again. What's wrong with this card? "Uh-huh."

"Especially after the list—that Gracen dude is an asshole. Why would he post it online?"

Great, now I'm gossiping.

I hum, which *should* be enough for the conversation to die, but after a long silence, she asks, "Do you work around here?"

"No," I say, eyes stuck to the buffering icon. "I have a farm."

Her eyes narrow.

"A vegan farm."

"Oh. That sounds cool. I've never been on a farm."

God, what's taking so long? And where is Primrose? I turn around, but can't see her past the busy tables.

There's a beep, and I release a breath, waiting for my receipt so I can walk away. Free of Cassidy, I notice Primrose sitting a few tables down, tucking her hair behind her ear as she looks down at her phone.

Thinking of the billion scrunchies disseminated all over my house, I join her.

Her eyes meet mine, and she excitedly wiggles on her chair. "How did that"—she jerks her head toward the counter—"go?"

"What, paying? My farm's doing like shit, but I can still afford coffee."

"No, not paying." She rolls her big blue eyes at me as if I'm supposed to know what the hell she's talking about, then wiggles her eyebrows suggestively. "Cassidy."

"What about Cassidy?"

"Logan, she was flirting with you."

"What?" I look back to where Cassidy is working behind the counter. She turns to me and smiles, so I quickly focus back on Primrose. *Was* she flirting with me? "She was just being friendly," I scold her. "Don't turn this into a whole thing."

"You seriously—" She scoffs. "Then why did you ask me to leave?"

"I didn't ask you to leave. I said I'd pay."

She looks up as if thinking about it. "Oh. So you're not interested?"

"No, I'm not . . ." I lean forward, then insist, "She wasn't flirting with me, okay? Just because she's a vegan, it doesn't mean we'll play together."

She widens her eyes. "Can't say I feel too sorry for Cassidy."

"Hm." I tap my foot, impatient for the food to arrive. The neon lights here give me a headache, and the noise is unbearable. People chatting, a service dog barking, children screaming. It's mayhem, and there's a nearby table of teenagers cackling like hyenas and driving me mad.

"Here's your food." Cassidy appears beside me and sets the tray on the table. She dishes out our orders, and I can feel Barbie's inquisitive eyes glued to the side of my face. What is she expecting to see, exactly? My eyes turning into cartoon hearts and thin red lines on my cheeks?

"And your coffee," Cassidy says, setting the cup before me.

"Thanks," I mumble. I keep my gaze on the dark brew until she leaves, and finally, I let out a breath, ignoring Primrose's *tsk*. What an annoying noise.

I set the napkin next to my pie on the table and start eating, but Primrose grabs it, and with an even more annoying "Ha!" she turns it around. "Looks like Cassidy wants to play with you."

I glance up at the words scribbled on the paper next to her number. *Would love a tour of the farm.*

Momentarily shocked, I blink, but that seems to amuse Primrose even more, and with a quick movement, I grab the napkin and ball it up. "Whatever. I'm not interested."

"You don't even know her!" she squeals. "What—you don't think she's pretty?"

Good god, why am I being punished?

"Leave it alone."

"Fine. I get it. You'd have to lose the whole 'grumpy guy angry at life' aesthetic if you were to have a girlfriend.

Her lashes flutter against her flushed cheeks as she takes a bite, a genuine smile curving her lips. Her emotions play out on her face as intensively as she feels them, and it's annoying. Inconvenient, even. But also impossible to look away from, for some reason.

Her eyes flick to mine, and licking the fork, she tilts her head. "Why are you smiling?"

"What? I don't know." My face scrunches, so I try to relax it into a neutral expression. Noticing a smear of chocolate over her lips, I ignore the instinct to clean it up with my thumb and hand her a napkin.

She wipes her lips. "Clean?"

No, not clean. I could lick that chocolate off her skin. She ordered off the vegan tray—I really could.

"Logan?"

"Here—" I point at the spot over my own lips, and this time she wipes it off.

"I made some candy for you." She sets the napkin down. "It's on the kitchen table."

Oh, so that's what that is. When I came back home for lunch today, I noticed the orange bowl filled with gummies, but I figured she was experimenting with her recipes for Marisol. "Let me guess," I say, thinking of the yellow candy. "Saffron and cornstarch."

"Lemon, actually." Her lips pinch. "I figured you'd appreciate it, given how sour you are."

I hide my amusement with another forkful of pie. "No thanks."

Why does she keep making candy for me? Is it because I didn't throw myself at her feet about it?

"Seriously? Can't you just try it?" She shoves a hand in her bag and takes out individually wrapped red hard candy. "How about this one, then? It's my favorite. I'm begging you," she insists. "Have mercy before this drives me crazy."

I think of making a joke about her definitely being nuts already, but it looks like I'm driving her up the wall, and I guess if I have to eat her candy, I want to see what her favorite is about. "Fine, Jesus."

I grab the candy, unwrap it, and pop it in my mouth. It mixes with the flavor of blueberries from the pie—another thing I'm eating because she asked me to—but once the strawberry overpowers it, I hesitate.

It's familiar—and excellent, of course—but I forget to even say something to Primrose, anxiously awaiting my feedback, because I can't figure out when or where I've tasted this before.

"So?"

I let the thought go and nod. "It's great."

Her eyes roll. "Thank you. I strive for that kind of lukewarm feedback." Gathering some chocolate cream on her fork, she mumbles, "So, why won't you give Cassidy a chance?"

Here she goes again.

I could tell her to fuck off. That it's none of her business, and

I'm not talking about this any more than I already have. She'd take it and eat her cake and probably look all sullen about it for a while.

But once again, it appears as if I care about how she feels, so I calmly say, "I don't think the love of my life is someone who'd give me her number while I'm with another woman."

"Who, me?"

"You are a woman, aren't you?"

She waves me off. "Women aren't usually intimidated by me. And besides, we're obviously not together."

I open my mouth, then close it. Why would that be obvious? Should I ask? It's not like she's going to offend me either way. I don't care.

"How is it obvious?" I mumble.

She keeps eating until, probably motivated by my insistent stare, she points the fork at herself. "Guys like you don't exactly date women like me."

Guys like me? Women like her?

I have no idea what she means.

My eyes flick to her blond hair, the strands fading into pink. "Women with pink hair?"

"No."

"With watermelons on their skirts?"

She rolls her eyes.

"What women, Primrose?" I ask in a bored voice as I break off another piece of pie.

She stares into my eyes, then sighs. "I just mean, I don't think I'm your type."

One corner of my lips lifts before I can do anything about it. I kissed her five minutes into knowing her. "Really? Was my tongue in your mouth too subtle?"

"You were going through a lot. It doesn't count."

Funny that she'd think she has any right to decide that.

"What's my type then?"

She taps the back of her fork on her lips. "Women with legs as long as highways and strong arms. Who look remarkably beautiful even in the simplest clothes and wear no makeup because they don't need it. With freckles and flattering smile lines and—"

What the fuck? "Is this someone you know?"

"Tell me I didn't just describe your ex," she deadpans.

When I look down at the blueberry jam on top of my pie, she lets out a smug "Huh," then adds, "Guess who fits that description?"

"Cassidy?" I ask flatly.

She taps the tip of her nose, and I roll my eyes. What an idiotic thing to believe. Not that I have anything against a tall woman with freckles, but that's not my type. I don't have a type. If I *had* a type, that wouldn't be it.

"Trust me, Barbie, your arm strength is at the bottom of the list of reasons why I wouldn't date you."

She shrugs, then slurps her pink drink. "Likewise," she says before she sets the glass down. Letting out a chuckle as if laughing at her own joke, she takes another forkful of cake. "And the top spot? No TV."

"Is that what you look for in a man? A TV?"

"Yes," she says with a playfully snarky tone. "How else are we supposed to watch a movie and snuggle?"

"Want to know my number one reason not to date you?" Without waiting for her answer, I say, "You keep using the word 'snuggle.'"

"I bet Cassidy would never," she teases.

I set my coffee down, then grab the balled-up paper and look around. Aiming for the bin to my right, I throw it in, then turn to Primrose. "Okay. You want to know what my actual type is?"

She nods.

"Smart women." I point at the counter behind me. "And any woman who thinks you're not a force to be reckoned with, Barbie, is a very stupid woman."

make me laugh when i'm sad

. . .

Primrose

DEREK
Meet me outside.

I STARE AT MY PHONE, eyes blown wide as my pulse quickens. The text came out of nowhere, and though I've been staring at the screen for a full minute, it doesn't become any less real. He wants to meet, but why now? It has to be about the piglets. About the fire.

I stand on shaky legs and walk out of the kitchen, abandoning my apron on the way. Since we came back from the mall, I've been making candy, and Logan has been working. Based on what I know of his routine, he won't be back for another couple of hours.

Wiping my hands on the skirt of my dress, I look around. The piglets are in the bedroom, and it's not like I intend to let him in.

When I open the front door and quickly slink outside, Derek waves at me. His copper hair has grown out since we broke up, and as much as I stare at his small, brown eyes, I can't see all I saw in him only a few months ago.

He surely doesn't hold a candle to Logan.

As I white-knuckle the handrail and walk down the steps, he smiles. "Hello. How's it going?"

"I'm fine." I come to a stop in front of him, and though the polite thing to do would be to ask how *he's* doing, I don't care and don't want to know. "What's up?"

"Well, I'm hoping you'll be more reasonable than Logan and agree to give me the pigs back."

I could laugh in his face. "What pigs?"

His smile falls like an autumn leaf off a tree, his bad mood sinking in almost immediately. "You know, once the investigation is over and you're in prison, I *will* discuss all of this at length with your audience."

Though the thought alone gives me shivers, I won't let him see he scared me, so I shrug.

"Come on. You have your list back—what do you want?"

"I'd love it if you could stop posting lies about me," I offer. "But no matter what you do, I still don't know the first thing about any pigs."

He shoves both hands in his pockets. "I *need* those piglets, Primrose. And if you give them to me right now, we'll tell the police that Logan acted alone. You'll be okay."

He just doesn't get it, does he? I'd never deliver the pigs to him, and the thought of betraying Logan feels unnatural. Sure, he's a moody guy, but he's been protecting me every step of the way.

"I won't do a single thing for you ever again." I turn on my heels and mumble, "Enjoy your followers, though."

As I close my fist around the doorknob, he asks, "Do you really think Logan will make all your dreams come true, Primrose? That he's any better than me?"

I spin around to face him. "Only in every way possible."

"Well, he's not. He's using you—that's why you're here. And even if he did like you, what will happen when he . . ." He gestures up and down at me, and instantly, heat rushes up my neck.

"When he what?" I bark.

"Look, let's be honest. You're not . . . you're not exactly hot. All

I had to do to keep you around was sleep with you, and if I couldn't do it for millions of followers, do you think Logan will? You've seen his ex, haven't you?"

It's important for my cover that I deny everything he just said. That I say that Logan loves me—that I show a united front and a strong relationship. But I'm stunned into silence. As it turns out, even if it comes from someone you hate, a knife to the heart makes you bleed all the same.

"He might act like he cares about you, but trust me, he doesn't," Derek insists. "And he'll be grossed out too when he eventually agrees to throw you one."

Without another word, I turn around and open the door, his words reaching me once more.

"But only an idiot would fall for the same scheme twice, right?"

Tears run down my cheeks faster than I can stop them, my mouth twisting as I sob harder and harder. It's like all the tension and doubt of the last few days have shifted to pain, and now that I've opened the faucet, it's impossible to stop the flow.

I hate it. I've always hated being a crier, but it keeps being my go-to response to any strong emotions. I cry when I'm happy, sad, angry, frustrated. I cry when I see something cute, when I'm on my period, when I'm in pain. It's inconvenient, especially when I need to pretend I don't care, and it makes me look weak.

"Strong girls cry when they're angry," I mumble to myself for the millionth time.

It's fine. Nothing of what Derek said is new, since he did *not* try to hide his contempt for me when we slept together. I'm perfectly aware that's the reason he decided to end our relationship. The way my naked body looks.

I've tried not to let it matter. I told myself I can't expect to be everyone's cup of tea, and I consoled myself with hopeful lies like 'someone, one day, will care about what's on the inside.' But the truth is that I want someone to desire me. To crave me. And I'm terrified no one ever will.

Sitting on the couch, I cry into a tissue until it turns black with mascara, and my nose feels stuffy and uncomfortable. Then I cry some more.

When something cold and moist taps on my leg, I flinch and see the piglet looking up at me.

It touched me.

I look down to confirm there's no bite, though I guess I would have felt it, as I quickly pull my leg away, but it just stays there, small black eyes staring at me.

Small, black, soft eyes.

"Do you want cuddles?" I ask, my voice hoarse. I've seen Logan pet the piglets several times, either behind their ears or on their backs and bellies. "I'm sorry, I'm not sure I . . ." It keeps staring at me, so I cautiously approach it with my hand.

Its tiny snout wiggles, and once my fingers are close enough, the piglet sniffs it tentatively. I hold back a whimper when its velvety snout nuzzles my hand, and feeling the softness of its fur, a gentle warmth spreads through my chest. Its oinks become smoother, more content, and slowly, I lower myself to the ground. With an endearing waddle, the piglet approaches me, and I find myself smiling down at it as it twists and turns to get me to pet its whole back.

Noticing a small brown spot on its ear, I lightly gasp. I'm pretty sure she's the girl. Now I'll be able to tell them apart.

The low rumbling of an engine startles me, and with a squelch, the pig rushes into the corridor. I follow it, then run to close the bedroom door behind me as I wipe my tears with the back of my hands. Logan is home early—today of all days.

I pace, holding my breath until I hear the front door open and close. There are steps, but I can't make out much else. That is, until I lean with my ear against the door, and a knock almost deafens me. I bolt back and let out a shaky breath. "Yeah?"

God, my voice sounds all nasal.

"All good?"

"Y-yeah, I'm fine."

I wait to hear him retreat, but nothing comes.

"What's wrong with your voice? Did something happen?"

"No, I—" Come on, Prim. Reasonable excuse. "I just got out of the shower."

"Really? Did you need to wash off after falling into a puddle of lies?"

Eyes rolling, I look at the ceiling.

"I don't want to talk about it, Logan. I'm fine," I say, though my voice breaks on the last word.

"You don't sound fine."

I'm not. Oh, and something else? Not wanting to talk about it is a lie too. I'd love to dump all my issues on him. To cry and whine about how the world is unfair, and men are the worst, and to have him soothe me and tell me that things are going to be okay. That what anyone else says doesn't matter if I love myself, especially not when Derek is the one to say it.

"Can I open the door?"

I press my lips together and look down at the floor. His voice is so comforting. Even when it's gruff, or he's using it to say very annoying stuff, it's still warm and reassuring.

Despite his rough edges and thick walls, Logan is sensitive and empathetic. But I also know there's some truth to what Derek said. I'm his ticket out of trouble—someone he needs to tolerate until I've done my part and can get out of his hair.

I can't let myself mistake this for something else.

As he walks away, I slink back to my bed, both regretting my silence and grateful I didn't let him in. Sure, I'm lonely and sad, but he gave up pretty quickly.

It's fine. I don't need him. I don't need anyone.

I hug my knees, feet pressing on the wooden edge of the bed

frame, when there's a little rattle at my door. Watching the handle move up and down, my brows scrunch. "What the . . ."

The door opens, and held between large hands is one of the piglets, belly-up and perfectly content with its legs stretched in the air. "Hello."

I can't help but smile. "Hey . . . piglet," I say. Logan's refused to give the piglets names so far, rejecting all of my amazing suggestions. "Did you open the door?"

Logan's hands tilt the pig forward and back in a slightly chaotic *affirmative*, and when he lets out a squelch, he pulls him back into the corridor. "Dramatic fucking pig."

The door creaks as it opens slowly, and on the other side, Logan stands against the doorframe in his usual dirty blue jeans and white T-shirt, his brows bent worriedly over his eyes. "Sorry about that. He has no sense for things like privacy or consent."

"Sure, with him being a pig."

"Right." He juts his chin out. "May I come in?"

I nod, and he slowly steps into the room. He sits on the chair and faces me, so close I can smell hints of cedarwood and pine from his soap. His eyes run over the clothes that pepper my floor, the half-eaten granola bar on my nightstand. "Now I know why the piglets like to sleep in here."

"Might be a stupid question, but what will happen to them? I mean, they'll be big soon. Will they still live here?"

Rubbing a hand over his mouth, he looks into my eyes. "If I tell you, will you tell me why you were crying?"

Oh, so it's as obvious as it feels.

"It doesn't matter," I say as I focus on the floor. "It's stupid."

"I'm sure it is. Probably a broken nail or some bag you wanted that sold out." When I glare, he smirks in response. "Whatever it is, if it makes you cry, I want to hear about it."

"Why?"

He raises one finger. "You get one question, and you already asked about the pigs."

"I . . ." I shake my head, resigning myself to the truth. "Derek . . . Derek came over."

"*Derek* made you cry?" His jaw hardens as he straightens in the chair. "What did he say?"

"That . . ."

"That?"

That he couldn't bear to have sex with me. Because he thinks my rolls, dips and curves are disgusting. Because he wants a skinny, hot woman, and I'm not it. That he thinks Logan wouldn't be able to do it either—maybe that nobody could.

It's too humiliating to say out loud.

"Barbie, you need to tell me."

"I can't," I whisper.

"If you don't tell me, I'll have to walk to that ass-wad's farm and punch him in the throat until he does." His teeth are gritted, his words almost slurred, as if anger has flared up his body.

"No!" I rush to say, holding a hand to his knee as my feet find the floor. "Please, you can't. What he said doesn't even matter. It doesn't—" My voice breaks again, and a tear falls down my cheek, quickly followed by a second one, then a third. "Doesn't matter."

"Then why are you crying?"

"Because—because . . ." I stand and pace to the other side of the room, but he follows me and grasps my shoulders. He's towering over me, and I'm forced to look at his face. In his deep, hooded eyes. "Because he was my first boyfriend," I confess. "Because I thought I'd finally found someone who . . . God, I'm so stupid."

"You're not stupid, Primrose, you—"

"But I am. I *slept* with him!" His jaw clenches, but he doesn't look all too surprised at the information. Bet that's about to change. "He's the first man that I ever slept with."

The gray speckles in his irises become even more noticeable as his eyes bulge out, then he sighs, head dropping forward.

"And it didn't go well."

I can feel how red my cheeks have become. Besides a couple of really close friends, the only person in my life who knew I was a virgin until six months ago is Derek, and though his reaction at the time was kind, it was probably an act.

Logan's shoulders tense until, with a groan, he turns around. "I can't fucking believe this."

"It's fine," I mumble. It's not like I can undo it.

"*Fine*? No, it's not fine. He took something from you that . . . goddammit, it should have been special, and now he goes around calling you leftovers. It's anything but fine." He straightens, and as if he's found a new sort of peace in his anger, he calmly walks out the door.

"Where are you going?" I say to his retreating back.

He ignores me, and once I see him head for the main door, I rush after him. "Logan, you can't. You can't go there."

"Bet, Barbie?"

Desperation claws at my chest as I step in front of him, blocking his path to the door. "Please, don't do anything rash," I plead, my voice trembling. "That's exactly what he wants—for you to do something stupid that'll get you in trouble with the police, so he can get his pigs back."

He tries to move around me, his frustration evident in every muscle of his body. But I stand my ground, refusing to budge an inch. "Get out of my way," he snarls, his face contorted with rage.

I meet his gaze, my own eyes pleading with him to listen, to understand. "You promised you wouldn't let anything bad happen to me. You swore."

For a long moment, he stares at me, his breathing ragged, his fists clenched at his sides. I can see the battle raging within him, the struggle to control the storm that threatens to consume him.

"I need you here," I whisper.

Slowly, almost imperceptibly, his features soften. With a heavy sigh, he lowers his gaze, the fight draining out of him like water from a broken dam.

"Fine."

I swallow past the lump in my throat. "Thank you," I say as I wrap an arm around me. "I'll just—I'll go take a shower."

Once he nods, I walk towards the corridor, quickly stopped by his voice. "You're not stupid, Primrose." I face him, and he looks anywhere but in my direction. "You're a smart, fun, and beautiful woman. And any man with sense would be ecstatic to call you his."

My gaze lowers.

"No, look at me." When I do, he holds my gaze. "I mean it. Okay? I need you to believe it."

I nod, and we watch each other for a while, neither saying a thing as silence and tension sizzle between us. For a moment, it looks like there's something more to it. Like maybe I'm not just Logan's ticket out of jail.

Clearing his throat, he walks past me and shakes the moment off. "I'll go make dinner. I'm starving."

He enters the kitchen, and a pink blur in my periphery catches my full attention. In trots one of the piglets, who circles my favorite T-shirt, abandoned beside the couch, and pushes at the soft cotton with its snout until it decides it'll do. Then, it proceeds to fall asleep in a heap on top of it.

"Wait," I say as I go after Logan. "You never told me about the pigs!"

introduce me to his family
. . .
Primrose

LOGAN STANDS before the imposing white picket fence that encases Aaron and Josie's house. The midday sun casts a golden hue across the perfectly manicured lawn, infusing the scene with tranquility, but not Logan. I've known him for less than a week, yet I can tell there's turmoil brewing under the surface.

I join his side, and though his expression doesn't shed light on how he's feeling, the fact that he's been motionless for several minutes now can only mean he's dreading this lunch as much as I am, maybe more. "You okay?"

He blinks. "Just need a minute."

I nod, turning to the house nestled between its neighbors on a tree-lined street. Its brick facade exudes a timeless charm, and the entrance steps lead up to a polished wooden door. A trimmed garden frames the front, featuring bursts of vibrant flowers in carefully arranged pots.

Perfect, if it wasn't for the fact that this lunch will mostly likely be a shitshow that will land us both in prison.

As a gentle breeze rustles the leaves of the nearby tree, Logan finally turns to me. "List?"

I look at his open hand and extract the list from my bag. "What for?"

He pats his pants, then pulls a pen out of his pocket. "Number thirteen."

Introduce me to his family.

Has he been . . . reading my list? I've left it on the bookshelf overnight, next to my plane ticket, and I can't help but wonder if he's studied it. Unless he's been seeing it online, the one time he's read it, he had it in his hand for a handful of minutes—there's no way he's memorized every single item. But why would he even care?

"At least this shitshow gets you to check one of the items off your ridiculous list," he says as he strikes through number thirteen, then hands the list back.

"Is there any way we can not do this?" I hush out.

"No. I promised Josie we'd come, and if we bail, she'll get suspicious. But I wouldn't worry if I were you. With me and my brother in the same room, the focus won't stay on our *relationship* for too long."

With a resigned nod, I follow him up the paved path to the front porch. Once he stands at the door, he straightens the collar of his black shirt and exhales. "You good with everything?"

"Yup. Act affectionate but *don't* use words like 'obsessed,' talk about our sexual life, or mention kicking," I say, repeating the speech he gave me back home word by word.

"Great." He knocks at the door, and nerves get the best of me too. "This is a great chance for us to convince her we're madly in love. Let's take it home."

I nod, but he's too ill at ease for me to relax. I've seen him uncomfortable before—at the mall, or every time I fire my questions at him. Sometimes, just the sight of me seems to make him tense up. But he looks downright terrified now, and I can't help but wonder if the issue is his relationship with his brother, or if he knows there's a high chance I'll screw this up.

How can I put up a convincing show? I'm a shitty liar, and Josie is trained to sniff out the truth. She and Aaron know Logan much better than I do, and I'm sure it won't take them more than a couple of pointed questions to find out this is a sham.

And once they do, the police will piece together everything else.

After what feels like an eternity, the door opens and Josie appears wearing a simple yet tasteful black dress. "Hey, guys! Come in, come in." She gestures at us to enter, the excited twinkle in her eyes matching the fiery red hue of her hair.

The aroma of a home-cooked meal wafts through the air, instantly making my stomach rumble with anticipation as Logan and I step into the entryway. After exchanging a glance with him, I offer Josie the bottle of wine we bought for today. "For you. It's—"

"My favorite. I can't believe you remembered, Logan," she says with a grateful smile. Then, she puts a hand on my arm. "Thank you so much."

"Of course. I also made some candy." I hand her the small transparent bag with a shrug. "For you or—Logan said you have a daughter."

She turns the colorful candy in her hands. "Sadie is going to lose her mind over this. Thank you so much."

A moment of awkwardness settles, and turning the bottle in her hands, she says, "Look, I know these circumstances are . . . peculiar. But I'm off the clock, and we won't discuss anything related to Derek or the piglets, okay?" She squeezes my shoulder. "Let's just have a nice family lunch."

Logan and I both nod and follow her into the large living room. The walls are painted in soft, earthy tones, complementing the gleaming hardwood floors that reflect the light streaming through lace-curtained windows. In the center of the living room, there's a vintage wooden coffee table displaying books and a vase of freshly picked wildflowers, and an inviting armchair sits by the fireplace, its mantle adorned with family photos and knick-knacks.

Aaron rises from a plush sofa, his tight-lipped smile accompanied by a doubtful expression. He and his brother look astonishingly alike, with their gray-blue eyes, dark hair, and strong jaws—it's almost like watching the same person before and after a five-year gap.

"This is my husband, Aaron," Josie says as she walks past him to a small table. "And this is Sadie." She ruffles the brunette child's hair, and her big brown eyes stare back at me as if she's seeing something incredible. "Look what Prim brought you."

Sadie's eyes become bigger than the moon as she reaches for the bag of candy, and as I turn to Logan with a grin, I notice his hateful glare is set on his brother.

Aaron's eyes flicker briefly to meet Logan's, and the room seems to hold its breath, caught in the tension that weaves a web around the brothers. "Hello," he says, and Logan answers with a light jerk of his head.

This lunch is going to last forever.

"Lono!" Sadie cries from a colorful, furry carpet next to the couch, and he walks to her and picks her up. I busy myself with checking out the mounted frames featuring Aaron and Josie over the years and Sadie as a baby. There's even one of Josie with Logan, and it must be from a decade ago. His beard is short, his body thinner, and his grin innocently happy, as if life hadn't broken him down yet.

Josie walks to me with two glasses of white wine. "Here," she sets one in my hand, then glances at Logan. "Let's get some alcohol inside those two *immediately*."

Probably a good idea.

"Lunch is almost ready—do you like falafels, Prim?"

"Love 'em," I say as I follow her into the dining room. "Can I do something to help?"

"Nothing to do," she says before disappearing into the kitchen.

Logan sits at the table, Sadie now in his lap, and I take a seat at his side.

"How old are you?" I ask when Sadie keeps staring at me, and with a timid voice, she whispers back, "Four."

Logan kisses her cheek. "Don't lie. You're one year old. Two tops."

"No!" She stands on Logan's thighs, then smacks his shoulder. "Four!"

He gives her a dry look. "Is that so? Then show me with your fingers."

Sadie pulls up five fingers, and he tucks her thumb against the palm of her hand. "*This* is four."

Holding on to his shoulders, Sadie starts hopping up and down, as if bored with their exchange. It can't be too pleasant, but Logan chuckles, hands gripping her sides to make sure she won't fall.

Damn him. Why does he have to be cute? And with a kid, of all things?

That's playing dirty.

"What?" he asks in a soft voice as he turns to me. He must have noticed I was staring.

"Nothing." I sip from my glass of wine, relieved when Josie walks back into the dining room with a casserole and squeezes it among the other trays and bowls.

"Here we go," she says. "Aaron. Take Sadie, please?"

"She's fine here," Logan interjects. Josie begins serving the casserole and describing one delicious dish after the other.

"And, of course, everything's vegan."

We all begin eating, the only noise provided by our cutlery and Sadie, who's telling Logan some rambling story about her favorite toy at kindergarten.

The tension is almost unbearable.

"So, how are you liking Pinevale?" Josie asks. "It's a pretty big change from Mayfield, huh?"

Setting what Josie said was pasta primavera on my plate, I nod. "Yeah, it's different. Especially the farm. Everything's so silent there, and I'm used to noisy, crowded places."

"Oh, well. If silence bothers you, I'm happy to bring Sadie over. Give it a night, and you'll be missing the peaceful cows."

We chuckle lightly, but as the laughter dissipates, she turns to Aaron where he's bending over his food and eating in silence. Then to Logan, whose full attention is devoted to Sadie, currently squishing his cheeks as he kisses her nose.

"You know, I can't *believe* you're doing long distance," Josie tells Logan, and she must realize it sounded like she doesn't think he could possibly do that, because she shakes her head. "I mean, that's great. You must care about each other a lot."

Is she referring to his ex? Logan said he was very resistant to being in a long-distance relationship with her.

Figuring my safest bet here is silence, I turn to Sadie and offer her another piece of pita bread.

"Yes. We're two lovebirds," Logan says.

I wish he would make more of an effort to sound like he gives a shit.

"So how did you meet?" Josie asks, ignoring Logan's obvious bad mood. "I know you met in Roseberg, and that you were there for work, but how exactly did it happen?" She elbows Aaron as if to invite him to join the conversation, and with a long sigh, he sips whatever hard liquor is in his glass.

I share a look with Logan, then bring the fork to my lips.

She's *just* asking to make conversation, I'm sure. She's desperately trying to fill the awkward silence or learn about her brother-in-law's life. Plus, we've prepared a meet-cute story about the two of us reaching for the same book at the library. My idea, of course.

But sweat forms on my lower back, and I remain silent, too scared to utter a word.

"She tried to kill me." My eyes nearly pop out as I turn to Logan. "Accidentally, or so she says. That's how we met. Right, snickerdoodle?"

My lips part. Is he serious right now? This is *not* the time to kid around.

"Kill you?" Josie's eyes narrow on me, a cautious smile taking over her lips. "How so?"

"It was a very windy day, and an orchid vase fell off the bannister of my hotel window," I blurt before he can say anything about the accident. He must have lost his mind, because Josie would definitely connect the dots between my rental and his bike. "I, uh . . . I noticed that it had almost hit Logan, so I"—I glare at him as he chuckles under his breath—"I ran downstairs to apologize."

"Apologize?" His face scrunches. "More like, scream at me."

Eyes widening slightly, I purse my lips.

Why is he making me sound like a lunatic?

"Well, to be fair," I hiss, "You *did* throw the vase at me."

A playful twinkle brightens up his eyes. "I was having a terrible day."

"Yes, you mentioned something about being headed for the strip club." With a wiggle of my brows, I purr, "Didn't you?"

"Uh-huh." He faces Josie, holding both hands over Sadie's ears. "Imagine my shock when she offered to give me a lap dance herself."

He did *not*.

God, I'm going to kill him.

"Imagine *mine* when he just burst out crying while I was—" I gesture at Logan to cover Sadie's ears, and once he does, I hiss, "grinding on his lap." With a satisfied jerk of my chin, I give him a pointed look. "Right, Bun-bun?"

Logan's lips are curled up, his eyes stuck to the table as if he knows the moment he looks at me, laughter will burst out of his lips. Josie and Aaron, instead, don't seem to be all too amused as they watch each other with horror and confusion.

"Then I kissed her," Logan offers. His voice has taken a softer edge now, and the amusement on his face has vanished in favor of a nostalgic sort of look. "It was the worst moment of my life, and I needed a . . ." His eyes search my face, and it occurs to me that he might no longer be joking, but actually talking about our first *real* encounter.

"An anchor?" I ask. We never talked about that kiss—not besides a joke here and there—and though I'm surprised he'd bring it up right now, I also want to know his thoughts.

"Yeah. I felt this overwhelming need to escape, to run away from it all. Then you took my hand. You were there, looking at me with these big, beautiful eyes filled with concern and guilt."

I remember, and I fight the urge to entangle my fingers with his right now.

He huffs out a laugh. "I don't know what came over me," he says, the words spilling out like a confession. "My heart was racing and my mind spinning, and all I could see was you. It just felt natural to kiss you."

The memory washes over me, vivid and raw. I can taste his lips on mine, feel the rush of emotion that followed.

"It wasn't about trying to escape the panic, you know?" he continues, his voice charged with emotion. "It was about finding something real, something to hold onto. And kissing you . . . it felt like coming up for air after being underwater for too long."

I swallow, blinking fast, and I forget all about Josie and Aaron and Sadie. I forget about our alibi, about Marisol, about Derek. For a moment, Logan is all I can bring myself to care about, and it's such a sudden, terrifying realization. That I *care* about him. That I hardly know him, but after six days, he matters to me in a way a few people in my life do.

"Well, that's . . . unconventional," Josie says, dragging me back into the moment. "But beautiful. Really."

Logan seems to wake up from a similar trance, and clearing his throat, he focuses on Sadie. "Yeah. I knew then and there that she was special. And I tried to run away from it, because . . . because I was scared, I guess. But, uh . . . I'm glad I didn't manage." He playfully pulls at her braids, then meets my gaze. "I'm glad we ended up here, Dumpling."

Everyone has stopped eating but Sadie, and she's too focused on her piece of pita bread to make any noise, so silence spreads like a thick blanket around us.

Does he mean all of that?

He looked sincere, but that stupid nickname he threw in is making me doubt the whole thing. Maybe he's just saying all of this because Josie is here—in fact, he probably is, and I just can't tell the difference between a heartfelt speech and a bald-faced lie.

This is a great chance for us to convince her we're madly in love. Let's take it home.

Thinking of the words he said before we came in, I decide it doesn't mean anything and resume eating. "So am I, Sweety-pie."

stand up for us

. . .

Primrose

"I'D LIKE to point out that, just like lunch, the dessert was made by Aaron," Josie says as she sets a chocolate cake at the center of the table. "I imagine it's hard to impress you when it comes to sweets."

"Please," I reassure her. "People think that because I make candy, I must be an excellent baker, and they're as wrong as it gets."

"How does one get into candy making?" she asks as she cuts the first slice.

"I started out in high-school and fell in love with it. Friends were always asking me to teach them, so I eventually opened a social media account and, well . . . the rest is history."

"So you can make anything?"

I take the plate she gives me with a grateful smile, then hand her Logan's. "I'm pretty sure I've made every single candy you can think of—and came up with plenty of my own too. Kale candy canes, cinnamon bun jaw crushers, bacon gummies, chili pepper—"

"*Bacon* candy?"

Logan's horrified gaze reminds me that I probably should

have left that one out. The man lives with pigs. "Uh, yeah. One of my best sellers, actually."

His mouth widens. He blinks. He scoffs.

Then, before he can say anything, Aaron mumbles, "What's wrong with bacon? It's yummy. Right, Sadie?"

"Love bacon!" she says excitedly.

"Aaron," Josie scolds before addressing Logan. "Don't engage. He had a bad week at work, and he's in a horrible mood."

"Is he?" Logan's gaze settles on his brother. "Didn't know the most boring job in the world came with problems."

"Plenty of problems. Thing is, I'm strong enough to face them." With a fake grin on his lips, Aaron sips his drink. "On account of all the protein I eat."

"I eat protein too, ignorant . . ." Logan covers Sadie's ears. "*Jackass.*"

"Guys," Josie tries to intervene, and as she cuts another slice of cake, my head bobs from one brother to the other. What the hell happened? We almost made it through the whole lunch without hiccups.

"Oh, give me a break. You and this damn veganism."

"What about me and veganism?"

Aaron smirks bitterly, and with my eyes ping-ponging between the two brothers, I swallow hard.

"If being a vegan was so important to you," Aaron hisses as he points his finger at the table, "then why did you take the farm, huh? Farms aren't vegan. When you decided to turn Mom's business into what *you* wanted, did you even think about everyone else?"

Josie meets my gaze as she smiles sadly, resignedly—as if it isn't the first time this has happened, and won't be the last. She stands and grabs Sadie off Logan's lap.

"Since when do you even care about Mom's business?" Logan spits back. "You split the second you could without looking back."

"Split?" Aaron stands, eyes flared, and his chair scrapes against the floor with a horrible noise. "You're not seriously sitting here telling me you wanted me to take over the farm."

I watch as Sadie waves goodbye over her mom's shoulder, and it looks like neither of the brothers even noticed Josie left. Should I follow her? Should I try to stop them?

"Fuck, no. You never loved it. If you did, you wouldn't have run to Uncle Jerry to work at his"—Logan grimaces—"accounting firm."

Aaron's face darkens. "You didn't *want* me there, Logan."

"You're right. I didn't," Logan says before shaking his head. "But don't act like it was my fault."

Aaron rushes around the table, and when Logan stands, I also jump to my feet. This has escalated so quickly that I wouldn't be surprised if they resorted to physical violence, and should that happen, I'd need to get out of the way quicker than I can breathe. Though Aaron isn't as big as his brother, he's nearly as tall and definitely as pissed off.

"I might not be as pious as you and your vegan ass, but I'm not an idiot, Logan. I *know* you're sinking her business," Aaron hisses, keeping his voice low so Josie won't hear him from the kitchen. "It's been successful for decades, and you're destroying it." When Logan looks away, Aaron nods. "I thought so. So what's the plan, huh? How do you think Mom will react to the farm failing? To her son being arrested again?" He gestures in my direction. "How do you think she'll feel when she finds out this is all a sham, and you're actually harboring a criminal who's stalking someone else?"

Logan's shoulders tense. "Don't say another word about Primrose. I let you spew your bullshit about her once, but I won't do it again." Then, gesturing at Aaron's chair, he mumbles, "Now sit down before I make you."

Aaron's lips harden, but he doesn't say a word, and I wish I could turn into wallpaper and disappear in the background.

When he takes a step forward, Logan stands in front of me.

"What, are you afraid I'm going to hit your girlfriend?" Aaron spits as he backs up.

Logan doesn't take his eyes off him. "She doesn't need to be the target to get hurt." He points his thumb at the kitchen door. "And I think you've hurt enough people today."

Silence envelops us, and from the kitchen comes a faint cry that makes my heart clench. Sadie.

Oh, god, they made her cry.

Aaron huffs out a breath, blinking quickly as if to hold back tears, and runs his fingers through his dark hair. "Shit," he mumbles as he walks toward the kitchen, and only once he's far enough, Logan turns to me with a frown.

"Let's go."

"Don't go anywhere," Aaron calls. "We're going to show Sadie we just had a disagreement. That everything is fine." He rubs the back of his neck nervously, then turns around and enters the kitchen.

Sadie's crying intensifies as she calls for her dad, and it's so sad, I almost want to cry myself.

"Are you okay?" I ask Logan.

He presses his lips together, his jaw sharpening under my eyes. "No."

Aaron and Logan are on the couch, Sadie tucked between them watching cartoons, and though she looks perfectly content, the tension in here is all but suffocating.

Josie has been gone for five minutes. When I saw her slip away with a bottle of wine, I figured she was headed for the recycling bins outside, but this might be a runaway situation.

Silently, I walk past the couch and to the back door. I find Josie there, sitting on the step with the bottle by her side.

I open the door, and her eyes meet mine over her shoulder. "How's it going?"

"Hey, Prim."

I sit beside her. "Are you doing okay?"

"Oh, yeah. I'm fine."

Her breath stinks of red wine, so I'm assuming the bottle she took out was not empty. It might be now, based on the droop of her eyes and the way she's grinning.

"We're all used to this. Which means you're officially part of the family."

I smile a little sadly, fidgeting with the hem of my dress. "Sounds like Aaron and Logan have a lot of history, huh?"

"Yes. They care about each other very much, and when there's that much love . . ." She brings the bottle to her lips and takes a big gulp of wine. "Conflicts hit hard."

Nodding, I look away.

"How's he doing?"

I meet her concerned gaze and ask, "Logan?"

"Mhm."

"Oh, he's fine." Actually, he seems to be the very opposite of fine. Isolated, lonely, distrustful. But I guess she knows that already. "He works hard."

"Yeah?"

She almost seems surprised, which has me rearing back. He's a farmer, possibly the most hard-working occupation I can imagine. And besides, Logan is all work, no fun. He wakes up at five in the morning, goes out for deliveries, stays in the fields until six in the evening, and is asleep by nine. Do these people know him less than I do?

"Good for him. Farming has always been his passion, but you know how he is." She shrugs, smiling affectionately. "A little irresponsible."

I nod, because I'm supposed to be his girlfriend, and his girlfriend would undoubtedly know that. But "irresponsible" does not sound like him. Maybe some version of his past that Aaron and Josie are familiar with, but not the Logan I've been getting to know these last six days.

"Sadie is gorgeous," I say in an effort to tread safer waters.

"Thank you. She just turned four a month ago." With an exhale, she shakes her head. "Crazy how time flies."

"How long have you and Aaron been together?"

She turns to me, her brows arched over her eyes, and her mouth opens in a surprised little O. "Uh, five—four years and ten months."

"Oh." Does that mean—"Oh, okay."

She huffs out an awkward chuckle. "I assumed Logan had told you."

Nice. I'm already blowing our cover. "He doesn't talk much about Aaron."

"Right." Hugging her knees to her chest, her black dress billowing out, she says, "It was supposed to be a one-time thing only. Then Sadie happened, and we made it work."

With a nod, I look away. I don't mean to sound judgmental, but that's the least heartfelt way I've ever heard someone talk about their relationship. "Well, you look like a great couple."

"So do you and Logan." She grabs the wine, takes another sip, and settles the bottle between her legs. "An interesting couple for sure."

There's a little resentment in her words, probably due to a mix of wine and, from what I can sniff out, personal dissatisfaction. And she must recognize it too, because she gives me an apologetic smile.

"I want him to be happy." The corners of her lips now seem hesitant, as if carrying the burden of long-buried sadness. "Both of us do. I just wish he could be happy with us in his life. Aaron misses him so much, and occasions like this, when we're all back together, make me hopeful and then . . . they just crush me."

Placing an elbow on my thigh, I rest my chin on a fist. "I'm sorry. I don't know much about what happened, but I can see there are a lot of emotions involved. I'm sure they need time. Eventually, they'll talk it out."

"Maybe. Or maybe some scars are just too deep to fix."

I let the silence spread until with a sigh, she reaches into her pocket and takes out a transparent bag. "Look, Prim. I'm not even supposed to tell you, but we found his keys in the small forest between his and Derek's property."

My jaw slacks, my mouth turning as dry as sand as I look down at the keys.

"We'll find more evidence." Her eyes are cloudy, and her voice soft, as if she's speaking out of worry for her brother-in-law and not as a cop. "And then there'll be nothing you or I can do to help him."

Lowering my gaze, I try to breathe through the crushing sensation on my chest. Of course, I can't tell her that I can't say a word without incriminating myself, but I wish she knew that I'm not just being careless with Logan's future.

"Look, I get it." Her hand cups mine, and once I venture a glance at her face, her green eyes sparkle with compassion. "You don't want to rat him out. Logan and I have been friends since we were eleven, and I know exactly what he's been telling you. That we won't figure it out, that we'll let it be." Lips stiffening into a hard line, she shakes her head, her fiery red hair swinging with the motion. "But we won't. Connor and Derek won't."

My stomach churns as I weigh my options, but doubt creeps in, clouding my judgment and making it difficult to see clearly. What if she's right and Logan is wrong? By withholding the truth, we're extending our punishment. We're getting into a sea of trouble. This was nothing but a stupid accident, and I can't lose everything because of it, but I also can't let Logan take the fall.

Maybe I should just trust Josie, tell her everything, and hope she'll help us. It's obvious she cares about him.

"I . . ."

She tilts her head, studying my eyes as she takes my hand. "Yes?"

"Okay. Look. What happened is—"

The door opens behind us, and as Logan peeks his head out, she mumbles a curse under her breath. "Ready to go?"

Was she hoping to catch me alone?

"Yeah, absolutely."

"Think about what I said, okay?" Her eyes are pleading as I stiffly nod her way. "It was so nice to meet you under different circumstances, Prim."

"Yes, it was," I say as I stand and straighten my dress.

She grabs the bottle, holding the railing for stability, then gives me a drunken smile before she hugs me. I meet Logan's gaze over her shoulder, but he looks away, a somber aura around him.

'Nice to meet you' my ass.

I can't *believe* I almost got played.

The phone rings, interrupting the silence, and the kiwi-pineapple gummy in my hands falls to the floor. Before I can even hope to reach it, one of the pigs enters the kitchen and swallows it without even chewing. "Hey," I scold weakly as I walk to the phone. "Your dad said I shouldn't feed you anything. He won't be happy when he gets back home, young lady."

The piglet watches me as if she's actually paying attention, and with a giggle, I bring the phone to my ear. Logan left an hour ago to do *something*—and despite my insistence, he made it pretty clear that I'm not meant to know what. "Hello?" I say as I bring the phone to my ear.

"Uh—you're not Logan. Do I have the wrong number?"

"No, this is the Coleman farm, but Logan is out right now. Can I take a message?"

"Yeah. Tell him Tom said he should buy a cellphone like a normal person."

I snort, quickly deciding I like Tom, whoever he is. "Will do, but I can't promise it'll work."

"Yeah, no kidding." There are some traffic noises, then, "Well, look, he was supposed to come by my office an hour ago, but he never showed. It's kind of urgent."

It sounds like Tom is deciding whether he can share with me whatever he needs to tell Logan, but I don't want to interfere with his privacy, so I offer, "That's probably my fault. I, uh . . . dropped in earlier in the week without warning and took over his house."

"Oh. *Oooh,* you're his girlfriend. Well, okay. Tell him we have a potential buyer, but we need to act fast. I got the feeling they were fretting, so we don't want to give them too much time to change their minds."

My brows scrunch, but I nod. "Sure, okay. Hope you guys make the sale."

"That's very kind of you. I wish you were my client instead of that grumpy ass."

I chuckle, leaning against the bookshelf. "I'll keep you in mind if I ever need to sell something."

"You do that. Apartments, villas, commercial spaces, and apparently, farms."

My heart stops in my chest as my whole body turns cold. Did he say . . . *farms*? As in . . . Logan's farm? Is Logan trying to sell?

"Hello? I think I lost you."

"No, uh, sorry. I'm here."

"Oh, guess who just parked in front of the office? Sorry to bother you; it looks like your boyfriend was just horribly late."

"Yeah," I say faintly. "Okay. Bye then."

Once I hang up, I bring a hand to my chest. Each new wave of emotion is chasing the last so fast that I can't fully feel anything. Is he seriously selling this place? His home?

Kyle and Simon can't possibly know a thing about it, or it would have come up. And his brother—his family. Nobody knows about this, I'm sure.

Why is he giving up on this farm? On what's most important to him?

The fresh scar of betrayal bleeds again as I slowly make my way over to sit on the couch. I thought he was starting to open up to me—that we were becoming something like friends—but maybe Derek is right.

Maybe there's no friendship, no affection or loyalty. Just an opportunity to escape jail. And I'm an idiot who's falling for the same scheme a second time.

your boobs distract me
...
Logan

WITH THE DOOR closing behind me, I exhale, my eyes bouncing from the candle on the coffee table to Primrose's makeup bag on the bookshelf and her tablet abandoned on the carpet in front of the small fireplace. Her book is face down as if she's using the whole couch as a bookmark, and all the lights in the house are on, though she's nowhere to be found.

I click my tongue, tossing away an empty yogurt cup. I'm not a neat freak, but living with this woman is like being swept up by a tornado.

As I approach the corridor, the phone rings, and I stop to answer. "Hello?"

"Hi. Farm Coleman?"

"Yes. Who am I speaking to?"

"It's Ashton Clifford. From Clifford's Vegotruck."

"Uh, yeah." I rub the side of my head, trying to figure out if I've ever heard of it. "How can I help you?"

"We'd like a quote. We heard your produce is vegan?"

Oh, fuck. A new client? We haven't had any requests in months. "Yes, we're certified by the Vegan Farming Association." I grab my notebook and a pen. "Happy to send you a quote. Give

Riding the Sugar High

me your contact information, and I'll have one of my guys call you."

He recites his number, and I say, "Thanks, man. We'll be in touch tomorrow."

When I hang up, I'm smiling. This hardly makes a difference in the big picture, but it's a new client. It's something. Especially seeing as the quote I got from the mechanic nearly gave me a stroke. Could it be the ads I set up throughout the region? Or maybe word of mouth is doing its job? Well, who cares? What matters is that I'm doing something right after all.

As I turn around, Primrose comes out of the corridor with a book held open against her chest. She drops on the couch, her eyes running down my mud-covered clothes, and begins reading without so much as a "Hello."

"Hi," I mumble. "All good?"

She ignores me, flipping pages like I don't exist.

Is she mad about lunch or something? She tried to discuss it as we drove back, after whining about Josie, who apparently tried and nearly managed to trick her into confessing. I managed to calm her down when she freaked out about the keys they found, though I'm most certainly concerned about it, then successfully avoided her billion questions about my brother and me.

I was rude, but nothing out of the ordinary. Normal-rude. So why does she look pissed off?

Glancing at the sweater on the chair, then the empty dish on the counter, I clear my throat. I'm not sure what exactly happened in the three hours I've been out of the house, but she's pissed. Seeing as I'm already annoyed after the day I had, I can't say I expect this to end well.

"Did you decide what recipe to send Marisol?"

She shakes her head but doesn't say a word. Seeing as she's physically incapable of silence, it's not a good sign. Maybe that's why she's in a shitty mood, though it seems targeted at me.

"Well, why not?"

When she shrugs, my patience wears out.

"Look, if something's bothering you—" I start, only to be interrupted by the male piglet, who welcomes me with a squelch as he bites the hem of my jeans. "If you have something to say—"

"What, Logan?" she asks in a snappy tone. "Do you want me to be honest with you? To just come out with it and tell you the truth?"

The spark of anger inside me flares, because you know what? This place is a mess, and having her around all the time is a constant and exhausting exercise in restraint. The situation with the police is stressing me out, and after my meeting with Tom, the last thing I need is to come back home and be screamed at for no fucking reason.

"You got a call," she says. Her voice is weirdly calm and collected, but somehow, I know it's because I'm standing in the eye of the hurricane, and the storm is just an inch away.

"Okay." I give her a dry look. "Who was it?"

"Tom."

"Oh." My eyes jump to the phone, then back to her. He didn't mention anything when I saw him today. "What did he say?"

"That you have a potential buyer."

Swallowing, I study her expression. I can't believe that idiot told her. I can only hope he didn't share more, and all she has is a suspicion.

"Mm. Well, whatever you're thinking, it's not it." I brush it off. "I'm just selling my bike."

She shakes her head, and I try to ignore the frantic beating of my heart. It's as if a bucket of disappointment is perched above her head and slowly drenching her, drip by drip. "Really? You should call him back, then, because he thinks he's selling your farm."

I stare at her for a long moment, my jaw tightening.

"Are you not going to say anything?"

"What's there to say?"

"You lied to me, Logan. You're lying to everyone."

"Oh, yeah?" My frown deepens. "Why should I tell you I've

put the farm up for sale? You don't work here. We're not friends—we're nothing. You're a guest."

She bites the inside of her cheek, and a light dims in her eyes. I'm being an asshole, but it's the truth. I told her from the beginning that I was not looking for friendship or romance. Whatever remains is what we are, and that doesn't grant heart-spilling or secret-sharing. I owe her nothing.

"What about Simon and Kyle? Are they just guests?"

"They're my employees. I'm under no obligation to—"

"Aaron, then. Does he know you're planning to sell the family farm?"

"Leave Aaron out of this," I snap back. "You don't know anything about him. He has no say on what goes on with my farm."

Eyes darting down, she frowns, which is just great. She went from pissed off to sad.

"Look," I mumble as I try to soften my voice, but the phone rings again, and I scoff. I usually get one call a week, if that.

I walk to the receiver, pick it up, and bark, "What?"

"Uh, hmm. Hello? Coleman Farm?"

Exhaling, I will my heartbeat to settle. "Yes, this is Logan. How can I help you?"

"Yes, hi. I'm calling from Eco Spot."

"Yeah?"

"We're a new vegan grocer that just opened in downtown Roseberg. We've been looking for a produce supplier, and . . ."

I tune out the woman's words, my face scrunching. This can't be normal. No new clients for six months, then two in twenty minutes? What are the chances?

"Hello?"

"Uh, yes, sorry. You . . . you wanted a quote?"

"Yes, if it's not too much trouble."

"Not at all. Let me get your number, and someone from my team will contact you tomorrow."

I hang up, rubbing my beard, and look down at the two new

potential leads. Is it possible? Have my efforts finally paid out? Maybe for once, I won't be an absolute fuckup, and I can pull through.

Maybe . . . or maybe not.

It can't be a coincidence. There's no way. And there's only one new thing around here.

I turn around, eyes laser-pointed at Primrose. "What did you do?" I ask in a low rumble.

"Hm?" She shrugs from her spot on the couch, then brings the book closer to her face. Hiding, the little rat.

"Tell me how you got involved. Right now."

"I didn't—" When she notices the murderous and unforgiving glimmer in my eyes, her nose scrunches. "Okay, fine. I featured Kyle chopping wood without a shirt on my social media to give a little shout-out to the farm."

Why did she even take a picture of Kyle? Was she planning to use it all along, or did she want it for herself?

No. Jesus, no. That isn't the point.

"How dare you?" I hiss. "Who gave you permission to do something like that? Because it certainly wasn't me."

"Wow, okay." Setting her book down on her chest, she scoffs. "That's your reaction?" She presses her lips tight. "Then I probably shouldn't tell you about the five other people who called."

Holy shit. Seven new clients? In one day?

I'm speechless, but it lasts no more than a second. Then, I have so many words begging to be shouted, gritted out, groaned. How *dare* this woman come here and revolutionize my life? She's messy, chatty, fucking hopeful and naive to an annoying degree. She's hot and smart and funny, and talking to her is as effortless as being alone, and she can do so much better than me. And now, she's getting involved with shit that isn't her business. She's doing my job for me.

Why is it that everyone can succeed at this but me?

And I thought I'd managed to do something right. Fucking idiot.

Pointing a finger at her, I snarl, "Don't you dare meddle in my business again."

"Seriously? *Seven* new clients." She sits up, then stands, setting the book face down on the couch. "Can't you just say thank you?"

I open my mouth to snap back, but my eyes stick to her chest. Staring at the faded white logo on the green cotton, I mumble, "What's that?"

"What's what?"

I point at her, and when she looks down at her shirt—*my* shirt—she crosses her arms. "Oh, yeah. I found it in the guest bedroom. I had to put my pajamas in the wash after Lola—or Paco—slept on them."

Lola? Paco? What the hell . . . ?

Reading the question in my eyes, she shrugs. "The pigs. You didn't like any of the names I suggested, so . . ." She shrugs.

So she named my pigs. Wore my shirt. Helped my farm.

I rub a hand over my mouth, knowing there's only one thing I can do. Only one thing I *should* do. Lock myself in the bathroom, take a shower, and, as shameful as it may be, jerk off. Because she's wearing my clothes, the green shirt reaching just above her knee, and she looks so hot I can't think. Can't reason. Can't cope.

"Take it off," I hiss despite my best judgment.

"What?"

"Take. My shirt. Off."

She squints, her shoulders rolling forward. "Is it . . . is it an important T-shirt?" She looks down at the faded white drawing. "You can give me another, or—"

"No. Wear your own clothes, not mine."

She stares at me for a couple of seconds, then, with a challenge in her eyes, whispers, "Really, Logan? I *helped* you. I posted about your farm while you've been lying to me. Now, because of a T-shirt—"

"End of fucking discussion, Barbie," I bark as I walk into the kitchen. I need to walk away from her. Maybe drink a beer. Or tea. What would work best against unwanted erections?

I opt for tea, and with heat climbing up my neck, I rummage through the cabinets for the infuser. Of course, it's not where I left it. Nothing is ever where I leave it.

I open the cutlery drawer, and she barges into the kitchen, arms bowed at her hips and a furious look in her eyes. "Stop pretending you're looking for something. What is your problem? It's a T-shirt." She puffs her chest out and sighs. "No. You know what? I'm done being nice to you. You're impossible. *That's* why I wouldn't date you."

"Oh my god, you can't be serious."

"I am, I—"

"Barbie," I say, drowning out her voice. "You want a reason not to date you? Look around." When she does, I gesture at the cabinets. "I'm not *pretending* I'm looking for something. I'm *actually* looking for the tea infuser. And I can't find it. You know why?"

"Because it's in the mug on the kitchen table, where I left it this morning?"

"Look at this." I grab a banana peel from the sink. "And your clothes are everywhere. None of my stuff is where I left it. Oh, and where, for the love of god, are all these candles coming from?" I snatch a pineapple-scented candle from the window frame. "Are you a witch? Why do you need twenty-five candles to be lit up at all times?"

Her lips open, but I raise a finger to stop her.

"And I get it. I really do. Neither of us has exactly chosen this situation, but what kind of fuckery is this?" I point at her shirt. "You have your boundaries, and I have mine. Spoiler alert? You're not allowed to wear my clothes, name my animals, or take my business into your hands."

"Fine," she yells back. "Just leave instructions on what I'm allowed to do, and I'll ignore them."

I stomp into the living room and grab the infuser. She didn't do any of it maliciously, but I can't stop the anger spewing from my mouth. I need her to stay away, but it's Primrose I'm dealing with. She won't.

"You know," she says, bursting out of the kitchen. "I have far more reasons not to date *you*."

Here we go.

I turn around and shrug. "Really?"

"Really."

"All right," I say, dropping the cup on the table. "Do tell."

"You're constantly grumpy. Moody. Angry." She widens her arms. "It's like you don't know how to smile."

"And you're always skipping around here like you don't have a single worry when we both know that's not true."

Her lips pinch, and I raise my brows in a challenge. "What else?"

"No TV? No internet? Why, Logan? Are you afraid the government will control you with their drones and *poisonous sky powders*?"

I suck my cheeks in, trying to fight a smirk.

"And . . ." She swallows, stormy blue eyes bouncing around as if she's running low on insults. "You . . ."

"I . . ."

"You wake up at five every day!" she squeals.

With a scoff, I lean with my back against the wall. "And?"

"And I have to wake up too, and—and it's too early, Logan."

She squares her shoulders as if she herself knows she's making zero sense.

"Then it's settled," I say as I roll my eyes. "Let the animals starve to death, because Primrose, the pink glittery Barbie princess, can't be woken up from her beauty sleep."

"You are the most frustrating person in the world." She grabs her book and walks away.

"Do I need to list my complaints again?"

She stops, shoulders hunched, and slowly turns to me. Her face is all scrunched up, red as if she's not breathing. As if she knows the moment she opens her mouth, she'll say something she can't come back from.

She sneers at me, then hisses, "You know what, Logan? You need to get laid."

I—*what?* "And what would you know about that?"

"Kyle mentioned you haven't had sex in—" Her eyes widen. "He just . . . Please don't kill him."

With a scoff, I look away, tracing my upper lip with the tip of my tongue. Unbelievable. I'm not just going to kill him—I'm going to skin him alive.

Glaring at her, I mutter, "Keep my personal life out of your mouth. Try to be ten percent less of an annoying roommate, and wear your own goddamn clothes."

She groans and looks up at the ceiling, fists clenched. When her gaze is back on me, she marches closer, and I brace myself for a smack. But she stops just an inch away, then pinches the fabric on her hips, pulling my shirt over her head. "Here. Take your *stupid* shirt back."

The shirt flies at my face and slinks to the floor between us. I don't move a single muscle, my eyes stuck to Primrose's heavy tits, lightly bouncing with her erratic movements. Her pink nipples, the same I felt rubbing against my chest that first night, almost instantly harden, and my brain flatlines. I can't think of a single thing as I stare and try not to drown in a pool of drool.

Everything about her is soft perfection. Her chest, with the faintest outline of her collarbone, the voluptuous curve of her hips and her belly, all the way down to the yellow shorts that could easily pass as underwear.

Gotta give it to her; this is a great way to win an argument.

When she breathes in a gasp, her body recoiling, I force myself to look away from her chest.

Is wearing a bra something one forgets to do? Because she looks as surprised as I am.

She regroups and lifts her chin in defiance, and I still say nothing, blinking again and again as more heat creeps up my neck and cheeks.

"Thank you," I choke out after a few seconds. Now, it's imperative I leave the room because I'm about to pitch a tent in my jeans. "Nice tits."

She jerks her head back, and with a horrified expression, mumbles, "Asshole," before scurrying away.

My shoulders only relax once her bedroom door closes behind her.

Silver lining? I don't think she'll be stepping over the line anymore.

Problem, though, is that now I want to grab the line and throw it out of the window. I want to cross it repeatedly until it fades away.

Fuck the fucking line.

act silly around me

. . .

Primrose

"REMIND me again why we're here," I say as I step out of the Uber. I rub a food dye stain off my wrist from this morning's candy-making session as Logan joins my side, nervously looking around.

"It was only a matter of time before my mom heard about you, and she's not going to give up until she meets my . . ." He grimaces. "My *girlfriend*."

"Don't look too happy about it."

"It's stupid."

I sigh, hoping this version of grumpy Logan is just an excerpt and not a preview for the whole day. He's been like this since last night, when I accidentally flashed him, though we've managed to mostly keep our distance. While he's been on the fields all morning, I've been working tirelessly on finding a recipe that I hope will please the people at Marisol. That is, until his mom called and threatened to come to the farm unless we *both* showed up for Sunday family lunch.

So here we are.

The single-story red-brick home in front of us sits on a manicured lawn, surrounded by a picket fence. It looks welcoming enough, and with the sun low on the horizon, it's the perfect setup for a nice meal. Though Logan clearly disagrees.

"Let's do this," I mumble, holding my hand out. Logan's eyes catch on my open palm, but he makes no movement, so I drop it down my side. "We're together, aren't we?"

"I don't hold hands."

"Right. *Arrr*."

One unimpressed glare later, we walk through the small gate and along the cobbled pathway that leads to the veranda. We approach the door, and it takes a full five seconds for Logan to actually knock. Tension vibrates off him, and it's making my hands sweat. Last time he was this nervous, the lunch ended in disaster, and today, I won't be lying to Josie and Aaron alone, but to his whole family.

The door opens, and Aaron fills the entrance, his smile slipping only a fraction. "Oh, hello." He turns to me, his grin back in place. "Primrose."

"Nice to see you again," I say with a timid nod.

He lets us in, and as I join Logan in the corridor, he says in my ear, "So you're polite to everyone but me?" but I ignore him in favor of Aaron, who asks how everything's going. We chat as he leads the way farther into the house and toward the cacophonic mix of noises. Through the sliding glass door in the living room, I spot people sitting at a long table outside, the smell of grilled meat making me salivate immediately.

"We're having barbecue," Aaron says to Logan.

"That's fine. I'll have a salad."

"There's probably cheese in it."

"Then I'll eat a tomato," Logan grunts out, obviously on the winning side of their glaring contest.

Clearing my throat, I step closer and lock arms with Logan. It gets his attention, and with a smile, I say, "How about we start with a beer and leave the tomatoes for later? Hm? Beer's always vegan, isn't it?"

"You'd be surprised," he mumbles, "but the one my parents drink *is* vegan. So, if you'll excuse me."

He walks away, and after throwing an awkward look at Aaron, I follow.

I hate to say it, but Logan might have a point about Aaron. He was hostile before we'd even stepped inside. Plus, he knew Logan was coming. Did nobody think to accommodate his diet?

I reach Logan as he steps through the back door—just in time to see a short, middle-aged woman stand and cup her mouth with both hands, a loud gasp escaping her smiling lips. Everyone else turns around in response, and there's a whole chorus of welcomes and hollering.

Nothing evil, not at first glance.

"See," I whisper as the woman—his mom?—rushes around the table. "Not that ba—"

His fingers slide between mine, though he keeps his gaze away. His shoulders are bunched at his ears, and he's chewing on his bottom lip. He's nervous. So nervous that he's holding my hand.

"Logan!" the woman squeals as she approaches us, her arms extended for a hug. Her eyes dart to our hands together and go comically wide, but she quickly recovers and throws herself at Logan.

"Hey, Mom." He lets go of my hand to hug her back, and I can't help grinning at the scene before me. Though I'm still very annoyed after yesterday's performance, this is cute.

"You're here!" She smiles at me over his shoulders as she gently rubs his back. "I can't believe you're here."

"Don't cry, Ma."

"Oh, let me be." She pulls away from him and brings a finger to her eye. "I'm old and sensitive." She turns to me, her eyes lit as if the sun itself were behind them. "And who's this beautiful woman?"

"Primrose Bellevue."

"Lucy Coleman," she says, shaking my hand. She waits,

clearly expecting one of us to explain, but it's not up to me to say, so I hold my breath as Logan awkwardly looks down at his feet, until eventually, Lucy claps her hands. "Okay, grab whatever you want to eat. I'll go fetch you a couple of chairs."

She sprints away, and we're soon joined by Logan's father, Darren, who just as warmly welcomes us. Before my hand even leaves his, he's introducing me to uncles, aunts, cousins, and only god knows who else, because I stop retaining information after the fourth person I'm dragged to.

"You're okay sharing a chair, yeah?" Lucy asks as she guides me to the table and fits a huge portion of eggplant on a plate. "We've had more people turn up than expected, and we've run out."

"*Moooom*," Logan drawls.

"What? I can't make a chair out of thin air, Logan."

With a resigned gesture, Logan sits and motions at me to come closer.

"No, Logan, I'm—"

"Say you're too heavy," he says as his arm drapes around my waist and he pulls me down, "and I'll start throwing you around like a juggler."

Fine, I guess.

I settle on Logan's legs, and my plate is snagged from my hand as Lucy begins questioning her son about his life while decanting the food they've cooked.

Though it's chaotic and my attention gets snatched by one person or another asking me questions, I feel Logan's tension. His discomfort. It's like he feels as though he doesn't belong. And it's not his family. It's him.

I discreetly tap his arm after some distant cousin I'm speaking to excuses himself from the table. "Hey," I whisper, his eyes meeting mine. "Are you okay, cowboy?"

"I'm fine." His eyes narrow on my face. "I thought you were mad at me."

I am, but seeing him this uncomfortable around his family makes my heart squeeze.

I grasp his hand, clenched in a fist over his mouth, and pull it down. "You know, I should take offense."

"Hmm?"

I keep my voice down and move my lips closer to his ear. "You didn't tell your mom we're together. You froze."

"I told you. It's stupid."

"Might be stupid, but it's our cover." I tap a finger on my lips. "Maybe you'd feel better if you yee-hawed."

That gets him to smile, and he settles his hand on my thigh. His thumb brushes over my naked skin, and at first, I figure he's doing it for our audience, but as he tilts his head and stares deeply into my eyes, I know he's picturing last night.

"Stop it."

His head jerks back. "What did I do?"

"You're picturing it—*them*."

His lips morph into a full-blown smile now. "Oh, you bet."

"Well, quit it."

"No. With no internet, that's the closest thing to porn I've gotten in five years."

"Then you better start paying me royalties."

"Too bad there's no *Be someone's jerk-off fantasy* on your list, because you'd be crossing that item off again, and again, and—"

When I smack him, he grabs my hand and explodes into laughter. Seeing as that was my initial goal, I settle on his thighs with a content sigh.

"Logan! Prim!" comes from behind us, and I turn around to see Josie walking out of the house with a casserole in her hands. "I'm so happy you're here."

We both stand, and after exchanging quick hugs, she puts the casserole down on the table and rubs a hand on Logan's arm. "I made a potato salad for you, Logan. And the corn pie is totally vegan too."

"Thanks, Jo," he tells her with a subtle bob of his head. "Where's Sadie?"

"With my parents today."

An awkward silence settles as I study her and she studies me. Seeing as last time we met she was half-drunk and trying to trick me into confessing, I'm not exactly sure how I feel about her, but I'll play my part.

Aaron comes to stand next to her, an arm draped over her shoulders and a beer in his hand. "Primrose, I wanted to apologize about last time. My behavior was inexcusable."

To me? That's who he wants to apologize to?

"Oh, thanks." I shrug half-heartedly. "Family drama. It happens."

He drinks a sip of beer. "Do you have a big family?"

Logan's arm wraps around my waist and pulls me down on our shared chair. Balancing myself on his legs—and ignoring the fact that my feet don't even touch the ground—I smile up at Aaron. "Uh, no. And we're not close anyway."

"Too bad." After a sip of beer, he shrugs. "To be fair, Logan isn't close to his family either."

Logan's body tenses beneath me. "And whose fault is that?"

"Yours."

"I don't think so, Aaron."

Here we go again.

"Oh, is it *my* fault?" He lowers his voice. "Are your felonies my fault too?"

I chew on my bottom lip, watching Josie as she exhales curtly, and Logan tips his beer back. "I have no idea what you're talking about."

Aaron narrows his eyes at Josie. "Will you say something? Tell him he needs to confess."

"I'm not saying anything at all," she quips back. Her eyes fill with resentment, and setting her plate down, she clicks her tongue. "This is supposed to be a family lunch. Why do you always have to ruin everything?" And without waiting for Aaron's answer, she walks.

Looking around, I notice the curious looks we've attracted and sink back, as if I can disappear into Logan's chest completely.

This is so embarrassing.

Aaron barely acknowledges his wife and keeps his eyes on Logan. "They're building a case against you. Do you understand? *Arson*," he snaps, his voice hushed so that nobody else can hear. "It's not just about two missing piglets anymore. It's a felony. Up to twenty years in jail."

My stomach twists with nausea.

"You're a good person, okay? And I'm sure Primrose is too," Aaron continues as he leans closer, concern painted over his face. "I know you don't want her to end up in trouble, but you can't go to prison for her."

Logan's hand protectively squeezes my hip, pressing me closer to him. "Primrose and I didn't do a thing. Even if we did, there wouldn't be any evidence to back it up."

"They *have* evidence, Logan."

"All right," Logan says, mindlessly rubbing my hip. "Looking forward to seeing what."

"Logan—"

"Look, Aaron," Logan hisses, "If you think there's anything you can say that would make me turn Primrose in, you're even more delusional than I thought."

"Huh." He pauses, studying my eyes for a long moment. "So you *do* like her."

I pull my shoulders back, Logan's thighs stiffening beneath me as his fingers stop rubbing. "Yes, I do," he says then, as if he's suddenly remembered about our cover. "Of course, I like her. She's my girlfriend. And besides, *look* at her."

I bite my bottom lip, heat rising up my cheeks as Aaron's expression softens.

"Okay, well. I'm happy for you. But we can't just ignore everything else that's going on. Like the farm?" He grabs a chair, then sits on the edge, elbows on his knees. "Let me help you. The money I inherited from my dad, you know we planned to invest part of it in the farm—"

"I'm not taking your money, Aaron," Logan says, a frustrated edge to his voice. "You can't fix everything with money, Jesus. I needed *you*, and you took everything from me. How can you possibly think . . ."

"Logan—"

"Look. I'm here for Mom, okay? I have my lunch," he says as he holds out his beer, "and my girl's ass on my lap." My eyes widen, butterflies rushing up my throat. "Just leave me alone."

Aaron shakes his head, then, with a final look at Logan, stands and walks away.

Though when we got here, he was acting like a total ass, it does look like he's trying to make up for his mistakes, and watching Logan tear his efforts down is heartbreaking.

Besides, he could use that money.

"Are you okay?" I ask as I gently twist on Logan's lap.

I hold a hand to his shoulder, and after a long moment, he mumbles, "Know why I wouldn't date you, Barbie?"

With my lips pursing, I gesture at him to speak. "Let's hear it."

His eyes narrow, then he shakes his head. "Sorry, what were we saying? I got distracted picturing your b—"

When I move to smack him again, he traps my wrist in his hand.

God, how I love the way he laughs.

"Elliot is having some car troubles," Logan's mom says in his ear before ruffling his hair. I set the fork back on my plate and watch him groan from my own chair—turns out there's enough for everyone after all.

"No, Mom. He's not."

"Yes, yes. The *carbonator*. It's broken—go, he's waiting for you in the driveway."

He tosses an apologetic look my way and moves to stand. "I want the record to reflect that a carbonator is a kitchen appliance, not a car part." Then before walking away, he discreetly mouths at me, 'Don't mess it up.'

"You should grab more food," Lucy immediately starts as she points at the table. "Did you try the zucchini pie? Oh, and that fancy cheese. Paul, Logan's cousin, has a dairy farm."

"The perfect family for a vegan to land in, huh?" I ask as I tuck my hair behind my ears.

I swear, with the way my heart is hammering, all this lying will send me to the hospital.

She laughs, nodding hard. "When Logan was a kid, the farm was much smaller. I only had a coup." Meeting my confused gaze, she chuckles. "With chickens, you know?"

"Oh, yes."

"Every once in a while, Logan would come downstairs for breakfast, and there'd be a chicken bleeding out in the sink." Her eyes, the same blue-gray as Logan and Aaron, moisten as she loses herself in the memory. "He would cry and cry—refuse to eat for days. And I couldn't understand it, because my parents were poor. We dreamed of a chicken dinner, you know?"

I do understand. Though my parents have always been absent from my life, they work harder than anyone else. They too didn't come from money and wanted a better life for me than what they'd had growing up. "Do you think he resents you for it?"

"Maybe. We *did* have a few hundred screaming matches about it. Then one day, he came out of his bedroom—I think he was twelve. He looked me straight in the eye and said, 'Mom, I'm a vegan now.'"

I can't help but grin. "What did you say?"

"I believe I said, 'What's that?' I thought it was a sexual orientation."

Chuckles burst past my lips, and she pats my knee with a fond look in her eyes. "You have a beautiful laugh. And smile. Are you a vegan, Primrose?"

"I'm not, Mrs—"

"Lucy." Her chin lowers, a complicit look in her eyes. "Mom, if you're lucky enough."

Oh, boy. Here we go.

"Uh, um . . . Logan and I, we . . ."

"Are you in love with my son?"

I suck in a breath, internally cringing at her friendly tone. I can tell she's asking in the hopes I'll say yes, not to warn me or scare me off. But I can't lie to this sweet old lady. I can't, in good conscience, tell her I'm her future daughter-in-law. It'll break her heart when I leave next week. "Well, we're, uh . . ."

I also can't tell her the truth, though. Can I?

Where's Logan?

When I look around in a panic, Lucy cups my knee. "Dear, I know my son, and he doesn't look at a lot of people the way he looks at you." She peers at me, holding strong eye contact. "Like he'll drop dead if he stops."

He does *not*. Does he? Last night, he looked at me like he wished *I* would drop dead. But the rest of the time? Just now, when he was making fun of my scene last night? There *was* a fond smile on his face. A sparkle in his eyes.

"You know he's been through a lot with . . ." She vaguely gestures behind her, and my eyes settle on Aaron, talking to Josie and an older man whose name I forgot.

"Yeah, I know."

"And she—"

"The *carbonator* is fixed," Logan says as he walks up to us, and his mom releases an annoyed sigh. "Did you get your intel?"

"Just eat your lunch," she says as she gently slaps the back of his neck. Once she turns her focus to the party, she gasps. "Oh, look, Theresa is taking pictures!" She frantically gestures at us to follow her. "Come on, I want one of the two of you."

"*Mooom*," he bellows.

Lucy's arm locks with mine, and when I flash a wide-eyed look at Logan, he follows, his back hunched as if he's been sentenced to death. Now that I think about it, there are no pictures in his home.

"I never want to forget the day I met you," she says as she props me in front of the camera, then tucks my hair behind my ear with the warmth reserved for a mother. It makes my heart ache, and if it's the last thing I do in this life, I'll take this picture for her. *We* will.

"Logan?" I call as he lazily walks toward me, making his disdain about the whole ordeal obvious to everyone, then pouting when his mom slicks his hair back.

"Let's just do this," he barks as he wraps an arm around my shoulders and unceremoniously pulls me closer until I bump into his side.

"Jesus. Manners," I mumble as I pinch his hip. "I'm not a rag doll."

He flinches away, then turns to me with a murderous look. His hand darts out, but I entangle my fingers with his, stopping him from pinching me.

"Logan, don't—"

His other hand approaches, but I hold that too, squeezing his fingers when he tries to free himself of my hold. "*You* started it."

"No, you did!" I squeal when his hand escapes and he tickles my side. "Logan—stop—no!"

I erupt into laughter as his other hand tickles my left hip. "You start wars you can't win, Barbie."

"I'm sorry!" I shout as I bend forward, his hands still mercilessly attacking my sides. "Please, I'm so—sorry," I manage in between waves of laughter as I slide onto the dewy grass.

The heat of his dark chuckle hits my ear, his hands still on my hips though he stopped torturing me.

I throw a look at his family, expecting to find them watching us with some degree of judgment—I know I would—but his cousin is taking pictures of us, and his mom's expression is that of someone witnessing a miracle.

We've attracted the attention of a few more people, Aaron and Josie included. Though Aaron isn't smiling, it's Josie's expression that catches my attention. Her lips are bent up, but her eyes aren't in it. Almost as if she were wishing this type of idiotic interaction for herself. I can't imagine Aaron is a "tickle you to the ground" kind of guy. It makes my chest squeeze for her.

"Ready for your picture?" Logan asks, and when I look over, I find him staring at me with something resembling a smile. His eyes are soft and curious, and for a moment, I wonder if that's the look his mom was talking about. Like there's something mesmerizing about me, though he can't wrap his head around what, and it's driving him mad. Since we've been crouched on the grass, has he taken his eyes off me at all?

"Yes," I mumble.

"Come on, you two," his mom calls, and with a sigh, he lifts me until we're both standing. I comb my fingers through my hair —I must look like an absolute lunatic— as his hand circles my hip, this time not to tickle but to gently pull me closer. I rest a hand and cheek on his chest and pose for the picture.

"Give us a kiss!" someone shouts, and I wish I knew who did it so I could incinerate them with my glare. I wouldn't kiss my real boyfriend in front of his whole family whom I *just* met—let alone a fake one.

But before I can protest, Logan's lips press against the top of my head, pulling me even closer. Sinking into him, I close my eyes for a second.

Moments like this one, when he's so gentle, make me like him even more. I like his rough edges too—how protective he is, how stubborn and direct. They're all parts of him that make my blood boil, and I'm learning to appreciate that too. The passion—the *fire* between us.

But when he holds me, when he strips himself of his hard

shell, I crave him in the most innocent way. It feels like the most dangerous too.

When Logan's cousin stops clicking away, I almost ask her for the files. It'd be weird, I guess. As a couple, we should have plenty of our own pictures. But I'll have to take one myself before I leave the farm. Though it's possibly the most stressed I've ever been, I want to remember this moment of my life—or rather, Logan. Logan and me.

"My turn now," Josie says as she walks closer. She wobbles a little, her eyes cloudy and unfocused, then stops next to the camera. Is she drunk? She and Aaron have kept away from us the whole day, so I can't say for sure, but she definitely isn't acting like herself. "Who's going to take a picture with me?"

"Josie," Aaron scolds as he grips her arm and pulls her back. "Let's go drink some water."

"No, *Aaron*," she snarls. "I want to take pictures, and if you don't, I'll take one with Logan."

My stomach twists as my fingers cling to Logan's shirt. Everyone is watching her, the chatter now nonexistent, and the tension is almost insufferable.

"Josie—" Aaron tries again, but with a strong pull, she frees herself from his hold.

"Let me *go*." She takes a step forward, tipping her glass to her lips and swallowing a big gulp of wine. She stumbles to the side, and before either Logan or Aaron can reach her, she falls, wine sloshing onto her dress. "Look!" she whines, lips twisted in a grimace. "Look what you made me do!"

Aaron slides his arm under her thighs and picks her up as Josie continues shouting at him. Lucy follows them inside, but I don't have the heart to meet her eyes as she passes us.

A low mumble among the rest of Logan's family morphs back into conversation, and before I've even noticed he left, Logan's back by my side with our jackets.

He hands mine over, and with any trace of joy vanished, he mumbles, "Let's go."

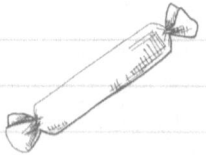

expand my horizon

. . .

Primrose

"*COME OOOON*," I drawl. "Number seventeen. *Expand my horizons.*"

"Nope."

I rest my back on the eroded concrete wall and frown. When he said he wanted to leave his parents' place, I figured we'd return to the farm. Instead, we got an Uber back to Pinevale, and after a long—and silent—walk through the small town, he sat on the stairs of a church and announced he'd smoke weed.

He won't let *me* try, though.

"Come on. Help me check an item off my list." He watches me as if trying to figure out which one, so I offer, "*Push me out of my comfort zone.*"

"Do you even know how to?" He taps the joint until the ashes fall off the tip.

"Yes, I smoked a cigarette just a couple of—"

Shit. Shouldn't have said that.

"You're joking, right? *That's* how you set Derek's trash on fire? How does that even happen?"

"It starts with an ill-advised cigarette disposal and a pile of dry leaves."

"Yes, and it ends in prison." When I pout, he rolls his eyes and holds the joint out. "Take a breath—not too deep, though. Start slow."

I nod, awkwardly holding the long joint between my thumb and index finger, the tip glowing softly in the dim light of the street lamps. Beside me, Logan leans back against the weathered stone wall.

"Are you sure we should be doing this here? We don't need another reason to be arrested."

"Nobody will arrest you for smoking a joint, Lady Arson."

Just like he told me to, I take a breath, and I don't feel a thing at first. Then my throat starts to burn, and I bend to the side in a coughing fit.

"Yep. Okay. That's normal." Logan takes the joint and pats my back as I look down at the concrete steps, trying to breathe through my nose.

"Oh, this is so gross," I croak before I cough some more. There's a weird taste in my mouth, and smacking my lips, I grimace. "It's like I've sucked on musk."

He snorts out a laugh, choking on the smoke just like I did, and even as he tears up, he throws an amused look at me. "It gets better."

"Does it?" I tilt my head. "I don't feel anything. "My vision isn't impaired, and my head doesn't feel light. If this is being high, then it's pretty disappointing.

"Well, you won't feel anything with one drag. Plus, it takes time."

I lunge for the joint again, but he holds it out of reach.

"Give it a minute."

"Fine," I sigh out. I think what happened at his parents' place has more than a little to do with his wanting to smoke a joint tonight, but I'm not stupid enough to bring it up. He would have mentioned it himself if he'd wanted to talk about it, but I wonder if he's thinking about Josie. I know I am.

From our vantage point on the steps, we have a perfect view of Main Street, lined with charming shops and bustling with activity.

People pass by, their voices mingling with the distant hum of traffic as they go about their daily lives. It's a scene straight out of a postcard.

"Make a decision about Marisol?"

I swallow, bringing my hands together. "Oh, no. Not yet."

"Seriously, Primrose? That apple stuff you made yesterday was great. Why don't you send them that recipe?"

"Apple cider caramels," I mumble. "I don't know if it's the right product. I can't just base my decision on what I like—or what you like, for that matter. I have to consider things like sellability. Marketability. Trends, and—"

"Primrose." He fixes me with an intense glare. "You're overthinking it. Believe in yourself and your product. If you like it, they will too."

"And if they don't?"

"Then they'll tell you, set you on the right path, and you'll try again."

"Or they'll think I'm an idiot who's way in over her head, drop me and smash my dream with a metaphorical hammer."

"Just like the FBI sending helicopters out here over the theft of two piglets and the stupidest arson in history," he says softly, "you can add that to the list of things that are never going to happen."

With his shoulder bumping against mine, he mutters, "Drama queen."

When I bring a hand to my shoulders to release some of the tension entrapped in my muscles, he brings a hand to his manbun. "Is it *that* important to you? Launching this . . . candy?"

Watching his freed hair fall down his shoulders, I nod. "Yes, it is."

"Why?"

I pause for a few long moments, looking for the right words. "Because I was denied candy most of my life."

"How so?"

"My mom and I aren't close. My dad and I aren't either, but

it's my mom I have the most troubled relationship with. Honestly, she made most of my childhood unbearable, because she's never been happy with the way I look."

Though his jaw ticks, he doesn't say a word.

"There's this candy store back in Mayfield, in the mall closest to my parents' place. But I was never allowed in, of course. With my body type, I couldn't afford to eat candy, she said." I smile, though the years of conflict and low self-esteem are heavy on my back. "One day, my mom and I had one of our fights. I was in high school. I jumped on a bus and went to the candy shop. Then I filled a bag with all the candy I could afford, sat by the bridge, and ate it. And the sugar high . . ." I remember that moment like it was yesterday. "It was incredible. Like getting a piece of my childhood back. All these colors, flavors and consistencies—and the *smell*. There's nothing like it."

When I turn his way, Logan forces his smile to flatten out.

"I pestered the owner until he gave me a part-time job there, thinking I'd learn how to make candy, which, of course, I did not —he just bought it." He smiles again, small wrinkles forming at the corner of his hooded eyes. "But I worked there for years, and I *saw* candy bring happiness to everyone. Cute couples bickering over what flavor to buy, kids darting left and right while their parents tried to contain their joy. Candy is a treat you use to celebrate something good or to feel better after something bad. It's a sweet, fluffy joy."

For a long moment, he doesn't say a word. Then he exhales. "I like listening to you speak."

When my mouth opens wordlessly, he cringes and clears his voice. "Uh, I also hate it when you ask a billion questions."

Oh my God. He likes to listen to me speak.

"So, hmm . . ." He uncomfortably glances at my shocked but pleased expression. "That's when you decided to be a candy maker?"

"Yup. YouTube tutorials." I widen my eyes and speak slowly. "YouTube is an *internet* where you watch videos."

"Funny."

He seems relieved about the change of topic, so I fish into my bag and take out a lollipop. I need this horrible taste off my mouth. "I decided I'd make candy for people who were told they couldn't have it, like me, because nobody should miss out on happiness. And one day, my candy will be at that very same shop in Mayfield."

His eyes dart to my lips, wrapped around the lollipop. "I have no doubt you're right."

God, I can't take it when he's so sweet. It almost makes up for his shitty attitude ninety-nine percent of the time. But now that I've answered his questions, surely he'll answer mine. "What is exactly the problem between you and your brother?"

"Barbie," he warns.

"Come on. I told you about my candy, didn't I?"

He groans, rubbing a hand over his beard, then probably deciding I'd eventually wear him down, he mumbles, "Aaron bailed on me. We were supposed to manage the farm together—he inherited all this money from his dad, and we'd agreed he'd invest part of it in the farm. He went to work for his uncle instead."

As he re-lights his joint and brings it to his lips, I ask, "Is your mom . . ."

"She's his mom too, yes. Aaron's dad died, and she remarried when she met my father. They come from money, and all we ever had is . . ." He sighs. "The farm. By the time he went to work for his pretentious uncle, Aaron and I already weren't on the best terms, and that just . . . sunk us."

"Well, it's a dick move," I whisper. And at least part of the reason why the farm is struggling, I'm sure.

"Yes, it *was* a dick move. The last dick move I tolerated from him."

My heart twists for him, but offering comfort would probably be met with some bark or grunt, so I ask, "Why weren't you on the best terms?"

He seems particularly annoyed by this question, his lips thinning as he clenches his teeth. I guess I must be close to the heart of the issue.

"He stole all of my porn magazines."

Of course.

"And my favorite pages were encrusted shut."

"So gross. If you don't want to tell me, just say so."

He winks. "I don't want to tell you, Barbie."

"Fine." I cross my arms, and when light gusts of cool wind whistle around us, goosebumps rise on my skin, and I rub my naked arms.

"You know, you should start throwing some real clothes on."

Eyes wide, I lift my head. "Excuse me?"

He shrugs. "I'm just saying. You're not in Mayfield anymore. It gets cold here at night, and watching you shiver drives me up the wall. Also, you don't live alone."

"And?"

He throws me a side-eye.

"And what, Logan?" I insist. Because it sounds like he's saying how I dress is inappropriate, and I do not need to be shamed by him over this. "If the sight of my body makes you so uncomfortable, then I suggest you look away."

His brow furrows. "Uncomfortable might not be the right word."

"Whatever. I can dress however I like," I mutter. "And you wouldn't be complaining if I were skinny."

His jaw unhinges, his eyes narrowing until they're slits. "If you . . . that's not what I meant."

"It's fine." I grab the joint from his hand, bring it to my lips and inhale, quickly exploding into another coughing fit. His hand cups my shoulder, but I shake it off, holding back my cough as much as possible until it stops.

"Look, I have no idea what I just stepped into, but you're grossly misunderstanding my words."

"Forget about it, Logan. I know you didn't mean anything by

it." I smile up at him, though his comment stings so much my throat burns, then take another puff of the joint and cough significantly less.

"No, Primrose, I didn't."

Noticing the concern on his face, I pat his arm. "Nobody ever does. Fatphobia is instilled in people—most of the time, they don't even mean to insult you when they do."

I feel his gaze on the side of my face, but keep mine in the distance. "Fatphobia?" he asks, his voice a low rumble.

"Yes. I've been told before that I shouldn't dress as I do. That I can't pull off a certain top or skirt. I'm constantly given side glances when I'm out shopping or told by shop assistants that I should go somewhere else because I probably won't find anything in my size." I huff out a laugh. "You know how many times I've been left out of pictures? In my line of work, image is everything, and mine isn't what people consider . . . perfect."

He doesn't say a word, and for the longest moment, he doesn't move either. Then, with a sigh, he takes the joint and inhales. "So why do you work with social media?"

"It's not just social media."

"Then what?"

With a shrug, I think of all the microaggressions I've experienced daily for as long as I can remember. "Well, men don't call you beautiful, even if you get all dressed up. They call you cute. And when you have a crush, it's almost sweet because they obviously won't like you back."

I swallow, and my saliva is thicker than usual. Maybe my throat is sensitive after coughing. Why can I feel the inside of my throat?

"What else?"

I glance at Logan, and the world wobbles before my eyes. "Uh . . . Doing anything that might imply I'm trying to be healthier usually calls for ridicule. And if I treat myself to something unhealthy, then I get looks. 'That explains why you're fat' looks." There's a sting at my hip, and I realize the step is digging into my skin from how I'm leaning. Straightening, I continue, "And children point at you and laugh. That's not fun."

"None of it sounds fun. People judging you before they even know you never is."

Though the way he says it makes me think he's relating deeply to my words, I'm suddenly and weirdly aware of the air coming in and out of my nostrils. That can't be normal.

"Oh my god, it's the weed!" I gasp. "Logan, I think I'm high!"

His face, initially frowning, splits into a wide grin I'm not sure I've ever seen on him. Usually, he smiles only with one side of his mouth. Sometimes, he smirks in an unruly, roguish way that makes him look disgustingly hot. But this is the first time I see his teeth peek through, his cheeks fully pulled up. He's smiling with everything he has. Smiling with his eyes.

"No shit, Barbie." He pulls me up again. "You're like the Leaning Tower of Pisa over here."

What were we talking about? It was something important. Oh, right.

"I spent most of my life hating the way I looked. But once I started feeling confident, once I fell in love with myself, these things . . ." I gesture vaguely, then think it's probably weird, so I tuck my hand under my leg. "They're no longer important. Now, when someone says something like . . ."

"Like 'your clothes make me uncomfortable'?"

I give him a one-shoulder shrug. "Yeah, like that. It doesn't feel as soul-crushing as it did before. It's just moderately annoying."

"What's the worst part?" he asks, his eyes laser-sharp even though he's smoked much more than me. "What hurts the most?"

Humming, I watch the light from the closest streetlamp dance across the cobblestone streets, casting long shadows against the colorful storefronts.

There are so many things I didn't mention, like the bias of medical practitioners who are quick to dismiss fat people based on their weight alone. Or the classic *You have such a pretty face* I've gotten a billion times in my life. But the scar that bleeds the most is the one that I thought Derek had healed, so I mumble, "Men keeping you hidden. A secret. How they'll flirt with you, and they'll kiss you, but they don't want anyone to know. It's happened . . ." My chuckle is void of any joy. "So many times."

He presses his lips tight as he stares down at the joint between his fingers. When he looks up again, his eyes are narrowed. "Feeling nauseous?"

"No."

"Head spinning?"

"No," I say again, and he holds the joint out for me.

"Then puff puff, Leaning Barbie."

I bring the joint to my lips and watch the smoke vanish into the night.

"Right. So, hm . . ." Logan rubs his hands together, avoiding my gaze and rocking back and forth before settling again, like he's gathering the nerve to say something. "Remember that woman at the mall?"

My mind struggles to focus, but yes, I remember her. And my stomach twists uncomfortably. Why did Kyle have to put ideas in my head? Why did his mom have to make that comment? Even though I tried to ignore them, they poisoned my mind irreversibly, and now I'm about to be, once again, the friend—the one who hopes he'll notice her while he's thinking about the skinny, gorgeous woman he doesn't even know.

"Primrose?"

"Y-yeah, Cassidy. I remember."

"When we talked about her, you described who you thought was my type."

"Yes. *Thall, tin.*" My brows scrunch because something feels wrong, but I'm too tired to know what. My eyes want to close. "*Tin*? Is that how you say it?"

"Okay, give me the joint."

Logan grabs it from my hand, then grips the side of my thighs and pulls me closer. I balance myself on his knees as his fingers pinch my chin. "Pay attention to me, Barbie."

I look into his gray-blue eyes, framed by long dark lashes. I like being this close to him. It's happened a handful of times, and it's weirdly comfortable. "Mm-hmm."

"You described my type. Thin, tall, smile lines—I can't remember. But that's not my type, okay? And when I said you're nearly naked all the time, I meant . . ."

"Yes?"

"I meant . . ." His eyes scout mine, left to right, then back again. His throat works hard, and he hesitates for a long moment when he opens his lips. "Short women with thick thighs and a spunky little attitude. I don't have a type, but if I had one, that'd be it."

I watch him, trying to process his words.

Does he mean . . . *I'm* his type? That he made that comment about the way I dress because . . .

His eyes drop from my eyes to my lips, and maybe I'm leaning again, because we're just inches apart now, and his short breaths fan against me.

"Do you understand what I'm saying, Barbie?"

My heart feels like a caged butterfly, wings hitting the metal bars again and again, desperate to break loose. "That . . . that you're attracted to me?"

"Yeah," he says, his breath softly fanning across my lips. "That the way you dress is, uh, distracting. You know how often I come into the living room to grab something, only to see you on the couch with no bra and those skimpy little tops, and instantly forget what I was looking for?"

My body shakes with the quick beats of my heart. "Sorry. I'll dress—"

"No, Barbie. I think—I think I was trying to . . . you know," he says with a vague roll of his wrist.

"Flirt? Is that what you were trying to do?"

"Yes. And I don't know why I did that, especially since I don't know how to." He lets my chin go, but doesn't move away. "Please, dress however you'd like."

I nod, and he releases a breath of relief, then throws one last look at my lips before turning away and lighting up the joint again.

"You know, you're not the bad person you want me to think you are."

He scoffs. "Don't mistake lust for kindness, Barbie. I'm not that kind."

Lust. That's what he said. He's *lustful* over me.

And I think he made sure I'd be too high to remember it tomorrow, but there aren't enough drugs in this world to make me forget. The awareness tingles through me, all the way to my fingertips.

He's so handsome, and he's so good, and he's a cowboy biker who smiles at me with his eyes.

"Logan?"

"Mm?"

"Do you think tomorrow we could . . . you know . . . take your bike?" I ask. My heart flutters, and my stomach shuts down so hard that it feels like someone is strangling it. But he already said he's attracted to me, so this isn't a vibe-check. It's an opportunity for us to end the ride *Top Gun*–style, and then . . . and then who knows.

Brows arched and lips parted, his jaw clenches, and my heart stops. "Sorry, Barbie." He looks away, shoulders tensed. "I don't ride with anyone."

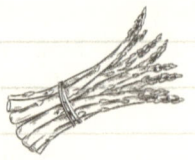

you won't let me sleep

. . .

Logan

I DID IT.

I told her I'm attracted to her, and nothing terrible happened. Hell, she looked pleased. Sure, she said she wanted to go home soon after that, but she'd smoked weed for the first time, and she was clearly exhausted.

She looked happy, though. It must mean she's attracted to me too. That she'd like something to happen between us.

Fuck, the things I want to do to her.

I rub my eyes, trying to fight the first erection of the day. I've been doing a lot of that since she came along.

The piglets aren't on their bundle of blankets. If I'm to guess, they're probably in Primrose's bedroom, and though it makes no sense, it feels like they're mocking me with the fact that they get to enter her bedroom whenever they please, day and night.

"Little fuckers," I mumble as I stand.

I walk out of the bedroom, and holy shit, I swear I'm standing taller than usual. My eyes keep darting to the corridor, waiting for Primrose to come out as I make coffee, then work on breakfast.

I ate the last of her candy yesterday, but the bowl has been filled again. Strawberry. I guess she knows she's found my favorite. As the pancakes cook, I eat a couple of pieces.

Not even the memory of Josie's freakout at my parents' place last night is enough to bring my mood down, though I plan on calling her later today and see how she's doing. I don't trust Aaron to be doing something about her drinking addiction, but she needs help. Quickly too, before someone at work notices.

By the time I enter the bathroom, Primrose still isn't out. It feels weird, as if something's missing around the house, and it's just another confirmation that I've let her in.

Worst part?

I don't hate it. Not completely.

Having someone to come back home to after work, for example, isn't that terrible. Cooking, knowing you're not just making food for yourself? Also not terrible. Primrose is right, this place can get very . . . quiet. And I guess sometimes, her voice filling it isn't the most annoying thing in the world.

I come out of the shower, wrap a towel around my waist, and march out, deciding I'll knock on her door. But as I step into the corridor, she silently walks my way while looking over her shoulder until she bumps into my chest.

"Sh—sorry," she mumbles as she bolts back, her forehead wet with the water droplets from my skin.

So now I know how her lips feel against my stomach.

Which, by the way, is not bad at all.

Her eyes run along my shoulders and arms, then the towel hanging low on my hips, and her whole face turns a lovely shade of pink.

"Good morning."

"G-good morning," she sputters.

"If you don't get a move on, there'll be some pretty fucked up chickens pecking at the door soon enough."

Uncomfortably wrapping an arm around her, she mumbles, "Uh, I'm not coming today."

My brows furrow.

What's wrong? She's . . . not herself. Her back is all hunched, like she'd rather be anywhere else but here. And why can she barely stand to look at me?

"Why not?"

"I'll just stay in and work on my recipes." She glances at my face, and her eyes, usually a warm blue, are as cold as ice. "You know, time is of the essence."

Yesterday, she said she needed some missing ingredients. Why is she lying to me?

My lips part as the painfully obvious answer strikes me like lightning.

She's *not* into me. She's rejecting me.

"What if Josie comes over?" I ask.

As her brows rise, and she stalls with a hum, I have the confirmation I need.

They say the worst thing that can happen is that she says no, right?

Wrong.

The worst thing that can happen is that she smiles. That she flirts back, that she looks at you as if she's begging for a kiss. That you fall asleep thinking you'll wake up to some gorgeous woman flirting with you during your car ride to work. Instead, you find out she was just high. Or trying to be polite. Or, what do I know, maybe she changed her mind. The point—though she hasn't flat-out said it—is that Primrose isn't interested. She wouldn't be blowing me off for no apparent reason if she were.

I can't *believe* I told her she's my type. That I had the goddamn audacity to talk about how every time I see her around the house, I lose any sense of self-control. That I nearly kissed her—probably would have if she hadn't been so high.

I told her I'm attracted to her, and now she can't even look at me.

"I'll just . . . uh, pretend no one's home."

Eyes harshly staring into hers, I remain silent for a few seconds. "Got it."

My heart is thumping hard against my chest, and with a shake of my head, I walk past her. But then I realize, though I can't unsay what I confessed to her last night, if Simon and Kyle find out she rejected the crap out of me, I'll never hear the end of it.

"Primrose?"

She turns around.

"Can I ask you . . . could we keep last night between us?"

Her expression darkens, but after a long pause, she nods. "Sure, no worries."

We stare at each other, and there's so much I want to tell her. That she's the first person I felt this attracted to in . . . god, in so long. That she made me think she was into me too. That she has every right to change her mind, but she hurt me.

But it doesn't matter, does it?

It's my fault, not hers.

I should have never let her in.

Sleep, Logan. Sleep.

It's been a shitty day, and I wish I could close my eyes and stop thinking, but I've been lying here for two hours. I've listened to Primrose work on her computer, then leave the house to settle on the front porch and call one of her friends back home. I've heard the click of her lamp when she turned it off, and since then, I've heard absolutely nothing.

Yet I can't fall asleep.

We've been avoiding each other the whole day. When I returned home for my lunch break, she didn't leave her room. And once I turned in for dinner, she'd already cooked and left food in the microwave for me.

So this is it. I guess we'll keep to ourselves until she leaves. She'll be gone in nine days, and I'll forget about this whole thing.

It's for the best, anyway. I have nothing to offer—my business is sinking, I have no real friends or family to bring to the table, and the emotional availability of a goose. Having sex with her would have made a mess of everything, and we don't need that.

I just wish it didn't make my stomach twist the way it does.

My eyes pop open at a faint sound traveling beneath my door, and I sit up. I hold my breath, straining my ears to listen for something—anything. It could have been Lola. Last I saw, she was asleep in the living room. Or it could've been a pipe. The wind, even.

It sounded like a sob, but I'm sure there's a perfectly—there it is again. Primrose must have left her door open, otherwise I wouldn't have heard it.

She's crying.

I shove a hand on my face, my chest hurting in a million different places.

Primrose is an easy cryer, right? Emotional too, so her crying isn't a big deal, and I should go back to sleep. But she's *crying*. And I don't care if she does it all the time, or if it's because of a stupid reason. I don't care if there's no reason at all.

I pull my covers off and walk out of my room and down the corridor. Though I've never been much of a sleeper, this woman has been stealing my peace in more than one way.

I raise my hand to knock on the door, but the bed springs squeaking stop me. Is she coming out here?

"*Hmm.*"

Nope. Back to sobbing.

"Oh, fuck..."

My eyes shoot wide as if I've just inhaled powdered coffee. That did *not* sound like a sob. It sounded like... like a moan.

I step back, my heartbeat racing like a runaway train, and hold my breath. There's more squeaking, then a whimper. I confirm she's *not* crying when she mewls, "Oh, Logan..." And I lose my ever-loving mind when I hear a click, followed swiftly by a vibration sound.

She's masturbating.

In my house.

Thinking about me.

I'm back in my room and sitting on the edge of the bed within thirty seconds, my cock poking at my stomach. What the hell is happening? She rejected me. Last night, she sent me all the green lights there can be, and this morning, a huge STOP sign. And now she wants me again?

Could I have gotten it all wrong?

The muffled cries continue, my erection growing stiffer until pre-cum leaks from the tip, and my hand itches to jerk off. Would it be creepy? She doesn't know I'm listening, and it feels like invading a private moment. But these walls are *thin*, and it turns out I miss porn after all.

I rub my dick over my sweatpants in a desperate attempt to soothe the ache, but it only makes it worse, and with a loud sigh, I throw my back on the mattress.

Ridiculous. That I'd be pitching a tent because my roommate can't keep her volume in check is just . . . ridiculous.

I pull a pillow over my head as her whines turn shorter and closer together. If I hear her climax, I'll need to dip my junk in iced water, but knowing I could be hearing her orgasm, and I'm choosing not to, might hurt even more.

Pillow back into a chokehold on my chest, I listen to the vibration increase, picturing her legs writhing together and her pussy clamping around nothing.

With our size difference, I know she'd feel better than good. Better than perfect.

My cock throbs, pleasure shooting from my balls and straight up, almost leaving me dizzy. I pull the pillow over my head again, and I might be going crazy, because I can still hear her. It's like she's in front of me, flushed, dimpled cheeks and hungry eyes, bringing herself to climax.

Fuuuuck.

She flirts with me. She teases me. Then she rejects me. And now she's picturing me—picturing me doing what? How? Why aren't we *doing* it?

No. No, Logan. You don't need the complication. It's better this way.

Except I'm so hard I might just come in my briefs.

"Primrose," I bark before I can command my mouth to shut. There's a few seconds of silence, then the vibrator is turned off.

"Y-yeah?"

"Can you hear me fine?"

"Uh-huh."

"Then so can I!"

Nothing.

I could kick myself, because I know I pissed her off—that she's probably embarrassed. And now I won't get to hear her come.

Well *fucking* played.

I close my eyes, not that I have any hope of sleeping now, and after a few seconds, the door of her room shuts. More noises follow, and I can't tell what she's doing, but she's up.

"Goddammit," I say as I stand and venture into the corridor, tucking my erection into the waistband of my sweats.

"Hey." I knock twice at her door. "What's going on now?"

"What's going on?" she shrieks in a sarcastic voice. "I'm leaving, that's what's going on!"

She's what?

Paco wobbles lazily beside me as I scratch my head. "What do you mean?"

"I mean, I'm leaving. I'm done. Being caught masturbating is where I draw the line, okay? I'm out."

Eyes rolling, I rest my forehead against her door. "Don't you think you're being a little dramatic?"

"No, not at all."

"Can I open the door?"

"I can't look you in the eyes."

"Then look away," I mumble before pushing the door open.

With a gasp, she turns around, then throws herself at the tiny pink vibrator on her bed before pocketing it. "Seriously? I said no!"

Glancing at the half-stuffed backpack on the desk, then her open luggage, I exhale. "Primrose, masturbating is normal."

"I know," she mutters, throwing more clothes into the backpack. Her cheeks are still red, her hair ruffled. It makes it *so* hard to think.

"Tell you what. Walk into my shower tomorrow, and you'll catch me."

She glares, which feels like an improvement.

"Come on. Stop packing."

With a deep sigh, she lets the shirt she's holding fall onto the floor. "Fine. Sorry about this. I guess this is just my week to gross people out."

Her sad frown does nearly nothing to soothe the immediate anger that fires up my mind. She does this all the time. She puts words in my mouth, twists the meaning of the ones I speak, assumes she knows what she's talking about.

I'm here, dying to touch her, my dick a rocket ready to take off, and she talks about grossing me out.

It's not a matter of self-esteem, because I've hardly ever seen someone stare at the mirror as much as she does. Her hair, makeup, and clothes are bold. Everything about her screams confidence. But with what she said about men keeping her hidden before, I guess it makes sense she'd be reluctant to believe anyone who tells her they're attracted to her.

"You know . . ." I rumble, but before I can continue, the word *people* echoes in my mind. She said this week she grosses *people* out. Who could she— "*Derek?* Derek told you you gross him out?"

She quickly looks away, and it's like a knife to my guts, twisting.

That's what she didn't want to tell me. Why she was crying after seeing him.

"He, um . . . He didn't even . . . finish. When we slept together." She sits on the edge of the bed, staring sadly at the floor. "He broke up with me after that, and it's been . . ."

Her lips wobble as I step closer. I want to kill him. Right now. But I also can't bring myself to walk away from her.

"It's fine, Logan. I don't want your pity, okay?"

"Well, good, 'cause you don't have it."

Her confused gaze meets mine.

"So . . . what? *One* dude can't get it up, and suddenly *you're* the problem?"

"It's not just that."

"Then what?"

Arms crossed, she huffs.

Does she really think I'll let this go? Yeah, fuck that.

I stride over and grip her arm, pulling her up to standing. Ignoring her protests, I drag her to the mirror on the opposite wall, and when she squirms, I hold both her shoulders to my chest. "So? What is it? Point at what's 'gross.' Let's talk about it."

"Stop it, Logan. That's not—"

"Come on, show me. What don't you like?"

"I love myself," she says, eyes brimming with confidence for a long moment before it dims out. "But I'm also aware that not many people like my body the way I do. They'd prefer it if I were slimmer, taller, or both."

"Yeah? Like who? Derek?"

She's so pretty without makeup. With it, she looks like a million bucks, and without it, she looks cozy. Warm and natural.

"Are we seriously acting like my belly is the benchmark for what men find attractive? The rolls on my back? The way my thighs brush together when I walk?"

I shrug. "I could keep them spread for you."

A faint blush tints her cheeks, the hint of a smile playing on her lips. "Logan . . ."

"You probably don't even notice men flirting with you half the time, Primrose. You—"

"I've been rejected because of my weight more often than I can keep track of. Online dates who couldn't handle their disappointment when they saw me in person. Men who wanted to kiss me, possibly do more, but didn't want to be seen in public with me." She exhales, her breath shaking. "A man once told me he liked me, but he'd always pictured himself being with someone skinny, and it bothered him that I wasn't. My first crush, a friend of a friend I met over the phone, walked out on me when he first saw me. Didn't say anything at all, just got on his bicycle and rode away."

I watch her, speechless. Uncomfortable, not because of what she's sharing, but because the only acceptable answer would be to tuck away that lock of hair bouncing over her eye as she speaks, then cup her chin and slowly lift it, until my lips are pressed on hers.

There's no other answer.

"Logan," she whispers, "I love myself—I do. I love my hair, my eyes. I have great boobs and, if I may say so myself, my ass is hot."

Good god, I know this is about her, but I don't need the reminder. "You may."

She chuckles, and it quickly dwindles. "But I also learned that most men don't feel the same. They don't find me attractive. Not until . . . well. I thought that Derek found me attractive, but he did *not*."

"*I* find you attractive."

She scoffs, rolling her eyes as if she doesn't believe me for a *second*. "Don't do this again. You think you're helping, but you're not."

As the memory of last night comes back to me, I groan.

Of course. That's what happened. For some reason, she thought I didn't mean what I said. That I'm not attracted to her.

That's why she pulled away this morning.

I get it now. She needs me to show her. She's been burned too many times to take my word for it, and that's something I can relate to.

"I find you attractive, and I think you deserve better than some pathetic piece of shit who thinks you're not worth his miserable moves." I fit my hand into the pocket of her shorts, then take out the small vibrator. Watching her eyes widen, I set it in her hands. "Finish."

"What?"

"Watch me," I whisper into her ear as I hold her gaze in the mirror, "watch you. Then you'll know."

A shiver makes her body tremble, her fingers tight around the small vibrator, and when she doesn't make another move, I press the on button and guide it to her shorts.

Brushing my lips against her skin, I breathe, "You moaned my name," and ignore the way she flinches at the realization I've heard that too. "It's my turn now." When her light blue eyes remain stuck on mine, I insist, "Number eighteen."

Make me feel pretty.

I'm not sure this is what she had in mind when she wrote that, nor do I want to pretend watching her orgasm won't be the best thing that's ever happened to me, but I mean it.

She needs to know there *is* a man who wants her.

And though it'll complicate everything—and I will inevitably mess it up—I am only human. I've wanted to revere every inch of her body since the night I met her.

I never stood a chance.

After another moment of hesitation, her hand disappears under her shorts and panties, and my mouth goes dry. The vibration intensifies and mixes with the wet noise of her pussy, followed by her worked-up breaths, though she's trying as best as she can to smother those. I can't say when I last blinked as my arm wraps around her to pull her closer.

Her legs spread, and eyelids fluttering, she lets out a strangled moan.

Fuck me, it's the best noise in the whole world.

"Barbie," I whisper as her hips swing back and forth. Her teeth snag her bottom lip, unbridled and honest desperation pouring out from her squinted eyes. Brushing a blonde and pink lock away from her shoulder, my lips drop to her neck, and I keep my eyes glued to her reflection. She's so gorgeous it hurts, her body writhing against mine as she looks for more friction. "Please, don't hold back. Let me hear it."

"Oh, yes." She pushes her ass back, rubbing it against me until I can *taste* an orgasm coming. "L-Logan," she whines, and with a moan, I sink my teeth into her skin.

I need her to stop saying my name. Stop moving. Stop moaning and holding that vibrator against her clit.

"Don't stop," I whisper in her ear. My hips buck forward, my cock straining against my sweatpants and using her perfectly round ass for friction. I can feel it moisten at the tip, feel my balls tighten with each of her needy whimpers. "Get your tight hole wet for me."

Her eyes widen for a moment, then turn languid, and her free hand reaches back to pull my hair.

I groan at the sting on my scalp, my fingers digging into the skin of her hip. "If that shocks you, you won't be able to look into my eyes once I'm done with you."

Will I ever be done with her, is the question.

When I wrap my hand around her neck, she gasps, her throat bobbing against my palm and her eyes searching mine in the mirror.

I have to keep reminding myself to go easy on her—that this is all new, and she might not be into the type of rough sex I like. But she looks pleased, her eyes rolling back, and it definitely makes me want to find out what her limit is.

"Let me watch you come."

She stares at my reflection, so I tighten my hold around her neck.

"Now, Barbie."

Before I come myself.

Her eyes roll, and her throat works hard, the sweetest noises coming out of her lips as moisture drips down her thighs.

"Keep your eyes on me," I whisper. Her head falls back, her eyes two dark slits directed at the mirror. "You've been driving me mad since the first moment I laid eyes on you, Barbie. And every day, I think I've reached the peak—that I can't possibly want you more than I already do. Then you wear one of your short dresses, laugh with your mouth open and your eyes shining. You talk in that low voice that's so sexy. And now, look at this," I say, jerking my chin toward the mirror. "You've never been more beautiful."

"*God*," she whines, digging her nails into the skin of my back. Her whole body shakes as she reaches the peak of her pleasure, her cheeks flushed, and a thin layer of sweat over her forehead. "Logan—fuck!"

When she lets go, I hiss. My cock hurts, my balls hurt, my head hurts. But the scratches left by her nails on my right shoulder sting so perfectly. She's perfect.

"Another reason why I'd never date you," she says as she catches her breath. She turns around, nervously pulling at her shirt, which has ridden up her side. "You make me do all the work."

you make me act crazy

. . .

Logan

"I'M COLD" are the words I wake up to. My eyes blink and try to adjust to the pale light coming through the gaps in the blinds as my mind runs through yesterday's events.

Primrose's fist weakly grasps my shirt. "Logan?"

"Yes. You're cold, I heard you." I stretch, then turn to her, big, watery blue eyes staring at me as she shivers. I'm nearly melting from her body heat, so the problem isn't the room temperature.

I check the alarm clock on my nightstand—it's one a.m.—and rub a hand on my face, trying to fight the sleepiness as last night's memories come back to me. Her orgasm trickling down her legs, then how she snuggled against my chest with those big blue eyes and asked me if she could sleep in my bed.

I rest my hand against her forehead, and she's definitely too warm. She must have a fever. "I'll go get a thermometer."

"Hmm?" she mumbles with a grimace.

Good grief, she can't even open her eyes, can she? I guess walking around half-naked finally caught up with her.

I gently move her arm off my chest, then tuck her under my side of the blanket. Maybe I should bring her to the hospital and let doctors deal with her. I'm not exactly the patient, nurturing person you'd want to take care of you when you're sick.

But I wouldn't be able to sleep if she wasn't here where I can see her.

I grab the medicine bag in the bathroom and bring it back to the bedroom. She's probably sleeping already, her chest rising and dropping quickly.

Taking the thermometer out, I turn to her.

"Huh." I look down at the small white device, realizing I'll need to put it under her armpit. Regret strikes me for not changing it to a newer model that goes in your mouth, but it's too late for that. "Primrose?" Nothing. "Primrose?" I insist as I gently shake her.

"Hmm?"

"I need you to put this under your armpit."

She blinks, her eyes red and watery.

"I'll need to . . . your shirt—"

God damn it, she came between your arms, Logan. Get your shit together.

She barely responds, her eyes closing, and I'd feel better if she'd consented to it. Still, I guess extreme situations call for extreme measures, so I fit my hand up her shirt, grazing the sweaty and hot—way too hot—skin of her chest before I position the thermometer under her armpit.

"Don't move, okay?" I tell her, but receive no answer.

I pace beside the bed, throwing a glance at Lola, who, probably bothered by the commotion, wanders out of the room. Once the thermometer beeps, I approach her, and Primrose whines as my hand touches her. I must feel as cold as ice to her.

"Holy shit," I mumble when I see the numbers on the screen. 102 degrees. We need to lower her temperature immediately.

I give her medicine and put a cold, wet cloth over her forehead. She tries to get it off and complains she's freezing, so I compromise on another blanket if she leaves it on.

After that, there isn't much more I can do, so I sit next to her on the bed, wetting the cloth with cold water every time it turns hot. I watch her sweat through the sheets, whine in her sleep, and wish there was more I could do for her to feel better. That there was an expedited way to make her get over whatever she has.

I guess for a while, she won't be leaving a mess all over my house, listening to her terrible music like she's at a live show while she works.

Why does that annoy me?

I let my hand trail down her arm, then rub her knuckles, her fingers tightly holding the blanket, and feeling the pressure of my hand, she lets go and entangles her fingers with mine.

Shit. My stomach drops, and quickly, I pull my hand away. For fuck's sake, this feels like more than physical attraction. Like her touch is infusing me with life.

What do I do now?!

"Have you been awake the whole night?"

Defensively, I square my shoulders and set the mug down when Primrose's head drops against the pillow again. Considering it's taken twenty minutes to get her to drink half a cup of tea, I don't think it's even warm at this point.

"You're sick."

"Aww. Are you worried about me?"

"Yes. You look like shit."

She lets out a sound that's probably supposed to be a chuckle, and I'm equally pleased to have made her laugh and concerned it sounds like a dying crow.

Biting my bottom lip, I watch her eyes close, my mind speeding as I consider my options. I haven't slept a second, and I'm not comfortable leaving her alone—or with Kyle. I guess someone else will have to take care of deliveries.

"I'm cold."

So she's been saying all night long, and I've added blanket

after blanket to the pile. "I don't think I have any more blankets, Primrose."

Her hand tugs at my shirt. "Come warm me up."

With a sigh, I lie next to her, then lift the layer of blankets. I gently pull her to me, her soft body relaxing against mine instantly. I must feel lukewarm at best to her, but she seems to like my proximity, and within a few minutes, her shivering subsides.

"Why can't I be your backpack?"

I freeze, my chest stilling against her cheek. Did she say . . .

I force a breath out and search for a possible answer in my brain. She's feverish. She might as well be high. She probably didn't even realize she said that out loud, and I should ignore her and wait for her to sleep.

But she said 'backpack.' Is that common knowledge?

"Kyle told me . . ." She breathes hard. "That you only let girls you're attracted to ride with you."

Kyle did *what*? I swear, I don't know why I keep him around.

"Wait, so, the other night . . ." She was testing me. I told her I'm attracted to her, then I told her I wouldn't let her ride with me, and she . . . she thought I was lying. "Is that why you avoided me all day?" My hold around her tightens as I bury my nose in her hair. How does she still smell like strawberries after sweating the whole night, I have no idea.

"You said you're attracted to me, then you said you wouldn't take me on a ride. At first, I thought you'd lied to make me feel better, but then, tonight . . ."

Tonight, I proved without a doubt that I'm attracted to her.

In fact, 'attracted to her' feels far too casual for the things I want to do to her.

"Barbie," I say, pulling the hair off her ear as if that will convey the message more clearly. "Riding together has nothing to do with attraction."

"It doesn't?"

"Well, I guess it's part of it, but not all." The muscles of my jaw tick. "I've been attracted to you since the moment you ran me over," I whisper as I softly brush my fingers through her knotted hair. "And none of what you've done since you've been here has helped in *any* way."

I swallow, my heart beating quickly against her ear. Can she hear it? Can she tell that I'm nervously sweating?

"Then why did you lie? Why did you say you don't ride with anyone?"

I lick my lips, thinking of the right way to express myself. It's not easy with Primrose, whose questions are always so targeted. "Before I ride with you, I need you to understand what it means. Sure, there's a certain component of attraction, but more than that? Intimacy."

"Oh."

I can't tell if she's disappointed or falling asleep, so I mumble, "It's like this, Barbie." I pull myself up on my elbow and lean closer as I rub her hip. "Riding with someone means becoming one. Being synchronous. Our bodies move together; your thighs press and release against mine, and the heat from your body emanates to my back. And adrenaline makes it that much more intense."

"It sounds a lot like sex."

"It's foreplay." I shift my waist, just in case. Talking about us riding together is so hot, and she doesn't need me to grope her while she's running a fever. "And for your safety and mine, we need to feel comfortable with each other. I need to know you'll understand my body language and respond accordingly with yours."

She pauses for a moment, then whispers, "So, Kyle was wrong. The women you rode with . . . you weren't just attracted to them?"

"No." I swallow, resisting the urge to kiss the soft, warm spot under her ear. "They're women I was intimate with."

Making herself even smaller against me, her breathing ragged, she blinks up at me.

I let my finger trail over the shape of her jaw, and both her hands encase mine, bringing it between us, against her stomach. She's as warm as a furnace, probably delirious, and whatever she has, it's safe to say I'm getting it next, but none of it feels inconvenient. There's no other place I'd rather be right now than in this bed, soaking up sweat and microbes from this infuriatingly beautiful woman.

"So, will I ever be your backpack, Logan?"

I breathe through the blood rushing to my groin, but focusing on that makes fighting other impulses tricky, and I lean down, pressing my lips to her shoulder. "Yes, Barbie," I whisper, though I'm pretty sure she fell asleep already. "You're mine."

A melodic laugh interrupts the hum of the tractor's idling engine, and I turn it off. I pull the bandana off my nose and mouth, inhaling the freshly cut grass, then wipe the sweat off my forehead with the back of my arm.

There she is, strutting by in her white boots. Primrose. Her blue skirt moves with the wind and her white top clings to her body, leaving her shoulders naked.

Her outfits have become the highlight of my day.

"No way!" she gasps, and trying to think past how goddamn beautiful she looks, I purse my lips. She was in bed all day yesterday, and now she's out here again, wearing scraps of fabric that'll hardly keep her warm during these chilly spring mornings.

My focus narrows on Kyle, walking beside her with a wide smile. This motherfucker. He's always finding excuses to be around her—not that I can blame him. I *could* punch him, though. I won't, but I could.

Kyle's eyes meet mine as he waves. "Mind joining us for a moment, boss?"

I *do* mind, but I hop off the tractor and reluctantly walk toward them. I'm not exactly in the mood to chat—not after I got a home visit from Tom, who was frustrated from not being able to reach me on the phone.

The buyer is becoming impatient, and Tom urged me to take the offer because there is no guarantee a better one will come. He doesn't need to tell me that—out of the dozens of farms in this area, the Gracen's farm and mine are among the few that haven't failed yet. And, besides, selling is my only choice. No matter how much it kills me, it's the right thing to do.

On top of all of that, there's been total radio silence from the police, and I don't know what it means. Is the case closed? Are they gathering evidence before arresting me?

It's unsettling.

Once I reach them, Primrose frugally looks my way, then, with a shy smile, turns around and sets her tripod on the ground. We've been sleeping in the same bed for the last three nights, and considering she got here ten days ago, my plans to keep a safe distance from her are, well . . . failing.

But she's been sick, and we haven't discussed what we did two nights ago. What she said afterwards, nor the fact that I told her she'd be my backpack.

"What's happening?" I ask, focusing on Kyle.

"Uh, we're doing a live."

"Great," I say flatly before cocking a brow at her. "Do you think you should be out here already? Wearing—that?" I say as I point at the blue, flowy dress that barely reaches the mid-point of her thigh. "You'll get sick again."

In fact, I'm surprised I didn't catch her cold.

"I thought you weren't going to tell me how I should dress," she says with a pointed look. "And the people at Marisol are waiting, so I had to get back to work. I'm perfectly healthy, don't worry."

I'm not *worried*. I'm annoyed that she's not taking care of herself, and, well . . . worried.

"Come on, kiss, and make peace," Kyle says as he gestures for us to come closer.

My stomach drops. Why—*why* would he say that in front of her? He promised he wouldn't make comments—I made him swear, before telling him briefly and vaguely about what happened between us. "Shut up, Kyle," I bark. "I've been looking for an excuse to punch you."

I venture a look at Primrose, and though she's definitely upset, it seems her anger is directed at me, glowering as she walks to some weird piece of equipment.

Kyle glares, then tilts his head toward Primrose. *Come on, man,* he mouths.

What did I do? Jesus, how am I messing it up now?

"Anyway," Kyle continues. "We were wondering—"

"You. *You* were wondering," Primrose says, avoiding my gaze like the plague.

"Right. *I* was wondering if you'd like to join us on the live. Maybe introduce yourself and the farm."

"No. I have actual work to do."

Primrose moves past me, grabbing something from the bag she's abandoned on the ground. "This is actual work, ass mouth."

"That's not . . ." I press my lips tight, watching her tilt the tripod. I didn't mean to insult her, but I can see where I fucked up.

Great.

"Kyle, go grab the hose."

"What hose?"

I narrow my eyes at him. "The *hose*," I insist, and with a small gasp, he nods, eyes widening.

"Oh, yeah. The *hose*. I'll . . ." He points toward the fields, then walks away, and once he's at an appropriate distance, I focus on Primrose.

"So, hm . . . sorry about that. Kyle is . . . an idiot."

"*Kyle* is an idiot?" she asks. I'm pretty sure the implication is that *I'm* an idiot. An idiot who should have kept his mouth shut instead of telling Kyle that I watched her climax between my arms and that I can't think of anything else since.

"Look, Logan."

Oh, no. Not 'Look, Logan.' I'll never hear her moan again, will I?

"Whatever this—" she points her finger back and forth between us—"is, we have a week left to explore it. I understand it's just fun. Casual." Her eyes darken, her lips pulling down. "But I won't be kept a secret, okay? I don't *care* how much you want me inside the bedroom. If you're freaking out because I told Kyle what happened, then—"

"You told him?"

"Not the details," she says in a scolding voice. "But if I can't tell anyone that there is something between us, then I don't want *anything* between us."

Jesus, again with this. I tell her I like her, and she doesn't believe me. I show her how my body reacts to her, and she still thinks I'm hiding her.

I get it. She's been hurt, and she struggles to trust men—we have Derek to thank for that—but I can't watch her feel this way about herself, and I can't stand that she believes any of it about me.

"Primrose, I'm not ashamed of you. Of . . ." My skin pulsates with warmth. "Of *us*."

"Sure you aren't. But you won't take me on a ride, you won't acknowledge in front of your friend that you like me." She scoffs. "The day after you confessed you're attracted to me, you asked me not to tell your friends."

"That's not—"

"Kyle!" she calls as she waves her hand in his direction. "We're done talking. You can stop pretending you're looking for a hose."

Kyle stares at me for confirmation, and with a shake of my head, I turn around and walk back to the tractor.

I sit and grab my bottle of lukewarm water, enjoying the partial shade from the tractor's cab. Primrose's voice reaches me from across the field, and I'm annoyed again that Kyle gets to hear her happy voice. I get the snappy voice, and for no reason.

What can I do to ease her concerns? To show her that I'm fully aware she's out of my league, and not the other way around? She's gorgeous, smart, a social butterfly. She's built a social media empire for herself, with nothing but raw talent and hard work.

I'm lucky she even *looks* my way.

Watching Kyle and Primrose chatting happily, an irrational wave of anger crests over me. I'm so jealous that I'm seething. Then I take in her bare legs, the fabric of her short skirt lightly flapping against the backs of her thighs, and my eyes stick to the hem, waiting for it to inch higher.

I want to kiss her. I kissed her once, and since then, I've wanted to kiss her again, and I'm pretty sure if I did it now, I wouldn't want to stop kissing her.

Every time I see her smile, every time I hear the hopeful lilt in her voice, a part of me wants to believe that maybe, just maybe, I could be what she needs. But I'm not the knight in shining armor she's looking for. I'm a tarnished sword, rusty and dull, incapable of protecting anyone.

She giggles over something he said, holding her stomach and shoving him playfully, and though it stirs my stomach, I can't even be pissed off.

Her laugh is so unique. It's infectious. Contagious. The laughter of someone who feels every emotion deeply. She's like a rainbow of color and feelings, while I've got one thing. Useless and consuming dark anger.

She turns her head, her eyes meeting mine across the field, and everything else fades away. I try to fight it, I really do. I tell myself that she's not meant for me, that she's looking for a Prince Charming with a white horse and emotional availability. But before I know what I'm doing, I grab the steering wheel and the back of the seat, launching myself out of the cab, then stalk toward her before I can change my mind.

I'm tired of pondering, of longing, of watching from afar. I'm tired of pretending she's just my alibi half of the time and my girlfriend the other half, while she's neither.

Most of all, I'm done with her thinking she's not good enough.

When Kyle's head turns to me, he lifts his palms and takes a step back, but I don't spare him a glance. Instead, I stop in front of her, cataloging her wide eyes and parted lips. Her chest is heaving, and I'm pretty sure I just scared her, which I'll have to apologize for. Later.

I cup her cheek, and though she flinches, she doesn't move back and instead stares deep into my eyes.

"What . . . what's going on?"

God, her voice. She doesn't sound angry anymore. Just surprised. And maybe . . . pleased. *What's going on*, I tell her with my eyes, *is that I want a chance.* Even though she'll be gone soon, and this will be over before I know it. Even though it's stupid, and I'll end up getting hurt when she leaves me behind. Even with all the reasons I have *not* to date her . . .

"Fuck it," I mumble as I lean forward, my lips falling on hers.

Holy shit.

She's stiff at first, even more so when I let my other hand roam down her back and yank her flush against me. But it lasts less than a second before she melts. And then it's . . . *holy shit* again. She fits so perfectly between my arms, like her curves were made to smooth my sharp edges. She tastes like summer and berries, and it's a familiar mix that makes my knees weak.

Her lips part, and I breathe hard at the implicit consent. Just like the first time, she's inviting me in, telling me she wants this as much as I do. That she's been waiting for it, craving it like I have. That this kiss is the *real* reason she's still here.

Her tongue grazes mine, and my fist bunches into her hair in response. All the blood has rushed to my groin, and I know I should stop, but I can't remember why. Especially when she lets out a moan, so soft I can't hear it, but I feel it vibrating against my lips.

I want to keep kissing her forever.

I never, *ever* want my lips to do anything else.

"Err . . . guys? The live?" Kyle calls.

Primrose bolts back, eyes wide and lips swollen as she looks between me and the camera.

She's so pretty.

I couldn't drag my eyes away if I wanted to, and anyway, there's nothing I need to tell the people watching. There's *one* thing I want to say, and only Primrose's meant to hear it.

I step back into her space, pulling her waist against mine. "Two million people just saw me kissing you." Leaning forward, I whisper in her ear, "How's that for being ashamed?"

let me help him

...
Primrose

WALKING AS QUICKLY as I can past the fish table, I spot Logan talking to a middle-aged woman. The tips of his ears are bright pink as he shifts from foot to foot, pointing at the pears stacked before him. This morning, he woke me up and told me to get ready for the farmers' market, which is excellent news—I'm sure people won't mind paying more for their fruit and vegetables if it means looking at him.

How's that for being ashamed?

My stomach clenches like it's done a million times since he kissed me yesterday. We haven't talked about it, because right after, he said he'd be going on a ride and vanished for most of the day. Kyle says it's normal, that he gets the zoomies when he's overwhelmed.

But he let me into his bed when I woke up in the middle of the night and couldn't fall asleep again. I might have asked for a cuddle. He might have said no, then done it anyway.

I've been waiting for him to bring it up, but he hasn't so far, which would send me spiraling if it wasn't Logan I was dealing with. He's been going about life burying every single feeling for years, isolating himself and exacerbating his anxiety. Now that he's allowing himself to feel something, he needs time to process it. I guess it's to be expected.

Still, I'm dying to know how he feels about it.

Once I join his side, the woman says a quick goodbye before walking away.

"Sorry," I say as I drop onto the stool and reach for my canteen of cold water. I appreciate the shade provided by the small roof, but it's not enough to keep my upper lip from sweating. I swear spring doesn't make sense in this part of the country.

"What for?"

"I think I just cost you that sale."

He looks out at the crowd, but the woman has already been swallowed by it. "That wasn't a customer."

"Then who is she?"

"Beth McMallen. She wants her sixteen-year-old son to work at the farm. He's been getting in trouble and could use an outlet."

"What did you say?"

He nods. "As long as the farm's mine, he can come over. It's not a big deal. I'll drag his sorry ass around and throw tomatoes at him if he annoys me."

"You know, you should stop downplaying every nice thing you do. People won't respect you any less if you acknowledge you're a kind person."

"Whatever you say," he mumbles as his eyes run over me. "But you can't leave my side again."

"Why not?"

"Some teenager saw me with you and asked me to TikTok."

"You can't use it as a verb."

He shrugs. "I won't use it at all, because I said no. Like a kind person."

When he smirks, I roll my eyes and adjust one of the precariously stacked eggplants. "This is a small town; and with this whole police business, I'm sure the news about our relationship spread like wildfire." I shrug. "My fame will rub off you, so you'd better get used to the attention."

Riding the Sugar High

He hums, throwing a sheepish glance at two women pointing at us. "I don't like attention."

I scoff. "Huh. You wouldn't guess." I cross my legs and fan myself with one hand. "Sorry to break it to you, but you're impossibly tall and gorgeous. You'll hardly ever go unnoticed."

He gives me a pleased smile and stands a little straighter.

"What?"

"You're tiny and gorgeous."

"Oh." I can't help the grin that takes over my whole face. "Thank you."

His eyes stay on me, but he doesn't say a word, even though I try to mentally will him to speak. It would be the perfect moment, seeing as it's just the two of us at the stall. But nothing comes, so with a resigned exhale, I take my tablet out.

"I think I know which recipe to send to Marisol."

A hint of a smile plays on his lips. "Let me guess. You know what *you* want to make."

"You were right. I keep worrying about what they want, what will sell, or what people like. But this is my candy—my dream. And I know exactly what I want to make."

"What's that?"

"Strawberry candy."

His smile turns warm and proud.

"I know it's pretty basic, but—"

"No." His head shakes. "I think it's perfect."

"Hopefully, Chloe will feel the same way."

"She will." When he notices my concerned frown, he rubs his thumb on my cheek. "She will, Primrose. She'd have to be an idiot to let you go."

An older man approaches the table, and after looking at the apricots, he moves on to the vegetables and grabs a couple of onions, carefully weighing them in his hands.

"Hey." Logan moves closer, his voice a whisper in my ear that sends my heart into a frenzy. "About that kiss . . ."

Yes, about that kiss.

This is it, *finally*. He wants to talk about it. What is he going to say? That it was a mistake and we should forget about it? That it was a mistake to wait so long to do it? I'm pretty sure my elbows are sweating, and I don't think that's ever happened before.

"Sorry I broke your rule."

My nervous tension eases as I burst into a heartfelt chuckle. "You're not much for rules anyway, are you?"

"No, I'm not." His hand brushes the hair off my shoulder; then his lips are even closer. "Did you check something off your list?"

"Take me by surprise."

"Ouch."

"What?"

"Well, I was aiming for number twenty-three."

Make my whole body tingle.

"When I wrote that, I pictured more than kissing."

He lets out a low rumble, his lips now an inch away from my neck as his beard scratches my skin. "Challenge accepted."

I press my lips together, chest heaving. Under different circumstances, I would beg him to drag me back home. I want to kiss him again. I want to kiss him all day long. But as it stands, we have another four hours here, and this market is important for Logan's business. Anything that could convince him not to sell takes priority.

"So . . . just to clarify," he whispers. "I'm your fake boyfriend. And your roommate. Your alibi. And . . ."

"And?" I tease.

"And for the next six days, I get to kiss you whenever I want?"

If this weren't so adorable, I'd be upset about the lack of a clear label. "Yes."

The tip of his nose brushes my neck, and my chest flutters, a wave of warmth coursing through my body. "Okay. That sounds good."

I turn to face him, and a loose lock of his hair tickles my skin. His eyes are hooded, and his shallow breaths fan over my lips. "So I'll kiss you now."

"Please."

He presses his lips against mine, soft and exploring. He tastes *perfect*, like man and nature. Like the stress of the last eleven days has been all for something. Like kissing him might be worth going to prison. Worth losing everything but him.

When I tease him with my tongue, his hand cups my cheek, and he pulls back. "Behave," he says, then kisses me again. "I'm not above putting on a show for these people."

I chuckle, and before I can press my lips to his a third time, the old man coughs loudly, and Logan stands. He rings through his products, and a small crowd forms around our stand in a matter of minutes.

"Can you grab the invoice from the organizer?" he asks as he finishes bagging cabbage for a woman. "His table is right there, and he doesn't exactly . . . *love* me."

Ah, great. Making enemies of the local farmer market's organizer. Smart.

I venture out again into the sun, an idiotic grin on my face, and approach the man. He continues his conversation with a blonde woman, who wears so much perfume that every one of her exaggerated gestures hits me like a blow to the face. When I glance back at Logan, he's staring back at me as if there's nothing else worth looking at.

"Yes, darling?"

I turn to the white-haired man, whose focus is now trained on me. "Uh, I'm here to collect an invoice."

"Sure thing." He grabs a folder. "Surname, please?"

"Coleman."

"Oh, you're with Logan?" He breathes through his teeth. "Do tell him it's nothing personal, all right?"

"Nothing personal?" I echo.

"Yeah. He was pretty pissed off when I rejected his application again. Good thing he still agreed to fill in for Julie today."

Mouth open, I stare dumbly at him as I take the invoice he's holding out. "How many times has he applied?"

He huffs. "Every time we open applications. But, you know, I can't choose his business over others. Only vegans care about vegan produce."

When he looks over my shoulder, as if he's done with the conversation, I ask, "Are there no vegan businesses in your market?"

He shakes his head.

"Not even one?"

He must notice the disdain in my voice because, with a huffed laugh, he squeezes my arm gently. "No, sweetheart. It wouldn't make sense to waste a stand on that, would it? Vegans can buy vegetables at any other stand."

But many vegans would prefer to support a business that shares their views, and everybody deserves access to food. Willingly denying it to some people in favor of what he thinks will be a more profitable offer is . . . at the very least, *yuck*.

I doubt, however, that there'd be a point in telling this man that as a business owner, food provider and human being, he has a responsibility to make his service accessible to everyone. That vegan businesses also deserve a chance at surviving.

If he cared, he wouldn't be saying this stuff.

"On the other hand," I mumble, "providing options that vegans struggle to find elsewhere would have them flocking to your market."

Waving at someone behind me, he chuckles. "I've been running this place for twenty years. I don't think I need advice from a little girl." He takes a step to the side. "Anyway—"

"Would you take the advice of someone with two million followers?" He stops in his tracks, his amused smile dissipating. "Would you take a shoutout? A nice video of your market?"

"You have that kind of audience?"

Ignoring his tone, I nod, and I can almost see the moment in which, in his mind, I'm no longer *sweetheart* or a *little girl*.

"And you'd do that?"

"I would love to tell my followers about an inclusive and

welcoming market." With my lips lifting slightly, I insist, "Can I tell them that, though?"

Rubbing his beard, he looks away, pondering. "I guess . . . I guess Logan can have the table permanently. Provided he pays on time and doesn't cause problems."

"He would never."

"I don't think you know him very well."

I step back, determined to walk away before he can change his mind. "I'll ensure my audience knows how much I love your market. And Logan will be here—every week."

With a stern nod, he watches me walk away until I turn around and reach Logan's side.

"All good?"

"Yep. Actually, Charles would like to offer you a permanent spot."

His eyes pierce mine. "Why would he do that?"

With a shrug, I look away. The last time I tried to help out his farm, he got angry, and I don't want to ruin the flirty mood between us. "I don't know. Maybe he realized introducing a vegan supplier at the market could attract a new crowd."

"*Really*? He got to that conclusion all by himself?"

I throw him a casual glance. "Yep."

He says nothing for a long moment, then he shocks me by pressing his lips to the top of my head. "Thank you."

Oh. This is new. And I like it. Like it a lot.

His strong arms envelop me as he hugs me from behind, my fingers briefly tracing the shape of his tattoos. It's like now that I've given him permission to kiss me as he pleases for the next six days, he plans to take advantage of every single moment. Not that I'm complaining.

But I slide out of his arm and take my list out. With a happy grin, I strike through number twenty, then show it to him.

"*Let me help him.*" He winks. "Don't get used to it, Barbie."

"Of course."

"Fuck," he grumbles as he tugs at my arm and pulls me

behind him. He says his next words from the corner of his mouth. "Don't speak, okay? I'll tell them you're indisposed, and—"

"Hello."

My muscles stiffen as I recognize Josie's voice and I peek past Logan, seeing her and Connor stand in front of our stall in their uniforms. With my stomach twisting into a knot, I cling to Logan's shirt.

"Hello, officers," Logan says. "How can I help you?"

"We were hoping to talk to Primrose."

Oh, shit.

I can feel the blood drain from my face as their inquisitive eyes study me. They want to talk to me. Why me? They must have found something. I'm screwed.

He crosses his arms. "Sorry, Primrose isn't feeling well."

Josie's brows arch over her eyes. "Oh no. Would you like a ride home?"

"No, it's—just a . . . a little stomachache."

She nods and awkwardly looks away. We haven't met since she made that scene at Logan's parents' place, and seeing her in full cop attire now is all sorts of weird.

"Or maybe it's guilt," Connor offers as he pulls up a plastic bag containing my pink scrunchie with yellow flowers. One of the dozen scrunchies I had in my bag the night I set that damn trashcan on fire.

Fear grips me tightly, squeezing the air from my lungs.

"Derek's dogs found this on his property, but he assured us Primrose was never there. To his knowledge." He smirks, pleased as if he's got me. "This is yours, though. We found a picture on Instagram of you wearing it, and your DNA will confirm it. So, do you want to tell us why you were there that night? Maybe you couldn't accept that Derek moved on, and you figured if you couldn't have him, then nobody would."

Oh my god, I'm going to be sick.

They think I wanted to kill him. That's attempted murder, isn't it? Far worse than accidental arson, which doesn't exist anyway.

"Oh," Logan says, casually, pointing at the scrunchie. "That's mine."

All eyes turn to him as Connor scoffs. *"Yours?* This pink scrunchie?"

"Uh-huh." Logan gestures lazily at his head. "Long hair. Need to tie it up sometimes."

"So why was Primrose wearing it in that Instagram picture?"

"I lent it to her."

With a sigh, Josie takes a step closer. Her eyes are soft on Logan as she whispers, "This isn't yours, Logan. And if you say it is, that places you on Derek's property. I appreciate that you want to help Primrose, but this is a serious crime, and—"

Logan huffs, then shoves a hand in his pocket and retrieves one of my scrunchies—the pink one with cute flamingos.

What . . . Why does he have that?

"There. See?" He pulls part of his hair up in a bun, then wraps the scrunchie around it. "Use them all the time."

"Even better," Connor says. "We'll need you to come down to the station for some questions. If the scrunchie is yours."

I shudder, sweat dripping down the sides of my face. I can't let him do that. He can't go to prison for a crime I committed. "Logan," I whisper, my voice trembling, but before I can say anything else, he reaches behind blindly and squeezes my arm tight.

"I'll see you at the station this afternoon. So you can ask all these pressing questions." Logan leans forward, his hand still gripping my elbow. "Now, if you don't mind, I'm trying to sell my produce here."

"Guess what, Coleman?" Connor sneers. "We *do* mind."

"Connor, it's fine. He said he'd come. Let's go." Josie motions at him to follow as she steps back, but he doesn't move a muscle, his hateful gaze still on Logan.

When Connor lets her drag him away, his fevered gaze is still on Logan like a rabid dog who can't let go of its chosen prey, until little by little, the crowd dissipates. Everyone goes back to shopping, chatting, and perusing the stalls—everyone but Derek, who stands on the opposite side of the market and wiggles his fingers in a corny 'Hello.'

"Ignore him." Logan's hand runs protectively over my side. "Or I could break his kneecaps. That's an option too."

"Forget about Derek, Logan," I scold. "What about the police? What are we going to do?"

"*You* won't do a single thing, Barbie. I've got this."

Does he?! Or does he think he's 'got this' while actually, he's burying a deeper grave for himself with each interaction? Now they know he was on Derek's property, and it would be one thing if he was getting caught for stealing the pigs, but my mistake? I won't let him go down for it.

Noticing the creases on my forehead, he squeezes my hand, a confident look in his eyes. "I've got you, Barbie."

share his passions with me

. . .

Primrose

THE FRONT DOOR OPENS, and my eyes shoot up. I lower the top of my laptop, wetting my lips as I put my lollipop in the glass on the nightstand. God, my heart is going to burst through my chest. He's back. He's *finally* back.

He left at two, and the police kept him for well over three hours.

I stand and walk to the corridor, the noise of drawers being opened and shut and things being moved around reaching me from the living room.

Crap. It didn't go well, did it?

I find Logan rifling through a cupboard in the living room, his helmet on. "Hey," I say tentatively as he slams it shut, then flips to the top drawer. "Is everything . . . okay?" I wince as that one slams too.

"I don't know where I left my keys."

I nod as he smacks books and knick-knacks from one side of the shelf to the other, but he doesn't seem in the right state of mind to be riding, flustered as he is. Even without seeing his face, I can tell. He's moving like there are bugs inside his clothes.

"Logan?" When he walks into the kitchen and begins a new search, I follow him. "What happened?"

With every one of his erratic movements, my heart beats faster and faster. Is this it? Have we been made? Maybe the police are right behind him, coming here to arrest me. Maybe they'll arrest him, and he wants to run away.

"Logan, please, just tell me—"

He snaps his visor up, his bloodshot eyes meeting mine. "I told you," he mumbles. "I'm looking for the fucking bike keys."

Shoulders falling, I walk closer. He's desperate, and that's much scarier than his anger. It reminds me of that first night, when he had a panic attack. Is he having one now?

I rest my hand on his jacket's faux leather sleeve, wishing there was some indisputable way to show him he can open up to me and trust me. But I know better than to try prying his mind open. All I need is for him to abandon the idea of driving the most dangerous vehicle he can get his hands on when he's *this* upset.

"How about we sit down for a minute? We don't need to talk. We could just . . ." I shrug, knowing that "snuggle" isn't the right word. "Just sit there and exist."

"No, I need to—" He moves past me, opening yet another drawer, the forks and knives clinking together as he roughly pushes them around. "I'm going out. Need to clear my head."

I guess these are the zoomies Kyle mentioned.

"Then let's take the pickup. We can—"

"I'm going for a ride, Barbie," he says, and fishing into the cabinet next to the stove, he takes out his keys. He turns around, his unhinged gaze set on mine. "I'm fine to drive. Promise."

I follow him to the door, my heart beating loudly in my chest. But I don't know what else to say to stop him, and he's not thinking straight right now. Watching him walk away, my stomach twists. I need to do something.

I shut the door behind me, then march after him. He turns as I approach his side, but I blatantly ignore him and step in front of the bike. Determined eyes set on him, I cross my arms. "You want to leave? You'll have to go through me."

He leans in an inch away from my nose. Through the gap in

his helmet, he stares down at me, and the disparity in size nearly makes me cringe. "My, oh my," he says flatly, a flicker of faint amusement in his eyes. "What will I ever do?"

"You'll do what any smart man would do once he's been overpowered." Tilting my chin up, I try to keep a straight face. "You'll listen to the much smarter woman telling you to come back inside."

"Yeah? You want me inside, Barbie?"

Look whose mood has suddenly improved.

Logan's head shakes, and backing up to walk around me, he says, "I'll see you later."

"No—no way," I say as I block his path again. I stare deeply into his eyes, though I'm not entirely sure he wouldn't run me over.

I'm *pretty* sure he wouldn't.

"I think I've already established I can move you around quite effortlessly, Barbie."

"Then do it," I say, not *solely* because I'm dying to feel his hands on me. I'd take anything to keep him off that bike.

"Okay." He approaches. "Hope you don't mind me locking you in the bathroom."

I take a step back and turn to face away. "Stop, Logan. This isn't fu—" I shriek when he lifts me from behind, then burst into laughter and kick my feet forward.

When he finally releases me, his eyes are considerably more serene than they were just moments ago. He brushes some hair off my cheek, slowly shaking his head. "You know what's really annoying?"

"Me?"

"That too. But I was talking about how you can turn my mood around in a matter of minutes." He thoughtfully stares at me, his gray-blue eyes shining. "Even when I have every reason not to be happy, you still make me smile."

"And we all know how much you hate that."

"Just worried about wrinkles."

I tilt my head toward the house. "Come on. Let's go in?"

"I have a better idea." He walks to the garage and emerges a moment later with a helmet and gloves.

"You want me to . . ." My eyes dart to the bike.

"Yes, if you're up for—"

"Yes!"

With a huffed laugh, he slides the helmet over my head. "Lucky you. You get the good helmet."

"*Good* helmet?" Unprepared for its heaviness, I wobble. Adrenaline courses through my veins, and my common sense slips away. "All your helmets should be good if you're riding *that*."

Jesus, I can't see anything with how dark the visor is, and it's so thick, it's setting me off-balance.

I slide the gloves on my fingers next, though they're easily two sizes too big. "What now?" I ask. I'm not even sure he can hear me through the helmet.

He reaches under and taps my neck, so I crane my head back. His fingers move to the clasp, but he pauses, staring at my neck for long enough that I wonder if there's something weird on it. A mole? Yogurt from breakfast? He brushes my hair back, his pupils blown, but he still doesn't move.

"Logan?" I whisper.

A grunt travels up his throat, and he snaps the clasp closed, then pulls the string until the helmet is tight under my chin. Once he's pulled my visor up, he straddles the bike and offers me his hand. "Done. Now, come on."

"Shouldn't I be wearing biker gear? A jacket—pants?"

"Well, it's always safer to use protection, but it feels better when you don't."

When my eyes narrow over his face, he smirks. "Are you still talking about the bike?"

"What else?"

He knows *what else*.

I squeeze his gloved hand with mine. "What now?"

Riding the Sugar High

"We're not holding hands, Barbie. Get on."

"Huh? I—yes. How do I do that? I don't know how to do that."

"First, foot here," he says as he points at a tiny metal piece jutting out from the side. "Second, push yourself up. Third, there is no third. It's climbing a bike, not metaphysics."

With an eye roll, I set my foot on the pedal. But—what if it breaks? Or even worse, what if the bike falls on me? "I'm afraid the bike will tip over."

"Nah, it's stable. Hop on."

"But I'm . . ." As I widen my eyes, he stares at me with the same blank, low-key bored expression, so I mumble, "Heavy."

His brows knit tightly over his eyes. "Again with this? You're one-foot-and-a-cucumber. You must weigh—"

Gasping, I smack the side of his helmet. "Don't you dare."

He grimaces. "Do you think you're heavier than the bike? Or me?"

My eyes run down his broad chest, his hips, the thick thighs straddling his bike. "No, I guess I'm not."

"No, you're not."

Right. The bike's heavy. He's heavy. Nothing will happen; it's fine.

But my stomach twists with anxiety, freezing me on the spot until Logan swings his long leg back over the bike and stands in front of me. With a sigh, he turns his back to me and crouches down. "Arms around my neck."

"Wh-what now?"

"Your arms. My neck."

I shift closer to him, then tentatively lock my hands at the base of his throat. When he reaches back and grabs my thighs, pressing them to his sides, I squeal.

My feet abandon the ground, and he pulls me up, ensuring we have a good grip on each other. My chest is pressed against his back, and I'm most likely choking him, but he doesn't seem bothered as he walks to the bike, then carefully throws his leg over and sits.

I land behind him with a gasp, my thighs still pressing the sides of his. My chest rises and drops quickly against his back, and I swear I can feel the heat of his body through both our clothes.

I'm sitting on what might potentially kill me, but Logan is in front of me, my legs hugging his, and it feels just a tad less scary.

"You good, Barbie?"

"Y-yes."

"Cool. This is your first time, right?"

If my heart beats any faster, it'll explode. "Yes."

"Feet." He twists to one side, moves my leg back until my foot comfortably fits on some other part of the bike, then does the same with the other. "Hands go here—you gotta let my neck go. It's called Backpack, not Necktie."

Right.

Carefully, I unlock my arms and move them to his waist. Suddenly, it makes sense why he'd call this "intimate."

"Yep, just like that. You'll have to hold on to the gas tank if I brake, or I'll get off this bike as a eunuch."

"Hm?"

"You'll crash my balls against the tank."

"Hands on the tank when you brake," I say, gripping his waist. "Got it."

"Cool. If I do this," he says as he taps the side of my thigh, "it means I want you to hold tight. I'll likely speed up, and my body will shift forward like . . ." His chest presses against the tank. "You'll need to do the same. Go on, try it now."

I lean forward, and when he straightens, my body follows.

"I probably won't do it this time, but you know anyway."

This time? As in, we'll do this again?

"Is everything clear? Got any burning questions?"

"Yes. Do they make pink helmets?"

He snorts, and the bike roars to life as if vibrating with anticipation, its engine emitting a low, rhythmic hum. My hands tighten around his shirt as he turns back to me.

"Remember my promise?" he calls over the gentle roar of the engine. With a deep breath, I press my helmet against his, the cold touch offering some comfort, and nod.

He's not going to let anything happen to me. I know it, because I feel safe around him in a way I've never experienced before.

"Okay, Barbie. One more rule." I meet his gaze again, and he snaps my visor shut, then says, "Never, for any reason, let go of me."

"Still talking about the bike?" I tease, raising my voice over the noise of the engine.

He winks, and before pulling his own visor down, asks, "What else?"

The bike moves, and with a shriek, my hands clench around his shirt. I close my eyes as the engine picks up, my heart thumping in my ears, and the world fades beyond the thick helmet.

It's unlike anything I've experienced before. As we reach cruising speed, the wind rushes past, tousling my hair and sending a shiver down my spine. I instinctively lean into the turns, mirroring Logan's movements, and the world blurs into streaks of colors—the landscape too fast-paced for me to keep track of.

It's terrifying at first. Then, not so much, until I'm confident enough to detach my face from Logan's back. I look around slowly, then a little more confidently, seeing the bike isn't affected by it. Every bump and dip sends a jolt through my body, and I cling to him, adjusting to the rhythm of the ride until I find myself enjoying the scent of asphalt mixed with the crisp air.

I look past Logan's shoulder, and a sense of liberation washes over me. The open road stretches out ahead, filled with unknown adventures. And the way he rides . . . How silly of me to think he wouldn't be in the right mind for it. It's like a synchronized dance between Logan and his bike, and I feel part of something powerful and dynamic.

I wish I could see his face. Or that we could talk. That I could ask him the million questions I have, or that I could comfort him, because he seemed so distraught when he got home.

I wonder what the hell happened at the police station.

Letting go of his shirt, I press a hand to his stomach. His body shifts, but it doesn't seem like he wants me to stop, so I use both hands to rub soothing circles, enjoying his closeness.

When his hand cups mine, I pull back, thinking he wants me to stop with the cuddles. But before I can inch my hand away, he's pressing it against his stomach tightly, his gloved fingers entangling with mine.

It's so hot. Why is it so hot?

Because he craves my touch. Because he's refusing to let go, as if he needs me. I've never been happier about a potentially deadly decision, especially when his hand moves up, dragging mine along until it's resting on his chest, right above his heart.

I move the other hand up too, and hug him tight, legs, chest, and arms, as he lets go of my fingers. Then he's back to gripping the handlebars, and feeling equal parts thrilled and calm, I close my eyes.

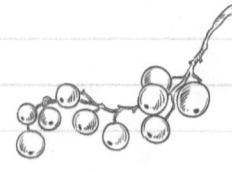

you want to ride my bike

. . .

Logan

STAGE FRIGHT. I've never experienced it, as I've never been on a stage before, but I'm pretty sure this is it. Riding with Primrose behind me feels like stepping onstage to perform. My hands are clammy inside the gloves, and her delicate fingers on my chest send shivers across my whole body.

It almost makes me lose focus, but I can't afford to, not while I'm riding and not with such precious cargo.

Regaining composure, I throw the bike into gear and drive at what I assume is an appropriate speed. I've never ridden this bike with someone, but Primrose is so light that she makes little difference.

"You can go faster if you want," she says, her voice reverberating through my helmet. She sounds out of breath, but in a good, exhilarated way, and as much as I want her to have fun, I'm not sure my mind's on the road as much as it should be.

I twist the throttle, and the bike speeds lightly as inertia pulls her backward. Her hold on my shirt tightens, the fabric bunching up in her fist.

Feeling more confident, I open the throttle completely, and her body tenses with nervous apprehension as we move through traffic. She draws closer as if she's afraid we'll hit the cars on either side of us, her fists pressing against me.

I could brake hard, make her bump right into me. I've been craving her so much it's painful, so I'd do almost anything to feel the soft curves of her body against mine. But I don't want her to get scared, nor do I intend to take advantage of the trust she's put in me by riding behind me, so I come to a gentle stop at a red light.

Once the road is mostly free again, I keep a cruising speed, wanting to prolong our time on the bike, but I miss the intensity of going fast and feeling her thighs clenching mine.

It's fucked-up.

Goosebumps scatter all over me at the heat radiating from the contact spots between us, and every time, I'm tempted to turn this bike around and bring her home. Continue where we left off at the market.

But we're almost at our destination, so I focus on the road until we slow to a stop.

My heart's still racing with the residual thrill as my helmet comes off.

I let out a slow breath and hang it on the handlebar by its strap when Primrose asks, "What is this place?"

Her hands are still on me, her thighs clenched against mine. And she's warm. Soft. I've been fighting a hard-on for most of the ride, and if she doesn't stop touching me right now, I'll lose that battle.

"Just a nice view," I say as her hands abandon my chest. But it's not just that, and I don't want to stop and think about why I brought her here, to the place I love the most in the world.

I let my eyes roam down the hill, enveloped by the breathtaking panorama that stretches before me. The air is crisp, and the gentle breeze carries the scent of earth and blooming flowers. The world unfolds in layers of greens and gold, a patchwork quilt of fields that seem to go on forever.

I twist to look back at her, but her visor is down, so I can't tell for sure how she's feeling. "Arms, Barbie."

"No, I'll get down by myself."

All right. I stand and give her my hand to lean on. She takes it and, awkwardly raising her leg over the bike, hops down.

"Chin," I say as I approach. Once the strap is snapped open, Primrose takes the helmet off, her flushed cheeks, ruffled hair, and misty eyes making my breath catch.

She looks like she's been fucked.

She looks like she's been fucked because she was riding behind me on my bike.

"Wow," she says as she turns to the view, and unable to look away from her, I nod.

Wow sounds about right.

"Logan," she whispers, and for the life of me, I can't imagine what she'll say next. "I think I want a bike."

Huh?

She chuckles, her eyes wide. I can almost see her blood pulsing. "It was like—like flying! Like I was free or . . . light as a feather. Like nothing else mattered except following the bike's movements with my body. Like . . . like . . ."

Huh.

She gasps. "When you turned, there at that big intersection, I was sure my knee was going to touch the ground, but it didn't, and then all I could think about was that feeling—like a buzzing in my veins . . ." She paces back and forth, her eyes darting around as she searches for the right word.

"Adrenaline," I mumble.

I can't believe she loved it. It makes me like her even more.

"Yes!" She points her finger at me. "That's it! Adrenaline. It was so cool, and—wait, do you think we can take a longer route back?" She gasps. "Oh my god, can you teach me how to ride?"

Woah. She's never riding my bike. Cute that she'd think she could even hold it up. But it does make my chest warm, how much she liked it. It's nothing special, right? Women love bikes. Some women must.

But she's not some women. She's Primrose.

"This place is so beautiful," she says, walking to the hill's edge as if the previous topic is done.

I join her side, anxiety slapping me in the face when she leans against the handrails. Someone who tends to fall without moving a single muscle should not be that comfortable this high up. Her eyes eat up the gorgeous view, and she slips into a contemplative silence, only the rustling of the wind and the melodic birdsongs to keep us company. As casually as I can, I place a hand on the railing in front of her.

"Can we see your farm from here?"

I turn to the lines of neatly planted crops forming geometric shapes. The afternoon sun bathes the landscape in a warm glow, casting long shadows, and birds soar overhead, riding air currents. Gently grabbing her arm, I move it until I point it home. From here, it looks doll-sized, and besides the red roof, it's hard to recognize anything else around it. "That's my house."

"Oh, yes, it is." She turns to me, her eyes dancing on my lips for a second. "So if that's your house, then are we looking at . . ."

I move her arm to the left, toward the fence I know is there but is invisible from so far away. "That's the end of the property."

She gasps, and it's the most sinful noise. I could hear it every day. Could wake up to it. Fall asleep to it too. Get her to make it in so many different ways.

"It's your farm. All of it."

"Only place you can see it all."

"Wow." The wind has her hair blowing over her face, and tucking it away, she exhales in a dreamy kind of way that makes me want to hug her. "It's perfect. Do you come here often?"

"Often enough." I ignore her smile as she watches the side of my face. "From up here, you're like a silent observer of the cyclical patterns of growth, harvest, and renewal. You watch it all happen, season after season. It's . . . I don't know."

"Humbling?"

"Yeah." I inhale deeply, then let it out. "And comforting. You look at all that, the life and the beauty, and you know your problems are just . . ." I pause, eyes darting over the fields. "Dust."

"Sure." She wraps an arm around herself. "But even dust has its place in the world, right?" When I throw a questioning look at her, she shrugs. "I just mean . . . You have the right to feel your pain. You don't need to remind yourself it's not a big deal."

"But I don't want to feel this pain. Any pain."

"Nobody does. But processing your emotions is the healthy way to—"

"I don't want to talk about it, Barbie," I interrupt. "So if that's why you came, we can just ride back."

She looks away, and my stomach drops when I watch her smile die. I deserve to trip over this hill. She's just trying to help. Just doing what she thinks is right, as she's done since she got here. Despite how horrible I am to her every single time. No matter how much I push her away.

It almost makes me believe she will never stop, but that's a naive thought. Everyone eventually stops. People grow apart, they get tired of each other, they betray and abandon and look only after themselves. People are always a disappointment, and despite how hard Primrose seems to want to prove the opposite, she's leaving in five days. Her ticket back home has been sitting on the bookshelf, reminding me of it.

Like my problems compared to the magnificence of nature, these two weeks together are just dust.

But even dust has its place in the world.

I stare at her, watching shivers break over her skin when another gust of wind strikes us, and slide my jacket off my shoulders. I hold it out, but her focus is elsewhere, so I drape it over her.

With a flinch, her eyes meet mine. "Oh, you don't need to—"

"I forgot how windy it gets up here."

Her bright blue eyes stare at me appreciatively as she lifts it off her shoulders and slides her arms inside the sleeves. "Are you sure? We both know how you feel about me wearing your clothes."

Horny, that's how I feel. So horny, I can't drag my eyes away from her. The jacket reaches her knees, her shoulders disappearing into the black fabric. No matter how ridiculous it looks on her, seeing her in something of mine stirs something possessive in me. She's wrapped in my smell, and when she gives it back, I'll be wrapped in hers.

"Number twenty-two."

"Lend me his . . . *faux* leather jacket." She pulls her arms up, the long sleeves flapping past her hands. "It's the first time someone else's clothes are too large for me."

Someone else's clothes.

An image of her wearing some other man's shirt has me nearly seething with jealousy, and I scrub a hand over my jaw, forcing the bile burning in my throat to settle.

She's leaving. She's leaving.

Only because we agreed to spend the next five days exploring this, I don't get to be jealous. To get attached more than I already have.

I'll repeat it until it settles in my brain.

She crouches down, sitting on the ground and holding on to the metal fence. Whenever I come out this way, I usually sit on my bike, but I'm not comfortable leaving her alone this close to the edge, so I settle beside her, resting my weight on my hands behind me.

"We don't have to talk about it," she says softly. "But can you just tell me what the police said? Am I in trouble? Are you?"

My eyes flutter closed. With everything else that's happened this afternoon, I completely forgot about the police. She must have been freaking out—god, I'm such an ass.

"They're still working the case, and from the look of it, they're hardly going to stop," I say as I think of the slew of questions Josie and Connor asked me. "They've made me repeat the same information we already gave them, and tried to scare me with the prospect of prison time." With a shrug, I meet her concerned gaze. "Nothing new."

"And the scrunchie? Did they test it already?"

"Remember that first night?" I ask as I think of the accident, then my panic attack. "You asked me for three movements, and—"

"You touched my scrunchie."

"Uh-huh. Left lots of big ol prints on it." I can't help but chuckle at the sheer luck of it. "They have no way of proving it's yours. And I could have entered Derek's property any time before or after Friday night."

"So they have nothing?"

I nod.

Her shoulders relax as she fidgets with a strand of grass. When her eyes meet mine, I can almost see the question flashing through her mind. *Then why were you so upset when you got home?* But she swallows it, and instead, points at my arm. "I like your tattoos."

God, it's hard to think when she looks at me like that. "You're about to ask me what they mean, aren't you?"

"No," she says pointedly. Then, jerking her chin up, she asks, "Are you calling me nosy?"

I smile wide. Too wide. "Yes."

"Then I *don't* like your tattoos." She pouts, but the uplifted corner of her lips betrays her.

"I have forty-six of them, so I won't tell you the meaning of every single one, but—" I sit up and show her my wrist. "I'll give you three."

"Today, or in life?"

My heart twists, but I smother it.

She's leaving. She's leaving.

"Just choose."

She perks up, her eyes scanning up my arm like she means business, and I know I'm playing a stupid, dangerous game. Now I've got her eyes on me, scrutinizing me with too much attention.

Making me want to do and say more stupid things. Dangerous things.

"This is only a minimal portion of your tattoos."

With a sigh, I bring forward my other arm, begrudgingly holding them side by side for inspection.

"Still . . ." she says as she points to my chest.

Lowering my arms, I cock a brow. "I just gave you my jacket. Now you want me to strip down?" I hold out my arms again. "Just. Choose."

"The word you have on your back."

Of course, she'd pick that one. When did she even see my back?

"What?" She shrugs. "I chose."

"That's . . ." I run my finger over the sharp edges of a small rock. "*Fratello*. Aaron spent a couple of years in Italy when we were younger, and I visited him for my eighteenth birthday. One night, we drank too much and got the Italian word for 'brother' tattooed." I hum, and the sound comes out gravelly as the memory of the tattoo studio we ended up at sours the taste in my mouth. "He got it on his arm because he carried me with him even when he was away. I got it on my back because I always . . ."

The words stick to my throat, and as I try to breathe through the stabbing pain in my chest, Primrose's small hand finds mine. She squeezes, and I glance up to see a compassionate look in her eyes—a patient understanding.

Her hair blows softly with the wind, and the strands trapped under my jacket frame her round face and rest along her neck. There's a reddish hue over her cheeks, probably because of the cold, and her plump, heart-shaped lips look delectable in that pink lipstick, like the candy she loves so much.

God, she's so beautiful it hurts. So close that if I leaned forward, I could press my mouth to hers. I could cup the back of her neck, feel her melt against me, and sink my teeth into her.

So perfect, I bite my tongue hard to make sure I'm not dreaming.

"Logan?" she whispers, and my eyes abandon her mouth. But she's not staring back—her gaze is on my lips.

It looks like the same thoughts running through my mind are going through hers too. Like whispering my name wasn't her calling my attention and reminding me I promised her the meaning of my tattoo, but an invitation. To kiss her, to take her.

"Because I always have his back," I mumble. "That's why I got the tattoo there."

She blinks, meeting my eyes. "You two were that close, huh?" she asks.

Yeah. We were that close before he ruined my life.

Glancing at the view of the farm, I move a hand to my chest. It starts with a subtle shift, almost imperceptible at first. A tingling sensation prickles at the back of my neck, then a spot in my chest begins hurting. Before I can do anything about it, it's throbbing as if I've been stabbed.

I breathe, but it feels like air can't move past the lump in my throat. As I set a hand on the ground for support, the world spins around me in a dizzying blur.

I think it's happening again.

I'm suffocating, trapped in a whirlwind and unable to stop it.

I close my eyes, trying to steady my ragged breathing, and Primrose's voice feels miles away. Much louder is my brother's voice, then the two of us shouting at each other as my mom cried and tried to keep us apart. The weight of it all presses down on me like a twenty-pound blanket, leaving me gasping for air.

A soft "Hey" reaches me, but I can't get my breaths to steady. Prim's sitting on her heels in front of me, terrified wide eyes and pale skin.

"You're okay," she says. I can't hear her, but I read her lips, then shake my head.

No, I'm not okay. I'm dying.

It's happening again, and I don't understand why. I don't know what's wrong with me, except that something is. I can't breathe—can't speak. Sweat gathers as I attempt to inhale, and I wish I could peel my skin off.

"Logan?"

When her hand gently grasps my arm, I cringe as if it's burned me, my wide eyes meeting hers as I open my mouth and inhale the biggest breath I can.

"I'm here. I'm right here with you." Her brows are taut, her lips twisted into a sad frown. "Remember the trick I taught you? You can do it."

Yes. Three things I can see.

I let my eyes roam over her, then jerk my chin toward her ear. "Ice cream cone earrings," I croak, My gaze dips down. "Yellow dress." Then down again. "White boots."

"Good. Great."

Aaron's voice echoes in the depths of my mind, nausea twisting my stomach as my head begins pounding. "I'm a fuck up—he's right," I say as I look up at Primrose. Though my eyes are open, everything's blurry. "I killed my relationship. I killed the farm. Everything I touch turns into failure and heartbreak."

I bring my shaky hands to the side of my head, pressing hard as if I'll get the noise to die out. But it doesn't work. It just gets louder and louder.

"You're worth *everything*."

My eyes meet Primrose's sad but determined gaze, and only then do I notice I've been repeating the very opposite out loud.

"I'm worth nothing."

"That's not true, Logan."

Yes, it is. If I was worth something, my brother wouldn't have betrayed me. Someone would have taken my side. I wouldn't have been dumped in such a callous way.

When everyone leaves you behind, you have to wonder if *you're* the problem.

Sitting beside me, she tentatively moves her arm around my shoulder, then pulls me closer. My muscles are stiff, and the thought of being hugged makes me claustrophobic, but I let her drag me down until my forehead rests against her neck, my ear to her chest.

Her smell is distracting, and as I focus on it, I hear the thumps of her heart too. "Your heart."

"Yes," she whispers, the word trembling out of her lips.

"Your voice." I hold back a sob, because I can't cry in front of her. But she sounds so sad, and it's because of me. "Your pain."

Her fingers run through my hair, and I wish I wasn't wearing it pulled back so she could do it all the way to the tips. It's calming. "Three movements now."

I raise my head, meeting her gaze from up close. The last time we did this, I kissed her. I'd love to do it again, and this time, I wouldn't stop there either. Goddammit, I haven't wanted to kiss a woman like this in the last five years.

"Three movements, Logan. You can do it."

When I wrap one arm around her, then the other, she looks up at me, her chest heaving. If I kissed her, she would melt against me like she did yesterday. Maybe I'd get her to moan again, to pull my hair.

But I don't want her to think she's a cop-out. I want her to know that I crave her all the time—not just when I'm going through shit.

Before I can make up my mind, she pulls me into a hug and whispers. "Come on, third movement."

I rub my hand on her back, run it up her shoulders and to the back of her head, pulling her closer. I stay in this twisted position, enjoying our hug, for far longer than it's appropriate. And then some more.

When I pull back, she carefully studies my expression, and I must be looking much better, because she smiles.

I squint down at the farm, the vast expanse tinted with an orange glow now that the sun is setting. "We used to have Sunday lunches on a big table in the backyard," I mumble. I don't know what exactly made me think of it. "The whole neighborhood would come to the farm. Sometimes, uncles, aunts, and cousins who lived far away. Kyle, Simon, and Josie. Aaron and me. It was the place that brought us together." I think back to the barbecues, Christmas lunches, and how my parents made it feel like everyone's home.

"You didn't keep the tradition alive?"

"No. Things changed." I press my lips together. "And they're about to change even more."

"When you sell the farm?"

I don't want to talk about this, but she deserves someone who isn't afraid to speak the truth. Even when it's hard and has the potential to ruin everything.

And there are a few truths I've been keeping from her.

Letting out a slow breath, I clench my teeth together to stop myself from tearing up. "It's done, Primrose. I sold the farm."

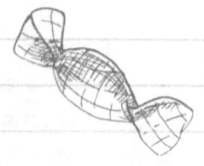

make my whole body tingle
. . .

Primrose

"WAIT, WHAT?"

His shoulders square as if he's preparing himself for my attack. "The documents aren't signed yet, but I saw Tom today and accepted the offer. It's done."

I swallow, but my mouth has gone dry.

Is this why we're here? I figured he wanted to remind himself what he's fighting for. Or that he came here because something happened, and the farm is what brings him the most comfort. Is it goodbye?

"You can't sell the farm," I mumble. It's pointless to say—he can do what he wants. But I've got no clever ace up my sleeve to make him change his mind, no inspiring speech to deliver that'll make him give this another chance; only my heartbreak and his, painfully present in this idyllic place.

He looks in the distance, his Adam's apple bobbing up and down. "Primrose, this farm is . . . is part of me. It's my legacy, my home, my passion. But there's nothing that counts more than the lives of everyone involved."

I slowly shake my head. "I'm not sure I understand."

"Selling a farm isn't an easy feat, Barbie, and if I wait to sell and *don't* find someone willing to buy, what happens then?" He shrugs. "I'd have to declare bankruptcy. I wouldn't be able to pay wages or insurance. You know Simon has a one-year-old? And Nadia, our accountant, has asthma and relies on us for health insurance. And Lou's wife needs monthly treatments at the hospital."

"But it won't get to that point, Logan," I say, though, really, how do I know? I'm asking him to put his faith in me, but we both know there's no guarantees.

"And that's only part of it. What happens to the animals if I fail? Or if I'm forced into a last-minute sale?" He rubs a hand over his face, the veins in his neck straining against his skin. "This will give me the time and money to relocate them. Make sure they're safe and don't end up—" He swallows. "It's the right thing to do. The responsible choice."

I scoot closer, then wrap my arms around his shoulders and pull him into a tight hug. We sit in silence, the leaves of the trees around us rustling. The buzzing of crickets grows louder, almost deafening. The world moves forward as if nothing's happened, while Logan loses everything.

And there's nothing I can do to stop it.

His forehead falls against my shoulder, and I press a hand to his back. If I could only scoop up some of his pain, some of the toxic black sludge in his soul, and throw it off this hill. If I could comfort or reassure him or know what magic words would fix this.

"I don't know what I am anymore," he whispers, and his words are so charged with anguish that my nose and eyes sting. "This is all I know how to do. All I've ever done. Who am I without the farm?"

"You're more than your farm, Logan," I whisper back. I try to break away from the hug to look at his face, but he strengthens his hold. "You're so caring, empathetic, and selfless that you'd give up something important to you to ensure everyone else is safe and sound."

"I'll never see any of them again."

"What?" I pull him even closer. "Of course you will. Your friends and co-workers won't ghost you because of this. They all love you, they—"

"The animals. I'll never see Paco and Lola again. Never see Tessa and Penelope and . . ." His voice is softer than a whisper. "I'll never see any of them again."

God, I can't breathe, the pain crushing my lungs and robbing them of any space for oxygen. He's hurting. I can't even pretend to understand how much, but I can see it, feel it.

"Please, give me a chance to help you fix it."

He straightens, clearing his throat as if that's also going to shake the pain away, then stares at the ground with a cold look. "I'm out of time, Primrose. You're leaving in five days. It's done."

"But you haven't signed the documents yet, and Kyle's picture performed so well—seven calls in one day! If we continue like this—"

"It's not enough."

"But it could be," I insist, rising to my knees. "We could try new things, and—"

His hand squeezes mine. "Barbie."

My heart beats frantically against my ribcage. There must be something that could buy us time, some way I could convince him not to sell. "What if . . . I'll lend you some money."

His brows scrunch. "What? Absolutely not."

"It's fine," I rush to say. "I have *some* savings. And my parents —I could ask—"

He lets my hand go, and squaring his shoulders, he glares. "This is not why I told you any of this." He stands, then brushes his hands together. "And there isn't a chance in the world I'm going to accept money from you. Let alone get you into debt with your family."

I stand too, rushing after him when he walks to the bike. "But it wouldn't be a big deal. You'd pay me back. All we need is some time to—"

"No, Barbie."

"We could try other things, then. The farmer's market went well, and you got a permanent spot, and—"

He breathes out, leaning against the bike with both hands. "Barbie."

"Your brother—he offered you money. We could . . ."

He holds out the helmet, but I cross my arms, and with a sigh, he lowers it.

"Don't push me away, Logan."

"This has nothing to do with pushing you away."

Doesn't it, though? I know for a fact that Kyle and Simon offered to stop cashing their checks for a while. I've seen him refuse his brother's help, and he doesn't want me to promote him —nor will he take my money. He *is* pushing everyone away. "There's nothing wrong in accepting help, Logan."

"God—I said I don't want to talk about it, Barbie."

"Well, tough luck." I step closer, pushing my chin up in challenge. "We *are* talking about it."

He sets the helmet on the bike, then drags a hand over his face before facing me again. Though I expect the usual aggravated expression, he smiles down at me with an atypical warmth. Well, I guess it's starting to be typical.

"What?" I ask, my own lips lifting.

"Just . . . you."

My cheeks burn, and struggling to focus, I mumble, "I . . . you—you're changing the topic."

"I'm not." He takes a step closer, my shoulder bunching when he invades my space. "But we could talk about it later. Do something else now instead."

I sheepishly glance at him. Though the answer feels pretty obvious, I'll ask anyway. "Do what?"

He closes the distance between us and cups my face, his lips pressing against mine with no hesitation. It's like a spark igniting a wildfire within me. I melt into him, my hands instinctively reaching up to grasp his broad shoulders, anchoring myself to him as if afraid he might disappear.

"Let's go home," he mumbles on my lips as his forehead presses on mine. "And I'll show you."

Oh. My stomach twists, a mix of apprehension and excitement coursing through my veins. Grabbing my helmet, I smile. "Let's see how many speed limits you can break."

As I straddle the sleek leather seat behind him, I feel a surge of adrenaline course through my veins. The powerful engine roars to life beneath us, vibrating with untamed energy and eager to devour the open road. I wrap my arms around his waist, holding on tight as he revs the throttle, the intoxicating scent of gasoline mingling with the crisp night air.

Shifting my hands from the tank to his jeans, I lean into the feeling of comfort. I rub until one of his hands joins mine, and with the other one, I keep massaging, then mindlessly dip to his inner thigh.

He squirms, then grabs it and leads it over his stiff erection, and though I've already felt it against my ass only a few days ago, I'm once again stunned at his dimension. And I'm pretty sure this is a "look what you've done" rather than an invitation to continue, but I take advantage of the confused message and press a hand over his shaft.

Yep, it's huge. And *so* hard.

He gently grasps my hand and sets it on his thigh, but as soon as we come to a red light, I rub his inner thigh, then his dick again.

Shoulders hunching, he leans forward. I think I hear him groan, but once the light is green and the one car behind us honks, he gives gas, and we begin riding.

Merely a minute later, after unsuccessfully shoving my hand away one more time, he slows to a stop, and I feel the bike come to a gentle halt beneath us. With a sense of anticipation tingling in the air, I watch him hit the off-switch.

"Is everything okay?" I ask innocently when he pulls the helmet off.

He chuckles, his gaze meeting mine over his shoulder. He stopped somewhere along the road leading to his farm, and there are nothing but fields on either side of us. Everything is utterly silent, too, the only background noise provided by the chirping of birds.

"You don't want to fuck around with me, Barbie."

"Don't I?"

"No, you don't." Kickstand in place, he dismounts. He unclasps my helmet and pulls it off me, and once I see the hungry look in his eyes, I feel like my chest could burst. Like I've been inflated with sweet, sweet air and now I'm close to floating away.

Hooking my helmet to the handlebar, he sits again, facing me. His forehead presses against mine as he whispers, "You're playing with fire."

"I've been known to do that at times."

His hands run up my thighs, pulling up my skirt in the process. "No kidding."

God, I want him. Right now. I've wanted him so badly since the day I met him, and I don't think I can wait another second.

His lips crash against mine, and I move my hand between us and begin undoing the button of his jeans until he interrupts our kiss. His eyes dart from my eyes to my hands. "Here? Are you sure?"

"Yes, please," I whisper. He tilts his head so he can have better access to my neck, and I squeeze my eyes shut to concentrate. But I have no hope to, especially as his fingers slide up and down against my opening and turn slick with my wetness.

I whimper when he fits them inside me, and he watches me close my eyes and exhale.

"Please, Logan," I whine. "I can't wait anymore. Just fuck me."

"Look at the size of me, Barbie. If I *just fuck you*, I break you," he says softly. It makes me clench around him, which should be a clear sign of how much I *want* him to break me. "Let me get you ready."

I nod, biting my bottom lip as his fingers push and pull, stretch and curl. My hips grind, roll, an orgasm orbiting closer and closer, until short of begging, I look into his eyes.

"Okay, okay," he breathes out. He stands and shucks off his jeans, then folds my legs up so they're against my chest. "Shit," he says with wide eyes as he meets my gaze. "I don't have condoms."

"I've been tested after Derek."

He swallows. "So have I after . . . my ex."

I give him an encouraging nod, my heart thrumming as he drags the tip of his cock along my entrance. He rubs it up and down, his eyes rolling back. "Fuck, Barbie. If you come on my bike, you're mine. Do you understand?"

I feel his tip against me, and breath catching, I nod.

"I want to hear you say it. Say you understand that if I fuck my backpack on my bike, I'm not sharing it." He teases my entrance but doesn't push. "You're *only* mine."

"Whose else would I be?" I whisper. It might not be the right thing to say, but it's the truth, and it makes his eyes grow darker as he stares down at me. "I'm already only yours."

With a deep groan, he pushes against the resistance of my muscles. I gasp, stretching around him as the sting makes way for pleasure, and inch after slow, painless inch, he buries himself inside me.

"Oh . . . my . . . god . . ." I breathe. I clench around him, over and over again, as his eyes flutter.

"Stop—stop doing—*oh*, that."

"I can't help it," I squeak. I really can't. I feel everything. Every inch of him, every twitch, every pulse. My fingers are buried in his muscular arms, my eyes lost in his. "You're huge."

His lips are parted, his brows bent. He halts, letting me adjust to him, then begins gently rocking into me. Within a handful of seconds, he moans and drops his face to mine, forehead to forehead. "*God*, Primrose. You keep squeezing me like that, and I'll embarrass myself."

"It's okay," I whisper. It's hard to talk, hard to focus on anything at all but the feeling of him inside me. It's better than anything I've ever experienced. "It's perfect."

"Can you take more?"

"*More*! There's more?"

He nods, eyes closed as if he's trying his best to restrain himself. "Yeah. There's more."

Holy shit. I look down, but I can't see just how much we're talking about.

"Yes, I can."

"Are you sure?" he asks, but even before I answer I feel him slide a bit deeper, his lips twisting before his jaw sets. "God, yes. Sorry. It feels so good—you. You feel . . ." His breath shakes out of his lips. "I fit so well inside you, Barbie."

I wrap my legs around his ass, pulling him until he's to the hilt. Until I can't imagine myself without Logan pressed on top of me.

"Primrose." He grits his teeth hard and sets a rhythm that evolves from stuttering to smooth and has me mewling and arching and whimpering on his bike. I can't imagine we'll be able to fully let ourselves go, not on here, not as hard as either of us needs, but he surprises me as he says, "I'm really going to fuck you now. Okay?"

I can barely nod.

His pace picks up, and every time he rubs that spot inside me, I moan louder. It doesn't hurt at all; it's euphoric. The highest I've ever felt. Better than all the sugar in this world.

"You can't feel this good, Barbie. It's not"—his eyes roll to the back of his head—"*oh*, shit, it's not possible."

I scratch at his arms, my knees hitting my boobs every time he pushes forward. He's got me all folded up for him, and watching his expression break every time he sinks inside makes me feel so powerful.

He needs me. He's trying so hard, the veins in his neck are strained against the reddened skin, but he needs to come, and I can help him.

"Come," I whisper through another push. His eyes meet mine in an expression that's half anguish and half delight. "Let yourself go, Logan."

"No, I can do it." He pulls back, then in again, his hands squeezing the bike seat on either side of my face. "I can do it. I can do it." At the next push, he grimaces, shaking his head. "I can't do it."

"Logan, please," I insist. I grab a handful of his hair and use it to pull his face closer. "Fill me up."

Goosebumps spread across my skin as he kisses me hard and fast. "Don't say that."

"I want to feel it dripping out of me."

"Stop talking," he pleads as his hips buck forward and he bottoms out.

"Show me I'm yours," I insist, my voice trembling as my back arches. "Please, cowboy."

With a grunt, he slows down, his movements stuttering until his jaw clenches. "I'm coming, Primrose. I—" He gasps, his eyes widening as if he wasn't prepared for the pleasure that's hitting him. "Should I—p-pull out?"

When I shake my head, he drives deeper into me, finally letting go as he releases one loud, feral moan after the other. "Oh —your cunt—god—" He spears his tongue into my mouth as his cock twitches, spurting his pleasure inside me. He whimpers—*whimpers*—as his hand grips my hip in a tight hold. Then his head falls next to mine, and slowly, I feel his orgasm trickle out of me.

He breathes hard, his whole body resting on mine and his hips jerking as if he wants to bury himself even deeper.

I've never seen anyone come this hard.

Twisting my neck, I kiss the side of his head as he catches his breath. "Are you okay?"

"Yes," he whispers. His hand rubs my side, and he kisses my shoulder. "Are you?"

"Yes." More than okay. I feel wanted. I feel sexy and lusted over. I feel his need for me tingle through every inch of my skin.

His chest rises, and looking down between us, he pulls out, then back in again slowly. "I'm not going to stop," he says as he continues thrusting. Is he *still* hard? Hard *again*? I have no idea, but this is the first time a man has come inside me, and feeling his cock push against the cum till it spills out . . . I groan and writhe against him.

"Are you sure?"

"Yes," he mumbles. His finger circles my clit, and when I squeeze him, his rhythm picks up. He reaches back, then with one hand only, slides his helmet on. "I want you to see how pretty you look when I bottom out inside you."

I breathe as he pulls his visor down, every nerve in me firing up. My eyes are bluer than normal as they stare back at me through the reflective surface, my cheeks red and my mouth open in surprised delight.

He sinks in roughly, and I force my eyes to untwist to watch my breath catch, my chest rising sharply.

"You see now, Barbie?" he says. "I've pictured what you'd look like pressed underneath me for close to two weeks, and not even in my filthiest fantasies would I have imagined this."

He pulls back, then rams in again, a moan slipping out of me as my nails sink into his arms.

"Isn't it perfect?" He fucks hard and slow. "Aren't. You. Perfect?" he continues, each word accompanied by a new snap of his hips.

"Harder." I almost can't speak, the words dragging out of my lips, exacerbated by desperation and need. "Fuck me harder." His cock slides in and out, hits all my nerves, and yet I need more.

"Harder, huh?" he asks, leaning forward and resting his weight on one hand. "You might just be made for me, Barbie."

With a long, low hum, I nod frantically.

Still punishingly thrusting into me, but at an excruciatingly slow pace, he says, "Ask nicely."

I grab the hair at his nape and grind my teeth as the pleasure intensifies. "*Please*, fuck me harder."

He holds my legs over his shoulder, and I relish the delicious stretch as his rhythm picks up. "How am I not breaking you?" he breathes, each of his motions landing with a loud thump of his body on mine, a pleasure I can't put into words.

He should be breaking me. He's thrusting so hard, I should be crying out in pain. But the strength of it just makes it better, makes me want to do it all day long.

"Oh my god!" Heat zips to the pit of my stomach, pleasure exploding like fireworks in the back of my mind. "Logan—Logan!"

Tears spill down the sides of my face as the orgasm rolls through me. I clench again and again, like it'll never end. Like this is the peak of my life.

His thrusts falter, his hands tightening on my hips. "Do you want my cum again, little backpack?"

"Please, yes," I whimper through the last echoes of my orgasm.

He groans, his cock sliding in and out of me harder and faster, and reaching forward, I pull his visor up. "Barbie," he whines. "This is my cunt. My—" The most delectable expression falls upon his face as his eyes bore into mine and he pours his moans out.

When his body relaxes, he gently sets my legs down and smooths the hair beside my face, then pulls out. One side of his lips lifts as he removes his helmet. "You should see what a mess I made of you," he says with a sigh.

"I can feel it."

He adjusts my panties, then holds his hand forward and pulls me up. His lips meet mine, and it feels like he kisses me for hours, though it's probably minutes. Like I could continue for days.

"You have a tissue on you?"

I fish into my bag, then take one out, and as he uses it to clean up the bike, I cock a brow. *"Really?* That's what needs cleaning up?"

He glances down at the paper, then at me. "Yes." Then, he presses a kiss on my cheek. "I'll clean you up. At home." The next peck lands on my jaw. "I want my backpack to ride home stuffed with my cum."

"Oh—kay." Heat rises to my cheeks, and he blows a breath against my neck, then lifts his sleeve to show me the spot where I clawed at him, and the scraping of my nails left a red mark. "Maybe you're ready for me to break you after all."

"Oops," I whisper. I press my lips tight, and with a dark chuckle, he tucks a lock of hair behind my ear.

"Primrose . . . you know why I'd never date you?"

"No," I say, souring lightly as I prepare for his quip.

But then he looks at me, eyes deeper than a well, the shadow of a smile that's so tender, it's nearly too intimate. Slowly shaking his head, he tucks my hair behind my ear and whispers, "Me neither."

go downtown

. . .

Primrose

WE STEP ONTO THE PORCH, hand in hand. My underwear feels wet and sticky, and though it's uncomfortable, it's hot in a way that makes me feel filthy—depraved in the best way.

When my legs twist for the hundredth time, he smirks. "How about we take a shower? Clean you up?"

I picture the harsh bathroom lighting and swallow hard, words like 'exaggerated curves' cutting my air supply.

He'll be grossed out too when he eventually agrees to throw you one.

I shake my head slightly, willing Derek's words to fade from my memory, my teeth sinking into my bottom lip. I figured when we'd have sex, there would be romantic lighting, a soft blanket, lots of eye contact. It worked out even better because I was fully dressed on his bike.

What he's asking right now is much different.

"Uh-huh, maybe." I follow him into the house, trying to bury my nerves under a smile, though I'm not sure it's enough to fool him. "We should probably check on the piglets first. They need to be fed, right?"

"They can wait." He pulls me to him, his lips tracing down my jaw and neck before closing the door.

God, it feels good. And scary. Terrifying, really.

"Do you want to eat?" I ask as I gently pull back.

We haven't had dinner tonight, so I don't think it's too weird of a question, but Logan clearly disagrees because his lips abandon the spot under my ear, and he leans back. "I do, Barbie." Gaze lowering to my lips, he whispers, "But my dinner keeps squirming away."

His dinner? *Am I* his dinner? "Oh."

"We don't have to shower together if you don't want to," he says, eyes narrowing on my face. "We don't need to do *anything* at all. We can hang out."

Great. Now he thinks I don't want to sleep with him, and I'm not about to tell him I'm worried about what he might think of my body. If there's something that *isn't* sexy, it's a trash heap of insecurities.

"You should go first."

With a resigned sigh, I walk past him. "I won't be more than ten minutes."

"Okay," he says as I open the bathroom door and slide in.

Amazingly done, Prim, I think as I wash off. What do I do now? How do I tell a guy I want to have sex with him without telling him I want it to happen in his bed, under a thick blanket?

I come out of the shower ten minutes later, still asking myself the same question. Did I kill the mood completely? I need us to have sex again. Actually, I need us to have sex all night long.

But how do I tell him?

"All good?" Logan asks as I leave the bathroom. He's standing with his back against the wall, his black shirt clinging to his muscles, and his eyes running down my towel as if he can see underneath it.

"The shower is yours," I whisper. I throw him a sullen look, wondering if there's any way I can fix it, as he steps beside me.

"Cool." He stops with his lips an inch away from mine. "Will you still be in that towel when I come out?"

Watching his hungry gaze, I frantically nod. "Yes."

"Good." He pecks my cheek, then closer and closer to my ear. "And will you be in my bed?"

"Sure." Relief pours out of me. "But where are *you* sleeping?"

"Watch your tongue, Barbie," he growls, his warm breath making shivers run down my spine.

I drag my hand along his leg, then over his shaft. "Or what?"

"Or I'll come on it."

I bite my bottom lip, the thought of his cock in my mouth making me drool. There's this urge in me to please him, to make him lose control. I want to find out every way I can.

"I'll see you soon," I say as he kisses my neck, his hand flattening my back and pulling me flush against him.

"Hmm." Begrudgingly, he lets me go. "Fine. Go. My bed."

He smacks my ass when I turn around, and with a flirty glance over my shoulder, I walk into his bedroom. The bathroom door closes as I hold the towel and slide under the blanket.

The rest of those ten minutes is absolute hell.

My heart jumps in my chest, and though anticipation pulsates between my legs, I question myself time and again until the water stops running, and it's too late to change my mind.

Panic rising as the door opens, I watch him walk to the bedroom through the gap left by the semi-open door, nothing but his jeans on.

This is a bad idea. Maybe I should leave.

But then his eyes meet mine through that gap, and he freezes on the spot. My heart is in my throat, beating incoherently, waiting for his next move until he pushes the door all the way open, and his eyes run along the blanket covering me. As we finally lock eyes, I throw the towel at him.

It hits him in the face and falls at his feet.

Two for two.

"Another reason I'd never date you," I say as if I'm not the most nervous I've ever been. His eyes move along my body, hidden by the blanket, eager and hungry. "Poor reflexes."

"If you're naked in front of me, the only reflex I have is to pin you down and fuck you."

"Really?" I ask, my heart thrumming. I make a show of moving my hand down until it disappears between my legs, and from his chest, he emits a low, rumbling noise.

A shiver of anticipation courses through my body. Seeing how much he wants me gives me confidence. How he's affected by the sight of me in his bed, knowing that my hand is on my pussy.

God, I wonder what he looks like when *he* masturbates. If he lets himself go. If he'd let himself go with me.

When my finger grazes my clit, I let out a gasp. My shoulders sink into the pillow, and I pull my knees up, spreading my legs as my eyes remain trained on him.

His jaw tightens, his sharp focus on every one of my movements, like a wolf ready to pounce on his prey and lock his teeth around its neck. Around *my* neck.

"What were you thinking about?" he asks as he takes another step forward.

"Hm?"

"When you moaned my name."

"You, of course," I say as I remember the night when he caught me masturbating. My eyes dart to his knuckles—white with the death grip he has on his forearms.

"What was I doing?"

"You were closer than this, for one," I say as I attempt to stabilize my voice through the sensation gripping me under his sheets. I crack a smile, but the tension in my body sucks it back in, my eyes wide as I press my lips together to hold back a whimper.

"How about this, Barbie?" He walks to the foot of the bed. "Is it close enough?"

Exhaling, I shake my head. The movement of my finger is now causing a wet noise that has his throat working hard.

I'm so sensitive to his presence. To him. I don't think I've ever felt this consuming, impending desire.

"No, of course not. I can't even see anything from here." He reaches forward, his hand bunching in the blanket, then runs his eyes up to me as if silently asking for permission.

He wants to pull it off me. Expose my body.

I bite my bottom lip, hating that this gives me pause, but it does. I'm not sure I'll be able to relax if I spend the whole night wondering what my body looks like from that angle, if he hates some part of me, if he regrets having sex with me.

"Barbie? Am I misreading your signals? 'Cause we fucked on the bike, then you climbed into my bed, butt naked, and that'll make someone think—"

"You're not," I breathe out. "Maybe . . . maybe we could turn the light off?"

"Oh." His jaw tightens as if he's only now realized the issue. "I'm not a cat, though. Can't see in the dark."

"We could turn this on, uh—" I look for the bedside lamp's switch. "For some softer, gentler lighting."

"Barbie."

I look back at him, his hand still clenched around the sheet.

"We rode together for the first time." When I nod, he does too. "Remember that feeling, backpack?"

Yes. Trust, intimacy, synchrony. Just the two of us, tightly holding on to each other as our bodies molded together. There was no talking, not even eye contact—only our fingers entangled on his stomach—and yet it was the most intimate experience of my life.

"How about when I filled you up? Remember that feeling?"

Of course. It was my first time doing that, yet I know nothing will ever come close.

"Think we can get to that place again? Right now?"

I honestly don't know. We've done so much already, and through it all, he's looked nothing but pleased. Hungry for more. But if I showed him everything, and he didn't like what he saw, I wouldn't be able to take another chance on men again. On intimacy or love.

If seeing me naked makes him change his mind, I'll die.

"I-I'm . . ." He nods, and though I don't need to say it, I do anyway. "I'm afraid."

"I know. And I want—Jesus, I *need* to see you, but it doesn't matter. What *I* want doesn't matter, okay?" He lets the blanket go, his movements slow as if it's the hardest thing he's ever done. "What do *you* need? What do *you* want, Backpack?"

I study the hungry gaze in his eyes, the tension in his body. We trusted each other enough to ride together—with our lives. I trusted him with my body. I think I can trust him with my insecurities too.

"I want you to see," I whisper. He doesn't move, a silent 'Are you sure?' in his eyes. Only once I nod does he pull the blanket down, until it uncovers my chest, then my stomach. With every inch of skin revealed, his lips part more, his body growing stiffer until he yanks the blanket off my legs, and his eyes land on my pussy.

"Fuck," he says before passing a hand over his mouth. I study him—inspect him, even—trying to find any sign that he doesn't like my dips and curves, but he barely moves beside his shoulders, rising and falling with each breath.

"How—how do you feel?" I ask, fighting the instinct to cover up. "If you've changed your mind or—"

"I . . ." His hands grip the bed frame. "There's no blood in my brain. I can't, uh, think."

My cheeks are burning up, my skin sizzling, but his eyes keep bouncing over me as if he doesn't know what to look at first, and it makes me feel just a little bit more confident. Confident enough to roll my wrist and let out a low moan.

"What happens now, Barbie?" He licks his lips, his eyes briefly bouncing to my breasts as if he can't help himself, before running back to my face. "You set the pace. Tell me what you need."

"I want to see *you*."

One side of his lips turns up as he breathes hard. He doesn't say a word, but moves his hand to his zipper and confidently drags it down.

I click my tongue, pointing at his briefs. "Aw, too bad. In my fantasy, those are pink."

"You don't say." He jerks his chin forward. "In mine, the only pink on you is the pussy I'm about to fuck." He lifts his gaze off my pussy for a fraction of a second, then tugs his jeans down his legs. He rubs his cock, hard and pressed inside his briefs.

Crap, that's hot.

I can't take my eyes off his erection. Though I'm trying to keep Derek entirely out of my mind, the comparison is inevitable. It almost feels like a reward. As if some deity decided that after having to go through that terrible first time with Derek, I deserved an ample—*so* ample—reward. "What do *you* need?"

He cocks a brow at me. "I think you're missing the point of this."

"No, I'm not." He wants me to feel comfortable and have the best experience possible. But he should have one too. It's been a while for him, and though Derek was horrible to me, his ex was just as despicable.

Plus, this is Logan. He loves to have control.

He tilts his head, his tongue rimming his lips. "Fuck your pussy."

I show him two fingers, then fit them inside my mouth and swirl my tongue around them.

His lips part in response, breaths coming out heavy and quick. When I remove the two fingers and slide them inside, he gives his cock a tug, his hips jutting forward.

My wet pussy clamps around my fingers as if they're Logan's, and my lips as my eyelids flutter. I writhe against my hand, looking for relief. "Take your briefs off."

He does, his hand firmly tugging at his erection and pre-cum wetting his tip. Though I know how it feels inside me, this is my first time seeing it, and . . . wow. Never thought I'd refer to a penis this way, but "humbling" seems like a fitting description.

When I focus on his face, I notice he's studying mine. "Like what you see?"

Heat rises to my cheeks. I'm not even sure how *that* fit inside me today, but I'm not complaining. "Yes."

"Good." He strokes slowly, and it's better than I pictured. His muscles are tense with restraint, but his hands keep rushing and slowing down, his eyes darkening dangerously. "See how hard I am? It's all you. Your curves. Your pretty cunt."

A shiver runs through me, my fingers quickening.

"Open up. Let me see."

I shake my head, slowly fucking myself as moisture coats my fingers down to the knuckles. "Come closer first," I whisper.

My voice is needier than before, on the verge of breaking, and pleasure cruises through me harder and harder as he complies and reaches my side.

"On the bed?"

"Yes, please."

This time, it sounds more like a whimper and less like a teasing request. Whatever game we're playing, I think we're both losing.

Getting rid of his briefs, he climbs onto the bed, and though I expect him to stop, he advances until his knees rest between my thighs and the skin of our legs is in contact, his muscles so perfectly hard against my soft skin.

He inhales deeply and grips his cock again, so I pull my fingers out and open myself up. It's positively sinful to know he's staring at my pussy, all stretched out for him. "So wet, Barbie. Look at that."

"Yes," I whine. "For you, cowboy."

The heat emanating from his body is drawing me closer, and I don't think I can wait any longer to touch him, to kiss him and feel his calloused fingers on me. Before I can beg him to do something about it, he leans forward as if he lost the same battle.

Our lips meet, and breathing in the scent of nature, I distinctly feel time slow down, then stop. My arm circles his neck, and the world around us is forgotten as the kiss deepens, our tongues entwining in a synchronized dance.

With a grunt, he says my name, but it's unintelligible as I tease him with the tip of my tongue. Our bodies press tightly together, leaving me breathless as he squeezes my breast, then pinches my nipple.

I arch against his chest, my pussy rubbing over his cock.

"Oh, you feel so good." His eyelids are heavy as he leans forward and kisses my chest. "Look at you." His usual unbreakable expression is gone, replaced by a rushed, eager desire that pours pleasure into my stomach. "I'm going to suck those pretty tits better than you do that damn lollipop."

My fingers dig into his shoulder. All I can think of saying is *yes, please*, but I figure it's redundant. Except he doesn't move. "Logan?"

"Hm?"

"Did you freeze?"

He shakes his head, his eyes running down to my pussy. "I could stare at you forever."

I breathe out shakily.

"What now, Barbie? What do you need from me?"

"Uh . . ." I clench my legs at the numerous filthy thoughts crossing my mind. I'm too nervous to voice half of them, so I mumble the only thing I can. "Number, uh, twenty-four."

"Ah, of course." One corner of his lips lifts. "Go downtown."

Anticipation swirls in my stomach, a heady mix of excitement and nerves.

"Switch with me."

"Switch with you?"

"On top. Come," he says as he tugs at my arm.

He guides me on top of him until I'm hovering over his erection, and with my hands on his chest, I impatiently wait for what comes next.

"Sit on my face," he says as he tugs at my waist.

"Wait, what?"

"You heard me." He pulls me some more, and my hands land on either side of his face, my boobs bouncing over his mouth.

"How . . . I don't know how to do that."

"It's easy, Barbie," he says as he pulls himself up on one elbow and peppers my stomach with kisses. "You press your pretty cunt on my mouth"—his tongue tails along my hip—"and when my beard is drenched, you know you've done it well."

I shake my head, wordlessly expressing my confusion, and with a third pull, he hauls me to his chest until my hands grasp the headboard.

"Okay, okay," I rush to say in a breathy voice. I have a feeling if I don't comply, the next tug will drag me over his mouth, so I might as well do it on my terms.

"But—" My protest dies in my throat when he leans to the side and licks the soft skin of my inner thigh. Shivers break over my skin.

Fine. I'll admit it feels good.

Suddenly, I'm hovering over his face, shaking like a leaf in a windstorm, but he doesn't seem to notice I'm nervous, or maybe he doesn't mind, because he breathes out, "God, you smell so good," and hooks his arms under my knees, holding on to my hips.

What do I look like from his perspective? Will I smother him with my thighs?

The flat of his tongue swipes through me, and my breath catches, every single worry dissipating. When it dances around my clit, I gasp again and again as each flick gets my back to arch more.

"You taste even better than you smell," he murmurs against my skin, his voice hoarse as he squeezes my sides.

"Logan," I breathe out. A second deep stroke of his tongue has my thighs shaking on either side of his face. "Oh my god."

"Ride my face now, okay?"

"*Ride?* Ride how?" I throw a panicked look down at him. "What does that mean?"

"It means grab the headboard and yee-haw, Barbie."

When his mouth wraps around my clit and sucks, I let out a

crazed whimper. I squeal, my resistance to his pull dwindling until I'm fully seated on his face. "Can you even breathe?"

He ignores me, his lips teasing me with soft kisses and delicate flicks of his tongue. I bolt up every time, and he tightens the hold of my hips to keep me steady until soon, we find a rhythm. An intense rhythm that has me quivering and crying out his name.

"Please—please," I whimper, my eyes squinted as I look down at his hooded eyes. I need more. Much, much more. "It's too slow," I cry as I lose any inhibition and grip his thick brown hair in my fist, pulling it so that his tongue will reach deeper.

It doesn't help, so I throw my head back in frustration, then push my hips forward.

And *yee-haw*, does that feel good.

I think that's what he meant when he said *ride*.

I do it again, back and forth, over his mouth. Watching his want-filled eyes is hot enough that I need to focus on holding my orgasm back, especially when his tongue ripples in stronger waves against me as if rewarding me for following his instructions.

I reach for the headboard, and with my nails painfully digging into the wood, I chant, *"Fuck, fuck, fuck,"* lost in the rocking movement. The more he licks and sucks, the more I grind, until I'm sure he's wet with me all the way to his cheekbones.

He sucks greedily, drawing even more moisture from my core, and I writhe against him. I can't think, can't breathe, can't *anything*. "Oh, I'm gonna—" My back arches, my toes curling on either side of him, and with pulsating pleasure, I moan loud and hard as my thighs press the sides of his face. I tremble, any semblance of control lost, as my stomach tenses and releases.

"Logan, oh—wait, I—" My eyes roll backward as I let my forehead fall lightly against the wall and my orgasm ripples. I'm so sensitive, especially with his tongue still rubbing my clit with maniacal precision.

Wave after wave, I ride out every bit of my pleasure, and it moves through me and echoes in him, moaning against my pussy.

When my body relaxes, he doesn't relent, his tongue causing me to twitch. "Okay, cowboy, enough," I say with a tired, hoarse chuckle.

Reluctantly, he lets me go, helping me climb off his face and nestle further down. I tuck my forehead under his wet chin and catch my breath, the scorching heat turning into a softer kind of warmth, a cozy moment rather than a fiery, passionate one. It turns attraction into affection, lust into something much different. Something comfortable and familiar, yet unknown at the same time.

I look up at him, and his soft and content eyes meet mine. Like I'm the most precious thing he's ever had grinding on his face.

I reach my fingers up and rub them over his jaw, chuckling. "I did it."

"Hmm?"

"Your beard. It's drenched."

He tilts his face down, then pecks my forehead, and by the time he speaks, I can feel myself drifting off. "You did great for me, Barbie."

you're too easy to miss

. . .

Logan

"LOGAN, PLEASE, ENOUGH," she whines as she comes down from her orgasm. Her hand smacks my face, and when she almost shoves a finger in my eye, I rise over her and lick my lips.

Sweat trickles down her forehead, her damp hair stuck to the sides of her face. I lean down to kiss her, and she frowns against my lips. So fucking pretty.

"What is it, Barbie? Tired already?"

"*Already*?" she asks as I peck her jaw, then the curve of her neck. "What the hell are you made of, titanium?"

"Even harder than that." I free myself of her hold and kiss her chest.

"Logan, seriously, what's with all the foreplay?"

I snort against the sweaty skin of her shoulder. "Said no woman ever."

"It's been all morning—"

"Forty-five minutes."

"Forty-five minutes is a long time to go down on someone!" she squeals.

I guess, but it's not like we didn't take breaks. We kissed, we laughed, we chatted. Plus, last night, we collapsed, and I wanted to show her all the fun ways in which I can make her shake. Really, she's making it sound much more dramatic than it is.

"Your jaw must hurt," she says as her fingers brush over my beard.

"I like eating your cunt, Barbie. Is that a bad thing?"

"No." Her fingertips massage my scalp. "But I think there's a line between liking and obsessing, and we crossed it ten minutes ago."

"Okay." I kiss her chest, making my way to her left tit. "Then I'm obsessed." I wrap my mouth around her small, pink nipple and suck. "With your taste." I let it go with a loud *pop*. "With you."

She breathes out, eyes shuttering. "You can go down on me whenever you want, Logan."

I lean down, but she grips my shoulders. "Later. Not right now." She gently pushes my chest until my back is on the mattress. "Now, let's try something else, okay?"

Watching her straddle me, I swallow. She's so gorgeous. I can't decide if she looks better like this, all disheveled, or when she's dressed to the nines.

I think I like every version of her.

"I hope you're ready for some moderate fun," she says as she leans down, her tits pressing against my chest as she hovers on my lips. "It would have been 'exceptional fun' two orgasms ago, but my muscles hurt now."

"Love it when you talk dirty."

She laughs, her hand cupping my cheek before she leans forward.

Her lips press on mine, and knowing she can taste herself on my tongue is driving me insane. My hands find her hips as my tongue swipes against hers, warm and wet and tasting like summer.

"Hmm," I moan into her mouth when she grinds over my cock, drenching me as she slides over. My balls tighten, an orgasm threatening to spill, and I try to focus on something else. Anything else. But then she does it again, and the only thing I can think of is the fact that she's wetting my cock. That she's so soft and warm. That I need to be inside her, and I need to come, and I need *her*.

She rises to her knees, and my dick throbs in anticipation. A shiver racks through me when she wraps her hand around it, then dips the tip in. I can't breathe. Can't move. Can't even look at her, because everything is so perfect, and I'm about to feel her cunt again.

Then there's a knock at the front door, and she freezes, wide eyes staring into mine.

Fuck. No.

"Ignore it," I say as I grip her hip. My cock sinks a little deeper inside her, and I groan. "I need you to ride my cock, little backpack."

"What if it's an emergency?" she whispers, her eyes closing as she lowers herself more.

"Unless it's a bomb, it'll wait until this afternoon."

There's another knock at the door, and she lifts off me with a sigh.

I want to die.

With a sigh, she pulls the blanket over herself. "Come on, cowboy."

"Fine, goddamnit." I stand and fit into my clothes. Whoever is on the other side of that door better have a good reason to be here, or I'll punch them in the stomach. "Don't you dare get dressed."

"I would never," she purrs.

I walk out of the room, but not before sparing her another look. My chest warms as I watch her head settle on my pillow, her blonde and pink hair ruffled, her eyes gleaming, and her smile full.

With a decisive step, I walk through the house and swing the door open.

"So you *are* sleeping with her," Aaron mumbles as he looks down at the open zip of my jeans. "Didn't see that coming."

Of course. It *had* to be Aaron.

"I'd show you proof, but I don't give a single fuck about what you believe."

His severe gaze meets mine as he fits his hands into the pocket of his gray suit, and I could barf. We used to make fun of corporate idiots, and now he's one of them. With his tailor, expensive aftershave, and hair pulled back with gel. It's ridiculous, and it's not Aaron. "Look, I'm here because . . ."

He looks down at his feet, and my blood pressure rises as my fists clench. "What?" I bark. "Are you pausing for effect?"

As he glances up at me, his throat works hard. For a moment, he seems to be deciding if what he wants to say is worth mentioning, and an uncomfortable tingling moves up my spine.

His shoulders drop, and with a sigh, he takes his hand out of his pocket, holding his checkbook. "Tell me how much you need."

"I'm not taking any money from you," I say flatly. I'm pretty sure this isn't why he's here, but it works just fine for me. Whatever gets him to leave faster.

"Logan, this is our family farm. Set aside your feelings about me for once, and please think about Mom. Think about yourself. Your life, your work." He steps forward, then scribbles in his checkbook. "Just take this. And next week, I can come over. We can figure out a plan to make it work. Maybe not one hundred percent vegan farming, but—"

As soon as he holds the check out, I grab it, rip it apart, and set it in his hand. "Good enough for you?"

He laughs, his lips bending bitterly. "Always the same Logan. Act first, think later. No matter who pays the consequences, right? Fuck everyone else."

I give him a shrug. "All I can say with confidence is fuck *you*. Now, if you don't mind, I was obviously busy."

I push the door to close it because, truth be told, I couldn't care less if he *does* mind. There's a woman in here I intend to do terrible, *terrible* things to.

Aaron holds his hand up. "Logan, wait."

There's an edge to his voice—something that feels a lot like desperation—and for that reason only, I open the door again, meeting his distraught expression.

"The farm isn't the reason why I'm here. Not—not the only reason." He can't even look at me, his eyes stuck on the floor as he mumbles, "I can't find . . . Josie."

A shiver runs down my spine. "The fuck does that mean?"

"She called in sick at work, picked up Sadie and went home. Then she called the babysitter, and she just . . . left."

"When was this?"

"Three hours ago."

I roll my eyes, exhaling in relief. "Good god, Aaron. She's probably running errands or grabbing a drink with a friend."

"The babysitter said Josie ran out without a word the second she arrived. That she was visibly upset."

Okay, well . . . that's weird. "Did you try her parents' place?"

"On my way here. They haven't seen her."

"I haven't either. Not since I went to the station yesterday."

He rubs his forehead, and now that I'm paying attention, he looks like shit. His gaze is weary, heavy in a way that wasn't there before. It's a sobering realization, witnessing the toll that life has taken on my brother and not knowing what caused it. We're strangers now.

"Aaron, what's going on with you and Josie?"

He shrugs but doesn't meet my gaze. "I better go. I'll give you a call once I find her."

There's a chasm forming between my mind and my gut. On one side, an eager want pulls me toward Primrose, back home, whispering promises that are hard to resist. And on the other, Aaron. He's an asshole, but a duty that tugs at my conscience. I love Josie, and Aaron is still my brother.

"Wait," I call. He stops, and by the time he turns around, I'm already slipping my boots on. "Let's go."

"What about Primrose?"

"I'll call her from the car." I advance toward his gray BMW—

pretentious, like everything he's taken up in the last five years of his life.

"You don't have to come with me," Aaron says as he reaches the driver's side. Our eyes meet over the car's hood, and for a moment, I don't say anything.

I know I don't have to go with him—in fact, he doesn't deserve it. But I will anyway, because he's my brother. Because he was my best friend for most of our lives, and that's not something you forget. It just stays there, stabbing you with pain and sometimes dragging you away from the woman you want to sleep with.

"I'm not doing it for you," I say as I open the car door. "This changes absolutely nothing between us."

"Okay, I'll see you soon," I say into Aaron's phone.

"Yeah, please keep me updated."

I close my eyes, letting Primrose's voice wash over me as the car struggles over the uneven terrain back to the city, my body wobbling from left to right. "I will. If you need to reach me, Aaron's phone number is in the black notebook next to the phone, okay?"

"I've been alone before, you know?" she sing-songs.

"Stop being yourself for a minute," I grumble.

"Why? Do you miss me too much?"

"Yes."

She sighs softly, the rattling almost comforting against my ear. "Help out Josie and Aaron. Then come back so you can show me how much you missed me."

I smile, quickly using my hand to hide it. "Yeah, deal."

"I'll see you later."

I hang up, then set my brother's phone on his dashboard stand. I'm not sure where we're going, but he's her husband, so he must have a better idea of where she usually hangs out than me.

We drive in silence for a while, my mind switching between worry over Josie and obscene thoughts of Primrose. I can still taste her. Still smell her. Still see the way she grinded on my face until she was screaming my name.

"So, how long has this been going on?"

With my daydreaming rudely interrupted, I glance at Aaron, whose eyes bounce my way before returning to the road.

"And don't try to sell me the story you gave Josie."

He's not serious, is he? He can't possibly think I'll discuss my life with him. "Unless you're up for brushing my hair, I'm afraid I'm not spilling my heart to you."

"Is it a serious thing? Just physical?"

I exhale, shifting position on the seat, and after a few minutes of silence, I ask, "Where are we going?"

"I have no idea. I'm just driving to Roseberg, but . . . no clue."

Great. I guess I forgot to account for my brother being a shitty husband too. He probably has no idea where she hangs out. "Who has she been spending time with lately?"

He shrugs, and it's tough not to smack him in the face. Josie deserves better than this. She deserves someone who knows her. Someone who cares. Aaron? He only cares about himself.

"Don't you think you should know this shit? Know what her routine is, and who her friends are, and—"

"Josie works part-time three days a week, including today. Usually, she picks Sadie up from school on her way home, then cooks dinner. She and Sadie spend the afternoon together—if it's sunny, at the park on Merrilord Street. If it's raining, she either tries to set up a playdate or they hang out at home. Draw, watch cartoons, read. We have dinner together when I'm home from work, and then . . ." He swallows. "And then I try to get her to do something with me. Go on a date somewhere, or stay in and watch a movie. I get her flowers or chocolates. Usually, the answer is no, which is either met with resignation or, sometimes . . ."

I look down, uncomfortable. "Sometimes?"

"Frustration." He doesn't sound proud of it, which I can relate to. "Either way, she doesn't spend time with anyone. Her life pretty much revolves around Sadie and avoiding me." He rests one elbow on the window, tugging at the root of his hair. "You think I don't give a shit, but you're wrong. That's hardly our problem."

Or that's exactly what someone like Aaron would say. Deflect and hang the blame on her rather than take responsibility for his actions. "Okay," I say, barely hiding my sarcasm. "Then what's the problem? Why is she drinking herself numb, and what are you doing about it?"

"What am *I* doing about it?"

"Yes, you. You're her husband, and she's clearly developed a drinking habit."

He shakes his head, chewing on his nails. I haven't seen him do that since he was a kid. "It's not . . . She doesn't even drink at home, you know? It's only when she's stressed, or . . ."

"Aaron," I scold. "That's a bullshit excuse, and you know it."

"How's it different from you smoking weed when you can't sleep?"

"It's different because I don't smoke weed until I stumble to the floor. I don't make a scene in front of a crowd of people because of weed. I don't up and vanish. *And* I'm not a police officer."

"She doesn't drink on the job," he barks.

I don't see how he can be sure of that since, by the sound of it, she doesn't share a whole lot about her life with him. "Even if that's true, I doubt they'd let her keep her job if they found out."

He doesn't say a word, but his teary gaze is like a punch in the guts when I look his way. I've only seen Aaron cry once when he was twelve, and some kid broke his skateboard. He didn't cry because of the skateboard—that happened later, when Mom grounded me for smacking that kid in the face.

"Yesterday," I mumble.

He turns to me, brows bent over his eyes. "What?"

"Primrose and I started sleeping together yesterday."

"Oh." He sniffles, his lips bending up. "Shit. I *really* interrupted you."

"Yes, you did." I look out the window. "And you wonder why I hate you."

"No, I know exactly why you hate me, Logan."

Shifting in my seat, I stick to silence.

"So, did you tell Primrose? What happened between us?"

"Parts of it," I mumble.

"Hmm." He rubs a hand on his jaw. "Why not all of it?"

What a question. I didn't tell her all of it because it's humiliating, that's why. Because it's too painful to talk about.

"You think it's a smart choice?"

"I don't know," I snap. "Was what you did a smart choice?"

Neither of us says anything for a while, until he parks in front of a small building and takes his phone out. "There's this one bakery Josie likes. I can't remember the address."

"What's it called?" I ask, checking the time. Businesses will close soon for lunch, so we'll have to rush.

"Desserts for—"

"Stressed People? Yeah, they're my clients." I point ahead. "Keep going another five minutes; it's next to that small square with the horse fountain."

He pulls away from the curb, and we silently head toward the square. I'm not going to let this one small interaction with Aaron change my mind about everything, but I guess I could admit to being partially wrong. I figured he was a shitty husband because he's always working, and Josie does everything by herself. But maybe that's what she wants, and the situation isn't as straightforward as I assumed. Maybe her drinking isn't on him.

But he's right. Not telling Primrose the whole truth immediately was a stupid choice. She needs to know the whole story—today. No matter how hard it is to bring it up.

"Do you think it'll lead to something more? You and Primrose sleeping together?"

"What kind of dumb-ass question is that," I mutter. "What are you, a teenager?"

"Jesus, Logan. Do you have feelings for her or not?"

"You still sound like a teenager."

He rolls his eyes. "Right. Because admitting you feel things is so immature. Real men only grunt their approval." With a shrug, he asks, "Do you know how she feels?"

Not really. She likes me and wants to sleep with me, but we hardly had time for that, let alone discuss what will happen when she leaves in four days.

All I know is that despite all the reasons I've given her, she hasn't turned her back on me yet. Despite how hard it is to be around me, she makes it look easy. But I also know better than to expect things from people, because people disappoint, just as Aaron himself has shown me on more than one occasion.

"She's leaving soon. She has her own life; it's not like she'll drop it all for me."

"You wouldn't go with her?"

I scoff. Me in Mayfield. I couldn't think of a worse recipe for happiness than throwing myself into a maze of concrete and skyscrapers. "No, of course not." And besides, it's not like she'd want me to go anywhere with her. "You heard the part where I said this started yesterday, right?"

He shrugs. "Sometimes, one day is enough to know you want to be with someone."

I wonder if he's talking about Josie, but I have no intention of asking, especially because we're here, on the opposite side of the square where the bakery is. "There it is."

I remove my seatbelt and open the door.

"Thank you," Aaron mumbles. "For trusting me with the truth about her."

Trusting him? As if. "The only reason I told you is because

even if you tell Josie, you can't prove it." I get out of the car, and before slamming the door behind me, I mutter, "I'll never make the mistake of trusting you again."

apologize after a mistake

...

Primrose

A KNOCK at the door has my chest fluttering. Could it be Logan? He said he'd keep me updated, but maybe he just came straight home.

I stand and walk to the door, my heart drumming. I don't even care what we'll end up doing today. I want us to lie down in bed and exist. I want us to chat and touch each other, and I want him to look at me the way he did tonight. So I straighten my dress as if the goal isn't to have him rip it off me as soon as possible, then open the door.

My gaze meets Josie's cloudy, unfocused green eyes, her frown turning into an excited grin as she takes me in.

"Prim!" she squeals, stepping forward and immediately tumbling against me in a cloud of rancid-smelling liquor.

She's drunk. Again.

"Hey, Josie. What are you doing here? Did you drive?"

"No, of course not! I took an Uber!"

"Oka—" She wobbles past me, holding onto the jackets at the entrance and pulling Logan's to the floor. "Careful—let me help you."

"I'm sorry," she whines. She throws her head back, groaning

loudly. "I like you so much, Prim, but I have to do this. You get it, right? Do you get it?"

"Uh . . . yes?"

"If I don't, I'll regret it for the rest of my life."

What the hell is she talking about? Is this about the case?

I close the door behind her as she nearly trips over the couch. "Wait," I call as she darts into the corridor. Once I hear the bedroom door open, I groan into my hands.

The piglets.

Lola trots over and throws herself at my feet. I don't know how, but I know she's telling me Josie disturbed her nap, and could I please get her the fuck out of here?

"I'm sorry," I whisper, leaning down to cuddle her. I can only hope Josie is too drunk to remember this tomorrow. Or, I guess, that her testimony won't count. I rub under Lola's chin, and her lips stretch as if smiling. "We'll need to be patient tonight, okay? She's . . . going through a rough patch."

Lola keeps looking at me, her black eyes sparkling with gratitude, and with a sigh, I walk to the phone and pick up the receiver.

I open the notebook, look up Aaron's number, and dial. As the line rings, I think about the last time I saw Josie. I've witnessed her *this* drunk on three separate occasions now. It can't be by chance, and someone needs to help her.

"Hello?" Logan's voice answers.

"Hey. Guess who showed up here?"

"Oh, thank god. Is she okay? Did she say what happened?"

"She just got here," I explain. "I figured you should know immediately. But I'm not sure she's in the right condition to talk."

"Is she . . .?"

I squeeze my eyes shut and shake my head. "Drunk, yes."

There's a long silence, then, "Give us twenty minutes."

"Logan?"

"Yeah."

"She said . . . she said she has to do something. That if she doesn't, she'll regret it for the rest of her life."

There's a moment of silence, then, "Okay."

"Do you have any idea what she's talking about?"

"Uh, yes. I think I do."

Goosebumps spread across my skin, an ominous feeling settling in my chest.

Logan is a private guy. Closed-off, distrustful, and despite everything we've been through together, we only met thirteen days ago. He needs more than that to open up completely, and I'm sure whatever *this* is about, it's not as bad as I'm picturing. I'm sure he had his reasons not to share.

"Do you think . . . you're ready to tell me?"

"Yes. Yes, I am. As soon as we get home, okay? We'll sort Josie and Aaron out, then we'll talk."

See? Nothing to freak out about. He wants to talk and open up; he just needs time. Though we only have four days left, I'll give him all the time I can get my hands on.

"Okay. See you soon."

I walk into the corridor, only to notice the light in Logan's bedroom is on. Josie is lying on his bed, her head hanging off the mattress and her body thrown across it. Her red hair, usually smooth, is now a messy nest over her head, and there's a little drool on her chin.

She's okay, but I'm not sure she's *okay*.

I fill a glass of water and walk it back to the bedroom, my body tense in a weird way after the conversation with Logan. No matter how much I try to convince myself that it isn't a big deal and that we'll talk things through, there's a heavy sense of worry hanging in the air around me.

"Hey," I say as I gently shake her shoulder. When that doesn't work, I try again with a firmer grip. "Hey, Josie?"

She blinks at me, her eyes glossy and tired. Pulling herself to a seated position, she looks around and mumbles, "I don't want to go home."

"That's okay. You don't have to." I help prop her against the pillow, then give her the glass. "Drink this, it'll help."

She slowly brings it to her lips. "Is Logan angry at me?"

"Of course not." I don't think so, at least. "He and Aaron are just worried about you. Why did you leave the house like that?"

She looks into my eyes, chin wobbling, and she shakes her head when a tear falls down her cheek. "Because some days, I hate it."

With a sigh, I sit on the edge of the bed. I knew something was off between her and Aaron, and after the scene at Logan's parents' house, this doesn't come as shocking news.

"Do you know what it's like to be with someone you don't love?"

My eyes widen, and I shake my head, trying to contain my surprise. "No, I don't."

One of her fingers brushes the rim of the glass. "We're both so unhappy, and the only reason we're together is Sadie. Which means that on the awful days, I regret having her." She brushes the sleeve of her cardigan over her cheek, a small sob making her shake as she tucks a frizzy lock of hair behind her ear. "And then I feel like a horrible mother, because she's the best . . . the best . . ."

"Shh." I cup her knee, trying to soothe her. "Josie, you're not a horrible mother. It's normal to wonder what-if, and if things with you and Aaron have been rocky, then . . . then I guess it makes even more sense."

"I messed up so bad," she says, voice quivering as if her pain is bleeding through her words. "All of this is my fault, and I can't do anything to fix it."

I exhale, my heart squeezing for her. I know so little about relationships, and I'm not the right person to give marriage advice, but I *do* know that a child isn't enough to keep a couple together. "My parents are divorced," I say as I fold my legs behind me. "And I remember how it was before they broke up—the fighting, the tension. My mom always says it was the best decision she and my dad could have ever made."

Josie looks up at me, tears streaming down her cheeks.

"They're on friendly terms too. We don't spend many holidays together because they live on opposite sides of the country, but when they meet at big family events, they chat like old friends." I shrug. "Of course, it's not ideal. A child always wants their parents together. But what they want more than that is two happy, healthy parents who can care for them."

Deep in thought, she bites her bottom lip and looks slightly calmer.

"If you don't want to go back home, you can stay here." Look at me, offering people a place to sleep in a house that isn't mine. "I'm sure Logan wouldn't mind."

With a slow nod, she whispers, "Do you think he'll turn me down?"

My mouth opens, then closes. Turn her down? As in . . . "You—you plan to . . .what do you want to tell Logan exactly?"

"That I love him." Tears well up in her eyes as she turns to face me, her words echoing through the room like a thunderclap and shattering the fragile peace of the night.

She's . . . in love with Logan. Josie. But she's married to his *brother*.

Suddenly, everything makes sense. From how she reacted that first night when she found Logan and me in the backyard to her sour comment about us as a couple when we went for dinner at her place. The scene she made at the barbecue when Logan and I were taking pictures, and even every single time she's told me how much she likes me.

She feels guilty because she's in love with my boyfriend.

My *fake* boyfriend.

"Do you hate me?"

I watch her blotchy, tear-streaked face and shake my head. Though my heart is pounding, I can't be mad at her when she's hurting this much. When her secret and her feelings are turning her into a drunk. What I am, honestly, is scared. Does Logan know? Is that the secret he's kept from me?

What if he doesn't know? Maybe this will change everything for him. Maybe he'll ask me to leave.

"How about you get some sleep, huh?" I say as I pat the pillow.

"No—no." She pulls herself up, her chest heaving. "I need to talk to Logan. I—"

"I'll wake you up once he's here, don't worry."

She shakes her head but struggles to keep her eyes open. "No, you're just trying to keep me from talking to him."

"I promise," I insist as I cup her shoulder. "I'll wake you up."

She nods, then slowly lies down. "You know what I miss the most?"

"What?" I ask distractedly as I tuck the blanket over her. I want to remove myself from this situation until Logan is back and I can talk to him.

"Riding bitch on his bike." She bursts out laughing as if she's just said the funniest joke, but my lips bend down. "And the sex, of course. The crawling and chasing and choking . . ." She half-laughs and half-cries. "You know what he's like."

A lump the size of an orange lodges in my throat as I think of the way I described Logan's type: tall, skinny, with smile lines, long legs, and strong arms. She's a woman who's beautiful without makeup, or in this case, drunk out of her mind.

Josie.

Is she . . . Logan's ex?

The door opens, then Logan and Aaron burst into the house, their steps echoing in the silence.

"Primrose?" Logan calls from the living room, and with a sigh, I glance over my shoulder at Josie, asleep. I haven't moved away from her side, afraid she'd vomit in her sleep, but I can't wait for someone else to be here.

My thoughts are incoherent, every piece of the lie forming a bigger picture.

Honestly, I don't know how I missed it.

Logan said he and Aaron were already on bad terms when his brother gave their relationship the final hit by pulling out of the work at the farm. And, of course, there's what he told me about his ex. How she's still with the guy she cheated with.

But I also remember what he said about their breakup. How he wanted to be with her, and she was the one to end it.

Since then, he's been single, and I assumed he'd kept away from women because of the break of trust he'd suffered, but maybe I was wrong. Maybe he's been single all this time because he's in love with Josie.

It would explain why he's so angry at Aaron, but not at her.

"Hey. Are you okay?" Logan asks as he enters the room. He kneels in front of me, chest rising and dropping quickly as Aaron circles the bed so he can tend to Josie.

"Primrose?" he insists when I flinch at the contact of his fingers on my skin.

"Who's your ex, Logan?"

I look up at him, and he's wide-eyed, watching me. "Did...uh, did Josie..."

"Yeah, she did. It was a matter of time. Wasn't it?" I ask, my voice barely a whisper. "She's drunk half of the time, and the other half, she's questioning me. But you didn't think I should know that?" When he lowers his gaze, I insist, "Why didn't you tell me, Logan?"

He can't bring himself to look into my eyes. It's a visceral sensation, like a knife plunged into my back, severing the trust I placed in Logan and leaving behind a gaping wound that refuses to heal. Every word, smile, and touch shared between us now feels tainted, poisoned by deceit and omitted truths.

"Barbie, wait," he says as I stand, and he jumps to his feet. "Please."

"Just tell me if you lied to me. If you made me think it was real when it was not."

"Of course, it's real."

My mind races with questions, doubts, and fears, each more painful than the last. Why didn't he tell me? Why can't he say something now?

He trails carefully behind me as I enter the guest room, and once I grab my backpack and begin shoving stuff inside, he whispers, "Barbie . . ."

My chest heaves as I face him, arms folded like a shield. "Are you in love with her?"

He swallows, then opens his mouth without a sound.

Not a single word.

"God," I whine as I turn around and zip my bag.

"I'm not in love with her," he says, and it sounds as if he's surprised himself.

Tears blur my vision as I struggle to make sense of the chaos raging inside me, the pain of his betrayal like a vice around my heart. "Really?" I ask, my voice quivering. "Then what was that full minute of hesitation?"

"I wasn't hesitating." He wipes his mouth with the palm of his hand, his back hunching as if pain is preventing him from standing straight. "Look, let's sit down and talk about this. You have nowhere to go, and—"

"I survived twenty-five years without your help," I cut through. "I'll be okay."

Anger surges through me like a tidal wave, fueling my every step as I march toward the door, my mind made up. I can't stay here—not when everything I thought I knew about us has been ripped away from me in an instant.

He blocks my access to the door, holding his hands up. He's as white as a sheet, and his panic attacks come back to me in a hazy blur. He looks even more desperate than he did then. Even more hopeless. "Just—wait, okay? I'll explain everything, I promise."

"What, Logan? You'll explain I was your second choice? The

one you had to settle for since Josie is taken?" I try to push him away, but he barely flinches. "Move."

His head shakes, his eyes closing as if he's fighting with his brain, trying to convince his mouth to let go of the words trapped in it.

"You finally found it, huh?"

My brows bend. "What?"

"The reason to believe I'm not into you. That I must have been lying all along." My ears are ringing, the slash in my chest bleeding with each of his words. "It's impossible to believe someone would be with you because they like you, right? Because they want you," he blurts. "And now you've found my real motive."

Unbelievable. *He* lies, but I'm the one at fault?

"Right. *I* fucked up." I hike my backpack higher up my shoulder. "You're unbelievable. Get out of my way."

"That's not . . .Shit, that's not what I'm saying, okay? I should have been honest. But I said we'd talk about it, and you *know* this has nothing to do with me being in love with her."

"Then what is it about?"

"About me being a mess, Primrose!" He shouts. He pulls his hair at the roots, his shoulders rolling forward. "I'm broken. I can't communicate, can't express my feelings. I only have anger—just blinding, exhausting fury. And then you came along and made everything else turn silent." He lowers his voice. "But I'm not your perfect guy with crayons and a white horse. I'm just some idiot who's worth so little, my own brother and girlfriend left me behind."

Bullshit. He could have been the perfect guy with crayons and a white horse. Hell, I didn't even need him to be that, but he was. He's gone through item after item on my list, and he made me believe it mattered. That *I* mattered.

"I'm not doing this." I sneak past him, and he moves out of the way before the door hits him on the ass.

"I know I should have told you already. I planned to, but if I did, we would have never . . ."

My eyes widen. "Never . . . Never slept together?"

"Yes," he confirms, and when he notices my wide eyes and parted lips, he shakes his head. "No, I—shit, that's not what I mean."

With a groan, I walk away, down the steps and onto the gravel.

Logan is a good person—deep down, I know it. But right now, he feels a whole lot like Derek. Like he used me. Like I'm his second choice, and if he was supposed to settle for someone he didn't love, he might as well go with the readily available girl. Delivered right to his front step.

"Primrose, stay. If you need space, I'll go, okay? I'll stay with Simon. But please—"

"No, Logan. No."

"Then let me drive you to a hotel. I'll get you a room, and—"

I flip around and stare at him, all my anger dangerously close to the surface. "You know, at first I thought that you and your brother . . . That it was a sibling thing. Then I thought that maybe you were right about him being a terrible person, and I couldn't see it. Never once did I consider that you were pissed off because she chose him over you."

"That's not what happened."

"Then what happened?"

"He stole her from me."

I look in the distance, unable to process my emotions. "It's funny."

"What is?" he asks, his hand reaching forward to touch me before I duck back.

"How you can't say a word when it comes to us. You stare at me with that scared, confused expression of someone who's been busted. You don't find the words, you don't fight for us." A sob racks my body. "But when it comes to her, there's not a moment of hesitation."

He takes a step closer, reaching for my face, but I again move away. The last thing I want is for him to touch me. I'll never forget how it feels to be touched by Logan Coleman.

"She's lucky," I say softly. She'll tell him she loves him sometime soon, and then have him for herself. And Logan is so good in so many ways. He cares so viscerally, like it's an instinct he can't turn off no matter how hard he tries. They'll be so happy.

"What, because she chose him?"

I laugh, but it carries no amusement. "No. She's lucky to have someone who loves her this much."

He shakes his head, his hand reaching for me once more. "Please," he chokes out.

"Bye, Logan."

I walk, phone in hand, to call an Uber. I need to step away from this situation and, most of all, from him. If I stay, I'm afraid I'll let him convince me. I'll believe that he didn't tell me because of his own issues, and not because of how he feels about Josie. Then it'll hurt again when she tells him there's still a chance for them to be together.

No. I'm out of here.

I'm done looking like a fool.

you're worth losing everything for

. . .

Logan

"WHAT IS WRONG WITH YOU?" Aaron asks as he joins my side. "Go after her."

Shoulders dropping, I watch Primrose disappear at the bottom of the driveway.

I knew it was just a matter of time before I fucked up. Before the reclusive, closed-off, anxious part of me would get her to throw in the towel.

This is it. Once again, I'm a letdown, and even someone as patient and loving as Primrose can't deal with it. Eventually, they all leave, because I can't open up. I can't face those ugly emotions that have kept me submerged in darkness for so long. Not even with Primrose, who's all light and fresh air.

"Logan? Do something, for fuck's sake."

Aaron's voice feels distant, my heartbeat deafening to the point where I can't hear anything else. Only my heartbeat and Primrose's disappointed voice.

Why didn't I tell her before? Yes, it's humiliating, but it's not like she hasn't seen me at my worst, weeping during my panic attacks. Why wasn't I honest from the beginning?

I can't follow her. What for? Whenever it's time to speak, I freeze. I look at her like some mindless idiot instead of pouring everything out like I should.

She's right to leave. God, she'd be stupid if she didn't.

And if I can't fight for her, then I don't deserve her.

"Will you react, Logan?" Aaron insists, grasping my shirt in his fist.

As I slump forward, my eyes finally meet his, and swallowing hard, he relents. I might need time to react, but he knows me well enough to imagine what will happen once I do.

Nobody puts their hands on me, *especially* not Aaron.

I pull my arm back and crash my fist against his eye, the crunching sound carried away in the spring breeze. With a groan, he goes slamming against the doorframe before sliding down to the porch.

He grimaces, then touches the abrasion under his eye. My heart is pumping blood in my veins faster than it should, and honestly, what people say about revenge is bullshit. It feels great.

"Five long years overdue," I grit out.

Gently moving his facial muscles, he nods and holds his hand out. "Is my debt paid now? Can you help me up?"

Fuck him. He's not fighting me back because he has no ground to stand on. Because he messed up, and he knows he deserves it. But he also didn't do anything tonight. He came here asking for help—hell, he's probably worried about his drunk wife.

And I *need* him to fight me.

I need to focus my anger on him.

"Get up yourself."

He stands one tentative step at a time, then keeps his good eye on me as he holds a hand over the injured side of his face. "So, are we finally doing this?"

"Yeah, we are."

"Good. Then let's sit down."

Sit down? "No, asshole. I don't want to *talk* to you."

"Fight me? That's what you want to do?"

My fists clench beside me, and with a scoff, he walks to the steps and sits. He runs a hand through his hair, his chest heaving as he grimaces. "You think I don't know how badly I messed up, Logan? I didn't just lose my brother. My relationship and marriage were cursed from the start because of what I did."

"I don't care," I growl.

"I know that too. You will never forgive me for stealing her from you. And she will never forgive me for taking advantage of a moment of weakness and ruining her relationship."

I open my mouth to quip back, but once I register his words, I shut it.

Why would *Josie* blame him? She went along with it—hell, she chose him when I begged her to stay. Aaron didn't make her do any of it.

"What? You think she doesn't blame me for it? Because she does. She hates me. Mom hates me. Kyle and Simon and you—" He holds a fist over his mouth. "It's only a matter of time before my own daughter picks up on it and I become the villain in her story too."

Fuck that.

Fuck *him*.

Why should I care? *He* did it. Nobody pointed a gun at his head and told him to screw my girlfriend. It was his choice, and now he'll pay the consequences for it.

"You think I don't hate myself, Logan?" He huffs out a joyless laugh as he rests his forehead on his fist. "But I love her. I've loved her for as long as I can remember, and I tried so hard to be the guy she'd fall for."

My jaw clicks. "No, you didn't."

"Yes, Logan. Yes. I introduced you two, remember?" He leans back, shoulders deflating as if he's been carrying the weight of this conversation for a long time. "She was my classmate's cousin. And I'd always see her at his place and thought she was so pretty. Until eventually I asked him to introduce us."

Right. Carl something. I'd forgotten about him. But this hardly changes anything.

"Why didn't you tell me?" I ask. "If you were in love with her, why didn't you say something when we started dating?"

"Why didn't a teenager tell his younger brother he liked a girl who didn't like him back?" He scoffs. "I didn't tell anyone. And then one day, I saw the two of you making out in the parking lot, and I knew I'd missed my chance."

He shakes his head, gesturing at me. "When shit went south between the two of you, I watched her be unhappy for months. You were immature, and she was a woman, and I..."

"You thought you were better than me," I finish.

He pauses, eyes burning into mine, then nods. "Yes. I thought I was better than you—*for her*. And I thought one day the two of you would break up, and I'd still never get my chance because I'm your brother."

I look away, because though I wish I'd known about all of this, it hardly wins me over. He doesn't get my sympathy, because there's a key difference in our situations. I had no idea he was into Josie, while I'd made no secret of my feelings. We'd been together for half a decade when he swooped in. I would have never chosen a girlfriend over him.

He broke me, fully aware of what he was doing.

"I'm an asshole," he says as he throws his arms up. "I betrayed you in the worst way possible. I fucked up, and I have no excuse."

No, he doesn't.

So what if he had feelings for her? If Josie and I weren't a good match? None of it matters. He's my brother, and he was my best friend, and that should have trumped anything else.

"I understand that you'll never forgive me, and there's nothing I can do about it." He drops his head in his hands. "I knew it the second I slept with her. But I wanted to make at least a good life for myself, Josie, *Sadie*. Make sure that all of it... that it was for something."

"Are you talking about that shitty job?"

He nods, looking in the distance. "But nothing will ever work. There isn't enough money to compensate for what's missing from our lives."

"What's that?" When he sniffles, the adrenaline and anger subside, and heartbreak takes over. Primrose's face filled with disappointment haunts me like a ghost, my stomach twisting as I picture her walking away.

What if it's my last memory of her?

"Love," he says coldly, dragging his foot over the gravel. "She doesn't love me. She will always love you, and I'll always be the one who broke the two of you apart."

My jaw slacks open, and quickly collecting myself, I watch him take something out of his pocket.

"We're divorcing."

Wait, what? Did I hear that right?

He takes out a paper. Once it's in my hands, he adds, "Just a copy. The original is already with the lawyers."

Divorce papers. I can't believe this.

I give them back, but my head is spinning with the overload of emotions, and I reluctantly sit beside him.

I've wanted them to break up for years, while hating myself for it. I yearned to see Aaron lose everything, then felt like shit because if he did, so would Sadie, and I never wanted *her* to suffer.

Now that it's happening, I don't feel anything but pain.

"You're a better man than me. You've always been. You're loyal, generous, strong." He slides the paper back into his jacket. "I'm sorry it took me so long to see it."

I rub my forehead, looking away. I can't forgive him—not when it took him thirty-five years to learn what Primrose understood in two weeks. "If you think this fixes anything . . ."

"No, I know." He releases a deep breath. "Divorcing Josie will not fix a single thing between me and you. And helping you with the farm won't do that either." He takes out his checkbook. "I'm not buying your forgiveness, Logan."

He scribbles on the check and hands it over. "I just want you to be happy—you and Josie—because I . . ." He looks down. "I love you both."

It's a little harder to hate him, knowing he and his family are going through what is probably the hardest time of their lives, but I'll manage.

"This money is yours. We always planned to invest it in the farm, and I left you high and dry." His eyes close for a long moment. "Spend it or not—the farm is yours. But so is the money."

I think of all the guys working at the farm and all the rescues living here. Though I wish I could throw the money at his face, I'm not willing to play with the fate of my farm. Of my friends and family.

We might make it without ever cashing this check, or we might need it eventually, but I'll take it. It's time I swallow my pride.

"Thank you," I say as I hold his gaze.

For a moment, he seems surprised, his eyebrows arching. "Wow . . . this Primrose did a number on you, didn't she?"

My tongue feels too heavy for my mouth, my head too light, my heart shattered. Now that he's mentioned her, I want to hit something again. I want to smash my fist against the wall, over and over again, until the pain is stronger than the regret.

For some reason, one of our first conversations comes back to me. The two of us sitting in my kitchen early in the morning, eating oats and talking about her candy. It was the first time she cried in front of me, and it's happened countless times since. I remember thinking she was acting pathetic. Crying over some . . . *boy*. She blamed it on anger, but it wasn't it. She was hurting.

You have every right to feel your pain.

Resting both arms on my thighs, I grimace. "Do you know why I still have a relationship with Josie, but not with you? Why I'm not angry at her the way I am with you?"

Tapping gently around his eyes, he hums. "Because you're in love with her?"

"Because *you* hurt me. She cheated on me, and it sucks." I shake my head. "But you are my big brother, Aaron. You were supposed to have my back."

He nods, looking down. When he doesn't say anything back, I run my fingers through my hair. I don't even know why I'm arguing with him right now—maybe in the hope of releasing some of the anger I feel at myself, but it's not working, and I want to be alone.

I stand, but Aaron offers, "Let me have your back now."

With a sigh, I watch him.

"If you're still in love with Josie, stay away from Primrose. I can tell she's into you, and unless you're ready to give her your all, you'll end up hurting her again." He rubs his jaw, looking away for a second before staring back into my eyes. "But if that's a closed chapter—if you think Primrose might be the right person for you, be honest, Logan. Don't let this good thing go because you're afraid. Just tell her how you feel."

I don't say a word, the memory of the pain disfiguring her face making me want to scream.

"But before you decide, maybe you could . . ." With a pleading voice, he whispers, "Talk to Josie. Please."

It feels like a beg. Like he's bleeding out, and he needs me to get this over with. To have the conversation that will finally put an end to all the drama and doubts.

And even though I hate him, I know how that feels better than anyone else. "Okay."

He nods, his shoulders shaking as he looks down at the steps.

I remember when I was right there, crying just like he is. When he and Josie caused me so much pain, every breath felt like dying.

It still doesn't compare to how I feel about losing Primrose, because tonight, I feel numb. By leaving, she's taken everything worthwhile in me. She's stripped me of the essentials, and I hate it.

I hate every minute of it.

I walk into the living room, all of Primrose's things still scattered about. Her cardigan is on the couch, and the piglets have chosen it as their bed. There's makeup on the bookshelf, books on the floor, and once I pull her scrunchie out of my pocket, the pain almost has me crouching on the floor.

The ghost of her. That's all I have left.

"Hi."

I twist my neck and throw a look at Josie, standing by the fridge. She's wearing one of my shirts, and her hair is wet after the shower I forced her to take. "Hello," I mumble as she walks closer.

This is so uncomfortable.

She is here wearing my clothes, taking a shower in my bathroom, then coming out here like this is still her house. Maybe it wouldn't have been weird two weeks ago, and we would have slipped into its familiarity. But it feels wrong today—like she's unsuccessfully trying to fill Primrose's spot.

"You know where the cups are," I mumble as I walk out of the kitchen and into the living room.

I drop on the couch as I hear her pour coffee, then open the fridge for milk. She probably realizes I only have almond milk, which she hates, and she closes it with a huff.

Just like a hundred times before.

She comes out, then slowly walks by my side and sits on the couch. There's a long silence in which she probably ponders what to say. What I think about, instead, is how I screwed up something that was barely even born.

I see all my mistakes one by one. Every single opportunity I had to tell Primrose, but I didn't, all the words I should have said but didn't leave my mouth.

They're heavy and thick on my tongue now.

"Look, Logan, I'm so sorry about tonight. I had a little too much to drink, and—"

"You're an alcoholic," I interrupt.

She doesn't say a word, so I turn to her, waiting for confirmation. "I've had a few incidents—"

"You've taken up drinking as an answer to your problems. You drink until you act irrationally or pass out. It's straining your relationships and ruining your life." I shrug. "So you're an alcoholic."

When she looks down at her lap, lips wobbling, I exhale.

"Aaron told me you filed for divorce."

Her eyes snap to me. "What . . . how do you feel about it?"

I ignore the *actual* meaning of her words and take a sip of coffee. "Worried about Sadie. I assume you'll have some shared custody agreement?" Her lips bend into a frown. "One week with you, one with him? Weekdays and weekends?" I shrug. "What happens when you have her? Will you drink if something happens? And if you're out of drinks, will you leave her alone to buy more?"

"Logan, I would never put Sadie in any danger."

"Maybe. Maybe you wouldn't today. But I'm sure you would have laughed six months ago if someone had told you you'd be making a scene at my parents' house and running from home to show up at my place."

She brings the cup to her lips and slowly sips without saying a word.

"You need help, Josie. We can get it for you so that you can go back to taking care of Sadie the way you're meant to."

Tears strike her face as she nods. "Okay," she says, her voice tinged with sadness.

Okay. I guess that's something, but I intend to ensure she follows through.

Neither of us says anything else for a long while, and Barbie's upbeat voice, blabbering all the time, is painfully absent. How can a place where I lived my whole life no longer make sense because she spent thirteen days here, then left? How is it possible?

"Does Prim hate me?"

My body twitches, and I shift position to mask it. "I have no idea. She dumped me."

"What?"

I'm not repeating it, so instead, I bask in my misery, in the unbelievable amount of pain compressing my lungs. I let the thought of it poison me slowly and thoroughly. How I lost someone who tried her best to get to know me. To understand me and give me comfort.

"So . . . you're single?"

My brows tighten as I turn to Josie.

"I know. You've just broken up," she says with a shaky voice. "But I need to say this now, Logan, because I don't think I'll get another chance."

"Josie—"

"I adore Prim, but you're the love of my life," she whispers.

Watching her distressed expression, I can recognize in her the same pain I felt for so long. It kills me to know she's going through it, but at the same time, I feel none of it. None of the heartbreak that has followed me around like a ghost for the past five years.

Hearing I'm the love of her life means nearly nothing to me.

"I know it's terrible that I only realized all of this when Prim came around. And if I'd told you three weeks ago that I love you, this would have been much, much easier, but . . ." She wipes her tears away, but more follow quickly after. "I had to try, Logan. You need to know before you choose."

Rubbing a hand over my mouth, I rest my forearms on my thighs. I keep my eyes on the silent fireplace, then whisper, "Timing has nothing to do with this, Josie. You could have said this a year ago, and my answer would have been the same."

She cups her face, shoulders shaking lightly.

"There's no choice, because there isn't a single doubt in my mind Primrose is the person I want to be with. But this has nothing to do with her. We were done the moment you chose my brother over me."

"I made a mistake, Logan, I—"

"I'm not punishing you or . . ." I wave dismissively. "Whether he loves you or not—even if he's given us his blessing—it'd hurt him. I don't care if he's done it to me, Josie. I'm not Aaron, and I would never, under any circumstance, date my brother's ex."

Tears create small dark patches on her jeans. "Yeah. And that's why I'm in love with you."

A bitter smile bends my lips as I turn to her. I think I spent the last five years missing her memory, before it was tainted by what she did. But seeing her for what she is is a sobering realization.

She's selfish. She *cheated* on me. And the fact that she'd decide to tell me all of this once I'm finally happy, careless of my feelings, of Primrose's, of Aaron's . . . "I think you should go."

Her face crumples at my words, tears flowing freely as she nods. "Okay. Yes." She sniffles, then stands and looks around. "I . . . uh, I'll—"

"Aaron is waiting for you outside. I'll make sure you get your clothes tomorrow."

She doesn't look at me this time and quickly walks to the door as if she can't escape fast enough. It reminds me of old times, when she ran away from fights. When she avoided confrontation until it exploded and tore us apart.

Not Primrose, though. She's not afraid of a fight.

As she darts out, Aaron's questioning gaze meets mine, then he nods with a half-smile. He points at the driveway and, with a wave, walks away.

Go after Primrose, he said. And I will. There's only one hotel in Pinevale, so it'll be easy to check if she's there. If not, I'll go through every single hotel in Roseberg. Her stuff is still here, so she can't be far, and fuck me, I'm going to find her and talk to her.

If I can punch Aaron in his face and reject Josie, I can talk to Primrose too.

I walk to the door, but just as I head out, the sound of a car engine comes from the driveway. My heart thumps as I wait for an Uber to show up and drop my Barbie at my door, but I'm hardly that lucky. Instead, the car parking in front of my house is a police cruiser with Connor at the wheel.

What the hell is he doing here?

"How's it going, Coleman?" he asks as he opens the car door and comes out. His cold and calculating eyes twinkle with joy as he pulls his pants up.

"What do you want, Harper?"

"I'm looking for your girlfriend, actually."

The blood freezes in my veins. "Primrose?" I scowl. "Why? What do you want with her?"

With a shrug, he thumbs his ear. "That's none of your business."

"She's not here," I mutter. I'll need to call the lawyers again, won't I? If only this asshole would let this go.

"Well, where is she? I need to see her right now."

My heartbeat quickens. I'm sweating, but I'm afraid the sun shining in the sky has little to do with it. I think I'm panicking again.

Why is he looking for her? They have nothing on us. They have nothing on *her*, and if someone should go down for this, it's me.

I will die before I let anything happen to my Barbie.

"Why are you looking for her, Connor?"

After a moment of hesitation, he picks his teeth with his nail. "Fine. I'll tell you, but only because, though I think you're a bumpkin, I'd want to know if it was my woman." As if his sudden display of humanity wasn't surprising enough, he takes on a severe expression. "We have a witness placing her on Derek's farm."

They . . . what? That's impossible.

There's nobody out here—who could have seen her besides goats and sheep?

"I'll need to arrest her, so if you could let me know where to find her, I'll be on my way."

No. *No*. He can't arrest Primrose. She can't be locked up—I'll do anything.

A surge of panic courses through my veins like a jolt of electricity, sending my heart into overdrive. My breath comes in short, shallow gasps, each inhalation feeling like I'm sucking in air through a straw. "I did it," I blurt without a second thought.

"What?"

"I set the fire, stole the piglets. It was me, and Primrose had nothing to do with it."

The words hang heavy in the air between us, and a deafening silence descends as the reality of what I've just done sinks in.

My mind spins. I'll need to call Kyle, make sure that the piglets are safe. He and Simon will take care of the farm, use Aaron's money, and fix everything. Primrose won't be arrested and'll get her dream job at Marisol.

Whether or not I end up in prison, *they'll* make it.

"*You* did it?" Connor comes to stand in front of me. "Do you understand—"

"Yes," I hiss. I understand that I'll be arrested. That I'm confessing in front of a police officer, and there's no coming back from that. "I did it."

"Logan Coleman, you're—"

"Wait," I say as I raise a hand. "You need to wait until tomorrow to arrest me."

He snorts, laughter exploding past his lips.

"Listen, if you arrest me now, I'll clam up. Won't say a word during the interrogation, making your job much harder." I can't be arrested before I talk to Primrose. She can't leave before I explain—before I tell her how I feel. "But if you give me today, I'll serve you my ass on a silver platter. I'll confess, give you all the dirt."

He shakes his head, gaze lost in the distance, until he turns to me with a click of his tongue. "Fine. You have until tonight.

I'll be back, and if you pull any crap, I'm arresting your girlfriend."

I nod, watching him walk to the cruiser and sit at the wheel. Only once he's gone, my eyes close, the back of my head hitting the doorframe.

This is it.

We've been made.

make sacrifices for me

. . .

Primrose

A NOISE WAKES ME UP, and with a gasp, I frantically look around to see where it's coming from, my eyes settling on the phone next to the bedside table lamp.

Right. I'm in a hotel room.

I rub my eyes as the events from yesterday hit me like a brick. Logan and Josie. His silence when I begged him to give me a reason to stay.

With a sigh, I pick up the phone and bring it to my ear. "Hello?"

"Yes, hi. I'm sorry to bother you, Miss Bellevue, but a man is here for you."

Logan.

The terrified look in his eyes comes back to me, and pulling the blanket closer to my chest, I swallow. "Tell him I won't see him, please."

"Oh, he didn't ask me to call you. He just won't leave, and he can't stay here any longer. I've waited as long as possible, but if he doesn't leave the property, I'll have to call the police. I figured you'd want to know."

Goddammit. "No, wait," I say as I peel the blanket off and set my feet on the carpeted floor. "Don't call the police. I'll handle it."

"Ma'am, are you sure?"

"Yes, quite." I think I'm done with the police for a while. I stand and look around, locating my clothes on the armchair. "I'll be right there."

I hang up, and on the way, I stop in front of the mirror, but there's little I can do with my hands alone to cover up the fact that I spent most of today crying.

I untie my hair, then ruffle it, and exasperated by the lack of results, I grab my key and walk down the flight of stairs.

When I enter the hall, the concierge points to the right. My eyes follow, and Logan is there, sitting with his back hunched and his elbows on his knees. He's staring at the floor, but as I step forward, his chin lifts from his hands and he stands, visibly nervous.

"Hey."

"Hi," I say when I reach him. Though I'm still very much angry, I also feel too tired for it, and pain has taken over sometime during the night anyway. "Logan, you can't stay here."

"I just wanted to see you."

"You can't *make me* see you. Make me speak." I shrug lightly. "Loitering in a hotel lobby for a woman who doesn't want to talk to you isn't . . . okay."

His eyes study my face, then he nods, as if it just occurred to him that this might be inappropriate. "You're right. You're absolutely right. I thought . . ." He shakes his head. "I don't know what I thought. I'll go."

I nod, surprised that's all it took, and the moment of silence stretches. His blue-gray eyes, filled with hurt and unsaid words, are hard to look at.

"Okay. Bye."

"Did you spend the whole day here?" I ask as he steps away.

"Uh, yeah." He rubs the back of his neck. "Sorry. It just made me feel better to be where you were. But I get it. It's creepy, and I should respect your wishes."

Yeah, all of that *is* true.

But he spent all day here, on this tiny plastic chair, not knowing if I'd even agree to see him. Not knowing if I'd listen to him, or talk. He tried. For me.

"Oh, you forgot this." He holds out my flamingo scrunchie. He never did tell me why he took it. "You only have fifteen thousand. I figured you'd miss this one."

I think of saying he can keep it, but he probably doesn't want it anyway, and heart twisting, I accept it and hug it to my stomach. If this is the last time I see Logan, this will remind me of him.

"Okay. I'll go now," he says, but he doesn't move. Instead, he rubs his jaw and presses his lips tightly for a moment. "Can I just say one thing?"

"Yes," I blurt.

"I'm not in love with Josie," he says, his voice steady. "Yesterday, when you asked, I hesitated, but it's not because I'm not sure." He pauses, and when I give him a nod, continues. "For the longest time, I was Logan, Josie's boyfriend. And then I was Logan, dumped for his brother. Logan who isolated himself from his family because he couldn't bear to be around her. Eventually, I found some balance in the everlasting unhappiness. But through it all, I was always Logan: in love with Josie. Unable to move on."

My heart squeezes for him. With the shock I felt yesterday, I didn't exactly stop to think about what happened between the three of them or how difficult it must be for him. Love or not, I don't think you ever get over your brother marrying your ex.

"Then you showed up."

My lips part, and his eyes soften when he notices.

"And since you came along, she never crossed my mind. Not in the way she used to. But I didn't think much of it. I didn't think about it at all—that's the point. She was the cop after us, and my brother's wife. But besides that, *you* consumed me. My whole mind." He sighs, chewing on his bottom lip. "For the first time in five years, yesterday I knew the answer to your question. I wasn't in love with her. I'm not. And I didn't know how to process it right then and there."

Tears fill my eyes.

I want to believe him so badly, and despite having this eerie feeling I'm headed straight for heartbreak, I think I do. But it doesn't mean I can play fast and loose with my heart.

I have no idea if Josie talked to him. What if she didn't? What if she does one month from now, when I'm even more used to his presence? When he's even more important?

What if he's saying all of this because he doesn't know she wants him back?

"Logan, I . . . I think you have a lot of things to work through. And so do I, after . . ." Derek took a hammer on my confidence and trust. "Anyway, we should probably work on that before we—we consider anything else."

"Oh." His shoulders hunch, and I can distinctly see the moment the meaning of my words hits him. "Oh-kay, yes. Sure, I get it."

He brings a hand to his face, rubbing his beard as his eyes bounce left and right over the floor, and tears sting at the back of my eyes, but for once, I refuse to cry. I know what it'll do to him if I start sobbing, and the last thing I want is to hurt him. Actually, the last thing I want is to lose him, but I'm afraid that ship has sailed.

"I'm *really* sorry," I insist. "I hope you know—"

"I know." His lips lift in a bitter smile. "And you're right. I do have a lot to work through. I understand that you didn't sign up for any of it."

"But maybe at some point . . ." God, I don't want this to be the last time I see him. What I want is to go back to the farm. Sleep against his chest. Wake up with his beard scratching my skin as he kisses me.

"Yeah. Maybe." He takes a step back, and it feels like my heart rips with the new inches between us. Then he takes one forward, and his arms spread. "Should we . . . uh . . ."

With a nod, I hide my face in his shirt and wrap my arms around him. His smell is comforting like it's always been, but I wonder if it will remind me of pain and heartbreak from now on.

"I'll work on it, okay?" he whispers into my hair. "On being a better man for you. And then I'll call you, and if you still want to see me, I'll come to you, wherever you are."

Don't cry. Please, don't cry until you're alone in your room.

"Thank you," he says as his hold tightens. "For everything." He breathes hard against my hair, then lets me go, and it feels against any logic to untangle my arms from behind him, but I do.

He needs to talk to Josie and make sure he has no feelings for her. He needs to process his emotions, as unpleasant as they may be, before I can trust him with myself. After being hidden by men, lied to, and used, I can't live my life thinking I'm his second choice.

Even though he's never made me feel like one.

"Bye," he says, and this time, he looks into my eyes for the briefest of moments. But it's enough for me to see the light in them dim.

For me to see him hate himself just a little bit more.

I settle on the chair and wait for my laptop to turn on. The hotel room is small, but still better than a porch for a meeting with Chloe. Of course, I'd rather be on that porch, smoking weed with Logan. In his kitchen, making candy, or in his bed, tracing the shape of his muscles with my fingers.

God, I miss Lola and Paco so much.

I open the video conference room and watch myself in the left corner. My skin is almost gray, the purple and blue hues under my eyes testifying to hours of crying. No amount of makeup could have covered this, and anyway, I left most of it at Logan's. At least Kyle promised to swing by and bring me my stuff later today.

Did Josie talk to Logan already? Are they back together, or did he reject her? Maybe I could ask Kyle.

"Hello?" Chloe's face fills the screen, and with a happy wave, she says, "Hi, Primrose! How are you?"

"I'm good, Chloe, thank you. How are you?"

She's joined by Jessica, whom I recognize as part of their HR department from previous interactions. "We're having a sunny day in Mayfield, so we can't complain." Jessica sits, and pulling her dark hair into a ponytail, she juts her chin forward. "When will you be back?"

"In four days," I say with a forced smile.

"Okay, Primrose, let me tell you," She chuckles on my laptop screen. "This recipe is incredible. We asked one of our cooks to make it for us, and"—she bumps Jessica's shoulder—"Tell her what I said."

Jessica's eyes widen. "'No way is this vegan.'"

My smile wavers, but I slide it back on. "I'm so glad you like it."

"It's brilliant."

Chloe nods. "This isn't candy—it's art."

"Look—" Jessica holds a hand up, her eyes narrowing—"we've seen some crazy flavor combinations on your page, so when you said *strawberry*?"

"Yeah, we were skeptical at best."

"Believe it or not," Jessica says as she smacks a hand against the white table. "This is my new all-time favorite."

My cheeks warm. It's everything I've ever dreamed of, but of course, I feel none of the happiness I should be experiencing. "This is music to my ears."

"We've already given it the green light, so we'll get to work as soon as you start. We plan to launch it before the end of the year."

"Wow, this is . . . incredible. I'm speechless." Drying my sweaty hands against my thighs, I wiggle on the chair. It might just be my bad mood, but being in this tiny room makes me claustrophobic. I miss the fields, the fresh smell of grass and moss.

Only a handful of days ago, I missed home—the busy streets of Mayfield, my frenetic routine, the place where I always get smoothies when the city gets too warm in the summer. Now, the thought of going back only means getting farther away from Logan.

"It's always been a dream of mine to work with Marisol. I'm so thankful for this opportunity."

"We're far more thrilled than you are, trust me," Jessica says.

Chloe bobs her head, then turns to the camera. "Okay. Now, onto our only issue."

As I swallow, my joy dampens. "Oh, uh . . . sure."

"Not an *issue*," Jessica scolds Chloe. "The sales marketing has reviewed your recipe and asked us to change a couple of ingredients."

"Okay." I don't think I hide my shock well enough before I realize I need to look collected. I'm sure this is all part of the process. "Sure, let's hear 'em."

"We'd like to use refined sugar instead of brown sugar. We understand that the recipe will need adjustments, but . . . we've made some projections, and that's the best way to ensure the highest revenue."

I guess I can live with that. Many vegans close an eye on refined sugar anyway, and if they do, so can I.

"And gelatine instead of agar-agar."

Gelatine?! "But that would . . . gelatine isn't suitable for vegans."

Chloe nods. "Yes, we understand that."

I must really be stupid, because the first thought in my brain is that Logan will never get to eat my candy. He won't be able to walk to the grocery store and buy a bag. Though the truth is, he probably wouldn't anyway.

But this goes beyond Logan. "You know . . . you know my whole brand is about making candy for people who can't typically eat it. And with gelatine, making it unsuitable for vegans, and white sugar, making it inaccessible for—"

"We get it," Jessica says, but her sweet smile feels awfully insincere now. "But we want to make this candy accessible to the masses, and we need to keep our costs low."

I get that, but they're talking about stripping my product of the *one* quality that makes it mine. I make candy for people who can't have candy. That's the one thing that I've never compromised on. Good god, I've been worrying about the recipe to submit when I should have been concerned about my whole brand being shoved aside.

"I'll be honest," I say as I fix them both with a cold look. "I'm a little surprised. I think I'll need a moment to consider this and get back to you."

"How about we send the contract over? I'm sure if you also look at the financial aspect, you'll—"

"The financial aspect doesn't overly concern me," I say softly. I've never been a very money-driven person, and I make a good living with my social media. "But please send the contract, and I'll go through it."

"All right. We hope you'll consider—"

"Thank you," I say curtly. "I'll talk to you soon."

I snap the laptop shut, then breathe out.

Of course, this is how these two weeks would end. With me losing Logan and my opportunity with Marisol. I would have accepted anything—any freaking thing—but this.

A new recipe. More or less of whatever ingredient. But to strip my recipe of its value would be an insult to me and my audience.

It's disrespectful they even suggested this.

Yes, my lack of the usual politeness might have something to do with what's happening with Logan, but what I said stands. I will *not* change the heart of my recipes.

I slump back in bed and scroll mindlessly on my phone. I expected to miss this much more than I actually did while I was at Logan's, and though it's nice to connect with the world again, I quickly get bored of social media.

Riding the Sugar High

There's nothing on there for me. Everything I want has already slipped through my fingers.

When there's a frantic knock at my door, I jump up and bring a hand to my chest. "Jesus," I mumble when the knocking continues. "Yes, I'm coming."

I walk to the door, then open it, Kyle's crazed eyes meeting mine. "Prim, you have to come back—you have to help me." He enters the room, pacing at the foot of the bed as he rubs both hands on his short brown hair. "I don't know what to do, and—this is so fucked up, okay? All he left is a message, and then I had to take the pigs and bring them home. And he said there's a check? This check—"

"Kyle?" I call, my heartbeat quickening as I try to understand what he's saying.

He shakes his head. "What am I supposed to do with it? Simon's kid is sick, and he doesn't answer his phone and—"

"Kyle!" I insist as I grasp his arm. I have no idea what he's talking about, but I can *feel* that something happened to Logan. And I know it's my fault. "What happened?"

He grimaces, worried wrinkles appearing on his forehead. "They took him away—the police. He got arrested."

love me

. . .

Primrose

"WHAT DO YOU MEAN?" asks the old officer as he leans over the counter.

"I . . . I was the one who set Derek Gracen's trash on fire—accidentally. And—and I stole his pigs. *Not* accidentally."

I've already told him this, but he keeps staring at me as if we're speaking two different languages, and I don't have time to chat. I need to confess, and I need Logan to be out of here immediately. I need him home with Paco and Lola. With all of his animals. I need him free, because if there's someone who would die in lockup, it's Logan. He'd perish, like a flower with no water and sunshine.

"*You*," the policeman insists. "You did all that."

"Yes, me."

"I thought we arrested Coleman." He looks to the right, through a door that leads into a small room. "Hey—Harper! Get back here!"

Harper. That must be Connor.

He steps out of the room, pulling up his beige pants, and pins his eyes on me. "Sugar High. What can we do for you?"

"She says she's here to confess about that whole Gracen

thing," the cop at reception explains. "I thought you got Coleman for it."

Connor exhales, and noticing the coy grin on his face, I know he won't take this seriously. "We did. He sold us a plausible story too, I'm afraid."

I swallow hard, wishing Josie were here. Even though I'm not her biggest fan right now, I have a feeling she's the only cop in this station who would be interested in hearing what I have to say. "But you *know* it wasn't him."

He shrugs. "I know no such thing."

Goddammit. After Kyle came to the hotel, I sent him to the farm and came straight here, but I didn't consider the resistance I would meet at the station. Connor is perfectly happy framing Logan for this—he doesn't care what actually happened.

"The cab driver," I blurt. "I—I took a cab to Derek's place. I don't know his name, but his parents live on the same street as Derek's parents, and—"

"Yes, we already talked to him. His records show he drove you to Derek's farm, but he swears he dropped you off at Logan's. That you gave him the wrong street number."

What?! Why would he do that?

"He also said that when he was laid off from his last job, Logan provided his family with fruit and vegetables—sometimes even money." He looks around before whispering, "Let me give you some advice, all right? Go home. Don't tank your career. Logan will take the fall, and it's not like he doesn't deserve it. The only reason we didn't arrest that hillbilly before is because we didn't have enough proof."

"Do you have it *now*?" I ask with an impatient gesture. All they have is a cab driver whose records reflect he's lying, and a scrunchie that obviously belongs to me.

"We don't need it. He confessed."

"Well, I'm confessing too! And you'll see, my story is much more convincing than Logan's. You have to take my statement—you can't just—you know what," I continue, my voice rising as panic stings my throat. "I want to talk to the captain. Or sheriff. Whatever you have here."

"Fine, fine. Calm down." He rubs his head, then, with a long sigh, grabs a form and begins filling it out. "Rob, is the interrogation room free?"

"What's going on?"

I flip as I hear Josie's voice, and if it wasn't for the fact that she wants to declare her love to the man I have feelings for, I could hug her. "Where is he? You have to take me to him—it was me, Josie. It was me all along. Logan didn't—"

"Stop talking," Josie says as she raises a hand. Turning to Connor, she sighs. "Why didn't you tell her?"

Tell me? "Tell me what?" My head bobs from one officer to the other. "Somebody speak!"

"Stop screaming in a police station," Josie whispers as she approaches. Her hand cups my shoulder, and she studies me with big, worried eyes. "Look, Logan was arrested this morning, but then . . . he had some sort of *attack*. We thought it was a heart attack, and we called the ambulance. He's at the hospital right now, but they assured us it wasn't—"

"Take me there," I say, my body shaking so hard I can barely speak. I can't believe I left him behind. I can't believe I broke his heart, and now he's at the hospital, waiting for the police to book him as soon as he feels better. "Please, take me to Logan."

She nods, but before we can step toward the exit, Connor says, "I'll come with you. Check on our inmate-to-be."

Over my dead body.

"Big guy with a scowl?" the nurse asks as she points to the right. There's a blend of antiseptic odors and bustling activity in the ER, making it feel terrifyingly real. "He's right there. If you could convince him he should spend the night here, that'd be great. We didn't manage." The young nurse takes a step forward, then seemingly changes her mind. "Oh, and if you happen to know what he's allergic to—"

"Strawberry," Josie says without skipping a beat.

Strawberry?!

"Great. Thank you. He was too worked up to talk." She walks away, and as Josie walks in the direction he pointed at, I tug at her hand.

"What?"

"He's not allergic to strawberry."

"Uh, yeah. He is." She looks past me, probably checking to see if Connor is still taking a call outside of the ER. "It's not a severe allergy, but before he found out, he ended up at the hospital because of it."

But he's been . . . he's been eating my strawberry candies. A *lot* of them. Even if it's not a severe allergy, why would he do that?

"Come on, let's go."

Josie walks and steps back once she notices I didn't follow.

Maybe he doesn't want to see me.

Maybe I'm the last person he wants to see, seeing as he was arrested because of me right after I dumped him.

"Prim?"

Plus, I have no idea if Josie talked to him already. If they're together. She could have told him this morning. She could tell him right now, or tomorrow, or—

"Prim." Josie's hand clasps mine, and with an encouraging tug, she says, "Come on. Let's go see him."

"I—I think I need a minute."

She nods. "Okay. I'll try to talk some sense into him. You . . . take your time." I nod, but she hesitates. "He needs to see you."

Once she disappears behind the blue curtain, I slowly step closer.

" . . . no need."

It's his voice.

I bring a hand to my mouth and exhale. He's speaking, and he sounds normal. He really *is* okay.

"Logan, the doctor thinks you should stay. Stop being stubborn and—"

"It's just because my heartbeat is *slightly* elevated."

"That sounds like a good reason!"

"It's not, trust me. My heart is fine. I just need to get this over with. Let's go back to the station, book me, and I'll pay the bail."

Exhaling, I take a step forward. There's no way I'll let any of that happen, and Josie's here. As an officer, she won't be able to ignore it if I confess.

With my heart in my throat, I pull the curtain open, my eyes landing on Logan, sitting on the hospital bed with no shirt and part of his tattoos covered by cables and electrodes attached to monitors around him.

"Primrose," he breathes out, but his voice is drowned out by the machines' beeps, which go from a soothing, stable rhythm to a rising, irregular cacophony.

The blinking light on the screen to his right turns red, and on the monitor, the numbers rise and rise until his heartbeat reaches one hundred and twenty. Unable to say a word, I meet his gaze.

Is his heart . . . beating faster?

For me?

"Are you okay?" he asks, and if I had the ability to utter a word, I'd point out the absurdity of *him* asking *me* that question. But his heartbeat is at one hundred and forty now, and genuinely worried about his well-being, I point at the screen.

"Should I leave?"

He swallows, a pink hue spreading over his neck and cheeks as he shakes his head, then takes the pulse ox off his finger and throws it to the side.

His heart beats for me.

So fast, so *honest*.

I rush to his side, then awkwardly set a knee on the bed and try to climb in, his hands gripping my hips to help me up just at the right moment. My face sinks into the crook of his neck, and throwing my arm over him, I feel his heart pounding against my chest.

His heart is my favorite thing about him.

"I'm sorry," he whispers into my hair, and my hold on him tightens. I don't care about anything else right now but the fact that he has feelings for me. And feelings that actively modify your vitals are feelings you can't argue with. "I'm so happy you're here."

I can feel it in his quavering voice, and smiling against his skin, I nod. Today, he had his first panic attack without me around. He must have been so scared. "I won't let anything bad happen to you. I *swear*."

He smiles softly, then his eyes dip to my mouth, and answering his silent question, I press a kiss on his lips. I've missed them so much.

Josie coughs. "Um, so . . . I'm sorry to interrupt, but you both don't seem aware of what the other has been up to, so I figured I should catch you up." She points at me, then at him. "You've both confessed to the same crime, then sworn again and again that the other was not involved."

"You what?" Logan hisses.

Right. I nearly forgot to scold him about that. "Why would you confess, Logan?"

"Jesus, Primrose. Why would *you*?"

"Because I can't let you go to prison for my crime, obviously," I whisper.

His chin jerks back. "Well, same!"

I should get off him, but he only lets me shift to a seated position before he turns to Josie. "Ignore everything she said. It was me who—"

"No!" I burst, my heartbeat picking up. "No, that's not true. I was the one who set Derek's garbage on fire, and—"

"Bullshit," he insists. "Why the hell would you have stolen his piglets?"

"Why would you be using a pink scrunchie?"

Connor joins us, a glare directed at Logan, whose lips thin until they're two straight lines. Turning away from him, he cups my shoulder. "Your life is too important, Barbie," he says softly. He cups my cheek, sliding his hand under the hair framing my face. "You'll do amazing things, and you need a clean slate for that."

My future isn't more important than his. It's just not. And I was the one to set that fire, so I should pay the consequences for it.

Folding my hand over his, I stare deeply into his eyes. "So . . . do . . . you."

"For Christ's sake," he explodes, throwing his head back on the pillow. "I can't stand the thought of you in danger—do you get that?"

"Logan, you *just* had a panic attack. You can't go to prison, you—"

"I had a panic attack because I was terrified they'd come for you," he says as he points at Josie and Connor. His eyes widen as if that'll help convey the message more clearly. "Do you understand that the thought of it is worse than hurting myself?"

"Do *you* understand that I love you?" I shout back, and just like that, we both fall silent.

I said I love him. Out loud.

I met him precisely two weeks ago, I'll be gone from his life in four days, and I just shouted at him that I love him.

Through the obvious surprise on his face, he opens his mouth. "I lo—"

"Don't!" I squeal as I cover his mouth with my hand. My heart is beating hard and fast, the weight of my fears melting away now that he's *almost* said it back. "Don't you dare. Not *here*."

I stare at him and try to breathe in and out. Even though he only said half of it, now I know how he feels, and there's no coming back from that.

Number twenty-nine. Love me.

"You almost said you love me while gaslighting me," I say through a half-sob, half-chuckle.

Tipping his head toward Connor, he mumbles, "So did you."

"You're *still* doing it."

"So—"

"Okay, enough," Connor bursts as he turns to Josie. "Did you put them up to this?"

"Me?" she asks, planting both hands on her hips. Her green eyes turn a shade colder as she meets her partner's eyes. "I didn't do anything."

"You did—you told them both to confess."

What is he talking about?

"Connor, quit it. I would never jeopardize my job. And look at them—they have no idea."

Our befuddled expressions must convince him, because he darts away in a cloud of swear words. After a stiff nod, Josie follows him, leaving Logan and me alone.

Immediately, my body crashes against his.

He almost said he loves me.

"I'm sorry I went behind your back," I whimper, my body shaking with a mix of adrenaline and pure terror. "I'm so—so . . . scared."

"Barbie," he says, pain bleeding from his words. "You've been really brave, you know?"

I look up at him, his thumb tracing my lips. "You don't mean that."

"I do," he insists. "I might hate that you confessed—might think it's the stupidest thing you could've ever done. But my god, Barbie, was it brave."

See? I love him. I just do. He's pissed off, I know he is. And yet he's complimenting me—telling me I'm brave, which I'm definitely not. I want to be brave for him, though, and not only when it comes to the police. I want to be fearless when it comes to us. "This is yours," I say as I slide my flamingo scrunchie off my wrist and fit it around his. "Never give it back, please."

"I don't intend to."

He pecks my forehead again and again, the scent of his body wash and fresh grass just about the most comforting cocoon. I could stay here forever, and as happy as I am, my heart also twists at the thought of my imminent departure.

"You know, this doesn't mean I'm not mad at you," I scold. "You still should have told me."

"You're right, Barbie." His hold tightens. "But *please*, come be mad at home."

Home. It feels like I'm home already, right here between his arms.

"Logan?"

"Yes?"

"Are you allergic to strawberries?"

His lips freeze against my forehead. "Uh, mildly. My throat gets a little itchy—no big deal."

"But then . . ." I look up at him. "Why do you keep eating my candy? I only made more because you finished it, then finished it again, and—"

"Because you keep eating it."

So? I also talk all the time, cry nearly every day, and wear pink skirts, and he doesn't do any of that.

His thumb presses on my lips, pushing the bottom one down. "Your lollipops—they're strawberry flavored, aren't they?"

Yes, it's nearly the same recipe as the hard candy.

When I nod, he cups my cheek. "You're always eating one, so your mouth . . . it tastes like strawberry. I couldn't tell the first time I ate your candy, but I knew it was familiar. And when we kissed again, I figured it out. You smell like it, you taste like it."

He ate something he's allergic to because the taste of it reminded him of our first kiss?

"Every time I wished I could kiss you, I ate your candy instead."

I blink, then blink again, too stunned to say a word. I spent most of two weeks thinking he wouldn't give me the time of day, while he was dying to kiss me all along? Why didn't he tell me? Why didn't I believe him when he did?

Now we have four days left, and the awareness that we wasted most of our time together is so bitter that no candy could wipe it away.

"Well, I think you're both free to go," Josie says as she pops into the curtained area. Though I didn't think there were any words in the English language that would get me to look away from Logan right now, those do the trick.

"We are?" I ask. "But—but Logan—"

"No charges will be filed against him."

What the hell is happening?

Connor comes back, his finger pointed at Logan. "Well played, but just know next time you won't be this lucky."

"What the hell is going on now?" he asks, and I share the sentiment. I don't understand what's happening, and I'm too tired to guess, so someone better bring us to speed.

"We have no way of proving which one of you did it, the scrunchie bears both your DNA, and the pigs are nowhere to be found." Her eyes dart to me and quickly move away, and I *know* she remembers seeing the piglets at Logan's place. She's saving our ass. "With both of you confessing—"

"Shut up," Connor barks at Josie, who responds with an eye roll.

"Do you need more proof that they won't turn against each other?"

When Logan chuckles, I watch him with a curious grin. It looks like he just lost thirty pounds of stress, his lips bent into an effortless smile. "You figured Primrose was my *one* weakness and lied to get me to confess because you have no hard proof." He laughs even loudly now, pulling my face to his with the usual lack of grace. "Except you're not my weakness, are you, backpack? You're my secret weapon."

I blush, still unsure of what's happening. But it sounds like we're not getting arrested today, and the police must be at their wits' end if they're pulling crap like that.

"Well, then. If you don't mind," Logan says as he wraps one arm around me. "I'd like both of you to leave now."

Connor is gone in a moment, and after a long look, Josie walks away too, leaving the two of us alone.

We're together again. We're free.

We're *so* fucking lucky.

"Did you know?" he asks as soon as they're gone. "Is that why you did all of this?"

I hum, brushing the skin of his hand with my thumb. "I'd love to impress you with my brain, but no. I had no clue."

"I definitely would have pulled you over my shoulder and spun you around, but . . ." His hand clasps mine, and it's like nothing else exists. Like I'm in the moment, at peace, and all those cheesy things people in love say. "Jesus, Barbie. You were willing to get arrested for me."

"I can't believe I told you I love you at the hospital," I mutter, dragging a hand over my face. "I can't believe you almost did too."

"Really?" he scolds, jerking his chin down. "Want me to take it back?"

"You can't—"

"I take it back. There. Done."

"Logan!" I smack my fist on his stomach. That was the first 'I love you' I got—he can't unsay it. "You didn't even *say* it, and it's not something you can take back!"

"But I did say it. The first half of it anyway. And now I take it back, like it never happened."

"Stop it!" I squeal as he traps my arms between us. "Come on, give me back my first half."

"So that you can complain about me telling you 'I lo—' at the hospital? Fat chance."

"You know what—"

He lets me go and pulls the electrodes off his chest.

"I take mine back. The full thing."

He stands and grabs his shirt. Once he slides it on, he shakes his head. "No, you don't."

"I do too!"

"Then look at me and tell me you don't love me."

I watch him slide his shirt on, speechless for a few moments. I can't say that—it's not true. I *do* love him, and I never want him to doubt it. "I hate you."

He walks around the bed, and even though I pull back, he presses his lips on mine. I can't even *pretend* I don't want it. "No," he whispers between my lips. "You don't."

you never have enough

. . .

Logan

I SCOOP the last bit of straw into the wheelbarrow, then grab the broom leaning against the wall, the familiar scent of hay and earth filling my nostrils. The sun casts a warm glow through the open stable doors, picking up the golds and yellows of the straw. The stables are quiet now, with the horses grazing in the field outside.

How am I *itching* to see Primrose already? With how pretty she is, she's made everything else unworthy to look at. With how smart and fun, she's made everything else dull. Every moment I'm not around her feels like being numb, and in three days, she'll be gone.

Which we still haven't talked about.

When we finally got back home from the hospital, we went straight to bed. We stayed there until this morning, sleeping and *definitely not* sleeping. Until there was so much shit to be dealt with around the farm, and I had to start my morning. It's been four hours since then, but they feel like forty.

Could I go with her? I hate big cities, and I'm needed at the farm. Now that I'm no longer selling, I'll have to find the best way to invest my brother's money and ensure the whole business doesn't fail. Plus, with summer approaching soon, it'll be the busiest time of the year.

But she can't stay either. Though she hasn't mentioned Marisol in a while, she's sent them her candy. When they do answer, I'm sure they'll love it, and she'll get the job.

What the hell are we going to do?

With a final glance around, I take a deep breath, and the silence is interrupted by light steps I've learned to recognize.

"Hello?" Primrose calls.

She can't see me from the entrance as I'm in the last box, so I call, "Here."

"Where are the horses?" she asks, joining my side. She's wearing a light-purple dress and a thin yellow cardigan, and though she's gorgeous, it's got nothing on how she looks naked, sweaty, whining my name as I fuck her with my fingers and suck her clit.

Or tucked under my chin, tracing the tattoos on my chest.

"Out back. Socializing."

"Huh." She walks closer, grabs the broom from my hand, and sets it down. "Kyle said that the piglets love his place."

I study her worried expression and stifle a smile. I had to move the pigs after Josie saw them. I'm not even sure if she remembers—maybe she was too drunk for it. If not, she's pretending she doesn't. "Are you worried they won't want to come back to you?"

"Maybe a little." She frowns, her lips sticking out. "I mean, they're not *his* piglets. He's going to give them back, right?"

And to think at the beginning, she was afraid of them.

When I give her a firm nod, she lets out a relieved sigh. "Have been missing you, cowboy."

"I don't know how I ever thought leaving the farm in Kyle's hands would be a smart idea. I was gone for one day, and the whole place went to hell." I rub the back of my neck, and I fit my hands inside my pockets as she approaches.

"Well, it doesn't matter since neither you nor the farm are going anywhere. That check your brother gave you . . . holy crap, that's a big number." She entangles her fingers with mine, then brings the usual red lollipop to her lips. "Did you hear anything from the police?"

My muscles stiffen, but I nod. "Actually, yeah. Josie called." I can't say hearing her voice is too pleasant these days.

"Oh? What for?"

"She said we're officially on our way to being a cold case," I say, her discomfort melting like ice cream in the sun. "No time or resources to keep digging, and apparently, there was a robbery at the jewelry store. Takes priority over piglets and improper trash disposal."

She chuckles, exhaling deeply. "I can't believe we made it."

"Told you," I whisper as I let my hand trail down to the small of her back, then lean forward to kiss her forehead. If I'm being honest, I've had my doubts here and there. But we *did* make it, and now we'll need to figure out everything else. "So, I thought that maybe we should talk . . ."

Her chin rests on my chest, and I can tell by the look in her eyes that talking isn't what she's here for. "Again, Barbie?"

After last night, I'm surprised she can even stand.

She bites her bottom lip, the telltale flush of embarrassment tinging her cheeks. "Maybe? Is it bad?" She shrugs. "We don't have much—" She presses her lips, as if we decided that our time running out isn't something we'll discuss, and now she's broken the silence. "I mean . . . There's still a lot we haven't done."

"It's not bad." I lean with my back against the box, pulling her with me. "I might shoot dust, but I'll fuck you as many times as you want me to."

"What if I don't want to fuck?" she asks, brows arching sweetly. "There's still something on my list we haven't done."

"What's that?"

"Teach me new things."

"Uh-huh." A heap of possibilities roam through my mind. Last night, I spun her around like nobody's business. We banged the headboard against the wall enough to cause a dent. Hell, with how I went at it, I'm surprised I didn't break the bed. Or her.

Yet there are so many things we should try. So many things I want to do.

She rolls the lollipop around her lips, then suggestively presses it over her tongue until it disappears in the back of her mouth.

"Oh," I breathe out. Is that what she has in mind? Because I've been picturing her mouth wrapped around my cock every single day since I ... well, met her.

My hands slide down her back until I'm cupping her ass. She likes it when I slap it, and I love to see my red print on her perfect skin.

When my fingers graze her asscheek under the skirt of her dress, she flinches. "Sensitive?"

"Yes," she breathes out. Her hand runs down my chest, settling on my stomach, while the other still holds onto the lollipop. "And nervous."

"Nervous? About what?"

"I've never done it before."

Oh. She's never given head? I can't even lie about it; the idea of being the first one to fuck her mouth fills me with a weird sort of pride. Makes me want to be the last one too.

"I think you'll be a natural." I press a thumb on her bottom lip, pulling her mouth open. "And besides, you don't need to be nervous about anything you do with me."

"Hmm." She swallows, her tongue twitching. I can picture it against my shaft, my head lodged at the back of her throat.

Once I let her mouth go, she softly exhales.

"Are you going to teach me, Logan?"

"Teach you what, Barbie?"

She tilts her head as if telling me she knows I fully understand what she's talking about. I still want to hear her say it. "Teach me how to suck cock."

"No," I say, ignoring her disappointment, "I'll teach you to suck *my* cock."

She nods, languid eyes lost in mine.

"Show me how you use your tongue."

When she doubtfully glances at the lollipop in her hands, then back at me, I nod.

"Like this?" Her lips wrap around it, then her tongue does, and my knees turn weak.

"Yeah," I whisper. I swear, I depend on her movements. I crave her like a shower after hours in the sun, like my bed after working in the fields. She's the natural conclusion to my day, and the only place I need to return to.

The fleeting thought of her imminent departure has my throat clamping down, but I sink my fingers into her hair and pull her closer. "Tongue out."

She obeys, her breaths coming out quickly.

"Rub it over your tongue."

Eyes fluttering, she rubs it back and forth. My cock hardens, painfully pressing against the zip of my jeans. "Once you're sucking my dick instead of candy, I'll drive it to the back of your throat until you choke on it."

She whimpers, her hand shaking as she presses her legs together. My Barbie. She gets hot and bothered so easily. One word delivered in the right way, one brush of my fingers where she likes it most, and she writhes against me, begging me with those sweet blue eyes.

Just like she's doing right now.

"Would this feel good?" she asks as she pushes the tip of her tongue against the lollipop and drags it over it. "On your, um . . . tip?"

"Yes," I wheeze out. "Don't stick anything *in* it, and keep your teeth to yourself. Everything else is pretty great."

"But what's the best?"

"Honestly? Watching you on your knees working my dick with your hand and tongue. Knowing you're mine—so mine that you let me take your mouth."

She looks lost in thought for a second, and I know she's fishing for much more specific information about what makes me go crazy, but I don't want her to put pressure on herself. Anything she'll do with my dick in her mouth will be extraordinary anyway.

I crouch slightly and circle my arms around her ass to pull her up, but she leans back before I can and slowly sinks to her knees.

It's like every drop of blood leaves my brain until I'm thoughtless.

Her hands move to my jeans, and my mind only snaps back into place when she pulls my briefs down, my hard cock bobbing out.

I breathe in relief. "Barbie?" Her tongue swipes over her bottom lip, and I could die. Does she want to do it now? Here? "Are you going to suck me off?"

She bats her lashes at me. "Well, I'm not proposing." She drops a kiss on my waist. "Yes, cowboy, let's put your lesson to practice."

"Fuck," I breathe out.

She tucks her hair behind her ear, then nervously looks up at me, an inch away from my erection. "Help me out, okay?"

When I grunt in response, she wraps her hand around my base, and everything I said about shooting dust is nothing but a memory. The first leak of precum moistens the head of my dick, and I feel my balls twitch.

"Just do what feels natural," I whisper when I notice her hesitation.

Tentatively, she runs her tongue along my shaft and swallows my tip.

Every single muscle in me squeezes. I want to look at her, watch her suck me, but my eyes roll to the back of my head, and without any restraint, I groan, loud and deep.

Crap, it feels too good.

"Is this okay?" Slowly, her warm mouth begins bobbing up and down, and my jeans crumple in my fists. It's not okay—it's so much better than I thought it'd be. So much better than I remember it.

"You can . . ." I try to fight against the torpor taking over my mind. "You can put even more, uh, pressure."

She makes a little noise of agreement, then her tongue rubs harder, and every time she moans, it vibrates against my skin and echoes into my goddamn soul.

"Barbie," I grit out. My hips buck a little every time she takes me halfway through, and unable to resist the temptation, I look down at her, working my cock with her small fist and tight mouth. Gorgeous.

When she speeds up, my hands abandon my jeans and move to her, and I stop myself just in time before grabbing her hair. She probably doesn't need to get my dick shoved down her throat the very first time she does this.

Tilting back, she breathes hard, saliva sticking to her chin. "You want to fuck my mouth, cowboy? Use me to come?"

Good god. I said it already, but this woman was made for me.

"Do it." Something rogue moves through her eyes—a flicker of her wild self. I'm not even sure if she's giving me orders or begging me.

Either way, I'm in. I've never been so *in* before.

I bury my hand in her hair, unable to process the simplest thoughts, and slowly drive my cock forward till I hit the back of her throat. She gags as her muscles spasm around my tip, and her tongue rubs along my shaft. With tears in her eyes, she stares at me, her skin turning redder the more she holds on. Watching her fight against her instinct to pull back so she can please me is enough to nearly throw me over the edge, and with a grunt, I shove her away just before I blow.

She inhales, and the second her gaze turns lustful, I push into her again.

"Just like that. Swallow me, Barbie," I say with a shaky voice. Drool drips down my balls, my cock twitching until it feels too good, and I jerk my hips back.

She's so excruciatingly pretty, whimpering with her short dress and big blue eyes. I want to free her tits, bend her over the nearest horizontal surface, and fuck her. But then she sucks greedily on my cock, and I know I won't be doing anything at all except spurting cum down her throat.

I try to slow her down, but pulling her hair just gets her to whine louder, until I can't hold off my pleasure any longer, and I thrust into her mouth hard, a gagging noise escaping her lips every time I slam all the way in. "Is this okay, little backpack?" I grit out as my balls hit her chin. "If it's not okay, just—"

She sucks, and the friction of the roof of her mouth has me crying out as she rubs her tongue on the lower side of my shaft. I try to stop it, try to hold it off for another minute, another second, but a tingle spreads along my cock, my balls squeezing.

"Barbie, I'm coming," I warn her, and the hungry look in her eyes is just about the best thing I've ever seen. "Barbie"—my voice breaks—"Bar—"

"Logan?" Kyle's voice calls, and with wide eyes, Primrose pulls back.

No. Fuck. No!

I groan, my orgasm wearing off before it even hits. The muscles of my stomach relax as I look up, meeting Kyle's gaze over the small door.

"Oh, there you are."

Yes, here I fucking am.

"What?" I bark, and it's aggressive even for my standards, because his brows scrunch.

"Dude—you have no idea. We need to find Prim *right now*."

"Why? What happened?"

"Is she home?"

Jaw clenching, I glare at him. He's fidgety, like he can't contain himself, so I assume whatever happened is good news. Which means it can wait. "I don't know. I'm busy. Get out."

"No, boss," he says as he wiggles his brows, an exhilarated grin splitting his face. "Trust me, you want to know."

I huff out my next words. "No, I don't." What I want is for Primrose to resume sucking my dick right now. To come in her mouth and watch her swallow every drop. Besides that, I can't think.

"I'll try her phone."

"Kyle," I scold, my eyes widening in a silent threat, but before I can do more, Primrose's mouth wraps around my tip and sucks.

My breath catches, and it feels like my body melts.

He huffs out in annoyance. "Nothing. Where did you see her last?"

Primrose fits more of my shaft inside her mouth, swatting my hand away when I try to gently coax her off me.

Shit, I'm about to moan in front of Kyle.

"Are you even listening to me?" he asks, his brows tightening over his eyes. "Are you sweating? What's going on?"

"Nothing," I say breathlessly as Primrose's mouth swallows me whole. I hold on to the door, my knuckles white with effort. "She's at home. Go there. Right now." My muscles contract. "Please."

Kyle's eyes search my face. After a moment of hesitation, he nods. "Okay. By the way, your mom called."

I breathe out, powerless against the friction of her tongue while simultaneously cringing. I can't think about my mom *now*. "Uh-huh."

"Oh, and there's a huge bug splat on your bike. So weird. Yellow and green . . ." He mock-shivers. "Gross."

I press my lips tight, nearly incinerating him with my gaze. Once I'm moderately confident I won't whimper like a schoolgirl, I open my mouth again. "Kyle, if you don't leave right now, I will knock your teeth out one by one."

His face, initially serious, splits into a smile, and he knocks at the door, laughing hysterically. "Prim, stop sucking dick! We've gone viral!"

With a throaty hum, she pops off my dick, wipes her face, and stands. I watch my last bit of hope wither away as she brushes the dirt off her knees and turns to face Kyle. "What? What happened?"

"Look!" Kyle opens the door, then holds his phone out, and it might just be me being difficult, but there's one person too many around my naked junk, so I turn my back to them and fit my slick cock into my briefs, then painfully squeeze it inside my jeans.

I swear, one of these days, they'll have to cut it off.

"Holy shit!" Primrose squeals. "It's our live!"

"Yes. Look. Look at these numbers. You two are basically the new social media couple—overnight!"

Wait, I'm *what*?!

I walk to where they're huddled over Kyle's phone, scrolling through videos. She's swiping so fast, it takes me a second to understand that I'm watching Primrose and I kissing during her live.

Nauseatingly sweet music accompanies a slow-motion video of me stepping in front of the camera and kissing Primrose. The video then turns black and white as I lean close to her ear, and the words of the song appear on the screen. "Wait—who made this?"

"I don't know."

"Someone remixed a video about us?"

Primrose looks up at me, and I can't tell whether she's disgusted or concerned. "Remixed a video?"

Oh, geez. "What would you call it?"

"I'd call it by its name, which is an edit."

"Fine. Why are people making *edits* about us?"

Her grin whittles down until it's an easy curve of her lips. She scrolls, and another rendition of the same video appears. Then again. And again. With one filter or another, with different songs and effects—the two of us kissing.

What sort of fuckery is this?

"Well?" Kyle says as he widens his arms. "What are we waiting for?"

Primrose shakes her head, an amazed expression on her face. "What do you want us to do? Let social media do its thing."

"Dude. Social media *is* doing its thing." Kyle says, and widening his eyes at me, he gestures at the door. "The phones are ringing. Let's go," Kyle says as he claps his hands. "And you"—he points at Primrose—"This is your chance at online redemption. Show these people you're *not* the 'psycho' Derek claims you are. Why would you, when you've got Prince Charming making you kneel in horse shit."

The stables are clean, but I don't care enough to point it out.

Primrose turns to me, her apologetic eyes meeting mine.

I sigh, admitting defeat. "Go. Get your . . . redemption."

"Are you sure?" She looks back at Kyle, then turns to me and whispers, "We can finish. It looked like you wouldn't need more than a minute."

I fight the instinct to smack her ass and kiss her instead. "Nah. I think I've been around him," I say as I jerk my head toward Kyle, "a little too long for my boy to come out and play."

Her nose scrunches. "Sorry I made it worse."

She did. So much worse. I think I need to sit.

But as she squeezes my hand and gives me a parting kiss on the cheek, I can't even pretend to mean it.

She makes everything so much better.

let himself go with me
. . .
Primrose

I STAND at the threshold of the guest bedroom. I haven't seen Logan in nearly twenty-four hours and haven't taken a break since. There was just so much to do. Yesterday went by in a haze between the comments and messages asking for information about the farm and the phone buzzing nonstop until late at night. Today, Kyle came to find me and told me that they're running out of produce.

Out of produce.

I still can't believe it, but Logan has been working on finding delivery companies, packaging materials, and extra arms to work in the fields—everything to meet this rapid and sudden increase in demand. At some point this morning, I was instructed to send any potential customer to a vegan farm a few hours away.

Everything is different now.

Logan already has his brother's money but won't be forced to use it anymore. Our kiss changed his life—and the lives of everyone on this farm, myself included.

As it turns out, people are fickle, and now that I'm no longer the weird candy lady obsessed with my ex, I'm back in the public's grace. Which is good, since social media will remain my source of income for the time being. Now, if I could only figure out what will happen between me and Logan once I leave in two days...

I should tell him about Marisol, but I haven't had the time. And to be honest, I'm terrified that once he knows I have no real reason to force me to go, he won't ask me to stay.

Maybe he wants his house back—his privacy.

With a sigh, I grab my phone from the bedside table. The notifications keep rolling in—last time I checked, the recording of our live had twenty million views.

Logan's bike roars in the distance, and with a squeak, I check the time. Kyle told me I had at least one more hour before Logan would show up—what is he doing here?

I throw one last look in the mirror and dart out of the room. I look like a child wearing her parents' clothes with his jacket on, but the fact that I'm wearing nothing underneath might help crank up the sexiness.

I hope so, at least, because I know Logan has been somewhat holding off due to my inexperience. I'm dead set on pissing him off and find out just how much.

I pull it over my breasts as I walk to his bedroom, then face the door and cross my legs in front of me. He's always talking about my thighs, so that's the first thing I want him to notice. My naked thighs under the black leathery fabric of his jacket.

The engine noise grows louder until it stops, and a few seconds later, I hear his steps on the porch.

He'll be proud of me—hell, I'm proud of myself. And sure, he used to hate it when I wore his clothes, but things were different back then, and I think knowing what it feels like to squeeze his ass while he fucks my throat gives me a certain kind of right.

The door opens, my heart beating like a drum in my chest. Sweat dampens my back as self-doubt makes me swallow nervously. Neither of us slept last night, so he might be too tired for this.

What if he doesn't take it as the playful show of disobedience I'm aiming for? What if he just gets mad?

"Hello?" he calls from the entrance.

"H-hey," I say back.

Come on, Prim. Confidence. What's done is done, so I might as well own it.

"Where are you?"

Oh my god, I'll have a heart attack if he doesn't just come in and see me. "Uh, bedroom!"

He enters the room, hands on his helmet to pull it off his head, then immediately freezes. His gorgeous eyes run over my body through the gap, and shoulders dropping, he lets his arm fall down his sides.

"Hello," I whisper. I was going for *seductive temptress*, but it sounds more like *schoolgirl caught in a fib*.

"What's . . . what's this?" he breathes out.

"I figured I'd try your jacket before buying my own. You don't mind, do you?"

Please play along. Please play along.

He says nothing, eyes running up and down my body as if he can't decide what to look at first.

I twirl around so that he sees the way his jacket stops right beneath my ass. "How do I look?"

His chest heaves as he slowly steps forward, like a hunter trying not to spook his prey. I think he knows I'm provoking him on purpose—that I want him to unleash his true self and show me the extent of what he likes in bed. That I'm dying for him to be rough.

If I'm supposed to leave in two days, then I intend to take full advantage of them.

"I thought we agreed you wouldn't wear my clothes."

"We did," I confirm, batting my lashes as he stops in front of me "Should I take it off, cowboy?"

His pupils are blown wide, his unwavering gaze set on me, and the smell of him is making me dizzy. "Run."

The growing pressure in my stomach has my thighs turning slick, and nearly out of breath, I ask, "Run?"

"Run . . . fast." His low, raspy voice shoots to my stomach. "'Cause I'll catch you, Barbie. And when I do, I'm going to fuck you like I hate you."

He lets me go, takes a step back, and flips his visor down.

My god.

He's terrifying. And captivating. And so . . . incredibly . . . hot. Does he really want me to run away?

Without a second thought, I dart past him, out the front door and down the porch stairs, an exhilarated giggle bursting out of my lips as the grass crunches underneath my naked feet.

I keep moving forward, adrenaline making me faster than usual, and dare a glance behind me. Logan is following, black helmet and gloves on. Though he's not running, one of his strides is worth three of mine, so I speed up past the gentle pain in my legs that reminds me I am not a runner.

I bolt toward the orchard, past the first few rows, until apple trees surround me.

Once I'm confident I'm deep enough, I stop, brace my hands on my knees, and wait for my heartbeat to settle.

I can't hear him walking, but I frantically turn left and right, peering through the gaps between the endless rows of trees. He was right behind me before I entered the orchard. Maybe he's hiding.

A noise to my right has me flinching, and without even turning to check if it's Logan, I take off again. I laugh, fully knowing I should remain silent, but unable to stop myself. Adrenaline thrums in my veins as I slalom between trees, my muscles growing tired with every step.

When I'm too exhausted to continue, I hide behind a trunk. I've run almost to the other side of the orchard, and he could be anywhere. I haven't seen him in a while—where is he?

"Gotcha."

A strong arm wraps around my waist, pulling me to the right, and with a squeal, I free myself of his hold and run. I don't make it far before both his arms squeeze my stomach, and I crumble down to the ground.

"Let me go!" I laugh, thrashing against the grass as he pins my body down with his weight. "I'm never giving it back!"

"If you keep the jacket, I'm keeping you."

With his free hand, he pulls my waist up, my chest still pressed to the ground. The jacket bunches around my hips, and the moisture between my legs is now exposed to the morning air. All the exhilaration of the moment fades in favor of a hungry need for him, especially as I throw a look past my shoulder and see the helmet still hides his face. From the way his head is tilted down, I know he's staring down at my ass, fully exposed to him, and just the sight of it makes me whine.

He lifts his visor, and the blue and gray irises have been swallowed by darkness, his brow tightly furrowed. I get lost in the way he looks at me. Like he needs me, like he owns me.

"*God*, I missed you." With a lightning-fast movement, his hand cracks down on my ass, the loud slapping noise hitting a moment before the pain.

I squeal, my body flinching, but the leather of his gloves quickly massages the raw skin of my ass as his other hand snakes around the back of my neck, keeping my cheek pressed to the ground.

"I missed this ass." His hand smacks my other cheek, my body flinching forward as I let out a gasp. His gloved hand rubs down my ass, over my drenched pussy, then down my thighs. "I missed you splayed out and completely at my mercy."

Bringing his hand up, he pinches the gloves with his teeth and pulls them off, then throws them to one side. My knees press against the dewy grass, my back arching as his hold of my neck tightens. I want him to overpower me so badly. I want his punishing touch on my body, the full weight of his desire, the entirety of his soul.

Once he's taken the helmet off, he meets my gaze. "If at any point you want to stop—"

"I'll tell you," I reassure him. "Now, please—"

His finger slides inside me, the inner walls of my pussy clenching around the intrusion. He rolls it inside me, then adds a second finger, stretching me.

"Is this why you wanted my attention?" he whispers as he leans forward. "Because you're so wet for me?"

"Yes," I whimper as I buck my hips. Though his fingers are deep inside me, he's not using them to fuck me, and I can feel myself growing needier.

"You want me to use you, little backpack?"

"Yes," I say, even more desperately. "Please."

"Are you sure?" he asks as his fingers continue their torturous movements inside me. "Because if you keep grinding your hips like that, I'm going to think what you want is to come on my fingers."

My erratic movements falter, my hands bunching in the grass beside my head. It's hard to keep still—he's giving me just enough to keep me wanting more. Like he's designed a game I'm meant to lose.

"I can make it happen for you, you know."

My eyes roll to the back of my head as he plunges his fingers in and pulls back hard, again and again. I spread my legs wider, hands clutching at the ground.

"Just like that. If you want to come, I'll let you ride my fingers. I'll feast on your pussy, and then I'll fuck you until you come apart for me. How does that sound, Barbie?"

"No," I cry out, though my body is in fervent disagreement. "No, please. Use me for yourself."

His left hand abandons the back of my neck as his fingers pull out of me. With one quick motion, my arms are pulled behind me, and my hard nipples brush against the dirt.

Once he grabs my wrists, I can't move at all. The side of my face is pressed against the ground as something soft wraps around them, and he entraps both my arms by making a second loop.

"I knew I'd find a good use for your scrunchies."

I listen to the whir of his zipper and peep past my shoulder at the pink flamingos wrapped around my wrists, my breaths running quickly out of my parted lips.

"You know why I don't want you wearing my clothes, Barbie?" he asks.

I blink, then swallow, but neither action seems to help my brain snap out of its trance. "B-because you're astonishingly possessive of your things?"

"I'm possessive of one thing only, and that's my backpack," he snaps. The fabric of his jeans presses firmly against my calves. "The reason I don't want you wearing my clothes, especially my favorite jacket, is entirely different." The crown of his cock rubs against me, dipping in before disappearing again.

"What is it?" I ask, out of breath. My heart is thumping, the anticipation making me pant as my every nerve tenses. "Why don't you want me to wear your clothes?"

His cock parts my lips, only the head moving past the resistance and making me shiver with pleasure.

"Because it makes me lose control."

I moan loudly as he slams his stiff erection to the hilt. My eyes water as he groans, my brain simmering in pleasure as I contract around him.

I feel so full.

"Did my pretty little backpack lose her tongue?" He pulls back. "Maybe I should fuck that bratty mouth of yours. Make sure it's still there."

"Yes," I whisper as he presses forward, cramming his cock deep inside me. Tears run down my cheeks as my mouth twists. "Whatever you want."

He rubs a hand along my spine, all the way between my shoulders, then fists my hair. "Here's what's going to happen, Barbie." He leans closer until his beard brushes my cheek, his voice laced with effort as he murmurs, "I'm going to fuck my favorite little hole until I shoot my load as far as you can take it."

I whimper, breathing in the scent of dirt and grass.

"You can come as many times as you want to. As many times as you manage. But I'm not going to stop for you. I will fuck you as hard, and as deep and for however long I wish to."

He groans when I move my hips to grind against him, looking for a release.

"And once I'm done with you, I'll flip you around and clean you up with my fingers. I'll push them deep inside you, get them coated with my pleasure and yours, then push them down your throat until you've cleaned up the mess you made."

My face rubs against the grass as I nod, and a whimper accompanies every breath from my lips. I can't think anymore, can't keep still. My nails dig into my wrist, and my arousal drips down my inner thighs.

"Watch me while I fuck you into the dirt, backpack."

With his hand still gripping my hair, my neck is angled to the right, and though every one of my muscles strains in this position, out of the corner of my eye, I can see him looming over me. And it's so worth it.

I keep my eyes on him just like he asked, but at the first thrust, they cross, the mix of pleasure and pain making lights explode in my brain. Then a second comes, and a third, and soon enough, I'm overwhelmed, only able to submit to him.

"Logan," I call, my legs shaking as an orgasm moves through me and takes over my body. "Oh my god—oh my—"

Pleasure ripples through me, his thrusts faltering when I clench around him.

He moans as his rhythm picks up again, and with my orgasm still echoing through me, I cry out. It's too much to take—too much pleasure, too much brute force—and then, it's not nearly enough. His cock works me up again, and before long, I'm on the brink of another orgasm, and his hand is tugging at my hair as a reminder he wants me to watch him.

Eyes struggling to stay open, I stare at his taut jaw, his hungry eyes. He stares back for a while, then looks between us, his eyes fluttering. "You should see this, Barbie. My cock disappearing into your drenched pussy."

With a loud hum piercing the silence, I call his name, and my orgasm explodes around his shaft for the second time in a handful of minutes. This time, he doesn't ease at all, his speed increasing as his hips slap against my ass.

I try to adjust to the unrelenting rhythm of his cock pushing inside me, and with every bit of my body tingling, I feel it start all over again. I could stop him with a word, and my shaking legs beg me to. But everything hurts deliciously, and feeling him relinquish control is what I've craved since the moment he kissed me on that deserted road.

I will lie here and take it until he comes, just like he asked me to. And I will enjoy every minute of it.

"Don't stop," I say through gritted teeth. "Show me who I belong to."

He growls, his cock sinking hard inside me. "Scream, Barbie. I want everyone to know you're mine."

you're perfect

...

Logan

SWEAT DRIPS DOWN MY CHEEKS, my arms, my back. My jeans are drenched in Primrose's cum, and more keeps dripping down her thighs, driving me crazy.

If I weren't impaling her with my cock, if I had any power to drag myself away from her tight, warm pussy, I'd lick it clean. I'd savor her tangy taste on my tongue and feel her stomach contract under my hand as I stuff my face between her legs.

But I don't have a hope of moving an inch away until I've released inside her cunt.

I rut into her, my pace quickening as I grit my teeth. I lift her leg, and now that she's all stretched up for me and has come a few times already, her pussy is so slick that I'm on the verge of losing it.

"Drench my cock, little backpack." I tip my head back as she pulses around me, my balls contracting hard. "Make"—I say as I sink into her—"a fucking"—I grip her ass in my hand and squeeze—"mess."

She mumbles something, her hands twisting behind her as her ass wiggles with each of my thrusts. She takes it so well, I might never recover.

"You're doing great." She's so tight, so perfectly made for me, that every thrust brings me dangerously close to spilling out, makes me hungry for more.

I see how badly she wants to please me. How she likes to be degraded, not with my words necessarily, but with my actions. She craves to be my little hole to play with however I want, and fuck if it isn't everything I've always dreamt of. Someone to forfeit all control. Someone to trust me completely.

"Hands on the ground," I say as I pull the scrunchie off her wrists, and her face rises from the dirt. "Come on, quick."

Her hands unlock from behind her back, and weakly, she holds her weight on her hands, her body shaking.

I grip her hip while keeping one of her legs up, and now that I can pull her to me while I sink inside her, I fuck her twice as fast, twice as hard.

Her shouts fill the silence, and they prompt me to keep going, to make her come again.

"You think they can hear you?" I ask as I try to maintain some semblance of control. "You think everyone knows that you're getting stuffed with my cock in the orchard? Hmm? That you lose all self-respect when it comes to getting my dick?"

She throws her head back, mewling as another orgasm has her fluttering around me.

It's the one that brings me over the edge, and I bottom out inside her, my movements turning erratic as she lowers her chest to the ground, no longer able to hold herself up.

"Here it comes, Barbie," I rumble. Pleasure mounts in the back of my brain and rushes down my spine. "I'm going to fill you up so well."

"Y-yes," she stutters. I can't see her face now that her cheek is pressed on the grass again, but a faint "Please, Logan," rumbles in the space between us.

"Oh, fuck, Primrose." I push deep into her, moans flying out of my lips as my movements stutter. I release inside her, losing track of time so deeply that once I'm done, my cock slides out nearly limp.

I breathe out, then set her leg back on the ground. The moment her knees are on the grass, she falls to one side, her back rising and falling as she catches her breath.

But a promise is a promise, and I'm hardly done with her.

I grab her legs and spread them so I'm kneeling between her thighs.

Crap, she's so beautiful.

My jacket falls open beneath her, and her soft, fair skin is covered in grass stains. Her tits and face and knees are rubbed raw, her legs and waist drenched.

What a perfect, dirty little mess.

Her eyes are half-lidded, and she's taking shuddering breaths. I push back the damp hair by the sides of my face, then, leaning forward, I do the same with hers. "You good?"

She nods, languid eyes looking into mine.

"What hurts?"

She huffs out a weak laugh. "Everything."

I bet.

I brush some dirt off her cheek, dropping a soft kiss on her lips as I let my hand roam down and push two fingers inside her, rubbing softly.

Her breath catches as her eyes widen, and it's as if she's reminded of what I told her before.

When I bring my finger to her lips and tap, her mouth opens, and she closes her eyes. Her tongue swirls around them, licking them clean. I push them down her throat, and she gags, moaning and drooling until I pull them out.

We repeat the cycle a few more times as our bodies cool down, and by the time she's reasonably clean, I'm hard again.

"Come, let's go home."

I slide painfully into my briefs, then button my jeans. With slow, sleepy movements, she also sits up, but when she tries to get on her feet, I scoop her up.

"I can walk," she says, her head snuggling against the nook of my neck.

"Uh-huh."

"I can," she insists, but she wraps her arms around my neck, her face cozily nestled under my chin. "Thank you, Logan."

"You're thanking me for sex?"

"No. Yes, also. Mostly for playing along. I was worried you'd get mad because I wore your jacket."

I didn't get mad, but I almost *went* mad. I missed her so much, and when I entered the bedroom, there she was, naked if not for my riding jacket. I don't think I've ever wanted someone more in my life.

I walk us toward the house, and by the time I open the front door, she's almost asleep. I kick the door shut behind us, then walk straight to my room and set her on my bed.

Turning to one side, she smiles up at me with sleepy eyes. "Cuddle?"

"You need to wash up," I say as I trace the dirt painted on her body with my thumb.

"In a minute," she insists, but I shake my head. As much as I enjoyed getting her dirty, now I want to clean her up, massage her sore muscles and kiss every bit of skin that stings.

I head for the bathroom, then run the faucets until they're the right temperature and sprinkle in some bath salts I find lying around. Once the whole room smells like lavender, I return to Primrose's side, dropping to my haunches to gently shake her awake.

"Where are we going?"

"I prepared the tub for you."

When I lift her again, she kisses my jaw, skating kisses along my cheek until she presses her lips to mine. Our tongues graze, and the taste of sugar and spring warms up my heart in ways I can't even process.

If I could keep her in my arms and kiss her like this forever, I probably would.

"Can you stand?" I rasp.

"Yes," she whispers and resumes suckling on the spot beneath my ear.

I set her down, then pull the jacket off her shoulders. "Get in, the water's warm."

"Did you put essential oils in?"

"Bath salts," I mumble. "I had some old ones here."

She leans forward, pressing a kiss to the middle of my chest. "Get in with me?"

"I don't think there's enough room for both of us."

"Really?" Tilting her head, she pulls at the sides of my shirt. "I think we've managed to fit bigger things in smaller spaces."

Snorting out a laugh, I raise both arms so she can remove my shirt. I wanted her to enjoy her bath in peace, but this sounds much better, so without further resisting, I strip off my clothes and slink beneath the water.

She follows, settling between my legs and resting her cheek on my chest, her soft body relaxing against mine. Slotting in like the missing piece of a puzzle. It makes no sense that we match so well. Whether we're fucking or fighting, pressing each other's buttons or pushing our limits, we work like magic.

And I seriously hope nothing will break this spell.

Steam rises around us, creating a cocoon of intimacy. I reach for Primrose's purple sponge and pour a healthy amount of soap as she pops the bubbles clinging to the water's surface.

Gently, I trace the contours of her skin, and in a way, it feels more intimate than sex. Touching her like she's mine while she's nestled between my arms and resting on my chest.

"Hey, now that the police are done chasing after us, do you think Paco and Lola can come back? I miss them," she says, breaking the tranquil silence.

I let out a contented sigh, reminded of when I found her constant chatting annoying. Now, it's relaxing. Soothing. "Sure, Barbie. I'll ask Kyle to bring them over tonight."

"Thank you," she says with a grateful smile as she traces the shape of my tattoos. Once she turns her focus to my arm, she asks, "How do you choose what design to get?"

"I've always known I wanted some of them, like the cow. With others, I just booked with my artist and chose on the day of my appointment."

"Is it your favorite animal?" she asks as she traces the shape of the cow's head. "Is that why you wanted it?"

I move the sponge to her neck, and she relaxes into me. "Yes. Cows are social, emotional. They're great problem solvers too, you know? Very smart animals. Kind of like the farm version of a dog."

"That mostly stays still."

I huff out a laugh. "You'd be surprised."

"What's this empty spot?" she asks as she touches the skin below my wrist.

"Hm? Oh, nothing. I haven't had time to get a new tattoo in years. It's the last free spot on my arm, but it's tiny. I'm not even sure what could fit there."

She snuggles closer, and I feel a rush of affection as I drag the sponge to her chest. "How about a cowboy hat?"

"Nope."

"Cowboy boots."

"No."

Laughter bubbles out of her lips. "You're no fun."

I bite her neck, and as she squirms away, her feet rise above the water. "Didn't look like it back in the orchard."

"Wait—I know just the right thing."

She walks out of the tub, dripping water all over the floor.

"No, come back. Where are you—"

She's already out the door, so I drop my head back, smiling at the ceiling. A minute later, she walks back into the bathroom and closes the door behind her, holding a Sharpie.

Watching her move around comfortably while completely naked is so good, she could draw a dick on my forehead, and I wouldn't say a word.

She relaxes against me again, and I watch her draw a small horse. She *tsks* when one of its ears turns out a little crooked. "There. I think it looks beautiful," she says as she releases my arm. Once her back rests on mine again, I bring my wrist closer. "Why a horse?"

"It's a white horse."

Ah, of course. A white horse, like on her bucket list.

I reach for my shampoo, pouring a generous amount into my hand before massaging it on her scalp. "How's that a white horse? It's a black Sharpie."

"Yes, but it's not filled in." She traces the edges of her drawing. "See?"

"So it's a transparent horse."

"It's a *white* horse."

I hum, tilting my head. "Maybe a *nude* horse."

The water laps gently against the sides of the tub, a soothing backdrop to her laughter. "Whenever I went through something as I grew up—from minor inconveniences to challenging times—I always pictured my prince coming to save me on a white horse."

"That's not very progressive of yo—"

Her elbow sinks into my stomach, and I sputter out a chuckle.

"He'd come back for me every time I needed." As she dips her fingers in the water and wiggles them, I push up off the edge and grab the shower head.

"What type of things did he save you from?"

"Just about anything. Not being invited to a party, my parents fighting, kids at school making my life hard."

Her hands slide along my thighs, gently massaging my muscles, and as the warm water descends over her hair, I drop kisses along her shoulder. "Is that why I get the horse tattoo? Am I your savior, little backpack?"

"If anything, you've gotten me into a whole lot of trouble."

"You've seen nothing yet," I mumble, brushing my nose against her neck. She chuckles, and I press my lips to her shoulder. "Perfect," I mumble. "Your laugh is perfect. Your skin is perfect. You . . . are . . . *so* perfect."

Her eyes are closed, her lips parted, and the freckles sprinkled over her nose and cheeks are even more prominent with the steam. She's so beautiful it hurts, so reactive to me it's fucking poetry. My erection stiffens behind her, and she responds by twisting to me and tentatively reaching for it.

I shake my head, holding her hand back. "Not now. I'm taking care of you."

A smile tugs at the corners of her mouth. "Okay." After a moment of silence, she touches my wrist. "Well, do you like it?"

I nod, staring at the little crooked horse nestled between a crow and an abstract tribal design. It's ridiculous, but I like it. Just like my Barbie.

"Thank you," I say as she tilts her head back. "For coming back."

With a soft sigh, she brings my hand to her lips and kisses my knuckles one by one, then mumbles, "So, uh . . . one more day, huh?"

"Yup. Less than twenty-four hours." Ignoring the lump in my throat, I peck the back of her head.

What are we going to do? She said she loves me, so she's definitely not casual about us, but that doesn't mean she'll want to have a long-distance relationship. What if she asks me to move? I'm crazy enough about her that I would. What would happen to the farm then? To the animals?

"Maybe I don't need to leave."

I tilt my head to the side to look at her, carefully studying her eyes. "What do you mean?"

"I'd still have my apartment in Mayfield, so it's not like—" She shakes her head. "I'm not saying I'd *move*, just . . . extend my stay. And I could get my own place. Get out of your hair, but stick to Pinevale—or Roseberg."

She would do that? For me? "But what about Marisol? Aren't you supposed to start next week?"

"Uh . . ."

"Primrose?" I insist. With the fight, then the hospital, then the video going viral, we haven't discussed this in days. Did something happen?

"I, um . . . I won't take the job."

What? "Didn't they like the strawberry candy?"

"No, they did. They loved it." With a sigh, she plays with the hairs on my arms. "But they wanted me to use white sugar and gelatine. To cut down costs, I guess."

So her candy wouldn't be vegan—it wouldn't be suitable for many people, actually. It'd be a store-bought candy like all others. "Oh." I rest a hand on her chest and pepper kisses on her ear. "I'm sorry, Barbie."

"That's okay." She swallows hard, eyes meeting mine. "At least I can stay. If . . . um, if you want me to."

If I *want* her to? I would commit crimes to keep her here. I would buy a TV. Get Wi-Fi. I'd sleep on a bed made of goddamn scrunchies if it meant she'd share it. "You shouldn't get an apartment. I already know you're a horrible roommate. Reason number one why I wouldn't date you."

"But you *are* dating me."

"Right. That's what I'm saying." When she narrows her eyes at me, I tilt her head back a little more. "Primrose, are you sure? Life at the farm isn't exactly your idea of a good time, and—"

"I love the farm," she scolds. "I don't love the no-internet part."

"But what about your dream? Your candy?"

"It's okay. I have social media, and I have you." She smiles dreamily and closes her eyes. "That's more than enough—more than I ever dared to dream of, actually."

I kiss her forehead, but the happiness I wish I were feeling isn't there. She's willing to stay here with me, at the farm. It's more than *I* ever dared to dream of, but it also feels . . . wrong. She's giving up on her dream, and she shouldn't. I won't let her.

Even if it means she'll leave me behind.

believe in me

. . .

Primrose

THOUGH I'M GETTING WEIRDLY USED to riding behind Logan for someone who's only done it a handful of times, riding along the farm's property line is new, and with the total darkness, a different experience altogether. Even more intimate, with the nothingness surrounding us.

My arms tighten around him, checking. Making sure this is real and I'm not dreaming.

He wants me to stay. In fact, he doesn't want me to get an apartment—he wants me to stay at the farm with him.

He wants *me*.

After I came out of the shower half an hour ago, he looked over at me from the couch and, with the softest eyes, told me to get ready because he was taking me out.

Where to? No idea, but to be honest, who cares? I want to be wherever he is. Which, from the look of it, is where nothing else is.

He comes to a stop, and once the bike lights turn off, I pull my visor up. I still can't make out a single thing around us. "I think we'll need the flashlight."

"We're fine."

"You *do* know I tend to fall even when visibility is ten out of ten, right?"

"Here," he says as he laughs, then helps me off the bike by my hips. "We wouldn't want you to fall."

Oh, I've fallen already. Fallen for him in a way I didn't think was possible.

"Hand?"

I find his fingers, and once they're tangled with mine, he gently nudges me forward. "So, can I know where we're going?"

"The valley."

"Huh." That's the place Kyle wanted to take me to on my second night here. "Is it an *actual* valley?"

"I guess. It's a narrow strip of land between two hills."

"And why is it special?" I ask. My boots sink in the mud, and with a grimace, I think of a much better question. Was a dinner date outside the realm of possibility?

"You ask too many questions, Barbie."

"Will I even be able to see anything?" I insist. He's only a step away, and I can't see him—how does he expect me to enjoy this valley?

"Too many questions."

"Fine." I follow him for a while longer until he comes to a stop.

"Come." He guides me closer, then settles both hands over my eyes. "We're almost there."

"I'd ask if my eyes need to be covered, but—"

"Just walk."

I amble along the uneven terrain until he tells me to stop, and I register a low buzzing in the background.

"Ready?"

Through the gaps in his fingers, I can see splashes of golden lights, and my heartbeat escalates as I try to identify the source. Fairy lights? Actual fairies? What the hell is going on? "Ready," I say breathlessly.

When his warm fingers finally release me, I blink a few times, adjusting to the sudden light.

Then I see the breathtaking valley stretching before me, illuminated by countless twinkling, floating lights. Are those... "Fireflies?"

Logan nods, but I barely even notice the bob of his head. There must be thousands of them, flickering up and down, left and right. "They show up in spring, and they're gone midway through the summer."

My breath is suspended as I take it all in, my eyes filling with the sparkling and dancing movements of the magical creatures. "It's like something out of a dream."

"Hmm." He walks closer and wraps both arms around me. I can't look away from the fireflies but gently sink my fingers into his skin, anchoring myself to him. "I feel the same way when I look at you."

With butterflies in my stomach, I twist to look up at him. "I love it. Thank you for showing it to me."

"You're welcome, Barbie."

Turning back to the fireflies, I stand there, speechless, my eyes wide with wonder. Everything about this moment is perfect–almost *too* romantic. It's as if he brought me here to say those words—the ones he nearly said but then took back.

Though he has every right to take his time, I've been dying to hear them.

Logan clears his throat, his body tensing behind me, and my heart palpitates.

"Hey guys."

I flinch as I turn to Kyle. Logan doesn't seem surprised to see him, and at first, my shoulders slump. I thought he'd brought me here for something romantic, and he called his friend?

But then I notice he's holding a cage, and with a gasp, I walk closer. "Oh my god! Are these—" I crouch, and Lola snorts as she saunters closer. "It *is* you! Hi, baby girl." When Paco joins her side, I give them both a cuddle through the bars. "I missed you guys so much. You have no idea."

I turn to Logan, who's smiling fondly at me. "Come on! Come say hi."

He lifts his chin in his friend's direction, and with a wave, Kyle excuses himself and leaves.

Once Logan is kneeling beside me, he smiles down at the piglets. "Want to take them out?"

"You mean it?"

"Sure." He opens the cage, holding Paco back with one hand while he hands me Lola with the other. I remember the first time he did that, precisely sixteen days ago. When I was hurt and heartbroken, and Logan was nothing to me but a dude who'd kissed me and then acted stupidly rude.

Lola's soft, warm body fits perfectly in the curve of my arms, her weight a comforting presence I've missed more than words can express. I press my cheek against her velvety fur, inhaling the familiar scent of hay and sunshine that clings to her coat. "Have you been good to Uncle Kyle? Did he feed you stuff you're not supposed to eat?"

I turn to Logan with a smile, but it quickly falls as I notice he's not holding Paco, and the tiny piglet is trotting in the direction of the closest tree. Sure, he's not exactly a jaguar, and even if he were to run, we should be able to catch up, but if he plans on taking the piglets out for strolls, maybe leashes are in order.

"Don't let him get too far," I tell Logan as I watch Paco push his snout on a big, flat mushroom.

"Barbie."

Logan's firm voice makes my stomach drop. His eyes are softly studying my face, a sad smile bending his lips as if there's something obvious I'm not quite grasping. What the hell is happening?

I glance at Paco, then back to Logan. "Are we not . . . taking them on a walk?"

"No."

My arms tighten around Lola, who squelches until I relent.

He wants to leave them here. He wants to leave them behind.

"N-no!" I step back, shaking my head hard. "Why? Why would we abandon them?"

"We're not abandoning them, Barbie." Logan steps closer, his hand clasping my shoulder to steady me. "They're meant to be here. To be free. The plan was never to keep them at the farm forever."

"But . . . but all the animals who stay permanently at the farm—"

"They're hurt, have been through something traumatic, or have been domesticated to the point where they wouldn't survive in the wild." He rubs behind Lola's ears. "But these two—they're young, healthy. They have a chance to adapt if we let them go now, so that they can grow and develop like they were always meant to be."

Lola lets out another screech, and once I look down at her, I notice that my tears are staining her coat. "Sorry," I whisper as I wipe them away with one hand. Though I've picked her up plenty before today, I'm suddenly realizing how much heavier she's gotten over the last sixteen days. How much bigger too.

But Logan must be wrong, right? They're only four weeks old—how can they survive in the wild?

"Waiting more time would only be detrimental." He pinches my chin. "Sometimes, you have to let someone go for their own good, backpack. You need to trust that somehow, at some point, they'll come back. You have to believe in them the same way they've believed in you."

He's clearly not talking about the pigs anymore, and this is starting to feel like a goodbye in more than one way. Did he change his mind about us? About me staying?

Throwing one more glance at Paco, now rubbing his side against a large trunk, I sniffle. Though he's the most sensitive of the two, with how easily he startles and the amount of cuddles he demands, the thought of letting Lola go is even harder. She's been my shadow over the last couple of weeks. She's the one Logan handed me that first night, and I like to think that going through that together brought us closer. She's slept on my shirts, eaten my candy, and followed me around the house every day.

But if it's for her own good, I suppose I should let her go.

I kneel, running my fingers through her soft, pink fur one last time. "You're going to be okay," I say, my voice thick with emotion. "You'll be happier here, I promise. Just keep an eye on your brother. You know how boys are."

Her black eyes meet mine and stare in the same focused way they always do.

"And we'll be back to check on you. So if you feel homesick or decide this whole wildlife thing isn't for you . . . you follow us to the car, okay? We'll bring you back home."

She doesn't understand a thing I'm saying, yet I feel like I should tell her so much more. "Don't eat weird berries, and avoid anything with sharp teeth."

When she wiggles in my hands, I set her on the ground and watch as she takes tentative steps forward, her trotters sinking into the soft earth with each stride. She pauses as if sensing the gravity of the moment before following Paco and disappearing into the dense undergrowth of the forest.

Logan joins my side, wrapping an arm around my shoulders, and we watch her until she's nothing more than a faint speck in the distance. Until I can no longer hear the rustle of her footsteps or the echo of her oinks in the breeze.

Then, Logan presses his lips on the spot over my ear over and over again, whispering a soft 'shh.' "You did amazing, Barbie. This isn't a sad moment, okay? It's a happy one. They'll do great things, and so will you."

There it is again. What is he talking about?

My brows tighten over my eyes as he reaches behind him and holds out something. He's acting oddly mysterious, and a veil of sadness covers his eyes, making my heart pound as I reach for the small paper.

"The money your brother gave you?" I ask when I notice Aaron's signature on the check intermittently lit by the fireflies. "What do you want me to do with it?"

He shrugs. "Candy for people who can't have candy."

"What?"

"Well, things with Marisol didn't pan out, and I know you said you can't do it by yourself because you don't have the infrastructure, but . . ." He points at the check. "Create it."

Wait—that's how he wants to spend the money his brother gave him? "You want to invest in me?"

"Invest?"

My eyes narrow on him. "Well, I'm assuming you're not just *giving* someone you've known for two weeks this much money."

"Uh, yeah. Yeah, invest." He awkwardly looks away. "Sure. We can write up a contract and everything."

Oh my god. He was totally trying to just give me the money.

I look down at the check, my stomach queasy as I stare at the zeros. It's a lot of money, and I *do* have some savings. I could easily fund product development, branding, and distribution channels with it.

This is the type of money that changes someone's life.

There's only one problem.

"I can't . . . I can't do any of it from here."

I'm not *telling* him. He knows—that's why he's in such a weird mood. Because by giving me this money, he's telling me to go. To leave the farm and go back to Mayfield, because that's where business deals are made. Where I have contacts I can turn to and, among other things, a working internet connection.

"You want me to go," I whisper.

"No, of course not," he says in a stern, decisive voice that turns soft and unsure as he continues, "But maybe . . . Maybe you should anyway."

Please don't cry. Please don't cry.

I look past him toward the apple orchard, trying and failing to hold back my tears. I need to remove myself from the situation.

My flight back home is tomorrow, and if I let him convince me, tonight will be our last night together. If I hear whatever else he's about to say, I won't be able to un-hear it.

"Barbie," Logan calls when I walk. He catches my wrist, then slowly spins me around. His eyes are filled with heartbreak, too hard to look at, but when I tuck my chin, he pulls it up. "Don't walk away from me. It kills me when you do."

"You're *asking* me to walk away from you."

"I'm asking you to follow your dreams."

His voice shakes hard, and the fact that he'd offer means the world, but the fact that doing it is killing him means even more.

I sink into his chest, throwing my arms around him, and just as quickly, he hugs me back. "Is my strong girl angry?"

Breathing through my nose, I nod, though we both know it's hardly anger making me tear up. "I think I finally found the ultimate reason not to date you," I mumble as I let go. I offer him a sad smile, then slump down on a mostly flat rock. "You want me to move to the other side of the country."

"But you will, right?" he asks as he sits beside me.

Hugging my knees, I try to breathe in the crisp night air through the lump in my throat. "I guess I will," I say in a whisper.

He gives me a somber nod, and I turn my cheek. I can't even look at him right now. I'm grateful for his generosity, and I can objectively recognize this is a huge opportunity. But I can't feel any happiness.

All I know is that tonight's my last night with him.

That tomorrow I'll get on a plane, and who knows if I'll ever see him again. Long-distance relationships are complicated, and with less than a week spent as a couple, do we even have the foundations we need to make it work?

When minutes pass, and neither of us has said a word, I glance at him and notice he's fidgeting with my flamingo scrunchie. Of the multitude I have, he picked the silliest one to steal, but I love that he has it—that it'll remind him of me once I'm gone.

With a long exhale, he turns to look at me. "I wrote my own list."

"Hm?"

He takes a piece of scrap paper out of his jacket pocket. "I know we . . . That this whole thing doesn't make sense in theory. We have nothing in common, we met a minute ago, and we have plenty of reasons to let this end now that you're leaving . . ." He nods at the folded paper, and I pinch it from him. "It's all there."

I blink through the surprise, then read the items one by one using my phone's flashlight. *"You can't drive. You kick during sex. Your boobs distract me."* I chuckle, my eyes roaming down. *"You want to ride my bike. You won't let me sleep."*

When I look up, a million questions on my tongue, he's gazing at me.

"All the reasons I wouldn't date you, down to the very last one."

I exhale, reading the last line. *"You're leaving."* When I look up at him, sadness is painted over every feature of his face. "I don't understand, Logan. Why are you showing me this?"

"Because they're all right there. Ink to paper. And I'm happy to add more if you can think of any, but I can't. I read them again and again, and they're just . . ." His head shakes left to right, and my heartbeat picks up. "It's not enough."

I smile, and almost instantly, he does too.

He only smiles like that at me.

"It's not?"

"No. I don't care if it's a bad idea or if we're going too fast." He glances down at the list. "There's nothing in there that'll keep me from you."

He points his index finger left and right as if he wants me to notice the valley again, with its hundreds of fireflies twinkling and buzzing around. "See where we are?"

"Yes?"

"It's the most beautiful place I know."

"Uh-huh."

"Definitely not the ER."

My heart tumbles as I connect the dots.

So he *did* bring me here to tell me those words. Of course, I already know he loves me. If he didn't, he wouldn't have offered to give me so much money or told me to go, though it's clearly not what he wants. If he didn't love me, he wouldn't have almost lost everything to protect me.

I've always wanted someone to tell me they loved me, but he's shown it with his every action, and that's much better.

"Primrose, I—"

"I love you too," I blurt, far louder than appropriate.

He half-smiles. "I haven't said it yet."

"You have. You've said it so many times." I throw myself at him, and his arms quickly wrap around me and pull me onto his lap.

"If it's okay with you, I'd like to say it out loud anyway."

I nod against his chest.

"Primrose, you and me . . . It shouldn't make sense, I guess, but it's shockingly easy, even when it's hard. Even when we argue. I like fighting with you more than getting along with anyone else. That's how I know without a doubt that I love you."

My heart is so full it might just burst. I will never understand how, in seventeen days, he became the most important person in my life, but I'm not questioning it. "I love you too."

"So you shouted," he says as his lips peck the top of my head.

I look up at the clear sky sprinkled with stars, then at the valley lit with fireflies. I'll miss this place so much—not as much as Logan, but almost.

"How is this going to work?" I ask with a pout. He hates technology, and we can't just use Kyle's phone to communicate. "Will you text? Will we talk on the phone and video call and all of that?"

He pauses for a long moment, then nods. "Yes. All of that. I was gone this afternoon because Kyle took me to buy a phone."

When I gape, his hands rub along my sides. "Barbie, I won't

let you vanish from my life. I want to talk to you after tomorrow. I want to talk to you as long as you have things to say."

My heart skips a beat, and for the first time in my life, I'm at a loss for words. Logan Coleman bought a phone. Family and friends have been begging him to, and he did it for me. "We'll be talking forever, then."

With a chuckle, he gives me a 'Don't I know it?' look. "So, can we do it? Kyle explained sexting to me. It sounded interesting."

With a half smile, I ask, "Did he explain phone sex?"

"I think I can figure it out." He pulls me closer. "I'm going to miss you like you've packed up all the oxygen in your ridiculous luggage," he says as he kisses my forehead.

I can't even answer. There's nothing to say, because the thought of leaving him and the farm behind feels . . . like leaving a part of me too.

"Hey, no. Don't be sad, strong Barbie." He pulls my chin up, his brows knitting dramatically. "You'll do great things, I know it."

I nod, though I'm not feeling it. "Maybe tomorrow," I say as I grind my hips forward. "I'd like to do *you* tonight."

His gaze locks with mine, intense and unwavering. "Want me to fuck the sadness out of you, Barbie?"

"Yes." I feel a flutter in my chest as he leans in closer, his warm breath brushing against my skin as my heart pounds faster with each passing second. Once his lips meet mine, a wave of electricity surges through our kiss, and my hands find their way to his shoulders, holding on to him as if he's my lifeline.

He grips the small of my back, pulling me closer, and a rush of heat spreads through me. When our lips part, I'm breathless, my lips tingling. Our eyes meet, and with a smile, I say, "I want you, cowboy."

He smirks, his hand moving my underwear to the side. "Save a horse, Barbie."

Ride a cowboy instead.

you're leaving

. . .

Logan

> Hey.
>
> Kyle helped me set the phone up.
>
> I'm on the porch.
>
> Your shower is taking too long.
>
> Come out here. I miss you.
>
> Where are you?
>
> Sorry, I thought I heard the bathroom door.
>
> Seriously, you don't need seven different lotions.
>
> Your skin is so soft, just come out here and fuck me.
>
> This is Logan, by the way.

I WATCH the screen impatiently as I shift on the step, but still no answer from Primrose. Until three dots appear on the screen.

PRIMROSE
Ten texts???

> **LOGAN**
> Too many?

> **PRIMROSE**
> That was quick. Were you staring at the phone, waiting for an answer?

Huh. Maybe I'm not supposed to do that.

> **LOGAN**
> Yes.

The front door opens, and Primrose comes out in a beautiful yellow dress that makes her look like summer. Her hair is still wet from the shower, and she must have used all seven lotions I've seen her use during her . . . *skincare routine*, as she called it, because her cheeks are glistening.

"'This is Logan, by the way?'"

I shrug. "You didn't have my contact saved yet."

She stands behind me, and as she gently pulls my hair back, I rest the top of my head on her legs and watch her.

"Though I do appreciate the sentiment and share the enthusiasm, I don't think we can have sex." She points at the house. "Your whole family is in the backyard."

I know, but a man is allowed to dream.

Why did I plan this lunch? I guess I felt like Primrose deserves a proper send-off, and I figured that with everything that's been going on with Aaron and Josie, we could all use a distraction.

But Primrose is leaving today, and I don't think I have it in me to pretend I'm fine. I'm anything but fine.

Sure, now I have a smartphone, and Kyle promised to teach me how much I'm allowed to call and the type of conversations that are appropriate to have via text. Primrose has shown me how to turn it on and charge it, and her contact is saved, which is all I need it for. She even promised to send me "nudes."

But it's not the same as having her here, is it?

It's not the same as waking up with her body on mine, not the same as cleaning up after her or knowing that she's past the orchard, making candy inside the house.

"Come on. Let's go."

I take her hand and watch her try to pull me up. Instead, her shoes slide along the porch until she nearly tumbles back. With a chuckle, I stand and follow her to the back of the house.

She waves her beautiful fingers at Kyle before she takes a casserole off his hands and brings it to the big table we've set up in the backyard. Simon follows, then tells her something that makes her laugh, which causes the skirt of her dress to sway as her chest gently shakes.

God, I'm going to miss the sound of her laugh so much.

"Lono?"

I look down at Sadie, pull her up on my lap and sit. "Hey, pretty girl. I like your dress," I tell her as I touch the pink sleeve. "Is it new?"

She nods, playing with a strand of my hair. "It's the same as Prim."

I nod, trying to hide the full extent of my anguish behind a smile. "You look just like her. Maybe she'll give you candy after lunch."

Her eyes widen, her face splitting with a full smile. "Really?"

"Uh-huh. Go ask her."

She jumps off my lap, then runs to the porch, calling Primrose's name. Once she crouches down to talk to Sadie, she looks back at me with a chuckle, and I swear my heart stops for a moment.

"Hey." My brother joins my side, and my cheek-straining smile hardens.

"Hey."

With a tired sigh, he sits beside me. "It's been a while, huh?"

I look at him questioningly, and when he gestures at the table, flashbacks of our childhood hit me all at once. Aaron, Josie, Simon and me, running around the table as our parents and their friends ate lunch. Then a grown-up version of us sitting at the table too, every Sunday, waiting for lunch to be over so we could smoke weed somewhere in the fields. "Yeah, it has."

Josie comes out of the kitchen with my mom, and she glances at me and Aaron before looking away. "Are you guys still . . ."

"Yes, still divorcing." He swallows, lips rolling over his teeth. "I don't know how . . . how we're going to explain it to Sadie."

"Would it help if I told you that, in the end, the happier you are, the happier she'll be?"

"I don't think it would," he says with a sad smile. "But it'd help to know you'll be there." Meeting my gaze for a moment, he shrugs. "For Sadie."

"I'll always be there for her. And . . . you." When he turns to me, I release the breath I've been holding for what feels like five years. "Got your back, remember?"

His eyes flare as they flick to my back, where the ink he inspired still sits, then he looks down at his hands. His eyes moisten, but with a sniffle, he looks away and finds his composure again. "I quit my job."

My mouth opens as I turn to him, and he chuckles. "What—seriously?"

"Seriously." He crosses his legs, stretching back, and now that I think about it, I haven't seen him this relaxed in . . . shit, years. "I'm done. I've worked twelve hours a day for five years. It's time to do something else—something that makes me happy."

"Do you, uh, want to come work at the farm?"

He studies me for a long moment, then shakes his head. "No, the farm is yours. I need to find my own thing."

I'm about to ask if he already knows what that might be when Primrose's melodic voice reaches me again, and I find her with my dad, Sadie between her arms as she whispers into her ear.

"What about you? Are you ready for her to leave?"

I swallow, wishing there was alcohol on the table already. "Do I look like it?"

"No, you don't."

Well, fuck, I'm not. How can I sit here and pretend to be okay with it? How can I go through driving her to the airport knowing this morning was the last time I'd hear that little gasp she makes when I bottom out inside her?

Not the last time, I guess, because we'll meet again. Soon. When winter hits, I'll see her in Mayfield, and my mom invited her to spend Christmas with us before she even set foot in the house earlier today.

But right now, it doesn't feel like enough.

"By the way, I wanted you to know, uh . . ."

"That you've given her the money?" Aaron laughs, rubbing his stubble. "Kyle inadvertently told me already."

Seriously, *why* do I keep that idiot around?

"I invested it in her," I specify. He doesn't need to know that it wasn't my original intention. "We'll draw up a contract and everything."

"It's your money," he says. "And Kyle also said you've had to pass on some clients because of the new volume of orders, so . . . you're free to choose how you spend it."

I nod. I should probably thank him—I still haven't—but I think it'll take me some time. The fact that we're sitting at the same table and no heads are flying is a miracle in itself.

With a long, deep sigh, he shakes his head. "She's been here for what, sixteen days?"

I'd tell him to back off, but he's right. And in that time, I've fallen for her harder and faster than I ever thought possible. Even so, I can't let her walk away from her dream.

She deserves to have it all.

"Seventeen." I shrug, then mumble, "She'll go. I'll be fine."

"No, that's not what I mean." He shrugs when he notices my eyes set on the side of his face. "I just . . ." He flashes me a playful smile. "Seventeen days ago, your farm was failing. You and I weren't talking, and I was in a loveless marriage. And today . . ."

"Today, I'm here, having one of our Sunday lunches for the first time in years."

He nods, huffing out a laugh. "Pretty fucking great."

He doesn't need to tell me how amazing she is. How everything she does is impressive. I know that very well.

Watching Primrose set Sadie down, I smile. "She believes in me so blindly." My throat constricts, tears burning in the backs of my eyes. "I needed someone to believe in me."

He squeezes my shoulder for a moment. "So . . . what are you going to do?"

"I'll drive her to the airport, kiss her goodbye, keep a smile on for her sake, and then . . ."

Then that's it.

I'll focus on work, maybe spend more time with Aaron and Sadie.

"Do you think you guys will be okay?"

I watch Primrose entertain our guests as if this is her house—it might as well be, goddammit. She's in everything, from the million candles to the pink containers, lipsticks, and creams in the bathroom to the scent of sugar in the air. She's embedded in me, so I know what she'd say if the question were pointed at her.

She'd tell me to believe in it. To believe in me and her.

She'd tell me to live life fully, to wear my heart on my sleeve, and not to brush off our seventeen days together because these moments might be as fleeting as dust, but even dust has its place in the world.

Before she got here, I hated my life. And it's much better now because of everything she's done, but not having her here feels like going back to those gray, meaningless days that blur into one another.

She's brought all variants of pink into my life.

And it turns out it's my favorite fucking color.

"Please, just let me carry your goddamn luggage, Primrose."

"I don't *need* you to," she insists as she drags the large suitcase along.

She doesn't need me to? She looks like David trying to cart Goliath around on tiny wheels. But her mood started worsening when we left, and by the time we reached the airport, she had a dark cloud following her around.

"Stupid—freaking—" She kicks the pink suitcase when one of the wheels gets stuck on a broken tile, and raising a brow, I watch her sigh and glance up at me. "Fine. Can you please—"

"Would love to, Barbie."

With her suitcase in hand, I follow her to the large screen showcasing the departures. Once she's located her check-in counter, we stand in line until a grumpy flight attendant takes her luggage. I wait by a bookstore for her to finish up, watching the people inside browse through books and magazines.

"You can go if you want," she says as she joins me.

"Hm? What?"

"You look uncomfortable. I know you don't like crowded places."

Yeah, I don't. I hate the fluorescent lights and loud noises, people screaming and crying and yapping. Of all the crowded places in the world, airports are my least favorite. So many emotions all around me. "It's fine. I'm not going to leave until your plane takes off."

"But we'll have to say goodbye at security."

"I know." I push the rising feeling of despair away, then point at the store. "Come on. I'll get you a couple of books for the trip."

"You don't need to."

"I want to."

She follows me into the store, but the usual bounce in her step is noticeably absent. "How about this?" I ask as I pick up a book with a dark cover that reminds me of one I've seen her read. "*The Hollow House*. Sounds intriguing, right?"

"I guess."

"Or romance? Huh? You want another one of your spicy books?"

"What am I going to do with them now?" she mutters. "You won't be there to take care of me."

"You can handle it yourself."

She pouts. "It's not the same anymore. Not after you."

Setting the book down, I turn to her with a sigh. "I know this is hard. Trust me, I'm not enthusiastic about it either. But we'll talk on the phone every day, and we'll text. And you'll be so busy with your sweets and social media, you won't even notice time passing before you're here again."

"Or I'll be too busy getting my product off the ground. You'll be too busy with the farm. We'll talk for a while, then we'll talk less. And then we'll be stressed out and start fighting. Until, at some point, we'll stop talking altogether because we can't stand each other anymore. And I'll never see this place again."

"Don't say that," I scold. "You know it's not true."

"It *could* happen."

"Barbie, you're just in a shitty mood."

She gives me a flippant shrug, and anger quickly boiling to the surface, I set the book back on the shelf.

"Okay, you want to fight? Would that help? Do you want me to scream at you and be an ass until you leave?"

She huffs out a light chuckle. "It might make it easier."

"Fine. Then I'm choosing your books, and I don't *care* what you want." I walk past her, ignoring her amused expression, then glance at the dozens of covers in front of me. "This one," I say as I point at a pink one. "And that one," I continue, this time not even bothering to check which one I'm pointing at. "Those are the books you're getting. End of story."

She hums, then grabs two different ones. "I want these."

Her tone is softer now, her brows pulled together, and her lips curved into a mischievous smile.

This woman loves to push my buttons.

I'm going to miss her so much.

With a nod, I grab the two books and walk to the cashier.

"Thank you," she says as I hand them to her.

"No problem. Ready to go?"

Her smile vanishes again, so I hold her hand. "Look, we still have those stairs over there, then a ten-minute walk before we get to security. We can fight a whole lot more." I snap my fingers. "For example, you shed like a border collie. I won't miss the blonde and pink hair all over my carpet."

She chuckles, and happy with the result, I walk up the stairs. "You know what else I won't miss?"

"What?"

"How you always put the milk carton back in the fridge even when it's empty. Or—oh, your snoring. And you're a total cover hog."

"I don't snore," she mumbles.

"You do." She doesn't. She's also the only one who drinks milk, so that was bullshit too. As for the covers, I guess that's true, but I run hot at night, so I never keep them on. "Your turn," I say as we reach the top of the stairs. "What are you *not* going to miss about me?"

"Uh, your, hmm . . . you . . ." She frowns, staring at the floor as we walk.

"My beard scratching your face?" I suggest.

"I love it. Not just on my face."

Not now, I mentally bark at myself when I picture her pussy opened up for me. "An internet connection."

"Turns out life without Wi-Fi isn't so bad."

We're approaching the security lines now, and my heart is squeezing too hard to pretend this isn't a big deal. She's leaving, and she's the best thing that's ever happened to me.

"I won't miss the stupid way you kiss me."

I look down at her, her teary eyes staring into mine.

"It's the worst. The way you always need to touch me everywhere. How you cup my cheek like I'm precious. How you pick me up all the time, but always hold a hand over my skirt or dress to make sure nobody can see my underwear."

I swallow hard.

"I won't miss sleeping with you either, with all those cuddles. You always scratch my back and twist your legs around mine. You breathe me in and kiss me until I'm asleep."

My eyes sting, but I try to smile. "I won't miss talking to you." When my voice nearly breaks, I clear my throat. "Your voice. Your questions. The million things going through your mind at any given moment. And I definitely won't miss waking up next to you."

"Morning breath?"

"The worst," I lie. "And your hair is messy. Your boobs are pressing against me. You're warm, with that peaceful expression on your face. Just . . ." Fuck, now *I'm* going to cry. "Awful."

"Yeah, you too."

We stop, and suddenly, I realize there's so much I forgot to tell her. Does she know I feel strong and confident whenever she calls me a cowboy? That every time she enjoys something I cook for her, it melts my heart? I don't think I ever thanked her for keeping a vegan diet while she stayed with me. And I definitely didn't tell her that she saved my life. That I will forever be grateful for it.

"I guess this is it," she says. Tears are streaming down her face, but she's almost expressionless, as if she's not even sure it's really happening.

"Yeah. For now."

She nods, then turns to me, and knowing what she needs, I lean forward and pull her up, a hand on her ass as she winds her legs around me.

"I wish we'd gone out on your bike more," she says. She chuckles, but a sob breaks through. "That we'd kissed more. And spent more time with your friends, and with the animals, and at the valley, and—"

"We'll do it all. This isn't the end."

She nods, nuzzling her face into my shoulder, and for a minute or two, I let her cry into my jacket. All her sorrows pour out as her shoulders shake, and I fight against my own painful breakdown.

I refuse to cry because this isn't the end.

"Okay, come on." I rub her back, then her hair. "Enough with this. Go, and call me when you get home tonight. All right?"

She nods, wiping her tears away, then her lips are on me a million times before she slides down. I kiss her again, then again, until she *really* needs to go, or she'll miss her flight.

"Do great things, okay?" I say as she takes a step back.

She nods and, with one last look, joins the line.

But the gut-wrenching fear that this is the last time I see her kicks the breath out of me.

"Barbie," I call, though most of the crowd turns to me. I walk over to meet her, thanking the couple of people who've already lined up behind her when they let me through.

Her nose is red, sobs shaking her shoulders. "Wh-what is it?"

I take my jacket off. "Take this."

"Your jacket? No—it's your favorite, Logan."

"That's okay." A tear falls down my cheek, and I harshly wipe it with my thumb. "Because we'll meet again, and you'll give it back to me."

The security guard tells Primrose to advance, and after a moment of hesitation, she takes my jacket. "What about you? I don't have anything to give you, Logan. What—" She opens her bag and frantically looks inside, mumbling something about her cowgirl boots. I'd never take them from her anyway.

"I already have something of yours," I say as I bring a hand to her arm to stop her. When I show her my wrist, she grimaces as she stares at the pink flamingos.

"But that's just a scrunchie. You gave me something so important, and I . . ."

She drifts off as I pull the scrunchie up, revealing the wonky horse beneath it. "Trust me, it's important. And it wasn't easy to convince the tattoo artist not to fix that line," I say as I point at the deformed ear.

"Logan," she breathes out. "When . . . when did you do this?"

"Yesterday. It was fading, and I needed it to stay there."

She brings a hand to her mouth and nods frantically before throwing herself against my chest. "If you ever need someone to save you . . ." Holding my wrist up, I force my lips to bend into a smile. "I'll be there in a minute. With my white horse."

"I love you," she mouths, and once I mouth it back, she turns around, eventually disappearing into the crowd.

Gone.

I walk, then walk some more, until I'm looking at the departures board, and I'm not even sure how I got back here.

Glancing around, I find an empty bench and sit. Her flight leaves in an hour, and I have nowhere else to be.

I cup my face, and for a while, I exist. I try to process the fact that she's gone. It feels like it's all been a fever dream—like it happened in my mind. Finding someone so imperfect for me that it just made sense. Finding her in such a weird way, then finding her again and again.

I kept finding her, and now, I've lost her.

"Hey." Someone sits beside me, and I turn to my brother with wide eyes.

What is he doing here?

Resting his back on the chair, he exhales. "Prim asked me to come. She figured you might need the support."

I look down, blinking hard and fast to stop the overwhelming emotions I feel from taking over.

I didn't lose her. She's right here.

She's still saving my life.

I let out a heavy sigh, and when my brother's hand rests on my shoulder, all my sadness and gratitude and relief erupt into tears.

fight for me

...

Six months later

PRIMROSE

"REALLY, I love your style. I've always hidden behind big sweaters and baggy jeans, but you've inspired me to dress how I want, regardless of what people say."

I smile at the woman in front of me, looking gorgeous in a fitted dress that hugs her curvy body. "Well, great choice. You look fantastic."

"I think so too," she says before grabbing the signed box of Uncandy and waving. "Tell your cowboy I say hi."

With a chuckle, I focus on the next person in line, a shy teenager whose mom keeps gently urging forward. The woman tells me about her daughter, how she's just taken up veganism, and though talking to fans is one of my favorite parts of the job, I get distracted by the thought of Logan.

My cowboy.

The cowboy I haven't properly talked to in two weeks, because I've barely had time to breathe.

But today is launch day. I've worked my ass off for six months, and Uncandy is hitting stores all over the country. After a few more weeks of promotion, I'll be back at the farm.

I know Logan feels neglected.

He hasn't said a word, of course. I miss most of his calls, but he never seems upset when I call back. The only thing he truly seems worried about is whether I'm eating and sleeping enough. The one question he keeps asking me is, *Are you happy?*

And I am. I really am.

I *mostly* am.

The only times I'm not exactly fond of is when I'm back home, between one trip or another. When I return to an empty apartment and hear traffic noises through the windows.

They never bothered me before, but they don't compare to the silence of the farm, interrupted only by Logan's deep voice.

I miss him. I miss him so viscerally that it feels like his absence is creating scarring tissue around my heart. Like I'm constantly deprived of the best part of my life.

Not to sound ungrateful, because my career trajectory has changed for the better, but it couldn't have happened at a worse time.

"Primrose?"

I flinch when the event organizer gently cups my shoulder, focusing on the young girl before me. "Oh my god, I'm so sorry. I—"

"Primrose has been signing autographs for several hours," she explains. "She's just a little tired."

"Yes, that's it," I rush to say. "Here." I autograph the girl's promotional box, then smile at her. "I've written down my phone number. My boyfriend is a vegan, and if you ever want some tips, or to talk about something—"

"Oh my God!" Her eyes widen as she takes the box. "I can text you?"

"Please do."

She smiles wide at her mom, who gently nods in a silent thank-you before walking away.

"Katie, I'm going to take a break," I tell the organizer as the next people approach.

"Of course." With a gesture at the woman helping with the line, she informs the crowd we'll be taking a short break, then points me to the back of the shop.

Thank god.

Just thinking of Logan has me craving the sound of his voice. We've texted this morning, and he's recently figured out voice messages, but replaying a mumbled "g'morning" doesn't cut it.

I take out my phone, tap on his contact and bring it to my ear, sitting at a small desk.

"—llo?"

Oh, his voice. I swear it has the ability to heal me better than Penicillin. "Hey, can you hear me?"

"Hello?"

"Logan?"

"Yes, hey. Hi," he says in a rough voice. "Is everything okay?"

"Everything's fine. I just wanted to hear your voice."

"I thought you had that signing today."

"I do. I'm still here."

"Missing me a little too hard today, Barbie?"

I smile, because it sounds like he's smiling. Every time he does, his voice takes on a softer, warmer edge.

"Always, cowboy. But I'll be there soon, right?"

"Right. Twenty days and sixteen hours left until you land." He clears his voice. "Kyle taught me how to use the phone's countdown timer."

I fight to hold back a chuckle. "Look at you. A real pro. Have you turned on the TV at all?"

"What for? I've got no one to snuggle. I set up all the streaming services the guys swore you'd want, though."

And an internet connection too. He's made his perfect house even more perfect for me, and I'm not there to enjoy it.

"What else is new?" I ask as I pull at a loose thread on my skirt.

"Uh, well . . ." There's a beat of silence. "We have a new goat. She's a feisty one, Julia. She kicked the crap out of Rob yesterday."

"Well, to be fair, Rob is a little . . ." I say as I think of the male goat.

He snorts. "Dense? He is. He could use a little goat to keep him on his toes. Or . . . hooves."

I drop my head back. "What else?"

"Kyle's grown an eight-foot zucchini. He might submit it to the Guinness World Record."

"Is he asking women if they want to see his massive zucchini?"

"No," he says with a low chuckle. "He's still going strong with Cassidy from the juice bar. He seems happy."

Even knowing I'm missing out on Kyle's relationship makes me sad. I wish I were there, checking on the progress of this zucchini, meeting Julia and watching her pester Rob.

"Simon's daughter started walking last week. Really, she skipped walking altogether, and she's just running all over the place."

"What about Aaron?"

"Aaron . . ." His sigh rattles against the microphone. "Aaron is lonely. Figuring out how to be a single dad now that Josie is in rehab."

My lips twist. Josie has been at the facility since the week after I left. I might be wrong, but it seems longer than usual. Is she hiding out? How is Sadie dealing with it?

"Are you there for him? For them?"

"Josie doesn't want any visitors, but you know I'm at Aaron's place nearly every day for dinner. Sadie is still going through her Barbie phase."

"Aw, just like me."

"Afraid it isn't exactly a phase for you, love."

"Fair enough," I concede, my lips curling at the nickname as butterflies overtake my stomach. Since I last saw him, there's been a whole lot of tastefully erotic pictures and filthy video calls, which are great but don't hold up against the real thing. They'll have to do for the next twenty days and sixteen hours, though.

"Do you think you might want to, hmm . . . give me two more minutes of your time?"

"Uh-huh, of course."

"And do something a little adventurous?"

"I'm feeling pretty adventurous today. What did you have in mind, Barbie?"

There's a bathroom down the corridor, and every time I hear his voice, I have to thank gravity for my underwear not automatically dropping at my ankles. "You know. Make me yee-haw, cowboy."

"Oh." There's a loud, high-pitched yelp on Logan's end, and focusing on the background noise, I hear more chatter. I check the phone, then bring it back to my ear. Twenty past eleven, which means he should be at the farm. "Where are you?"

"At the mall."

At the *mall*? He hates the mall.

"Is someone pointing a gun at your head?"

"No. Just trying to buy some candy."

"You are?" I smile wide. "Is it for me?"

"It's not for you, but it's *from* you."

"My candy?"

"Yeah."

I close my eyes, my grin increasing with every passing second. "Why are you buying it? I can make it for you when I get there."

"Yeah." He pauses. "But I was hoping to get it autographed."

My brows scrunch. "But I'm . . . I'm in Mayfield."

"So am I."

"What?" I jump up, my heart beating so fast in my chest it might just explode.

I rush toward the door, then stop, my hands shaking as I look for a mirror.

"The line is long, and apparently, Primrose needed a break."

Shit, he's here. I'm about to see him again after six whole months.

"Did you faint? Crawl out the window?"

"N-no, of course not." I run a hand through my frizzy hair. "I just—I left my makeup at the table, Logan."

"Ohh. Well, that's a real tragedy."

"It *is* when you haven't seen me for six months."

"I've also seen you sweat through your clothes and run away from a fire. Saw you covered in mud, and, uh, well. Myself."

"But it's been half a year!"

"Which means, come through that door before I break it down and take you on the first horizontal surface I find." He clears his throat. "On second thought, vertical stuff will do too."

"But—"

"You know I like the chase more than I should, backpack."

I do know. Not that I have any intention of running away. "Yes. Okay." An exhilarated, nervous giggle moves past my lips. "I'm coming. You—you stay right there, okay? Because I want to kiss you and touch every bit of your face, so I know you're really here."

"How about instead of telling me, you—"

I grab the handle, then rush back to my bag and grab his leather jacket. Despite how ridiculous it looks on me, I might have been using it almost every day and sleeping in it a couple of times. "Don't move."

"I'm right here. Big guy in the pink cowboy hat."

Pink cowboy hat?

No, he didn't.

Logan

The white door opens, and Primrose comes out with my jacket in hand, frantically scanning the crowd left and right. It's my first time seeing her since I got here, because even with how much taller I am than anyone in this store, there's only so much distance I can cover, and this line is *long*.

Fuck. She's beautiful. She also looks like she lost weight, which is not surprising with how she's been working herself silly these last couple of months. Between all the new partnerships that popped up and these promotional trips for her product, she hasn't stopped for a minute.

Our calls diminished in intensity and duration, and I won't lie and say it's been easy. The only reason I haven't freaked out is that I could tell it wasn't for her lack of trying. But I'm pretty sure she teared up yesterday when she heard my voice, and I decided I'd had enough.

She needs me, so I'm here. With a pseudo-white horse.

She quickly walks across the room, getting closer, but I don't wave, as she hasn't looked in my direction yet.

Come on, Barbie. I'm not exactly hard to miss.

Her fans stop her and try for photographs, but she just kindly waves and moves on, stepping closer and closer in her pink outfit.

If she weren't so obsessed with her clothes, I'd rip it off her with my bare hands.

Her head turns, and when I feel like she's about to look my way, I raise my hand, then bring it to my hat as her eyes meet mine. Her smile widens, and stepping to the side, I leave my spot in line and jerk my chin up. "Howdy, Barbie. Get your sweet ass right here, right now."

I can't wait another minute.

She runs, which, in those heels, has the potential for disaster, but before I can tell her to slow down, she crashes against my chest, the smell of strawberry all around me as she melts into me.

"Shit," I whisper as I wrap both arms around her and lean down to kiss the top of her head. I can *feel* her presence—my whole body's reacting to it. My lungs expand more, my shoulders become lighter.

She's here. Between my arms.

Her hold tightens, and though I'm vaguely aware of the crowd squealing and the infernal clicking of pictures being taken, I can hardly bring myself to care—especially when Primrose's shoulders start quaking.

"Hey—Barbie," I say, pulling her chin up. She fights my hold, hiding her face against my shirt. "Come on, let me look at you."

She tentatively glances up, her eyes swelling with tears and her chin wobbling. "I'm sorry," she says in a frustrated voice. "Why do I cry all the time?"

I, for one, love it. Not that she *cries* specifically, but how strongly she feels. How deeply. I don't think we'd be here if she didn't. That we would have fallen in love in a little over two weeks, then survived six months apart.

"You're so beautiful. I'd forgotten how beautiful you are."

She shakes her head. "Not true. You tell me every single day."

"But I forgot it was *this* beautiful."

"Why are you here?" she asks, something between a laugh and a sob escaping her. "You hate malls. And airports. And planes."

"I hate a lot of things, Barbie. I'd still live through them all for you."

Someone in line goes *awww*, and I roll my eyes.

"How long are you staying? Did you get a hotel? Please cancel the booking and stay with me."

"Actually, I . . . This is the reason I'm here." Her brow furrows, so I quickly add, "Of course, I wanted to celebrate your launch, and I was *dying* to see you. But, um, I'm here to tell you that I just . . ." She moves against me, her breasts brushing my stomach. "I can't do long-distance anymore."

"What?" she squeaks, a horrified grimace appearing instead of her smile. "You're dumping me?"

"Dumping you?" My head jerks back. "Why—"

"You can't do it anymore?" she asks, her pitch rising. "Are you serious? I'm here because you told me to go—we're launching the candy today. We made it all this time, and three weeks before I'm back, you—"

I pull her closer and look deeply into her eyes. "Do you think

I'd squeeze myself into a metal box that shoots through the sky for six hours, then wait in a line for two more wearing a pink cowboy hat that doesn't fit my big head—all of it, to dump you?"

She pauses, her wide eyes blinking as if she's realizing it sounds peculiar at best. "Right."

"Right."

"So, wait . . . what do you mean?"

Gently coaxing her closer, I lick my lips. I've thought about this speech for hours, and all the words I carefully crafted now seem light-years away.

"I've been miserable, Primrose. I mean—you're part of my life, and that makes it . . ." I can't even put the feeling into words. "*So much better.* But I also miss you all the fucking time. When I talk to you, I miss you even more. It's like a clock that never resets, just ticks faster and faster until I can't think of anything else but the fact that you're not there, next to me."

Her mouth opens, and for a few seconds, she stares at me. "Therapy is working out for you, isn't it?"

It is. I've had three panic attacks since I started, but I was more prepared to face them. And I'm working on expressing my emotions. On processing them.

"The point is, I've done it for six months. I'd do it for six more —hell, I'd wait a whole lifetime for you to come back."

"But?" she whispers.

But she's been calling less and less. She used to text me all day, every day—to the point where Simon and Kyle started calling me Cyber Logan, because I was always staring at my phone. And now, she doesn't have the time for it. It's hurting me, but most importantly, it hurts her. "You're too busy for a long-distance relationship, and I won't let us grow apart. I won't stand here and watch the most important thing in my life fall into pieces only because I didn't do anything about it."

"So, um . . ." She shakes her head. "Are you here to talk about us? To set some boundaries and—"

"I'm here to stay."

Her eyes widen again. "Stay? In Mayfield?"

"Yes, for now. Then we'll go back to the farm, and then . . . I'll be wherever you are. The work at the farm has been good, but now winter is approaching, and they can handle it without me. After that, we'll see. But I'm not leaving your side for as long as you need to stay away."

She smiles, which immediately relaxes my shoulders. She doesn't seem to think I'm crazy, which was my main concern. "But, Logan, your whole life is there. You can't just leave everything behind."

I tuck a lock of hair behind her ear, my fingers rubbing the pink tips. I've missed those pink tips. "My whole life is right *here*."

Tugging at my shirt, she smiles. "Why haven't you picked me up yet?"

I lean forward and, with the usual protective hand, pull her up against my chest, her legs wrapping around me.

"I love you," she whispers then. "I've been so miserable too."

"Yeah, I could tell." I brush a thumb over her cheek. "But I'm here now, okay? And I love you, so I'm not leaving until you ask me to."

She sniffles. "Okay. Three more weeks, and then we'll be back home."

"I *am* home."

She leans forward, her lips pressing on mine, and the crowd immediately cheers, their claps and excited yelps turning into a *oooh*s and *aaah*s once I deepen the kiss and taste her tongue.

Her hazy eyes meet mine when I pull back, and I jerk my head to the right. "Think we're going viral again?"

"So be it," she says before diving back in.

I pull back before it turns heated again, because the last thing I need is to have an erection in front of three hundred women holding their cameras to me.

"I love you," I mumble into her mouth, our noses grazing. "I love you so much, Primrose. Reason number one why I *would* date you."

She closes her eyes, pressing her forehead against mine. "Are you sure you'll be okay? My apartment is a mess, and this city is chaotic. It smells, it's loud, and people can be so rude."

"I'll be okay." It might not be ideal, but being here for her doesn't feel inconvenient. It feels right. "Take as long as you need, and I'll be by your side every step of the way." I gently put her down and smack her ass. "Now go get 'em. We'll talk about everything else later."

"Okay." She reaches for my neck, so I lean down to kiss her. "I'll see you soon. For real, this time—like in two hours." Happiness is bursting out of her, and she breathes as if to expel some of her adrenaline. I call her name when reminded of my gift for her. "Yes?"

I wait until she spins around, then set the pink cowboy hat on her head with a wink. "Yee-haw, Barbie."

epilogue

...

One year later

LOGAN

"YOU'RE SO FUCKING ANNOYING."

"Am I? Or are you mad because I'm right?"

I stare into Ian's blue eyes and shake my head. "Hmm . . . no, you're just annoying."

He points at the crate of zucchini between us. "Look, I don't know much about vegetables, but—"

"Clearly."

"But zucchini is one of the few green things I eat. And these don't look good. Come on, look at them." He grabs one and holds it close to my face. "They're yellow."

I know he's a client, but this is it. I'll smack him. "You *do* know these are yellow zucchini, right?"

His eyes dart from me to the zucchini, then back to me. "Uh, what?"

Good god. "Why don't you go back to marketing and have your wife, the *actual* chef, handle this?"

"Amelie is busy. We're starting a new venture, and it's been consuming a lot of our time." When I blankly stare at him, he smiles wide. "Well, since you asked. Private chefs. I'm very excited about it—lots of new opportunities. In fact, we're hiring. If you know of anyone who—"

"Do you want the zucchini or not?" I hiss.

"Yes. But, I *will* tell Primrose that customer service has been lacking."

"You do that," I mumble as I gather my things.

Though I'm happy Barbie finally made friends in the area, did she have to get along with these people? I could even get on board with Shane and his wife, Heaven. Her name infuriates me, but when we had dinner at their place last week, Shane and Primrose spent most of the night talking, so I ended up with her and her kids. Cute little things, the two of them.

And Amelie isn't that bad, either. She's smart and knows to respect my silence. But this guy? He never, *ever* shuts up. He never relents.

Unfortunately, Primrose is crazy about him.

"Do you want to come over for the game tonight?"

Game? What game?

I throw him a glance as I grab the pickup keys. "I'm busy. Taking out Barbie for our anniversary."

"Oh, congrats." He follows me to the back door of the restaurant. "Shane and I meet every Saturday. Neither of us gives much of a shit about the game, but that's when the girls have their 'kids and husband-free night,' so we made it a thing."

I think of Primrose scolding me for not giving Ian a chance, then nod. "Fine. Next Saturday."

"Really?" Brows arched high, he smiles. "Nice. Amelie always leaves us snacks. I'll make sure they're vegan-friendly."

After studying his face for a few seconds, I nod. "Thank you."

"See ya," he says as I turn around and walk. "Oh, and really, if you know of anyone looking for a job, we have several open positions."

I stop in front of the pickup. "My brother has been looking for something."

"Great. Tell him to check our website."

"Will do." I enter the pickup, and I swear I wouldn't be surprised if he waved until I disappeared behind the corner. If I'm a Doberman, and Primrose is a chihuahua, this guy is a golden retriever.

And I'm more of a cow person.

I grab my phone and tap on my text thread with Barbie.

> **LOGAN**
> On my way back.

> **PRIMROSE**
> I'm in Roseberg for a meeting. Did Amelie give you some documents for me?

> **LOGAN**
> Haven't seen her. She left Ian in charge.

> **PRIMROSE**
> Oh-uh. Were you nice to him?

My eyes roll.

> **LOGAN**
> Yep. We kissed and all.

> **PRIMROSE**
> I'll let it slide this time, but you're only supposed to kiss me. See you later, cowboy. ILY
>
> Sorry. I forgot you hate that. I LOVE YOU!

"Yes, I *do* hate that," I mumble with a smile. If she's going to tell me my favorite words in the whole world, she should *actually* say them.

I start the pickup and drive towards the farm. Work has finally slowed down after a very intense summer, but I can't complain. I get to do the best job in the world and fall asleep next to the most perfect woman.

I have family and friends around—even when I don't want

them—and I'm healthier. This reminds me that I'm seeing my therapist tomorrow.

Tapping on Kyle's contact, I relax into the seat.

"Boss?"

"Hey. All set for tonight?"

"Absolutely. Enjoy your dinner out, and I'll take care of everything here. Primrose is going to *freak*."

Yes, she will. I've been freaking out too, in fact, but I simultaneously can't wait. I've been thinking about this for a while, and I know it's the right moment. Hopefully, she'll feel the same.

"Great, thank you," I say as I stop at a red light. "I expect to not be able to work much tomorrow. You and Simon have it covered?"

"Hey, I'm the vice-boss for a reason."

"That's a title you made up."

"Yes, but isn't it accurate?"

I guess it is. He's been working like a donkey at the farm. "Sure. I'm still not calling you that."

"Just get your ass back here. Big night tonight."

I hang up, then exhale as I grip the steering wheel. "Yep. Big night tonight."

Primrose

"Hello?" I call as I enter Desserts for Stressed People. They're closed today, and seeing the bakery not bursting with customers is weird.

"In here!"

I follow Amelie's voice to the back, my nose scrunching at a weird smell. I can't identify it precisely, but it's terrible. Are they having a sewage problem?

"Hi, Prim," Heaven says with a tired voice. She's nursing her newborn, Marty, and though she looks at peace, I can tell she's exhausted. Especially next to Amelie, who's always quite energetic.

"Sorry to bother—"

"Please," Amelie stops me. She hands me the documents beside her and squeezes my shoulder. "Thank you so much for looking at these. The lawyer is out until next week, and we need to get the papers started."

"Of course." I've done all of this already when I launched Uncandy, and though it's not exactly complicated, I remember feeling overwhelmed when I first started the application to open a business. "I'm sure you've done everything right anyway."

"Hey," Heaven says as her eyes narrow. "Isn't it your anniversary today?"

I nod. I briefly mentioned it when we had dinner last week, but with everything she has going on, I'm surprised she remembered. "It is. Logan is taking me out for dinner. And apparently, he has a surprise for me."

"Surprise?" Amelie's eyes widen. "What surprise?"

When I give her a shrug, she scoffs.

"Come on. You must have at least a suspicion."

I guess I do, but I'm a little afraid to voice my thoughts. If I admit it might be what I think, and then it *isn't*, I'll be devastated.

"Please, tell us," Heaven whispers as she shifts Marty against her breast. "I'm dying to talk about anything other than baby stuff."

After a moment of hesitation, I smile. "Fine. Okay. I think . . . maybe, uh . . . maybe he'll propose."

"What?!" Amelie whisper-screams. "Propose?" She gasps, turning to Heaven. "Oh my god!"

Heaven smiles. "Amelie is quite fond of weddings."

"No kidding. If he does propose, I'll need help planning it, so . . ."

"I volunteer."

I smile, and I'd normally stay and chat for longer than this, but this smell is giving me a headache. "Is everything okay with the bakery?"

"Uh, yes? Why?" Heaven asks in a doubtful voice.

"No, nothing. It's just—" I point my finger around me. "The smell?"

"What smell?"

I turn to Amelie, and she's as confused as Heaven. "Did Marty poop?" she asks. "'Cause at this point, I can't even tell anymore."

"No, it's like, um . . . sewage, maybe? Do you guys really not smell it?"

"Oh." Amelie points her thumb behind her. "Did you get here from the square? They're doing some work on the fountain and, holy stink. Maybe it just rubbed on you."

I guess that must be it. "Crazy—it feels like it's right under my nose." I brush the thought off. "Anyway, I'll text on the group chat tomorrow. Wish me good luck."

"Good luck, Prim. Text first thing in the morning," Ames says with an encouraging smile, but when I turn to Heaven, her brows are tight over her eyes.

"Is everything okay?"

"Oh, yes." She shakes her head. "I was just . . . do you really smell that in here?"

I nod. "It's making me nauseous."

"Hmm." Heaven glances at Amelie, who gasps.

"What? What is it?"

Amelie rubs her brow, mumbling something about how 'it's happening again.' Seriously, they're freaking me out.

"It could be nothing, Prim, but . . . A heightened sense of smell is a very common sign of, uh . . . I found out I was pregnant with Nevaeh because Shane was cooking at home, and it felt like he'd shoved an onion in my nostrils."

I swallow, blinking. Logan and I had to go back to condoms a couple of months ago because my gynecologist wanted me to stop taking contraception for a while. We've been careful, though.

Could she be right? Could I be pregnant?

"If you want, I still have a few tests back home," Heaven offers.

My first reaction is to shake my head, but it's not a bad idea. I want to run to Logan, but I'm not sure how he'll react to this, and I don't want to take the test by myself. "Y-yeah, okay."

"Don't worry," Amelie says as she cups my elbow. "It could be nothing. And if it is, you'll take it one step at a time. You're not alone."

"Right," Heaven confirms. "And let's not panic or celebrate before you know for sure." She stands, adjusting her bra and shirt. "Come on, let's go. We got you."

I follow them out of the bakery, unable to process any thoughts. I've always wanted a big family, and Logan wants kids too. But is now the right moment? We've only been together a year.

And how is *he* going to take it?

LOGAN

"Are you sure you enjoyed dinner?"

Primrose nods, her hand tightening around mine. "Yes, I'm just not very hungry." She gives me an apologetic smile. "Sorry."

"No, you're fine." It's just . . . she was also weirdly silent. I never have to carry the conversation, yet she looked distracted tonight. Maybe she guessed what's about to happen and she's nervous. "Ready for your surprise?"

"So ready." She smiles wide, looking gorgeous in her light blue dress. She's gotten a whole collection of cowgirl boots, pink included, and tonight, she's wearing an indigo pair.

"Great." I step behind her and then cover her eyes with my hands. "Let's go."

We walk around the house, and once we get to the backyard, I see Kyle's setup and mentally thank him. It's perfect.

"All right. Hope you're prepared."

She nods, excitement making her whole body vibrate. "Stop stalling!"

I lift my hands off her eyes and watch her face. Her excited smile turns into shock as she blinks, and once her lips bend in a slight frown, I turn to the pink bike sitting at the center of my backyard. I got her a Yamaha YZF-R3, perfect for beginners, then spent the last week custom painting it pink. The pink helmet is there. So are the pink suit and the pink boots. It's everything she's been wanting for the last year, so I don't understand why she looks ... disappointed.

"Oh my god, Logan. This is ... perfect."

"Yeah? Does your face know?"

She gives me a scolding look. "I love it. Wow, look at that." She walks to the bike, tentatively touching it as if she's afraid it'll fall. "I can't *believe* you got me a bike."

Me neither. I might start having panic attacks again. "You're not allowed to take it out without me."

"Am I not?" She cocks a brow at me. "Then you're not allowed to take yours out without me."

"Deal." I don't care if I have to sacrifice a ride here and there. There's no way I'd be able to cope with her riding by herself.

Her fingers brush the helmet and the suit. She looks at them dreamily, but there's something wrong. I expected her to be screaming and jumping up and down, to be already trying to get it off the stand, turn it on, and maneuver it. But her head seems somewhere else.

"Backpack?" She glances at me over her shoulder. "Tell me what's wrong."

"Nothing's wrong," she reassures me. She walks closer and hooks her arms around my neck. "I'm sorry. I promise I love it."

"Are you not ready to talk about whatever is going on?"

She bites her bottom lip. "Yeah. I'll need a minute."

Okay. I'll respect that. I might die from anxiety, but that's not her problem. "But you won't dump me, right?"

Her eyes narrow. "They'll have to pry you out of my cold, dead hands."

Good. "And you still... LM?"

With a chuckle, she pulls me closer, and once her lips are an inch away from mine, she whispers, "Yes. ILY."

I kiss her, and she responds in the usual enthusiastic way, which immediately soothes me. Though I want to know what's wrong, I can deal with whatever it is as long as she's with me.

"Do you want to take your new bike for a spin?"

Her eyes blow wide, her hand cupping her belly. "Uh, n-no, not now."

"Are you nauseous?"

"What?" I point at her hand, and she sucks in a gasp. "Oh, no. I'm fine."

Weird, weird, weird.

"Okay, then. Let's go back in?"

Her hand sinks into mine, and she follows me inside the house.

"I know what you need," I say once the backdoor closes behind me, and I circle her back with my arms. "Snuggles and a movie. Get settled under the blanket and choose what we're watching. I'll get some snacks."

"I love you, you know?" She looks up at me, and her eyes are misty. Is she feeling emotional? I mean, I guess I am too. When I woke up this morning, I couldn't stop smiling. We've been together for a whole year, and it's been the best year of my life. Through arguments and filthy sex, soft moments and new traditions, we've made a whole life together. A life I'm pretty freaking proud of.

"I love you." I rub my thumb along her cheek. "I wouldn't change a single thing about our life."

Once again, though I expect a smile, I'm surprised by a frown. "Well, *some* change is good, though, right?"

"Sure. I just mean . . . I think everything's perfect already."

Her lips twist, and I know I said something wrong, but before I can ask, she leans closer and tilts her chin up. After I kiss her, she smiles and walks toward the living room. "I'll pick a nice movie."

"Popcorn incoming."

I turn to the counter and breathe out. What matters is that she's mine. That she loves me. Whatever change she's thinking about, we'll deal with it together.

PRIMROSE

Marching past the orchard, I walk to the stables. The guys meet here every morning for their meeting, and I woke up feeling like I would explode if I didn't talk to Logan. So I will. Right now.

Kyle and Simon are leading the meeting, while Logan is with his back to the stables, and the rest of the workers are scattered around them. As soon as Simon spots me, he snaps his fingers in Logan's direction and jerks his chin toward me.

Logan's brows tighten as I stomp closer, until he walks to meet me halfway. "What's—"

"A *bike*, Logan? That's your surprise?"

His mouth opens, then his eyes dart left and right. "You've wanted one since we met. You've asked for one nearly every day, and you said it *had* to be pink, and—"

"I know all of that!"

"Then why are you screaming at me?"

I don't know. Hormones? Panic? Who's to say. After I took those two tests at Heaven's apartment and two more back at the house, I figured . . . He'll propose to me tonight, and I'll tell him I'm pregnant. Hell, it'll be the best night of our lives. I was sure of it, even though I had no evidence. Then he showed me the bike.

I'm pregnant, and he got me a motorcycle.

"Are you ever going to propose to me?"

A 'holy shit' echoes from where the guys are standing, but Logan barely reacts. "That's what you're upset about? You never told me you wanted me to propose."

"*You* should want to propose."

Why am I being such an idiot? We've been together for a year. One. Year. Yes, I thought he would propose, but I have no reason to expect him to.

I still can't stop myself. I was scared of how he'd react yesterday, but after the bike? I'm terrified. I figured he was ready to settle down, while he was thinking about teaching me wheelies.

"What the hell is going on, Barbie?"

I shake my head, then notice the workers staring at me with wide eyes and amused smiles. Bet they think I'm a *psycho*. God, maybe I am. "Nothing. Just—" I shake my head. "Just forget about it." I turn, but Logan calls my name, so I face him again. "Seriously, Logan—"

My voice fades out as I see him kneeling. He looks up at me, and my heart goes into a frenzy.

"No, you shouldn't propose because I told you to."

"I don't follow rules, and I barely take suggestions." He fishes into his back pocket, then takes out his wallet. As he extracts a ring, my mouth drops open. "Remember?"

Holy shit. So I *was* right!

"You—you—"

"Looks like you're done screaming, huh?" he mumbles. He holds his hand out, and with cheers from every one of his employees, I cringe and walk closer. Once my hand rests in his, he smiles. "Hi, giant red flag. Wanna tell me what's wrong with you before we do this?"

I shake my head firmly.

"All right, then." He swallows. "Primrose, I've had this ring for the last six months. I bought it the day of Uncandy's launch, when I moved to Mayfield to be with you. I knew back then that if I was willing to leave the farm for you, I was in love beyond what

I ever thought possible." When I smile, he does too. "And I knew you were the woman I wanted to marry when you didn't *ask me* to leave everything behind for you."

Seriously? I can't believe he's had the ring for six months.

"So, on my way to see you, I went to a jewelry store and bought this."

I look at the ring for the first time—a thin golden band with a light pink gem. Perfectly me. "I love it."

"I knew you would." He inhales and exhales, watching my eyes with content ease. "I kept this ring with me all the time, and the only reason I haven't given it to you yet is that I didn't know you were ready for it. You haven't talked about it besides saying that you'd like to get married at some point, and I didn't want to spook you."

I wish I'd had the same thought when I shouted at him that he should propose in front of all his employees.

"But I *do* want to marry you. I want to be with you forever." He smiles. "I also want to get up, because the guys won't let me live this down, so . . ." He kisses the top of my hand, eyes stuck on mine. "Primrose Bellevue—"

"I'm pregnant."

A shrieked 'What?' emerges from the group—it sounded like Kyle—but I can't look away from Logan. He seems confused, as if he's suddenly forgotten how to speak English.

"You . . . you . . ." His lifted arm drops. "Is it mine?" When my fear morphs into anger, he shakes his head. "N-no, that's a stupid question. I, uh . . ."

I'm going to stomp on his head.

"We're having a baby," he whispers. His shoulders rise and fall fast, and though I wish he hadn't said *that*, I can't be mad at him. He's doing so much better these days that I forget he's still working on his anxiety. On his trauma.

I kneel in front of him and take his hand in mine. "Are you okay?"

He's as white as a sheet as he lifts his gaze off the ground. "Are you?"

"I think so." Though I definitely planned to wait a little longer, after sleeping on it, I can confidently say I'm happy about it. And Logan just proposed, which means he must be somewhat ready for the next stage in our lives. Doesn't mean he's ready to be a dad, though.

"Because you know I'll support you no matter what you decide—about this or anything else."

"I know, but I . . . I want this." I tuck his hair behind his ear. "How do *you* feel about it?"

He blinks, and tears fall down his cheeks. I think they're happy tears, but I need him to say something.

His arm wraps around me, gently pulling me forward. Once my face is buried in his chest, he fits his in the nook of my neck, and his soft tears turn into full-fledged sobs. I rub a soothing hand on his back, and he peppers my shoulder with kisses. "I was so afraid, Barbie. I was terrified."

"I'm . . . I'm sorry. I just needed some time to process it. I hate that I worried you."

"No." He sniffles, grasping my face with both hands. "Before I met you, I was so scared this would never happen." He kisses my chin, my lips, my cheeks. "And now I have you." Another peck on my nose, my forehead, then my hairline. "And you love me so much you want to marry me." The kisses keep raining down on me, and I fight against the overwhelming emotions I feel. "And now I'm going to be a dad."

When he breaks into sobs again, I hug him. I've never seen him cry like this—never seen him so happy either. It makes me wish I'd told him immediately.

Clearing his throat, he pulls back and smiles. "Okay, let me do this right." He shows me the ring, then cups my face with the other hand. "Primrose Bellevue, I found the ultimate reason not to date you."

"Is that so?"

"Yes." He kisses my lips. "Because if that's okay with you, I'd rather marry you."

I nod, and though I don't have it with me, I mentally strike through the last item on my list. Not 'marry me,' no.

~~Give me a happily ever after.~~

THE END

also by letizia lorini

Desserts for Stressed People

The Wedding Menu

acknowledgments

It's the third time I get to write these, and it never gets easier. It's the moment an author looks back at the last year(s) of their life, feels grateful for the people they met along the way, and sad for those they lost. Which is a long-winded way to say, bear with me.

My first huge thank you is for my beta readers. Especially with this one, I've dragged you through hell and back with a million different changes and versions (what's new, am I right?)

A special shoutout to Heather, who says I edge her on purpose, but I don't. She beta-read RTSH in a week. Queen.

Another, just as big thank you to my editor, Britt, who took a horribly unpolished book and turned it into what I think is a little masterpiece. I'm sorry I rescheduled forty billion times, and thank you for not making me feel bad about it.

For the third time, thank you to Sam for creating the most beautiful cover. I'd say it's my favorite, but the next one would come, and everyone would be rolling their eyes at me.

Now, onto more personal stuff.

'More (I wrote Caroline at first, but it felt wrong), you've been patient for so long and in so many ways. I promised you I'd make it worth it in the last two acknowledgments I've written . . . and then I did it? Here's to the future, to working one job instead of three, and to us getting to enjoy the results of our hard work.

Thank you, mom and dad. The last year has been the most beautiful and stressful time of my life. You've never failed to push me when I needed it and to remind me you're incredibly proud of me every step of the way. Sorry for all the calls I missed.

Mary, Claire and Stef, you're always and forever my sisters.

Thank you for accepting my absence and never holding it over my head.

Elodie, WH, Becky, and Heather, you're my rocks. The number of times you've distracted me with your shenanigans, listened to my dramatic outbursts, talked about everything and nothing, and supported me in a million other ways is something I will never take for granted.

Oksana and Madison, there are no words for the two of you. You're my biggest cheerleader and two beautiful humans I get to call my friends. I know it has nothing to do with RTSH, but you told me on day one that a big publisher would pick up my books, and you'd get to see them in stores. I need you to know that I smiled every time you said that, but I also rolled my eyes big time. And f*ck me, you were right.

I'm a creature of habit and lucky to have the most fantastic bestie in the world, so she once again gets mentioned close to last (that's when dessert happens; look it up.) L.H. Blake, you're one incredibly talented author and a precious friend. We've been doing this side-by-side since the beginning, when I fell in love with your writing and found a friend for life. We'll be doing this together until the very last word.

Finally, to my readers. Holy crap, how can I even thank you?! You've shown up for me on multiple platforms. You've commented, DMed, liked, reviewed, bought, and shouted. I've had the pleasure of meeting some of you, I've chatted with loads of you, and I'm constantly amazed by the work you put into supporting authors and the whole book community.

I hope that with my books, I make you smile, cry, and feel. It's not enough to thank you, but it's a start.

Once again, I'm closing with a gentle request (how crass.) If you have any platform where you review books, I'd appreciate it if you could leave a line (or a rating) about Riding the Sugar High. If you don't have any, I'd be endlessly grateful if you recommend this book to someone. Even if you hated it! In that case, buy and deliver a copy to your enemies' houses. Not only will they read a bad book, but they'll also have a constant reminder sitting on their bookshelf!

For that and more petty advice, you know where to find me. Until then, thank you so much for reading Logan and Primrose's love story!

about the author

Letizia Lorini is an Italian rom-com author who lives in Malmö, a quaint town in the south of Sweden. There, she lives in her lovely apartment with her partner and their fluffy Japanese Spitz.

When she's not writing or reading romance, she's cooking up some new story, researching the indie business, or wishing she was better at marketing or graphic design. She's also a criminologist, speaks three languages and loves coffee.

Oh, and she's a hybrid author.

That's right. She signed with Gallery, Simon & Schuster, and she thinks that's a pretty big deal.

- facebook.com/letizialorini.author
- instagram.com/letizialorini.writes
- tiktok.com/@letizialorini.author

www.ingramcontent.com/pod-product-compliance
Lightning Source LLC
LaVergne TN
LVHW091657070526
838199LV00050B/2188